THE BLACKBOARD JUNGLE

A NOVEL BY

EVAN HUNTER

POCKET BOOKS

New York   London   Toronto   Sydney

POCKET BOOKS, a division of Simon & Schuster, Inc.
1230 Avenue of the Americas, New York, NY 10020

This book is a work of fiction. Names, characters, places and incidents are products of the author's imagination or are used fictitiously. Any resemblance to actual events or locales or persons, living or dead, is entirely coincidental.

Copyright © 1953, 1954 by Evan Hunter
Copyright renewed © 1982 by Evan Hunter
Introduction copyright © 1999 by Hui Corp.

Previously published in hardcover in 1999 by Simon & Schuster, Inc.

All rights reserved, including the right to reproduce
this book or portions thereof in any form whatsoever.
For information address Simon & Schuster, Inc.,
1230 Avenue of the Americas, New York, NY 10020

ISBN: 0-7434-9368-0

First Pocket Books paperback edition October 2004

10 9 8 7 6 5 4 3 2 1

POCKET and colophon are registered trademarks of
Simon & Schuster, Inc.

Cover design by Rod Hernandez
Photo of classroom © Lorna Clark/Photonica
Photo of broken glass © Johner/Photonica

Manufactured in the United States of America

For information regarding special discounts for bulk purchases,
please contact Simon & Schuster Special Sales at 1-800-456-6798
or business@simonandschuster.com.

BCID: 866-5154519

WRITTEN BY EVAN HUNTER

NOVELS

*The Blackboard Jungle** (1954) *Second Ending* (1956) *Strangers When We Meet* (1958) *A Matter of Conviction* (1959) *Mothers and Daughters* (1961) *Buddwing* (1964) *The Paper Dragon* (1966) *A Horse's Head* (1967) *Last Summer* (1968) *Sons* (1969) *Nobody Knew They Were There* (1971) *Every Little Crook and Nanny* (1972) *Come Winter* (1973) *Streets of Gold* (1974) *The Chisholms** (1976) *Love, Dad* (1981) *Far from the Sea* (1983) *Lizzie* (1985) *Criminal Conversation** (1994) *Privileged Conversation* (1996) *Candyland** (2001) *The Moment She Was Gone** (2002)

SHORT STORY COLLECTIONS

Happy New Year, Herbie (1963) *The Easter Man* (1972)

CHILDREN'S BOOKS

Find the Feathered Serpent (1952) *The Remarkable Harry* (1959) *The Wonderful Button* (1961) *Me and Mr. Stenner* (1976)

SCREENPLAYS

Strangers When We Meet (1959) *The Birds* (1962) *Fuzz* (1972) *Walk Proud* (1979)

TELEPLAYS

The Chisholms (1979) *The Legend of Walks Far Woman* (1980) *Dream West* (1986)

*Available in paperback from Pocket Books
** Available in hardcover from Simon & Schuster

When The Blackboard Jungle *was first published in 1954,*
Dragica Dimitrijević was a little girl
in a little Serbian village.
She is now my wife.
This new edition of the book is dedicated to this gentle,
loving woman who has brought so much joy
to my life.

What are the roots that clutch, what branches grow
Out of this stony rubbish? Son of man,
You cannot say, or guess, for you know only
A heap of broken images, where the sun beats . . .

THE WASTE LAND, T. S. Eliot

Introduction

I'm always amused by the American myth of Overnight Success. I suppose it does happen sometimes. Here's this kid without any acting training, for example, and he's working in a car wash when he gets discovered by a famous director who gives him the starring role in a multimillion-dollar movie, after which he immediately becomes America's favorite male star. Listen, it could happen.

That's not what happened with *The Blackboard Jungle*. The book was published in October of 1954. Ten years earlier, I hadn't even dreamed of becoming a writer. Back then, all of my ambitions were art-oriented. In high school, I'd been Art Editor of the Literary-Art magazine and cartoonist for the school newspaper. In a citywide competition, I won a six-month scholarship to the Art Students League. I was later accepted at Cooper Union, one of New York's two prestigious art schools. I was studying there when I enlisted in the U.S. Navy. In November of 1944, I was called to active duty, and sailed to the Pacific on a destroyer the following summer.

Word gets around fast on a small ship. I was soon

doing pencil drawings of everyone in the crew for all of them to send home to their wives, girlfriends, mothers, police dogs. When I ran out of live subjects, I made drawings of the smokestacks, and the torpedo tubes, and the gun mounts, and the depth-charge racks, and the radar antennas—and then there was nothing left to draw but the sea, which was boring. I borrowed a typewriter from the radio shack, found an empty storage compartment with some sort of countertop in it, set myself up, locked the door, and began writing, don't ask me why.

A radioman's typewriter has only capital letters on it. Everything I wrote had the look of an urgent bulletin from the front: JOHN WOKE UP AND LOOKED AT THE ALARM CLOCK. Everything I wrote was also somewhat lousy. It wasn't until 1952, after almost two years in the Navy, and four years of college and months and months of odd jobs as a vocational high school teacher (remember that occupation!), an Automobile Club telephone dispatcher, and a lobster salesman, that I landed a job at the Scott Meredith Literary Agency and finally learned how to write. I must have published something like sixty or seventy short stories, three young-adult science-fiction novels, and two mystery novels in the several years during which I worked at the agency. All of this *before* I wrote the novel that truly launched my writing career and made me an overnight success, ha.

The road to Simon & Schuster began with a submission of a novel I'd written titled *Tomorrow and Tomorrow.* This was a science-fiction novel, the only truly good science fiction I'd ever written. You have to understand that the science course I elected in college was Geology. If you have ever elected Geology to fill your science requirement, you know exactly where science and I stood in relation to each other. Which goes a long way toward explaining why the science fiction I wrote had very little to do with nebulae or electromagnetic fields, whatever they may be. The agency had a very good science-fiction list, and I was learning from all the writers on it, but I never truly caught on to the genre until I read a novel titled *The Demolished Man* by Alfred Bester, who was not an agency client. Inspired, I wrote a novelette that was published as *Malice in Wonderland* although my original title had been *Tomorrow and Tomorrow*. Encouraged by the magazine acceptance, I expanded it to novel length and Scott sent it to Peter Schwed, who was then a senior editor at Simon & Schuster.

The rest is history, right?

Wrong.

Simon & Schuster did not publish science fiction.

Peter explained this to Scott in a nice letter, and then added that if ever Hunter wrote anything outside the genre, he would be happy to take a look at it.

Up to that time, with one exception, *all* of my writing had been genre writing. The pulp stories I'd sold were Westerns, mysteries, adventure, or science fiction. The exception was a short story titled *To Break the Wall*, which told of a violent encounter between a vocational high school teacher (keep remembering that occupation!) and his uncontrollable class. It was published in an experimental magazine called *Discovery*, which published quality fiction in a paperback format. The paperback house was Pocket Books, Inc., a subsidiary of Simon & Schuster. Stick around, it gets better.

In May of 1953, I left the agency to freelance.

I had saved $3,000 by then, and I figured this would last me at least six months. A lot of editors were buying my work, and I truly felt I had an honest shot at making a go of it. If I wasn't earning a living as a writer by the time the money ran out, I would either go back to the agency (if Scott would have me) or else seek work elsewhere in publishing. Three thousand bucks. Six months. What the hell!

Well, the pulp magazines decided to fold.

Most of them, anyway.

I had lucked into the end of an era!

I wrote a mystery novel about a literary agent, which had been my nine-to-five occupation for the past almost two years, but it didn't immediately sell, perhaps because it was lousy, and I was down to about five hundred dollars, with a wife and three young kids to feed, and a mortgage to pay, and the winter coming on, and I thought, Gee, maybe I ought to expand that Qual Lit short into a novel, try my hand at something truly serious before I walk off into the sunset.

I wrote ninety pages and an outline of a novel called *The Tiger Pit*. The title was from a line in a T. S. Eliot poem: The tiger in the tiger-pit/Is not more irritable than I. The tiger pit was a vocational high school, and the hero was a teacher, and Evan Hunter was the "I" who was irritable. I fired the manuscript off to Scott with the suggestion that he send it to that nice editor at Simon & Schuster, whatever his name was, who'd said he'd be happy to take a look at anything I wrote outside the genre.

We were in a bakery shop on East 86th Street, my wife and I. I don't know why we were on 86th Street. I know we once took jobs as counselors at the Y on 92nd, but I think that was earlier, when we were first married. I know we were living in Hicksville, Long Island, when I wrote *The Tiger Pit,* so I can't for the life of me imagine what we were doing in a bakery shop on 86th, but that's where we were when I decided to give Scott a call, see how the book was doing up there at S&S. My wife had taken a ticket and was waiting to be served. I told her I was running up to the phone booth on the corner, and would be right back.

The receptionist put me through to Scott at once.

"I've been trying to reach you," he said. "Where are you?"

I told him I was on East 86th Street.

He said, "Peter Schwed is buying *The Tiger Pit.* Can you deliver it in six months?"

I learned how to fly that day.

I came out of that phone booth flying. I flew to the bakery shop and I scooped my wife into my arms and flew her up to the ceiling, babbling, repeating every word of the conversation with Scott, over and over again, flying.

The Tiger Pit, of course, became *The Blackboard Jungle.*

It was published in *Ladies' Home Journal,* in a special issue devoted to education.

It was sold to MGM while it was still in galleys.

It was published in paperback by Pocket Books, Inc., who had first published the short story that became the penultimate chapter of the book.

Sometimes, there's symmetry.

Evan Hunter
Weston, Connecticut

PART ONE

1

The building presented a not unpleasant architectural scheme, the banks of wide windows reflecting golden sunlight, the browned weathered brick façade, the ivy clinging to the brick and framing the windows. His eyes passed over the turrets on each corner of the building, green-tiled in the sunlight. It was a nice-looking building, he thought.

He walked through the Cyclone fence and into the empty yard stretching before him in endless concrete monotony. It was still hot for September, and the sun glared off the concrete except where the building cast a turreted black shadow near the entrance steps. He was a little nervous, but he knew that would pass once the interview started. He was always nervous before an interview. He would feel all bottled up until the first few words were spoken. Then the cork would be drawn, and all the nervousness would spill out, leaving only the confidence that always lay just beneath the bottled surface of the nervousness.

He paused on the shadowed steps, partly to reassure

himself of his confidence, and partly to look up at the chiseled letters in the triangular arch over the doorway.

NORTH MANUAL TRADES HIGH SCHOOL

Leave us gird our loins, he thought.

He sucked in a deep breath, the way a man on a diving board will just before taking the plunge, and he started up the steps. He pulled open the wooden door, surprised to find marble steps behind it. He started up the marble steps and saw the sign GENERAL OFFICE. Beneath the sign, in sprawling crayon, someone had scribbled the timeless epithet, and an industrious summer custodian had succeeded in partially scrubbing away every letter but the bold, black *F* of the first word. He smiled and followed the arrow beneath the sign into a cool, dim corridor. There was another sign with another arrow in the corridor, and he followed that dutifully. The halls were freshly painted and spotlessly clean. He admired this with an air of proprietorship, almost as if he had already won the job. *A clean school is a good school,* he mused, and then he wondered in which education class he'd picked that up.

He made a sharp right-angle turn at the end of the corridor, following the instructions of another sign, and then walked rapidly to an open doorway through which sunlight streamed. A sign to the right of the doorway read GENERAL OFFICE.

They believe in signs here, by God, he thought. He expected to step into the room and find a desk with a sign reading DESK, and a chair with another sign reading CHAIR. Mr. Stanley would undoubtedly wear a cardboard placard strung around his neck, and the lettering on it would say MR. STANLEY. He wondered if he should put a little button in his lapel, like the ones they gave you at Freshman teas.

My name is RICHARD DADIER; *what's yours?*

Josephine of France.

Not tonight, Josephine.

He sighed impatiently and stepped into the room. It was a long rectangular room, with the entrance doorway on one long side of the rectangle. The other long side was directly opposite him and covered from short wall to short wall with windows. Five feet back from the wall with the door in it, a railing divided the room, stretching across its entire length. Behind the railing, he saw a group of desks. A distinguished-looking man was talking to a frightened-looking man at one of the desks. A time clock hung on the wall to the left of the doorway, behind the dividing railing. Racks for cards were hung beneath the clock, but the racks were almost empty.

He stood in the doorway for just an instant, and then walked to the railing. The railing had a counter top, except where a gate was set into it near the time clock. A blonde with an upswept hairdo and a pencil stabbed into the hair was busily scribbling something on an official-looking form, her elbows on the counter. He walked to her, glancing quickly at the row of cubbyholes which were labeled TEACHERS' MAILBOXES.

She did not look up. He cleared his throat, and she still did not look up. She continued scribbling on the white official-looking form, and she did not deign to notice him until she had finished. She looked at him exactly as she had looked at the official-looking form.

"Yes?" she said.

"I have an appointment with Mr. Stanley," he said, smiling.

"Your name, please."

"Mr. Dadier."

"If you'll take a seat, Mr. Dadier, he'll be with you in a moment."

She looked past him to a bench against the wall near the cubbyhole mailboxes.

"Thank you," he said.

"Not at all," she answered, and he immediately figured her for one of those efficient women who always have to get the last word in. He'd known an executive like that once. If he got a letter saying, "Thank you for your kindness the other day," he'd immediately get off another letter saying, "Thank you for thanking me for my kindness the other day." Pit two people like that against one another and you'd get an endless round of "Thank you for thanking me for thanking you for thanking me . . ." Which was probably the best way to keep two such crackpots occupied, anyway.

Having made this astute judgment, Richard Dadier, sizer-up of women with pencils growing out of their heads, promptly walked to the bench and took a seat. There was another fellow sitting at the far end of the bench, but he gave him only a cursory glance and then turned his attention to the two men seated at the desk beyond the railing.

The distinguished-looking man was doubtless Mr. Stanley, and the one with fear all over his face was undoubtedly applying for the open English teacher's position. Stanley seemed completely bored. He was a blondish man, with a thin, angular face, and a precise mustache that formed an unobtrusive cushion for his slender nose. His eyebrows were blond, and slightly raised now, like the eyebrows of someone politely listening to a joke he's heard before.

The fellow opposite him droned on endlessly, using his hamlike hands to illustrate pertinent points in his undoubtedly illustrious career. Every time the fellow waved a hand, Stanley flinched, and Rick made a mental note to keep his hands clenched tightly in his lap.

He heard the slightly louder words "student taught," and Stanley nodded, with his eyebrows still raised in polite anticipation of a punch line he already knew. The fellow went on, and Stanley hastily penciled a few notes on the pad before him, glanced at his watch—the gold cuff links glittering in the sunlight when his jacket sleeve pulled back—and then leaned forward smiling.

"Don't call us, we'll call you."

Rick could almost make out the words as they formed on Stanley's almost feminine mouth. Those words, or a reasonable facsimile, like the box tops always said. He wondered what the box tops had meant. Ten cents and a box top or reasonable facsimile thereof. Did that mean you could draw a box top on a sheet of cardboard and send that in with your dime? He wondered. He had wondered the same thing when he had been a rabid sender-inner. Especially for the Tom Mix stuff. He had received a magnifying glass, and a ring through which you could look and see people behind you, and a six-shooter. And he could never remember finishing a box of Ralston. He had also received the Little Orphan Annie shaker by sending in the aluminum seal from a can of Ovaltine, together with twenty-five cents. He would always remember the Little Orphan Annie shaker because there was a picture of the little orphan herself on it. And in the picture, she was holding a Little Orphan Annie shaker upon which there was a picture of Little Orphan Annie holding a Little Orphan Annie shaker. He had wondered if the thing would go on forever, orphans holding shakers with pictures of orphans holding shakers. He had used his Tom Mix magnifying glass on it, and was vastly disappointed when the series of pictures within pictures petered out after a few tries.

He looked back to the desk now. The frightened-looking fellow had still not moved. He had leaned forward earnestly, and was now entering on the second stage of his illustrious career, with Stanley looking more bored than he had before.

"Richie?" the voice asked.

He was surprised because he had not been called Richie since he was fifteen. He turned to his right, and the fellow on the end of the bench was beaming broadly and extending his hand uncertainly, the way someone will when he's not sure he's identified the right person.

"Richie Dadier?"

"Yes," Rick answered, striving to recognize the fellow at the end of the bench. He was a short man with tightly curled hair and a broad nose. He had blue eyes that were crinkled into a smile now, and Rick studied the eyes and then the smile, and suddenly he knew who the man was because the wrinkles dropped away as did the dark circles under the eyes, leaving only the youthful face he had known many years ago.

"Jerome Lefkowitz," he said, using his full name, as if that was the way the name had come back in his memory. He reached over and took the extended hand, sliding closer on the bench. "I'll be damned! How are you, Jerry?"

"Fine, fine," Jerry answered, and Rick noticed that he still possessed the same mild manner he'd had in high school. "What are you doing here?"

"Hoping for a job," Rick answered. "Gee, how many years has it been? I haven't seen you since we graduated."

"That's right," Jerry said, still smiling.

"Are you still playing the fiddle?"

"On and off," Jerry said, still smiling.

"You certainly could play that fiddle," Rick said. "Say, what are *you* doing here?"

"There's an English teacher's job," Jerry said, smiling.

"Oh no! How do you like that?"

"Are you applying for the same job?"

"Yes," Rick said, overwhelmed by the coincidence.

"Maybe there are two of them," Jerry said, smiling.

Rick nodded. "Sure, maybe there are." It seemed unfair somehow that he should be placed in competition with someone he had liked so well so many years ago. It seemed doubly unfair because he was certain he would get the job instead of Jerry, and the knowledge left him feeling a bit guilty. "There probably *are* two jobs," he said hastily. "Vocational schools always need teachers."

"Sure," Jerry said, smiling.

He wanted to stop talking about the job because Jerry was such a hell of a nice guy, mild and even-tempered, and vocational schools didn't want nice guys who were mild and even-tempered. He wanted to get as far away from the subject as possible because the unfair coincidence of the competition had caused a tight knot in his stomach, and he was nervous enough without having tight knots to worry about.

"What have you been doing with yourself?" he said.

"I'm married," Jerry said, smiling.

"Well, that's grand. Who'd you marry? Anyone I know?"

"I don't think so. Shirley Levine, did you know her?"

"No, I don't think so. Well, that's swell. I'm married, too, you know. I don't think you know the girl."

"Congratulations," Jerry said, smiling.

"It's a little late for that," Rick answered pleasantly, wishing he had not been placed in competition with Jerry whom he truthfully and honestly liked. "We've been married close to two years."

"Well, that's wonderful," Jerry said. "I've got two kids, you know."

"Two kids! No, I didn't know. Two kids!" He was very happy to learn this because Jerry Lefkowitz was just the kind of nice guy who should have two kids, but at the same time he remembered he was in competition with Jerry for the same job, and the two kids didn't make him feel any happier about the whole damn mixed-up situation. "Boys or girls?"

"One of each," Jerry said, smiling paternally now,

smiling the smile that always preceded the showing of snapshots in the gatefold of a wallet.

He rapidly changed the subject because he did not want to see the pictures of the children. It was bad enough he knew they existed. If he saw their pictures they would become real flesh and blood, and that would make taking the job away from Jerry even harder.

"Jesus," he said, "remember the time we played Monroe? Do you remember that football game, Jerr? Jesus, did we raise hell!"

"The school had a good team," Jerry said mildly.

"Only City champs," Rick added expansively. "Remember the Elf? Brother, could he run!"

"He was very good," Jerry said mildly.

There was movement behind the railing, and Rick saw the frightened-looking man rise and shake hands with Stanley. He thought he saw Stanley heave a heavy sigh, but he wasn't certain. The blonde with the pencil in her hair came to the railing and said, "Mr. Lefkowitz?" and Jerry rose rapidly.

"I'll wait for you, Richie," he said.

"All right," Rick said, wishing Jerry hadn't wanted to talk more after the interviews. "Good luck, boy."

"Thanks," Jerry said, smiling. He walked to the gate in the railing, and then directly to Stanley's desk. He still walked like a duck; that big wide-toed amble, and Rick watched Stanley appraise his walk with slightly raised eyebrows. *He likes a man who walks proudly,* he thought, and then he felt immediately ashamed of his analysis. It was somehow unfair of him to benefit by Jerry's mistakes. If there was to be a competition, he would make it a completely honest one. Having set the rigid rules of the game firmly in his mind, he turned sideways on the bench so that he could not see the interview going on behind the barrier of the railing.

It seemed like a very short time, but that may have only been his imagination. The blonde said, "Mr. Dadier?" and Rick turned and rose, and saw Jerry crossing the room behind the railing. Jerry smiled and winked and indicated the corridor with a slight movement of his head, and Rick knew he'd be waiting for him out there.

Rick wet his lips, the bottled-up nervousness moving up against the cork of the bottle, swelling up into the neck, bubbling frothily. He threw his shoulders back, remembering to walk proudly, reminding himself that he was taking advantage of Jerry's mistake, but telling himself that he had learned that before he made up the rules of the game. Stanley appraised him as he came closer to the desk, and Rick kept his hands tightly clenched because he knew they would tremble if he loosened them. Stanley followed him all the way across the room, his eyes inquisitive.

"Mr. Dadier?" he said, and his voice was very soft, like the roll of distant thunder in purple hills.

"Yes, sir," Rick said.

"Sit down, won't you?"

He sat stiffly, fastening his eyes on Stanley's face immediately. Stanley's eyes were gray, a pale gray. His hair was not as blond as it had looked from the other side of the railing. He wore a soft button-down collar, and a simple gold pin held his narrow tie to his shirt. His suit was expensively tailored, and he looked the complete picture of the chairman of the English Department at Princeton or Harvard, except this was North Manual Trades and not Princeton or Harvard.

Rick made a mental note of that, with the nervousness bubbling noisily within him now. He wanted to get on with it, wanted the cork to pop.

"Why do you want to teach here?" Stanley asked suddenly. His gray eyes narrowed for just an instant, and then his blond brows went up inquisitively, as if he were surprised by his own question.

"I have to teach in a vocational school," Rick said honestly.

"Would you rather teach in another type of school?" Stanley said suspiciously.

Rick smiled a bit tremulously, wondering if he were taking the right tack. "Sir," he said, "I would rather teach at Princeton . . . but so would a lot of other people."

Stanley smiled briefly, and Rick knew he'd hit the right spot, and suddenly the cork popped. The nervousness flooded over the lip of the bottle, a green bilious stuff that dissipated into the air. He felt his hands unclench, and he knew he could take whatever Stanley had to offer now. *Fire away*, he thought, and he waited impatiently.

"You said you *have* to teach in a vocational school. That means you have an emergency license, doesn't it?" Stanley asked.

"Yes, sir," Rick said. "A year in vocational high schools to make the license valid for *any* high school."

"A good move on the Board's part," Stanley commented dryly. "We need teachers in vocational high schools." He paused and smoothed his thin mustache, patchy in spots Rick saw, now that he was closer to it. It's probably a new mustache. A department chairman must look older, and he figured Stanley for no more than thirty-eight or -nine.

"Which college did you attend?"

"Hunter, sir."

"Oh?" Stanley's brows went up in interest. Everyone's brows always went up in interest. It was better than having a Harvard degree. It always caused interest, and interest was what separated the men from the boys, interest was what made one face stand out from all the thousands of other hopeful faces. "That's an all-girls' school, isn't it?"

"It was, sir. They took in veterans after the war. It was difficult to find a school, so many of us were returning at once."

"You're a veteran then?" Stanley asked.

"Yes, sir. Navy."

"I see." He could tell Stanley was pleased. The veteran hook always pleased people. Do their bit for the boys, you know. "Where did you student teach?"

Stanley pronounced it "styu-dent," and Rick suddenly remembered his diction, and he recalled the Speech I and II classes. He knew he possessed a sibilant *S*, and he reminded himself to watch that *S*, and when he spoke, his speech was letter perfect, as if Stanley's "styu-dent" had given him an invisible shot in the arm.

"I taught . . ." and he hit the *T* perfectly, touching his tongue to his gum ridge, pulling it away quickly, trippingly . . . "at Machine and Metal Trades, sir."

"Oh? A vocational school, eh? That was thinking ahead."

"Yes, sir," and he watched the *S* carefully, cutting it off the instant it began to hiss.

"How'd you find it?"

"I enjoyed it, sir. It wasn't at all as bad as they'd painted it."

"If you liked Machine and Metal, you'll like it here. Who was Department Chairman there?"

"Mr. Ackerman, sir."

"Mmm, yes, a good man."

"He helped me a lot, sir."

"You speak rather softly," Stanley said suddenly, lifting his brows again. "Can you be heard at the back of a classroom?"

"Well, I did a lot of dramatics in college, sir, and they could always hear me in the last row of the theater."

"Really?" Stanley asked, seeming truly interested.

"Shall I project a little?" Rick asked, smiling.

Stanley leaned back and smiled with him. "Go ahead. Project."

Rick felt for his voice at the pit of his diaphragm. *"Once more unto the breach, dear friends, once more,"* he quoted loudly, strongly, *"or close the wall up with our English dead. In peace there's nothing so becomes a man as modest stillness and humility: but when the blast of war blows in our ears, then imitate the action of the tiger."*

He stopped there, hoping Stanley would not want him to go farther because he could not remember any more of the quotation. The blonde at the railing had turned and was looking at him curiously.

"An aptly chosen quotation for this particular example," Stanley said smilingly, pleased. "*Henry the Fourth*, wasn't it?"

Rick hesitated for the first time during the interview. The passage he'd quoted had been from *Henry V*, Hank the Cinq as they'd called it in school. Was it possible that Stanley, the chairman of the English Department, did not know this?

"I think it's *Henry the Fifth*," Rick said politely, smiling, gambling that Stanley knew and was simply testing him.

Stanley nodded knowingly, more pleased now. "Damn right it is," he said. He did not hear Rick sigh. "Can you be here Friday for an Organizational Meeting, Mr. Dadier?"

"Certainly, sir," Rick said, still not realizing the job was his.

"Fine. Give your license to Miss Brady in the adjoining office. She'll list you on the books and make out a time card for you. You know how to punch a clock, do you?"

"Yes, sir," he said happily.

"Fine. The meeting is at noon Friday, but I'd like you to be here by eleven or so. I'll introduce you to Mr. Small, our new principal, at that time. You can report to the English office. That's on the fourth floor, Room 439. Any questions?"

"Just one, sir," Rick said. He hesitated, and then asked, "The discipline problem here. Is it . . ."

Stanley's eyes tightened. "There is no discipline problem here," he said quickly. "I'll look for you on Friday."

He rose quickly and took Rick's hand, and Rick rose uncertainly.

"Yes, sir," he said. "Thank you, sir."

He strode briskly from the desk and through the gate, remembering to keep his shoulders back and his head high. He went directly into the adjoining office and asked for Miss Brady, who turned out to be a spinsterish sort of person with mouse-brown hair pulled into a tight bun at the back of her thin neck. He handed her his license, and she asked for the book the Board of Education had supplied him with, the one with all the dates listed in it, the one that would keep a record of the days he had worked. He handed it to her, and she explained that she would keep this in her possession, even though the listing of the dates was a mere formality when it concerned a regular substitute as differentiated from a day-to-day substitute. She also told him he could have his license back in about ten minutes if he cared to wait, but he abruptly remembered Jerry standing outside in the corridor, and he told her he'd pick it up when he came in on Friday. She nodded noncommittally, and then gave a birdlike shrug which plainly said, "It's *your* license, mister."

He did not want to leave the security of her office, nor did he wish to meet Jerry. He still felt irrationally guilty about having taken the job from his old friend. He decided, though, that it would be worse to put it off any longer. He squared his shoulders and walked out into the corridor.

Jerry met him with a smiling face and an extended palm. "You got it, didn't you?" he said happily. "Congratulations."

Rick took his hand, feeling even more guilty in the

face of Jerry's obvious sportsmanlike joy. "Thanks," he said. "I'm sorry I . . ."

"Say, what did he have you doing in there? Reciting poetry?"

"He wanted to know if I could project or not," Rick said embarrassedly.

"I knew I didn't make it the minute we started talking," Jerry said sheepishly. "I could tell he didn't take to me."

"Hell, there are other jobs," Rick said.

"Oh, sure." Jerry smiled. "I'll find something."

"Have you tried New York Vocational?"

"No," Jerry said. "Where's that?"

"On 138th Street and Fifth Avenue. I was going to head there right after I left here. I think they have an opening." He felt better about revealing this information. He knew they did have an opening, and it somehow took the onus off his having stolen this job from Jerry.

"I'll try them," Jerry said, happily, thankfully, gratefully.

"And I think Samuel Gompers may have something. I know a guy who was hired there last week, and he said they were desperate."

"I'll try them, too," Jerry said gratefully. "Did you student teach in a vocational school, Richie?" They were walking down the dim corridor now, walking toward the door through which Rick had first entered the building. Their heels clacked on the marble floor, and the corridor seemed very lonely and very dim.

"Yes," he said, "I did."

"You were lucky. I student taught at Taft, up in the Bronx."

"That's a good school," Rick said.

"Yes," Jerry agreed, "but it doesn't train you for coping with juvenile delinquents."

"Oh, it's not that bad," Rick said. "I got along fine at Machine and Metal Trades."

Jerry looked at him admiringly. "Is that where you taught? I heard that was a very rough school."

"I never had any trouble there," Rick said, basking in the glow of admiration on Jerry's face.

"Still, it's a tough school." They were walking down the marble steps now, and Jerry shoved open the scarred, slashed wooden door and held it open for Rick. He gestured with his head toward the corridor they'd just left, and said, "This one isn't any finishing school, either, you know."

"Stanley said there's no discipline problem here," Rick told him, stepping out into the sunshine.

Jerry nodded solemnly. "There's no discipline problem at Alcatraz, either."

The door slammed shut behind them, and they started across the schoolyard. *This is my schoolyard*, Rick thought. *My students will play in this schoolyard.*

"I've heard pretty good reports about this school," he said, disturbed by Jerry's Alcatraz allusion.

"Really?" Jerry said agreeably. "Well, perhaps I'm wrong."

"I'll soon find out, I guess," Rick said.

"Yes."

They walked in silence to Third Avenue, and then

Jerry said, "I'll take a cab to New York Vocational. It's getting late and if there is anything, I don't want to miss out. Can I drop you anywhere?"

"No," Rick said. "I get a bus across the street. Thanks, anyway."

"We should get together," Jerry said, smiling.

"Yes, we should." He paused, and then popped with sudden inspiration, "Look, let me know how you make out at New York, won't you? Give me a call."

"All right," Jerry said happily. "I will."

"It's Tyrone 2-9970," Rick said. "Like in Tyrone Power."

"That's a funny exchange."

"It's a new one," Rick said.

Jerry jotted down the number in a small black pad. "I'll call you," he said. "It was real good running into you again, Richie."

"Same here. Good luck, Jerry."

They shook hands awkwardly, the way two people will when they have recalled an old friendship for just a brief while, and are ready to commit it back to the limbo from which it had come.

"There's my bus," Rick said.

"Go ahead," Jerry said, smiling. "You can catch it."

They terminated the handshake abruptly, and Rick ran across the street under the El structure. He caught the bus at the corner, and when he was seated and looking through the window he saw Jerry wave and smile from the other side of the street.

It wasn't until then that he remembered he hadn't called Anne, but he told himself it was better this way, he'd surprise her.

And then the bus belched carbon monoxide, pulled out into the thick traffic, and left Jerry on the corner where he stood, smiling.

When the old-fashioned twist bell in the metal door sounded she was standing at the sink with her hands in soapy water. There was a nice breeze here on the eleventh floor, and it lifted the plaid curtains at the kitchen window, touching her blond hair lightly, loosening a wisp near her throat.

She called, "Just a moment," and then opened the cabinet to the left of the sink, removing a dish towel from its hook and drying her hands rapidly. She dropped the dish towel on the kitchen table, walked down the long foyer past the living room and to the front door. She lifted the metal flap of the peephole in the door, and then said, "Oh, Rick, it's you." She said it happily surprised, and then she dropped the peephole and unlocked the door, wondering why he hadn't used his key.

He stood there with a little-boy look on his face, both hands behind his back. The light from the bulb down the hallway struck the planes of his face, touching on the high cheekbones and the strong nose, putting a pinpoint of light in each of his deep brown eyes. He was grinning broadly, like a kid on Christmas morning, and she knew then that he'd got the job, but she would not have spoiled his surprise for all the tea in China.

"Hello, Anne," he said softly, secretly.

"Hello, darling," she answered, smiling, almost not

able to contain the fact that she already knew his secret. "Why didn't you use your key?"

"I couldn't," he said secretly, a mischievous twinkle in his eyes. His hair was still cropped close to his head in an even, militaristic fashion, like the bristles on a brush, the way he'd worn it all through college. It added to his secretive, little-boy appearance, and she wanted to hug him to her breast, and she thought, *God, I really am getting the maternal urge.*

"Why couldn't you?" she asked, playing along with the game, still standing in the doorway, waiting for him to break the surprise.

"My hands are full," he said. *"Voilà,"* he popped, and he pulled one hand from behind his back, and there was a bouquet of red roses in that hand, six of them, with ferns and crisp green wrapping.

"And *voilà!"* he popped again, and he pulled the other hand out, and she saw the bottle of champagne, and she could read the delicately scripted *Domestic,* but that didn't matter to her at all.

"You got the job!" she said ecstatically, pretending surprise, not having to pretend vast joy because she was truly excited, the way she had only been excited on several occasions in her lifetime.

"Did I get it? Did I get it?" He pushed through the doorway and scooped her into his arms, lifting her off her feet, with the champagne and roses clutched tightly behind her back. "Did I get it, honey? Did I get it?"

He swung her around, and she shrieked girlishly and squealed, "Rick, your son and heir!" and he answered, "Nuts to my son and heir."

But then—remembering that she was six-months pregnant, remembering that you don't go swinging six-months pregnant women around in the air, even if you did get a job at Manual Trades, and even if this was the first goddamned break you'd had since you got out of school, even so, you did not go swinging pregnant women around in the air, not if you indeed wanted a son and heir, or a daughter and heiress, though he would have vastly preferred a son and heir—he put her down.

He put her down, and when her feet touched the asphalt tile floor covering, he kissed her resoundingly on the mouth, thinking how sweet her lips were, and thinking there was no one on earth he would have rather come home to with the news that he had got the job at Manual Trades. No one on earth, and that included Hedy Lamarr and Rita Hayworth and anyone else you might care to name, sir.

"Oh, Rick," she said, "that's wonderful, truly wonderful!"

"And are you going to worry about money anymore?"

"No," she said softly, pleased, smiling.

"And are you going to call me a lazy loafer anymore?"

"Rick, I never . . ."

"And are you going to love me?"

"I love you, Rick," she said.

"Are you going to really love me?"

"I really love you, darling."

"Have you cooked supper yet?"

"No, I . . ." She put her hand to her lips because she hadn't even begun supper yet, and here Rick was home with wonderful news, news that rated at least a supper begun. Her green eyes clouded. "I . . ."

"Good! Because I am going out for supper. I shall bring supper home to you as befits the wife of a new English teacher at North Manual Trades High School, Incorporated, of America."

"Rick," she said, chiding and laughing at the same time, and feeling the happiness swell inside her like a blossoming flower.

"How about ravioli?" he asked, his eyes sparklingly excited. "How about that? That goes well with champagne, doesn't it?" he asked. "Ravioli, and a good antipasto before. And we'll put candles on the table, and these roses, by God, these good American Beauty roses!"

"All right, Rick," she said, watching him happily, loving the excitement in his eyes, and the high flush on his cheeks. "All right, Rick."

"And I want you to wear your black strapless, and I'll wear my blue . . ."

"Rick, I'd never get into it!" she complained.

"The hell you say, Skinny." He swept her into his arms again and kissed her lingeringly this time, and she tightened her arms around his neck, not wanting to let him go, wanting to preserve this bubble of complete happiness forever, wanting to coat it in bronze and put it on the living room end table, the way people put a baby's first pair of shoes on the living room end table.

He released her suddenly, holding her at arm's length. "That new maternity thing then, the pink one. I want this to be dressup, Anne. Do you understand?"

"Yes, darling," she said. "I do."

"Good. Are you happy, Anne?"

"Yes, I'm very happy." She could not keep the happiness off her face, and she knew he must have seen it there because it was reflected on his own face, in his eyes, in the smile on his lips.

"Good. Now you set the table, and don't forget the candles. You can use those goddamn brass candlesticks your mother gave us. By God, I knew they'd come in handy someday." He laughed aloud, and he danced a little jig across the kitchen floor, and then he pointed a finger at her like a commanding officer and said, "Hop to it, wench! I'll go get the vittles."

He kissed her again, swiftly this time, and she said "Be careful, darling," and he left the apartment like a whirlwind, leaving a curiously empty silence behind him.

They could not have asked for more from the evening.

The candles cast a warm glow onto the stiff regularity of a City Housing Project kitchen, and the food looked inviting and tempting. They ate with relish, and he related the entire interview to her, still excited, leaving nothing out, telling her all about the frightened jerk who was there when he came in, and then all about Jerry and how guilty he'd felt about him (to which Anne said, "That's silly, Rick. Someone had to get the job"), and then all about how he'd recited Hank the Cinq, and Stanley calling it *Henry the Fourth* to trip him up. He told her all about it, and she listened while she ate, listened excitedly, enjoying the experience vicariously because he told it so marvelously, leaving no details out.

And afterward they turned on the radio and danced

in the living room, with the cool breeze blowing off the East River, and across Bruckner Boulevard, and up Soundview Avenue, into their eleventh-floor window. They danced with her belly big against him, and he held her tightly, and they didn't speak, just listened to the music and felt the breeze and were content in the tight little happy vacuum they had built around themselves.

In bed, they were not awkward. It had become awkward this past month, sometimes so awkward that all the pleasure was lost in their near-adolescent strugglings. She had begun to curse her mountain of a belly because she had always enjoyed bed with Rick, and now it was rapidly becoming anything but a pleasure. But tonight, there was no awkwardness. There was something about both of them tonight, something that transcended the hill of flesh that could have made things difficult. She was slender again for him tonight, the way she had always been, and she did not even realize she was pregnant, this thing in both of them changed all that.

They did not know what this thing was. They accepted the gift gratefully, moving with the casual abandon of expert ballet dancers, but with none of their scientific aloofness. This thing that miraculously surrounded them was all a part of Rick's getting the job, and the impromptu supper suggestion, and the dancing afterward, and now the sex in this beautifully tender way they had almost forgotten.

They did not stop to realize that this thing about them was simply being in love.

Solly Klein had been to Organizational Meetings before. In his twelve years at Manual Trades he had been to plenty of them. And in his own words, they were all just so much horse manure. The Boss would get up there like the coach of a football team between halves, and he'd tell them all how he wanted them to get out there and fight. He'd tell them all what a fine school this was, as if they all didn't know this was not a fine but a ratty school, and then he'd tell them all to get out there and fight again.

Solly had been getting out there and fighting for twelve years, and he prided himself upon the fact that he was still not punch drunk. He did not know why he was not punch drunk, but he imagined it had something to do with his attitude, and his attitude was damn well not shaped by any stupid Organizational Meetings. It always amazed him how The Boss could get up there in front of all those fairly honest people and lie his god-damn head off so baldfacedly. It was like using an advanced form of Orwell's doublethink, he supposed, but he always wondered if The Boss really believed everything he said about the vocational school system and the need Manual Trades filled in that complex, complicated system.

This year, there was a new Boss, and so the between-halves talk would probably be more spirited. He remembered back to when Ginzer had come in as principal, and the talk then had really set a mark for spiritedness. Ginzer had come to Manual Trades fresh from an administrative assistant's job at Evander Childs, which was a fairly decent academic high school. He had read all the books about the vocational high school, and he had proceeded to tell the gathered teachers—some of whom had been at Manual Trades for close to twenty years—all about it. They were very polite, and they did not laugh at him. Perhaps because the talk had had so much spirit in it. Besides, they were all returning from summer vacation, and facing the fall term after summer vacation is certainly not a laughing matter. Not at Manual Trades.

Of course the new Boss, Small was his name—and he was anything but, if Solly was any judge of height—had come from another vocational school, and so he should know the score. He had caught a glimpse of him this morning as he'd gone into his office, and after that Stanley had led in his bevy of new English teachers, all shined up and spruced, the way the new English teachers looked every year. Kalbenstadt had followed Stanley in with a new science teacher, and Morley trailed behind both of them with the two new history men, and that was probably the fall lineup as picked by Red Barber in *Collier's*. Thank you, Red Barber.

The meeting had been called for noon, and it was quarter past that now, but these damn things never started on time. The tables in the library had been situated so that they formed a rough semicircle around one table over near the fiction section. The Boss, naturally, would sit at that table, together with Mike Angelico and a few of the other wheels. Solly had greeted all the old-timers, and they'd exchanged the usual prattle about how was your summer and how was *yours,* and then he'd found an inconspicuous spot at a table off to one side of the Boss' table. He'd also found an old copy of *Today's Woman,* and he was leafing through it, musing over the crap women would read and wondering what a copy of a woman's magazine was doing in Manual Trades, when Stanley came in with his train of English teachers again.

He found a table for them close to the Boss' table, and then seated them with all the maternal care of a mother hen, while Solly watched with all the disinterest of the barnyard rooster. It wasn't until he noticed the girl that he dropped his magazine and took out his reading glasses, perching them expertly on his broad, flat nose.

The crew-cut Kid College had not interested him, nor had the intense-looking, bespectacled boy with the dark hair and the serious eyes. But the girl was something else again.

Her hair was very black, and she wore it trimmed close to her face and neck, and the neck was delicately curved and very white. Her face was a pale white, too, like a flawless piece of alabaster, or an untouched, rounded bit of balsam. She had large, liquid brown eyes which dominated the paleness of her face, and she wore a light crimson lipstick which contributed to the fragile, delicate appearance of her features.

There was nothing delicate or fragile-looking about her body, though, and Solly scrutinized it from the insurmountable, protected heights of middle-age. She was big-breasted and narrow-waisted, and she wore a thin nylon blouse through which the delicate lace of her slip and the slender straps of her brassière could be clearly seen. Solly wondered if she would wear that blouse on Monday, because if she did, there would surely be a rape. Either from the students or the teachers or maybe both. Unless they locked her up in the bookroom where no one could take advantage of the view.

She wore a straight black skirt that followed the line of her flesh-padded hips. The skirt was very tight, and the rolled line of her panties showed through the skirt where it tightened over her buttocks. *This one*, Solly thought, *has never even heard the words Vocational School*.

Or perhaps this is just for today, just so she will be the star of the North Manual Trades picnic, Organizational Meeting, and chowder party. On Monday, the beginning of the school term, she would come in wearing a dress down to her ankles, and up to her throat. She would also wear gold-rimmed glasses and no lipstick and the boys would look upon her as a spinster aunt, provided she did something about the line of her panties tight against her behind.

Still, a girl as young and as pretty as that in a vocational high school. Solly shook his head in muted wonder.

There was a hushed murmur at the back of the library, and then the door opened and Mike Angelico rushed into the room, like a page in the royal chambers. He walked briskly down the aisle which had been left between the tables, and Miss Brady, the Boss' secretary, followed behind him. Hawkner, who had been at the school for close to seventeen years, entered with a broad smile on his broad face, and behind him was William Small, the new principal, God bless him and keep him, and heal his head.

The men teachers rose, and Small accepted this small tribute with a small nod of his rather large head. He was rather large all over. He looked like a misplaced fullback, and Solly hoped he was as tough as he looked. He still remembered the time Juan Garza, a little bastard of a troublemaker, had thrown an inkwell through the window in Ginzer's office, and then almost thrown Ginzer out after it. They'd have a tough time throwing Small through any windows, unless the meat was just meat with no spine in it. He watched Small as he deposited his notes on the table top, Mike Angelico on his left, and Miss Brady on his right. A thin scar ran from Small's right temple to just below his cheekbone, and Solly wondered if it were an occupational wound.

Small did not sit. He kept standing, and when the room was absolutely silent, he said, "Well now," and that was all.

Martha Riley, who was a lady of about fifty, and who had been teaching math at Manual Trades since before Moses, giggled and then stifled it immediately, and

Small smiled like a benevolent despot, and cleared his throat.

"First, welcome back to all the old faces," he said in a rhetorical voice, "and welcome for the first time to all of the new faces. Since I'm a new face, welcome to me, too."

The assembled teachers, remembering Martha Riley's recent outburst, hesitated. Then Mike Angelico gave out with a hearty chuckle, and accepting this as their cue, the staff of Manual Trades acknowledged the Boss' razor-sharp wit with a polite round of subdued laughter.

"I mean it when I say 'Welcome,' " Small said. "I mean it because I mean to make this school one of the best damned schools in the vocational educational system, and a school where knowledge and practicality will always be welcome."

There was a stunned silence, and then Mike Angelico nodded his head in appreciation, and the staff buzzed appreciably, showing they appreciated Mike's nod of appreciation.

"Oh, I know vocational schools," Small said. "I taught for two years at Bronx Vocational, and three years at Manhattan Aviation, and three at Manual Training in Brooklyn, and I even taught at Benjamin Franklin, which is not a vocational high school but which gave me a little memento that made me grateful there were such things as vocational high schools." He touched the thin scar on his face here, and everyone nodded in tribute to his heroism under fire.

"I've taught at New York Vocational," Small went on,

"and Central Commercial, and Brooklyn Automotive." He paused here for the gasp of acknowledgment, because Brooklyn Automotive was possibly the worst goddamn school in the whole setup, and they all knew it. When the gasp did not come, Small said in a voice like muted gunfire, "I was administrative assistant at Brooklyn Automotive for seven years."

Mike Angelico flinched at this, but not because he was admiring the courage or skill of the new principal. Mike Angelico had been at North Manual Trades for eighteen years. He had been administrative assistant at the school for ten of those years. He had been administrative assistant when Anderson was principal, and he had been administrative assistant when they dragged in Panucci from Chelsea Vocational for the principal's spot, and later when they brought in Ginzer from Evander Childs. He had been administrative assistant all that time, and now they had brought in another outsider for the principal's job, and Solly knew that Mike did not wholly appreciate this incontestable fact.

Even so, Solly reflected, *Brooklyn Automotive is no goddamn picnic and maybe Small is a good man after all, despite his half-assed jokes.*

"So I know vocational schools," Small said. "I know them very well, and I know what they're supposed to be doing in the community that is our city, and I also know what they are doing. Now understand this. I don't care what North Manual Trades *was* doing, but I know damn well what it's *supposed* to be doing, and that's what it's *going* to be doing, starting this term, starting this day, starting right this minute!"

Mike Angelico started to applaud, but Small cut him short with a withering glance. It was apparent The Boss had not finished.

"We've got a good staff here," Small went on. "The teachers who have been here all these years are some of the best to be found in the system. I've checked the records of the new ones, and I think we've got a fine crop of level-headed people who can handle any situation that may arise.

"The point is this," and here he stabbed the air with a large forefinger, *"I do not want any situations to arise!*

"When those kids come into this school on Monday morning, I want them to know immediately who is boss. The teacher is boss, and I want them to know that, because we are not running any goddamn nursery school but we are running a school that will teach these kids to be useful citizens of a goddamn fine community, and pardon my French, ladies, but that's exactly the way I feel about it."

The ladies present, of which there were four, smiled in a virginly, ears-unused-to-such-language manner, and the men chuckled a bit, and then Small cut the nonsense with a slicing wave of his hamlike hand.

"So here's what I want. I want a well-disciplined school because we can't teach a disorderly mob. That means obedience, instant obedience. That does not mean delayed obedience, or tomorrow obedience, or next-week obedience. It means instant obedience! It means orders obeyed on the button. The teacher is boss, remember that! And I'm sure I don't have to remind a great many of you of that fact."

He paused to consult his notes and then shouted, "Troublemakers? I want troublemakers squelched immediately! If a teacher can't handle a troublemaker, I want him sent to the department head. That's what department heads are for. And if the department head can't handle a troublemaker, I want that damned troublemaker sent to either Mike or myself, and you can bet we'll know how to take care of him, you can bet your life on that. I don't want any troublemakers in my school. There are reform schools for troublemakers, and that's where I'll send them as sure as I'm standing here, as sure as I am Principal of North Manual Trades High School."

Small nodded his head emphatically, and Mike Angelico unconsciously nodded his head simultaneously.

"So on Monday morning, we come here ready for trouble. If there's no trouble, fine and dandy. If there is, we step on it immediately. We step on it the way we would step on a cockroach. I want no cockroaches in my school, the same way I want no cockroaches in my kitchen. Now as soon as this meeting is adjourned, and I promise you I will not keep you very much longer, there will be departmental meetings, at which time programs will be distributed. Now I do not wish to hear any complaints about programs. I'm an old hand at this game, and I know that free hours and lunch hours can be juggled, and I know there are desirable classes and undesirable classes, and I know all the little tricks, believe me.

"But our department heads and the head of the program committee have made these programs out fairly and honestly, and we've tried to combine the good with the bad, and where you get the dirty end of the stick in one spot, you get the mink-lined end of the stick in another spot. So no complaints about programs, please. It took a long time to figure out the schedule, and I can assure you no changes will be made at this late date, no matter how things used to be before.

"Now on Monday we will greet the students in the auditorium, at which time each teacher will call off the roll for his official class, and then lead them to the official room. I expect that this will consume the major part of the first two periods, if not the third period also.

"We are giving ourselves leeway, and saying that it will also consume the third period. At the end of the third period, the fire gong will be sounded twice. This is not a fire drill, and please warn your students beforehand so that we will not have a mad rush out of the building, an excuse they would readily seize upon. This is simply the signal for change of classes, and it will be the beginning of the fourth period. You had best make this clear to the students in your official class, or they'll all head for the first period, and things will really get fouled up.

"I guess that's all for now. I won't bother to introduce everyone in the room to everyone else in the room because I've no doubt you will all know each other within a matter of days, and I know I can count on the older teachers here to lend whatever orientation assistance is needed to the newer teachers.

"If we'll all go with our department heads now, we can get the routines set, distribute the programs, and then see that our rooms are all ready for Monday. Then we can all go home, except poor me," and here he smiled briefly, "because Monday is the big day, and I want you to relax over the week end and forget all about Manual Trades and come in fresh and ready to handle anything that comes up. All right, now."

He left the desk, and the teachers applauded, all but Solly Klein who watched Small walk to the back of the room and out of the library, followed by Mike Angelico, Miss Brady, and Hawkner.

Yay team! Solly thought.

And I'll bet it's me who got the crappy end of the stick.

Whether or not Solly Klein got the crappy end of the stick was not a matter of great importance. He had been teaching for twelve years at Manual Trades, and one more crappy end certainly wasn't going to break him after all that time.

Richard Dadier, however, was a new teacher, a teacher of English in a vocational high school, and the end of the stick he grabbed might very well make or break him.

He examined his program with more than curious interest, and after he'd studied it he could not but admit it was a fair and a good one, in fact a better one than he had hoped for. He did not realize that he had received the crappiest end of the crappiest stick, and that his program was the worst one distributed in the English Department.

He had, of course, seen a good many programs of different shapes and form throughout his many years of schooling, the years that had prepared him for his present exalted position. It *was* an exalted position to him because, as short a time ago as June, when he had still been at Hunter College, he was a student and the other people were teachers. Now, he was a teacher, and the roles were reversed, and this reversal of roles made him feel damned fine.

As did the program.

The program was divided into eight forty-five-minute periods. There were five minutes allowed between each period for change of classes, and fifteen minutes allowed at the beginning of the day for his official class. All told, he reported for work at 8:30 A.M. and his day ended at 3:25 P.M. A short day, even counting the lesson plans that would have to be prepared at night on his own time, and even counting the traveling time, and even allowing for the fact that he'd have to be at school by about 8:15 and wouldn't leave, most likely, until 4:00. Even so, it was a short day.

His official room was Room 206, the room in which he would teach all day long. His official class was a second-term class. There happened to be nine second-term classes at North Manual Trades, and the official classes at the school were differentiated by numbers. The figure 2, then, designated the term, and any figure from 1 to 9 designated the specific official class in that term. His official class was officially titled 27, the term figure and the group figure wedded in holy matrimony. On his program, the appropriate spaces for the appropriate periods were filled in with a figure indicating the term he'd be teaching, another figure indicating the period in which he taught them, and then—because many teachers taught in several different rooms throughout the day—the number of the room in which he taught. In short, if he taught a second-term class during the second period, in Room 206 (which he did), the space on his program card would be filled with the numerals 22–206.

The program looked like this:

8:30–8:45	*Home Room*
1—8:50–9:35	*English 21–206*
2—9:40–10:25	*English 22–206*
3—10:30–11:15	*Hall Patrol*
4—11:20–12:05	*Lunch*
5—12:10–12:55	*English 55–206*
6—1:00–1:45	*Unassigned*
7—1:50–2:35	*English 77–206*
8—2:40–3:25	*English 78–206*

And that was it, and it looked good to him.

He did not realize that it was undesirable to have two English 2 classes. It was undesirable because 1's and 2's at North Manual Trades followed a block program, a so-called exploratory course. This meant that they, unlike the upper-term classes, did not follow individual programs. They traveled in a group, and that group was a well-knit, solidified thing. It was undesirable because 2's are beginning to feel their oats, are beginning to feel familiar in the school, are beginning to know the score, their "exploration" being almost at an end. The 1's still haven't cut their teeth, and they'll take whatever you have to hand out. The 2's have already cut their teeth, and

those teeth are getting sharp now. They are just marking
time until they're sixteen and can get working papers and
drop all this horse manure by going to continuation
school while they're out earning money. The 2's are four-
teen and fifteen, and you can't smack around a fourteen-
year-old without feeling like something of a tyrant. And
2's, in short, simply do not give a damn about learning a
trade and especially about learning English.

Rick did not realize this. He was, in fact, pleased that
he had two English 2 classes. And he was especially
pleased over the fact that one of those classes was his
own official class, 27. He did not know that this, too,
was undesirable for the simple reason that a prophet is
never appreciated in his own backyard, and his official
class would never appreciate him as an English teacher,
even if he were the best English teacher in the school, or
the system, or the world—which he was not.

The Hall Patrol period did not disturb him, either. He
knew that there were so-called "duty" periods in every
high school, and a hall patrol was a nice time to sit on a
chair and catch up on lesson plans while the monitors
did all the work.

He did not as yet know that his hall patrol was in the
short end of the first-floor corridor L, and that there
was an entrance at the end of that L, and also a toilet.
Even if he had known this, it would not have bothered
him because he didn't know the locks on every door to
that entrance were broken, and he didn't know that this
particular toilet was a gathering place for every kid in
the school who was cutting, smoking, or just generally
killing time.

He was glad they'd given him an English 5 class. Perhaps he would still have been glad if he had known a little about English 55–206, but that is doubtful. Most of the boys in 55–206 had started as freshmen in Ginzer's reign. A good many of them had traveled in a block program with a freshman named Juan Garza, and Juan Garza had raised delightful sorts of hell at Manual Trades, culminating it by throwing an inkwell through Ginzer's closed window and attempting to throw him after the inkwell. Nor was Juan Garza without disciples, and most of those disciples were in 55–206, and those disciples were reported to be some of the worst trouble-makers at Manual Trades, even now that Garza was safely ensconced in a reform school. Rick did not know all this.

He vaguely surmised that it would have been more desirable for his unassigned period to immediately follow his lunch period, and he didn't like the idea of lunch at 11:20. It would have been better if English 55–206 had not separated these two periods. However, he could always eat lunch in his unassigned period, which was at one o'clock. God knew, there were millions of people who ate lunch at 1:00. And besides, a fellow couldn't ask for everything. His program looked fine, especially when he saw that he had two English 7 classes.

Now everyone knew that English 7's were ideal. They'd come to within a term of graduation, and they sure as hell didn't want to get thrown out of school for fouling up at this late stage of the game.

This was ordinarily true.

It was, unfortunately, not true at the present time.

Because most of Rick's English 7's were boys of eighteen and nineteen, and most of them were expecting to be drafted into the Army of the United States at any moment. They were really not interested in English or Manual Trades because they would soon be carrying guns—a prospect most of them looked forward to—and if there should be another outbreak any place on the globe, they might very well have their goddamned heads blown off.

In the meantime, most of them worked after school, so it was doubly unfortunate that one of the English 7 classes was during the eighth and last period. A last-period class is always a restless one, and when a boy is thinking about the money he can be out earning, it can become a torture, even if the English teacher is the best English teacher in the world—which Rick was not.

Nor can you push around a nineteen-year-old boy when he sometimes outweighs you and outmuscles you and outreaches you.

Rick did not think of all these things. Rick was immensely pleased with his program, and after Stanley had spoken to the gathered English teachers, including the lovely brunette with the peekaboo blouse—a blouse which seemed to unruffle Stanley until he finally advised her to wear something "less feminine" this coming Monday—after Stanley had spoken to them about the books they would be using and the classroom procedure and the conferences he would like to have with each of his staff before the first week was out, after all that, Rick had gone down to the general office to pick up the roll book for his official class, to see just what sort of a crew he was getting.

The older teachers were all lined up like bums at the Salvation Army, and Rick wondered what this was all about until he realized they were probably waiting for their August checks, the one real reason they all looked forward to the Friday Organizational Meeting. He picked up the roll book, a heavy leather folder with the numerals 27 lettered on its front in white ink, and then crossed from the metal rack where the books were kept to the key rack near the time clock. He took the key to his official room, and then walked out into the corridor, passing the lined-up, chatting teachers.

"What did you think of the new Boss?" a thin man with rimless eyeglasses asked the shorter, stouter man with him.

"So-so," the short man replied, rubbing his broad, flat nose with his spatulate fingers.

"You didn't like him, Solly?" the first man asked.

The one called Solly shrugged. "He sits when he goes to the can, doesn't he?" he asked philosophically.

Rick smiled and walked down the corridor to the elevator that had been pointed out to him earlier. He buzzed for it, and then realized it probably wouldn't be running until Monday, so he took the first stairwell he came across and climbed the steps to the second floor. Room 206 was situated on the long stem of the L that was the floor plan of North Manual Trades High School. It was close to the elevator and close to the stairwell, and it received sunlight from six large windows that faced the street. It was also directly below a

machine shop on the floor above, a fact Rick would discover shortly. The machines were not running since the
school term had not yet started, so the corridor was
absolutely still as he inserted his key into the door and
twisted it now.

He shoved back the door, pushing the metal prong in
its back against the metal forks set in the wall behind the
door, holding it open. He noticed that the upper half of
the door consisted of four panes of glass, and he
thought that was sensible and wise in a vocational high
school, where any passerby could look through the glass
and see if the teacher inside were perhaps being pinned
to the wall or stomped into the floor.

The room was absolutely silent. The sun streamed
through the windows, and the dust motes floated lazily
on the broad golden beams. There was something
almost sanctified about the room at this moment, and
Rick walked solemnly to his desk and looked out over
the rows of empty seats, feeling something like a priest
in a new parish awaiting his Sunday congregation. He
pulled back his chair gently, and then opened the drawers in the desk, looking into each one. There was a pencil in one of the drawers, but aside from that, they were
empty.

He put the leather-covered roll book on the desk top
and opened it. For each boy in his official class, there
was a plastic-encased white card in the book. The plastic
cases were lined up vertically, with each one overlapping
the one beneath it. The boys' names were lettered at the
bottom of each white card. The only full card that
showed was the top one. After that, only the names of

the boys were visible in a row down the length of the book. Rick glanced down the list of names quickly.

>Abrahms, Morris
>Arretti, Louis
>Bonneli, George
>Casey, Frank
>Diaz, Alonso

There were more, a good many more. He did not bother looking at them now. He would make a list of the names before he left the school today, and study them when he got home. He flipped back the plastic cases, choosing one at random in the center of the row. The white card was divided into sections for each month, and each month had a row of boxes, one box for each day of the month. The attendance was kept in these little boxes, on these white cards which were easily slipped out of the plastic cases. It was a simple matter.

Rick flipped the cases, and then closed the book.

He sat at the desk quietly, looking out over the empty classroom. When the voice came from the doorway, it startled him.

"Makes you feel good, doesn't it?"

He looked toward the door and the voice, and recognized the new teacher Stanley had introduced him to earlier that day. The man was small and meek-looking, with intense brown eyes and heavy spectacles. Something burned in those brown eyes now, and there was a smile on his round, wide face. Rick tried to think of his name, but he couldn't remember it. He felt a little embarrassed, too, at having been caught staring out over an empty classroom. He almost resented the small, beaming man's intrusion.

"Yes," he said, trying to sound less frigid than he felt. "It makes you feel good."

The small man walked into the room, still beaming, as if Rick's words had somehow served as an invitation, and as if he wouldn't have considered entering if Rick hadn't spoken those words.

"I didn't think it would affect me that way," the small man said expansively. "I mean, you know, it's just a job."

"Yes," Rick said. He estimated the new teacher to be about twenty-eight or so, and he wished he could remember the fellow's name. Hell of a thing not knowing whom you were talking to.

"But the minute I stepped into my room, I felt differently about it. Like reaching a goal, you know? Like— like here I am." The small man's grin widened. "Damn, if I don't feel good!"

Some of the small man's enthusiasm was beginning to rub off on Rick, despite his earlier resentment. "I'm afraid I've forgotten your name," he said.

"Edwards," the small man said. "Joshua Edwards. The man with the two first names, like Harry James. Do you like swing?"

"Well, yes."

"I do, too. I have a good collection. I plan on bringing some of the records in for the kids to hear sometime. Do you think they'd like that?"

"Well, yes, I suppose they would."

"You can call me Josh," the small man said. "Your

name is Dadier, isn't it? Richard, I think. Shall it be Dick, Rick, Rickey, or Richard, or what?"

"Rick," Rick said.

Josh extended his hand, and Rick took it. "I'm right across the hall," Josh said, "if you should need any help."

Rick smiled. "I'm not looking forward to any trouble."

Josh withdrew his hand. "I'm not, either. My God, I'm excited. Are you excited?"

"Yes, in a way."

"Well, I'm excited. I can't remember ever being so excited, except the time I almost drowned, and that was different. Hell, I can hardly stand still."

"It'll pass. Wait until Monday."

"Have you ever taught before?" Josh asked.

"No. Just student teaching."

"Me, too. My God, I can't wait." His brown eyes burned intensely, like the eyes of a man who's found religion. "Do you think it'll be okay?"

"I imagine so. The new principal sounds on the ball."

"He is, oh he is that. He'll be all right, a good man to deal with. Knows how to handle this type of kid, don't you think?"

"Yes, I think so."

"But I'm not expecting trouble anyway."

"Did you student teach in a vocat . . ."

"Yes, Central Commercial, do you know it?"

"There's a nice bunch of kids there, isn't . . ."

"Yes, very nice. These kids will probably be rougher, but they're just kids, you know. I mean, damn it, you won't mind if I hop around a little? I swear to God, I can't stand still."

"That's all right," Rick said, smiling because he was beginning to like this little man with the restless feet and the round beaming face.

"I figure you can handle any kids if . . ."

"If you can handle them," Rick finished for him.

"Yes, exactly," Josh said, beaming. "Say, that's right. You just have to handle them, that's all. I can't wait until Monday. Can you?"

"I'm looking forward to it," Rick said, his own enthusiasm a bit overshadowed by Josh's.

"Me, too. You think we'll have trouble?"

"I doubt it," Rick said. "I'm just going to get up there and teach. Hell, I'm not looking to be a goddamned hero."

3

Rick was certainly not a goddamned hero at 8:30 on Monday morning when he walked into the auditorium together with the host of other teachers who sallied forth to meet the foe. Nor did he even suspect he would become a hero, if you looked at it from a certain viewpoint, by the end of that day.

He had entered the building at 8:15, punched the time clock with a curious sense of efficiency, and then gathered up his roll book and walked confidently toward the auditorium, smiling at several students he passed in the hallway. His confidence had momentarily wavered when he entered the high-ceilinged, student-filled room and heard what he considered an unruly murmur of many voices. He figured, however, that this was the customary fall exchange of summer experiences between the students, and he imagined the same murmur would be filling the auditoriums of every academic high school in the city on this first day of school.

He had walked to the left side of the large room, and then down the aisle there where the teachers seemed to be congregated up front, near the piano. He had found Josh Edwards sitting up front, his hands clenching and unclenching nervously on his roll book, had exchanged greetings with him, and had nodded pleasantly at the pretty young woman teacher whom Stanley had introduced yesterday, noting with amused satisfaction that she'd exchanged her sheer blouse for a severely tailored beige suit that still did not quite hide the obvious thrust of her breasts.

"When do we start?" Josh wanted to know.

Rick shrugged. Now that the moment was actually here, he felt no real excitement.

"Look, there's somebody now," Josh said.

Somebody, or something, had indeed climbed the steps to the stage and was now fiddling with the adjustment of the microphone there. Each time the Somebody twisted the adjustment, the microphone squeaked. And each time the microphone squeaked, Rick winced.

He studied the Somebody with interest. The Somebody was very tall. He owned a thatch of unruly hair that sprang up from his forehead like crab grass. His brows were thick patches of chickweed. His mouth was a ripe slice of watermelon, and his nose could have been a banana, though Rick shied away from the obvious metaphor.

Mr. How-You-Gonna-Keep-Them-Down-on-the-Farm, Rick labeled him. He watched the man as his long, disjointed arms struggled with the intricate mechanism of the microphone. The man thrust his long jaw closer to the head of the mike and then said, "All right, testing, one-two-three-four, one-two-three-four."

A boy at the back of the auditorium shouted, "Five by five, Mr. Halloran," and this started a series of shouts, cries, laughter, and catcalls which Rick felt would soon get out of hand unless somebody took control of the situation.

Somebody did. It was Somebody himself who did. Somebody, or Mr. Halloran to be exact, picked up the mike in his beefy red hands and shouted, "SHADDUP!"

Rick himself was startled by the outburst, so it did not surprise him that the gathered students immediately quieted down.

"All right," Mr. Halloran said in a normal, gravelly, chipped-rock, wood-splinter voice. "All right, now dat's the end of any nonsense like dat anymore, you follow? Just can it 'cause we're here on business."

"Who is *that*?" Josh whispered behind his hand.

"Superintendent of Schools," Rick said, smiling.

"No," Josh said, "I think he teaches public speaking here."

"By dis time, you've all said hello to ever'body else, so le's calm down and get on wid the business before us," Halloran said. "We're here to get dis business over wit, and not t'dally aroun' all day, so le's get on wit it, and dat way get over wit it."

The students were very quiet now, and Rick wondered what power Halloran wielded over them.

"Dere'll be a assembly in the middle of da week for de extreme purpose of meetin' the new princ'pul, Mr. Small, so we'll dispense wit any conjecture as to wedder he'll be here now or not. He won't, and dat's dat, so put it out of yer minds. We're here for just two tings. The

first ting is to wish you all a good welcome back to
Manyul Trades . . ."

And here all the students groaned audibly.

". . . and so I'm doin' dat right now. Welcome back,
and I hope dis'll be one of de best terms we've ever had.
So much for dat. Dat's over and done wit, and now we
come to de second point as to why we're here t'day, and
that's to start the school term. So, witout any further
ado, le's start the school term. We will start it by havin'
all the teachers call the rolls for dere official classes.
When your name is called, you fall out in de center aisle
wit the rest of the boys in your class, and your teacher
will den lead you up to your official room. We don'
want any monkey business now because we want to get
dis term under way as soon as possible. And I can guarantee I know how to take care of any you guys who feel
like a little monkey business, I'm sure you all know dat."

The students laughed at this, and Rick continued to
stare at Halloran, wondering if his speech pattern was
simply affected in order to establish rapport with the
boys.

"We'll start wit de seniors," Halloran said, " 'cause
the seniors got priority, and den we'll work our way
down to de freshmen. Any complaints you should regis-
ter wit your official teacher after you're up in your official room, so don't start talkin' it up now, we got business t'attend to. We'll start wit a teacher you all know
well, and dat's Mr. Clancy from Carpentry and
Woodworking. The floor is yours, Mr. Clancy."

Rick watched the red-thatched, rotund Mr. Clancy
mount the steps to the stage, and he heard whisperings

in the audience which he could only interpret as "Ironman Clancy." Then Clancy's voice, in comparatively brilliant English diction, rolled forth over the assembled throng, and the seniors he called began filing into the aisle, slapping each other on the back occasionally, clasping hands, all friendly classmate gestures. And then Clancy's voice ended as abruptly as it had begun, and he stepped down off the stage and walked back to join his class who immediately calmed down as he approached.

Halloran was back at the mike, and he shouted, "Shaddup, shaddup," and the students who had deigned to open their mouths quickly closed them. "De nex' teacher is a new one in d'school, and she'll be takin' care of the other senior boys. Miss Hammond, please."

Perhaps Halloran's choice of language was unintentional, or perhaps it was part of his pitch to the boys, the we're-all-brothers-under-the-skin pitch, and I-know-your-problems-well, fellows. Rick had to admit, however, that his choice had been an unfortunate one. For after having introduced the woman who would "be takin' care of the other senior boys," Halloran stepped back and the new English teacher started mounting the steps to the stage. Her skirt, even though it belonged to the severely-tailored suit, was straight and perhaps too tight. At any rate, it rode up over her calves and the flawlessly straight seams of her stockings as she climbed the steps, and a loud wolf call whistle arose from several thousand throats simultaneously.

She was a pretty woman, and Halloran's injudicious choice of words had put an anticipatory flush of excitement on her pale complexion. To make matters worse, she dropped her roll book, started to stoop down for it, and then seemingly realized what such a stoop might do to the riding-up-over-nylon-knees quality of her skirt. She pulled back her hand, looked to Halloran imploringly, and then was forced to stand by in embarrassment while Halloran retrieved the errant roll book for her.

Halloran grandstanded it all the way. He handed her the book, bowed from the waist, and then grinned out at the boys, who whistled and cheered in appreciation of Halloran's chivalry, and who were all too aware of Miss Hammond's reasons for not wanting to stoop down for the book.

Miss Hammond suddenly seemed to regain the composure she had all but lost. Like a follies queen whose breasts have been insulted by a drunken third-row heckler, she threw her shoulders back defiantly, tossed her black hair impatiently, and strode purposefully to the microphone.

She opened her roll book, and the kids packing the auditorium were dead silent as she prepared to speak. She opened her mouth, and her voice caught in her throat, and she succeeded in getting out only a mouse-like squeak which positively convulsed the kids. Hell, this was better than Martin and Lewis. This was one of the best goddamn first-days-of-school ever.

Rick thought back to what Stanley had said about there being no discipline problem at Manual Trades. Perhaps this was so. And perhaps it was so because the people who were supposed to be looking for problems were casually ignoring them. When Miss Hammond, completely rattled now, the composure she had regained all gone again, hardly able to control her tongue, finally blurted the name of the first boy in her class, a cheer of congratulation went up from the assembled kids.

The senior who'd been called leaped into the aisle and shouted, "Lucky old me!" and this caused a fresh outburst of laughter. Man, this was terrific. This was grand! Let's just sit here all day and have laughs at this piecy new English twat.

Rick writhed in his seat, wondering when Halloran was going to step in and take over the ball again. He didn't have to wonder long.

A prolonged "SHADDDDUPPP!" burst from Halloran's watermelon lips, and the kids heard the rumble of impending doom and promptly shut up like obedient little clams. Halloran kept his lips pressed firmly together, casting an evil eye out over the crowd. He nodded his head once in emphasis, a nod which plainly told the muted kids they'd better keep shut up or it would be their asses. Miss Hammond smiled tremulously, and then began calling the roll in a very quiet voice while the kids listened in cowed respect.

When she'd called the two dozen or so seniors in her class, she stepped down from the stage, and every eye in the auditorium was on the nylon sleekness of her legs. She walked back to her class stiffly, trying to hide a walk that was very feminine, but succeeding only in emphasizing the emphatic swing of her well-padded hips. When she'd finally left the auditorium with her class, Rick breathed a sigh of relief, and he nodded his head in disgusted agreement when Josh said, "That was an exhibition, wasn't it?"

The party was over now, and the kids all settled down to listen to the droning voices of the less inspiring teachers as the rolls were called one after the other. Rick chatted quietly with Josh until it was Josh's turn to call up his class, a fourth-term group. When Josh had left, Rick sat impatiently in his seat, almost dozing. When he heard Halloran call out his name, mutilating it as only Halloran could, he picked up his roll book and his briefcase, walked quickly to the steps, and mounted them with his shoulders back and his head high. He paused dramatically for a moment, and then began calling the roll in his best Sir Laurence Olivier voice.

"Abrahms," and he saw movement out there in the seats, but he did not pause to focus the movement.

"Arretti," and another blur of movement.

"Bonneli," and "Casey," and "Diaz," and "Di Zeffolo," and "Donato," and "Dover," and "Estes," and on, and on, and on, until he flipped over the last card in the book. There had not been a murmur while he spoke, and he was satisfied that he had been accorded the respect due an English high-school teacher. He slapped the roll book shut, and walked down the steps and then into the center aisle, conscious of the curious eyes of the kids upon him.

When he reached his official class the same curiosity was reflected in their eyes.

"Follow me," he said, unsmiling. "No talking on the way up."

That, he figured, was the correct approach. Let them

know who's boss right from the start, just the way Small had advised.

"Hey, teach," one of the boys said, "what did Mr. Halloran say your name was?"

Rick turned his head sharply. The boy who'd spoken was blond, and there was a vacuous smile on his face, and the smile did not quite reach his eyes.

"I said no talking, and I meant it," Rick snapped.

The boy was silent for a second, and then Rick heard him say, "Dig this cat. He's playin' it hard."

He chose to ignore the comment. He walked along ahead of his class, feeling excitement within him now, feeling the same excitement he'd felt when he got the job, only greater now, stronger, like the times at school when he'd waited in the wings for his cue. Like that, only without the curious butterflies in his stomach, and without the unconscious dread that he would forget all his lines the moment he stepped out onto the stage in front of all those people. He felt in complete control of the situation, and yet there was this raging excitement within him, as if there was something he had to do and he simply could not wait to get it done.

He could best compare it to the excitement he had felt a long, long while ago, when he'd first entered Hunter College and had planned the seduction of Fran Oresschi. Exactly like that night, that payoff night, when he would find out if his plans would succeed or not. Just like that, only without any of the slyness or the feeling of conspiracy.

He led the class to the stairwell, and aside from a few whispers here and there, they were very orderly, and he felt that everything was going well. He could hardly contain the excitement within him, and he wished that Anne were there to share it with him. And thinking of Anne, he thought of telling her about this, his first day, when he got home that night, and this made the excitement inside him flame.

When they reached the door to Room 206, he inserted the key expertly, twisted it, removed it, and then pushed the door back.

"Sit anywhere," he said brusquely. "We'll arrange seating later."

The boys filed in, still curious, still wondering what sort of a duck this new bird with the Butch haircut was. They seated themselves quickly and quietly, and Rick thought, *This is going even better than I expected.*

He walked rapidly to his desk, pulled out his chair, but did not sit. He looked out over the faces in the seats before him, and then sniffed the air authoritatively, like a blood hound after a quarry. He cocked one eyebrow and glanced at the windows. Then he turned and pointed to a Negro boy sitting up front near his desk.

"What's your name?" he asked.

The boy looked frightened, as if he had been accused of something he hadn't done. "Me?"

"Yes, what's your name?"

"Dover. I didn't do nothin', teach. Jeez . . ."

"Open some of the windows in here, Dover. It's a little stuffy."

Dover smiled, his lips pulling back over bright white teeth. He got up from his seat and crossed behind Rick's desk, and Rick congratulated himself on having handled that perfectly. He had not simply given an order which would have resulted in a mad scramble to the windows. He had first chosen one of the boys, and then given the order. All according to the book. All fine and dandy. Damn, if things weren't going fine.

He turned and walked to the blackboard, located a piece of chalk on the runner, and wrote his name in big letters on the black surface.

MR. DADIER.

"That's my name," he said. "In case you missed it in the auditorium." He paused. "Mr. Dad-ee-yay," he pronounced clearly.

"Is that French, teach?" one of the boys asked.

"Yes," Rick said. "When you have anything to say, raise your hand. We might as well get a few things straight right this minute. First, I want you to fill out Delaney cards. While you're doing that, I'll tell you what it's going to be like in my classroom." He swung his briefcase up onto the desk top, reaching inside for the stack of Delaney cards. He took them to the head of each row, giving a small bunch of the cards to the first boy in each row, and asking him to take one and pass the rest back.

"The official class is 27," he said, and then he walked to the blackboard and wrote "27" under his name. "Please fill the cards out in ink."

"I ain't got a pen," Dover said.

"Then use pencil."

"I ain't got a pencil, either."

"I have some," Rick said coldly. He walked back to his briefcase again, silently congratulating himself upon remembering to think of an emergency like this one. He pulled out eight sharpened pencils, handed one to Dover, and then asked, "Does anyone else need something to write with?"

A husky boy sitting near the back of the room said, "I do, teach."

"Let's knock off this 'teach' business right now," Rick said angrily, his sudden fury surprising the class. "My name is Mr. Dadier. You'll call me that, or you'll learn what extra homework is."

"Sure, Mr. Dadier," the boy at the back of the room said.

"Come get your pencil."

The boy rose nonchalantly. He was older than the other boys, and Rick spotted him immediately as a left-backer, a troublemaker, the kind Small had warned against. The boy wore a white tee shirt and tight dungaree trousers. He kept his hands in his back hip pockets, and he strode to the front of the room, taking the pencil gingerly from Rick's hand.

"Thanks, teach," he said, smiling.

"What's your name?" Rick asked.

"Sullivan," the boy said, smiling. His hair was red, and a spatter of freckles crossed the bridge of his nose. He had a pleasant smile, and pleasant green eyes.

"How would you like to visit me after school is out today, Sullivan?"

"I wouldn't," the boy answered, still smiling.

"Then learn how to use my name."

"Sure," Sullivan said.

He smiled again, a broad insolent smile, and then

turned his back on Rick, walking lazily to his seat at the rear of the room.

"I want those pencils returned," Rick said gruffly, feeling he had lost some ground in the encounter with Sullivan. "Fill out the cards as quickly as you can."

He cleared his throat and walked over to one of the boys, looking over the boy's shoulder to see that he was filling the card out properly, and then turning away from him.

"To begin with, as I've already told you, there'll be none of this 'teach' stuff in my classroom. I'll call you by your names, and you'll call me by mine. Common courtesy." He paused to let the point sink in, remembering Bob Canning, who'd graduated from Hunter the semester before him, and who'd taught in a vocational school, only to leave the job after five months. Bob had allowed the boys to call him "Bob," a real nice friendly gesture. The boys had all just loved good old "Bob." The boys loved good old "Bob" so much that they waited for him on his way to the subway one night, and rolled him and stabbed him down the length of his left arm. Good old bleeding "Bob." Rick would not make the same mistake.

"I've also told you that there will be no calling out. If you have anything to say, you raise your hand. You will not speak until I call on you. Is that clear?"

The boys made no comment, and Rick took their silence for understanding. All of their heads were bent now as they busily filled out the Delaney cards.

"We'll be together in this room every day from 8:30 to 8:45. Then, as you probably know, you'll come back to this room during the second period for English, which I will teach."

The boys' heads bobbed up, and he read the puzzled looks in their eyes and realized he had not yet given them their programs. They did not know he would be teaching them English, and he had broken the news to them in perhaps the worst possible way.

In defense, he smiled graciously. "Yes," he said. "I'll be your English teacher, and I'm sure we'll get along fine." He paused. "I'll give you your programs now," he said, "while you're filling out the Delaney cards. I might add you've got a very good program this term." He had barely glanced at the individual programs, which were carbon copies of each other since the boys were second-termers who still traveled in a group during their exploratory adventures, and he truthfully didn't know if it was good, bad, or indifferent. But he felt it sounded fatherly for him to say the boys had a good program. He got the program cards from his briefcase and rapidly distributed them, calling the boys' names and taking the cards to their desks while they worked.

"You all know the rules about lateness," he said. "I won't tolerate lateness. If you come in one second after the late gong sounds, you go right down to the General Office for a late pass. And I won't listen to sob stories about absences. You can tell those to the General Office, too."

He glanced out at the class, whose interest was alternating between the Delaney and program cards. "You can look over the programs later," he said. "Let's finish the Delaney cards."

He paused and said, "When you come into this room, you put your coats, jackets, hats, or whatever you were wearing outside into the coat closet at the back of the room. I don't want anyone sitting in this room with a coat or jacket on. I don't want pneumonia in my class."

"Hey, what's our official class?" one boy asked.

"Twenty-seven," Rick said, "and no calling out." He turned his back to the boys and chalked the numerals 27 on the board again, remembering the vocational school adage which frankly warned, "Never turn your back on a class." But he obviously had the situation well under control, and he saw no reason for demonstrating distrust at this early stage of the game. He put the chalk back on the runner and said, "Dover, you will be in charge of seeing that the windows are adjusted every morning when you come in."

"Yes, sir," Dover said respectfully, and Rick was a little surprised, but immensely pleased. He remembered something he'd been told back in one of his education classes, something about giving the difficult boys in the class things to do, like raising windows and cleaning blackboards and erasers, or running errands. Dover did not seem to be a difficult boy, and perhaps he'd been wrong in giving him the window assignment. He remembered then that someone had to bring down the list of absentees each morning, and he decided Sullivan, his good friend in the rear of the room, was the ideal man for the job.

"And you, Sullivan," he said, looking directly at the boy, "will take down the roll book each morning."

"Sure," Sullivan said, smiling as if he'd won a major victory.

Sullivan's attitude puzzled Rick, but he decided not to let it bother him. He picked a blond boy in the third row and said, "Will you collect the Delaney cards, please?"

"Sure, teach," the boy said, and Rick realized he'd made a mistake. He should have had them pass the cards down to the first seat in each row, and then have the boy in the first row go across taking the cards from each row. Well, it was too late to correct that now. The blond boy was already making the rounds, picking up the cards dutifully.

"What's your name?" Rick asked him.

"Me?"

The answer irritated him a little, but that was because he did not yet know "Me?" was a standard answer at Manual Trades High School, where a boy always presupposed his own guilt even if he were completely innocent of any misdemeanor.

"Yes," Rick said. "You."

"Foster, teach."

"Mr. Dadier," Rick corrected.

"Oh, yeah. Sure."

"Hurry up with those cards, Foster."

"Sure, teach."

Rick stared at the boy incredulously. "I don't want to have to mention this again," he said. "The next boy who calls me 'teach' will find himself sitting here until four o'clock this afternoon. Now remember that."

The boys stared at him solemnly, a wall of hostility suddenly erected between Rick's desk and their seats.

He sensed the wall, and he wished he could say something that would cause it to crumble immediately. But he would not back down on this "teach" informality, and so he stayed behind his side of the wall and stared back at the boys sternly.

The door opened suddenly, and a thin boy with brown hair matted against his forehead poked his head into the room.

"Mr. Dadier?" he asked.

"Yes?"

The boy moved his body into the room, walked briskly to Rick's desk, and handed him a mimeographed sheet of paper. "Notice from the office," the boy said.

"Thank you."

"Y'welcome," he answered, turning and heading for the door instantly. Rick was impressed with the boy's efficiency and apparent good manners. The boy walked to the open door, stepped out into the hallway, and then thrust his head back into the room. He grinned and addressed one of the boys near the front of the room.

"Hey, Charlie, how you like Mr. Daddy-oh?"

He slammed the door quickly, and was gone before Rick had fully reacted to what he'd said. Someone near the back of the room murmured, "Daddy-oh, oh Daddy-oh," and Rick turned toward the class hotly.

"That's enough of that!" he bellowed.

The boys' faces went blank. He looked at them sternly for another moment, and then turned his attention to the notice from the office.

It told him that the roll-calling had been accomplished much faster than they had expected, and that a

gong would sound at ten-thirty summoning the start of
the third period, rather than the fourth as anticipated. It
advised him to instruct his class that they should proceed immediately to their third-period class, ignoring
any instructions they may previously have received con-
cerning the fourth period.

Luckily, Rick had not given any instructions concern-
ing departmental as yet. He was aware of the sudden
attentiveness in the classroom, and he realized the boys
wanted to know what was in the notice from the office.
He glanced at his wrist watch. It was ten-fifteen.

"A gong will sound in fifteen minutes," he said. "The
gong will announce the start of the third period. When
the gong sounds, you will leave this room and go
directly to your third-period class, is that clear?"

The boys began talking it up, looking at the programs on their desks, which told them their third-period
class was Civics.

A boy in the fourth row raised his hand.

"Yes?" Rick asked.

"Does that mean we won't have you for English
today, Mr. Dadier?" he asked.

"Yes, that's what it means. You go directly to Civics
when you leave here," Rick said, consulting his copy of
the boys' program. He smiled, pleased because the boy
had used his name and raised his hand. "Say," he said
conversationally, "we'd better hurry if we want to get
seated before it's time to go."

He opened his Delaney book, and then his roll book,
and he began calling the boys' names alphabetically,
seating them one behind the other. Several boys com-

plained when they were separated from lifelong buddies, but he ignored the complaints and went on with
his seating plan. Belatedly, he realized it would have
been simpler to have the boys hold their Delaney cards
until they were seated properly. Then he'd just collect
them by rows, ready to slip into the Delaney book. This
way, he had to alphabetize the Delaney cards, jotting
down the name of the first boy in each row, and arranging the cards in the book on his own time later. Well, he
would not make that mistake again.

He gave the boys an opportunity to discuss the program among themselves while he started to alphabetize
the cards. He had alphabetized all of them and was
beginning to put them into the Delaney book when the
gong sounded. He rose swiftly.

"You go to your third-period class now," he said.
"Remember that. Civics, Room 411." He paused and
added, "Be sure to have all your subject teachers sign
your program cards." He smiled. "I'll see you all tomorrow morning."

Some of the boys had already filed out into the corridor and were lingering outside near the open door. Rick
heard someone shout, "Not if we see you first, Daddy-
oh!" but when he turned to the door, the boys were
gone. He let out a deep breath as the remaining boys
filed out of the room, and then he consulted his own
program.

Hall Patrol.

Quickly, he began packing his stuff in his briefcase.
He had been a little Caesar, true, right from go, and in
the best possible little Caesar manner. He had done it

purposely, though, because the first day was the all-important day. If you started with a mailed fist, you could later open that fist to reveal a velvet palm. If you let them step all over you at the beginning, there was no gaining control later. So, whereas being a little Caesar was contrary to his usual somewhat easy-going manner, he recognized it as a necessity, and he felt no guilt. As Small had advised, he was showing the boys who was boss. He finished packing, locked the door, and then started for the General Office, where Stanley had said a Hall Patrol schedule would be posted.

He fought through the swarm of students in the hallway, abruptly remembering that Dover and Sullivan had not returned the pencils he'd loaned them. He cursed his own inefficiency, making his way toward the stairwell. He thought he heard several shouts of "Daddy-oh!" in the thronged hallway, but he could not be certain. When he found the *Down* staircase, he walked quickly to the main floor corridor, and then to the General Office. The schedule was posted near the time clock, and he studied it carefully, located the position of his Hall Patrol on the diagram beneath the schedule, and then started for his post.

The General Office was located approximately in the middle of the long side of the L of the building. He walked toward the intersecting short side of the L, turned right, and then headed for the end of the corridor. His Hall Patrol post was directly opposite the entrance doors there.

Two boys stood flanking the wide entrance doorways, and the yellow armbands on their biceps told Rick they were monitors. He walked directly to them and said pleasantly, "Hello, boys. My name is Mr. Dadier. We'll be working together on this post during the third period every day."

The two boys nodded obediently, and Rick knew he'd have no trouble with them. Monitors were selected from the cream, such as it was, of the school.

One of the boys, a fat kid with streaked dungarees and a striped tee shirt, kept staring at Rick, as if he were expecting further instructions. Rick said, "Would you get a chair for me in one of these rooms, please? Tell the teacher it's for Mr. Dadier."

"Sure," the fat boy said pleasantly.

Rick watched the boy go down the corridor, and then he turned his attention to the doors. There were four of them set side by side. On the other side of the doors a flight of marble steps led to the outside doors of the building. He looked through the glass panels on the inside doors, nodded his head briefly, and then said to the second monitor, a tall boy who stood with his hands behind his back, "You haven't been letting anyone in or out of these doors, have you?"

"No, sir," the boy said.

"Good. And no one is allowed in the corridor without a room pass."

"I know," the boy said.

"Good," Rick said again. He clapped the boy on the shoulder, the way a commanding officer will do to a particularly obedient enlisted man, and then he looked down the corridor to see if the fat boy was returning with his chair. The boy was not in sight. He bit his lip and then studied his end of the corridor, noticing the toilet there for the first time. He walked to the battered wooden door, read the gold-lettered STUDENTS' LAVATORY, and then pulled the door open.

"Chiggee," someone shouted, and Rick heard the instant flush of a toilet. The room was smoke-filled, and his entrance started a mad scramble among the ten or twelve boys who'd been standing around smoking.

"All right," Rick bellowed, "let's just hold it!"

The kids stopped dead in their tracks, dropping their cigarettes and stepping on them. One made a rush for the door, but Rick blocked the boy and shoved him back into the white-tiled room.

"What's going on here?" he roared, squinting through the smoke. "What is this, the Officers' Club?"

One of the boys snickered, and Rick cut him short with a dead cold stare.

"Now clear out of here," he shouted. "I'm letting you all go this time, but if I catch anyone else smoking or loitering here, your name goes to the principal. Now just remember that."

The boys, thankful to be let off the hook so easily, filed out of the room swiftly. Rick watched them go, and then turned to face two boys who lounged near the sinks by the windows.

"What's the matter with you two?" he asked.

One of the boys was a husky Negro with an engaging grin. He had a wide nose, and thin lips, and clear, large brown eyes. He wore a white tee shirt and tight dungarees, and the rich brown of his skin glistened against the white of his shirt.

"We ony just got here, Chief," he said.

"Well, you can only just get right out of here," Rick mimicked.

The boy with the Negro was obviously Puerto Rican. He grinned and a gold-capped tooth in the front of his mouth gleamed.

"Sure," he said, "we jus' get here, Chief."

"Look," Rick told them, "I don't want a debate. Let's clear out."

The Negro boy continued to grin engagingly, continued to lean against the sink. "Can' a man take a leak, Chief?"

"Take it and get out," Rick said.

"Sure, Chief," the Negro boy answered, still grinning pleasantly. "You goan to watch me leak, man?"

"Listen," Rick said, "I don't go for wise guys. If you came here for trouble, you'll get it. If you came to urinate, do it fast and then get out."

"He come to ur-ee-nate," the Puerto Rican said, smiling.

Rick turned on the thin Puerto Rican. "What's your name?" he asked.

The boy blanched. His eyes got suddenly frightened, and he said, "Me?"

"Yes you. What's your name?"

"Emmanuel," he said.

"Emmanuel what?"

"Emmanuel Trades," the Negro boy said. "Man, don'-choo know? This boy yere, he got the school named after him." Again he grinned engagingly, and Rick turned on him furiously.

"What's *your* name, wise guy?"

The boy lifted one eyebrow, and he continued to slouch against the sink. "Gregory," he said, defiantly. "Gregory Miller."

"I'll remember that name," Rick said.

"Sure, Chief. You do that."

"Or maybe you'd like to take a walk to the principal's office right this minute? Maybe you'd like that?"

Miller shrugged, and then smiled, showing those brilliant white teeth. He was a good-looking boy, with the build of a weight lifter and an easy, nonchalant charm. "You holin' all the cards, Chief," he said. "You wanna take me t'see Mistuh Small, that's your choice."

Rick reconsidered. Hell, there was no sense getting a boy into trouble on the first day of school. "Well," he said slowly, "I'll let it pass this time. Just get back to your classroom."

"This's my lunch hour, Chief," Miller said.

"Knock off that 'Chief' routine," Rick said. "If it's your lunch hour, what are you doing in the building?"

"Had to take a leak, man, like I tole you."

"Well then take it."

"Sure, Chief. Thass what I been dyin' to do all this time now."

Miller stepped over to one of the urinals, and the Puerto Rican boy followed him like a shadow. Rick turned away while they urinated, and then Miller, buttoning his fly, said, "Okay for us to drift now, Chief?"

"If you're on your lunch hour, you're supposed to leave the building by the exit near the auditorium. Isn't that right?"

"Yessir."

"Then head down that way. And don't let me catch you in this toilet again."

Miller smiled. "Suppose I got to crap, man?"

"That's different," Rick said instantly.

"I figured," Miller answered, smiling.

"All right, take off."

"Sure thing," Miller said. He walked to the door with the Puerto Rican behind him, and Rick followed them both into the corridor. He watched them walk slowly and naturally down the corridor, and then turn left into the long side of the L. When they were out of sight, he turned to find the fat boy with his chair.

He took the chair, placed it against the wall, and said, "Thanks a lot." The fat boy nodded, and then took his place on one side of the doors. Rick sat, unzipped his briefcase, and took out the Delaney book, hoping to arrange the cards in it for his official class. He was reaching for the Delaney cards when the outside doors were thrown open, and he heard several voices floating up the marble steps and approaching the inside doors. He got to his feet as three boys came through the inside doors, still talking and laughing. They spotted Rick and stopped, seemingly deciding whether to stick it out or run back toward the outside doors again.

"What's this?" Rick asked sternly.

The boy standing in the center of the trio, obviously the leader and spokesman of the group, opened his eyes innocently and asked, "What's what, teach?"

"Where are you boys coming from?"

"Outside, teach."

"You're not supposed to enter the building through this entrance," Rick said sternly.

"Oh no?" the boy asked, surprised.

"No," Rick said.

"We was just havin' lunch," the boy answered.

"Well clear out and go around to the auditorium entrance, the way you're supposed to."

"Sure, teach," the boy said. He smiled and made a slight movement with his head, which the other boys instantly obeyed. Together, the three went down the marble steps and out of the building.

"How'd they get in?" Rick asked the fat monitor.

"Through the doors, I guess," the boy answered.

"I know, but aren't the doors locked?"

"Gee, I guess not."

"Go down and lock them, would you? Just pull them tight against the door jamb."

The fat boy hesitated. Then he said, "I can't, Mr. Dadier. The locks are busted."

"What do you mean busted?"

"On all of the doors. That's how the kids get in."

"How long have they been broken?" Rick asked.

"Long as I can remember," the fat boy answered.

"Mmm," Rick said, making a mental note to tell the custodian about the broken locks. "We'll just have to be careful then, that's all."

"Yes, sir."

Rick sat down again and began slipping the Delaney cards into their slots in the Delaney book. Two boys sauntered down the corridor, passed him quietly, and went into the toilet. When he finished inserting the cards into the book, he sat back and relaxed, and then realized the boys had still not come out of the toilet. He rose and walked to the wooden door, pulling it open.

The two boys, as he'd suspected, were standing near the windows, smoking. He bawled them out heartily, sent them back to their classroom, and then went out into the corridor again. He was seated for about thirty seconds, when the outside doors flew open and a swarm of kids started up the marble steps. He dispatched them quickly, sat down for a full minute, and then rose again when a new gang started up the steps. By the time he'd sent them around to the auditorium entrance, the toilet had gathered five loiterers and smokers, and Rick flushed them out angrily, giving them all warnings. He didn't get a chance to sit down again because the third period was almost over, and the outside doors were opening and closing with rapid regularity now as the kids began returning in force to the building.

When the bell announcing the end of the period finally rang, Rick was exhausted. He promised himself he'd have to figure out a way to cope with those broken locks. Perhaps post one of the monitors outside the building to steer away any kids who tried to use those doors. He'd also have to do something about the smoking in that toilet. Maybe he'd ask some of the other teachers. He reached into his briefcase and consulted the program he'd Scotch-taped to the inside of his small black notebook.

Fourth period: LUNCH.
Allah be praised.

Of course, he had still not become a hero. Dashing into
the toilet to put an end to the tobacco habit was not
exactly an occupation of heroic proportions, even
though it was fatiguing disciplinary work. Nor was
charging up and down marble steps, even if he had done
it on a splendid white stallion, a task that was heroic in
its nature. He had simply behaved in a normal vocational schoolteacher manner, attending to the little tire-
some details that sent vocational schoolteachers babbling incoherently to the nearest booby hatch. But he
had done nothing heroic, and he was still not looking
for trouble, and he was still resolved not to be a "goddamned hero."

As he walked up to the third floor, having lingered a
while to avoid the student rush, he congratulated himself upon what he considered almost perfect behavior
thus far. He had made a few mistakes, true, but on the
whole he had done well. He had shown a tough exterior
to the kids, and whereas tough teachers were not always
loved, they were always respected. He was not particularly interested in being loved. Mr. Chips was a nice
enough old man, but Rick was not ready to say good-by
yet. He was interested in doing his job, and that job was
teaching. In a vocational school you had to be tough in
order to teach. You had to be tough, or you never got
the chance to teach. It was like administering a shot of
penicillin to a squirming, protesting three-year-old. The
three-year-old didn't know the penicillin was good for

him. The doctor simply had to ignore the squirming and the protesting and jab the needle directly into the quivering buttocks.

It was the same thing here. These kids didn't know education was good for them. There would be squirming and protesting, but if the teacher ignored all that and shot the needle of education directly into all those adolescent behinds, things would turn out all right.

To do that, you had to present a tough exterior, no matter how you felt inside. There was the danger of becoming so goddamned tough, of course, that you forgot you were also supposed to be a teacher. Rick would never carry it quite that far. He intended to lay down the law, and then to relax, never letting discipline establish itself as a problem. Once discipline became a habit, there would be time for joking, time for a few laughs while he injected the educational needle. But not until discipline was an ingrained response.

Stanley had explained how the teacher's lunchroom could be reached. You could go directly to a deserted staircase on the main floor, and take that up four flights. Or you could go to the gymnasium on the third floor, cut across and through that, and then climb one flight of steps to the lunchroom. Since Rick had not yet seen the gym, he chose the latter approach.

The gym was situated on the short side of the L, directly at the end of the corridor. Twin wooden doors were set side by side, and the inevitable gold lettering announced that they opened onto the GYMNASIUM.

Rick opened one of the doors and stepped into the high-ceilinged, wire-mesh-windowed room. The floor was highly polished, and Rick noticed that all the boys lined up before the teacher's platform were in their stocking feet. He imagined this was the teacher's method of preserving his polished floor on this first day of school when the boys would not be carrying sneakers. The teacher was a tall red-headed man with muscles bulging under and around his white tee shirt. A whistle hung from a lanyard around his neck, and he stood on the platform with his hands on his hips, talking out over the heads of the lined-up boys.

Rick crossed the gym, his shoes clicking noisily on the polished wood floor. He passed between the teacher's platform and the boys, smiling up at the teacher, who waved slightly and went on laying down the law to the kids. When he reached the door at the opposite end of the gym, he opened it and stepped onto a landing. He closed the door on the hollow, echoing voice of the gym teacher, and then started up the steps to the lunchroom.

He had formed no preconceived notion of what the teachers' lunchroom would be like, so he had no reason to be surprised by what he found. He was, nonetheless, surprised. The lunchroom consisted of two rooms, actually. At the top of the steps there was an open doorway, and Rick stepped through it into the first room.

One wall of the room was lined with windows. The opposite wall was bare. A long table ran the length of the room. The table was bare. A refrigerator and a sink occupied the wall facing Rick. An old gas stove was on the other side of the doorway that divided that wall in half. A tea kettle was on the stove, a blue flame curling around its metal sides.

Rick stepped through the doorway, walking between the sink and the stove, and into the second, smaller room.

This room was occupied. This room was the dining room, as differentiated—he supposed—from the other room which could be classed as the galley or the kitchen.

A table was in the center of the room, and there were chairs around the table, and there were men sitting in the chairs, and each man had a sandwich in his hands. There were windows on two walls of the room. The third wall held the door through which Rick entered, and the fourth wall boasted a bulletin board and a cupboard. Rick saw cups hanging on hooks inside the cupboard, and saucers stacked in neat piles. Looking through the glass doors, he also saw a small tray with silverware stacked in it. A couch was against one of the windowed walls, and a leather lounge rested beneath the bulletin board. The lounge was occupied at this moment by a man who lay face down on the leather, his shirt-tail sticking out of his trousers, a bald patch at the back of his head.

A short stout man with a flat nose was standing near the bulletin board, looking over some of the notices there. He turned when Rick came in, and he smiled and said, "Sit down anyplace. The waiter will take your order shortly."

"Thanks," Rick said. The other men at the table glanced up, smiled, and then went back to demolishing their sandwiches. Rick pulled out a chair, dipped into his briefcase for the sandwiches Anne had prepared, and spread them on the table before him. The man at the bulletin board continued looking at him.

"My name is Solly Klein," he said. "You're one of the new English teachers, aren't you?"

"Yes," Rick said. He wasn't sure whether he should offer his hand to Klein. He decided against it. The man was on the opposite side of the table, much too distant for a handshake. "My name is Rick Dadier."

"Welcome to the Forbidden City," Solly said. "How's it going so far?"

"Not too bad," Rick said.

"Give it time," Solly answered. "It'll get worse." He smiled, and then the smile vanished, and Rick wondered if he were joking or not. He slipped the rubber band from one of his sandwiches, and then began unwrapping the waxed paper. He spread the paper, and then lifted the top slice of bread, smiling at Anne's thoughtfulness when he saw she'd given him ham, his favorite cold cut.

"Can I get anything to drink?" Rick asked.

"You mean non-alcoholic, I take it," one of the men at the table said.

The man was small and wiry, with a curling crop of hair that hugged his head like a Navy watch cap. He had a long, hooked nose, and black-rimmed bop glasses behind which intense blue eyes sparkled. He held a sandwich in one hand, and an open history book in the other. Rick estimated his age at thirty-one or so.

Rick smiled. "I don't suppose there's beer available, is there?" he asked.

"You're lucky if you can get the water tap to run," Solly said, and the small, wiry man with the history book chuckled.

"This your first teaching job?" the small, wiry man asked.

"Yes," Rick said. He had somehow been put on the defensive, and he didn't like the position at all. And simply because he'd asked if he could get anything to drink, which seemed like a normal, civilized question.

"I'm George Katz," the small, wiry man said. "Social Studies. Taught at Christopher Columbus before I got appointed here."

"You should have stayed there," Solly said. "Even if they had you sweeping up the toilets."

"They didn't," Katz assured him, smiling.

"Well, not to change the subject," Rick said, "but *can* I get something to drink?"

"You get a choice," Solly said, walking to the table and looping his thumb through his suspender. "You can bring your own container of milk and stick it in the refrigerator. That's if you drink milk. If you drink coffee, you can bring instant coffee and use the hot water from the tea kettle outside. That's if you drink coffee. If you drink tea, you can pay Captain Schaefer a scant ten cents a month, and he'll let you use the tea balls he buys for us thirsty bastards. The hot water is still free."

"Well . . ." Rick started.

"In any case, you will have to pay Schaefer your dues. He'll pop in any minute and put the bite on you, as soon as he has his gymnasts climbing ropes or playing basketball or pulling their dummies."

"Is he the gym teacher?" Rick asked.

"You saw him downstairs?" Solly asked. "Captain Max Schaefer."

"What are the dues for?" Rick asked.

"The cups. The Captain buys the cups. Then he takes the dues we pay, and he replenishes his pocketbook. He also uses the dues to replace chipped, cracked, or broken cups. The Captain is a non-profit organization, or so he tells us."

"How much are the dues?"

"Ask the Captain," Solly said. "They change all the time."

"He charged me a quarter," one of the men at the table said.

Rick looked down the length of the table to the man who'd spoken. He was a tall, handsome boy, with midnight black hair that spilled onto his forehead in small ringlets. He had a perfect nose, high cheekbones, and sculptured, almost feminine lips. He was no older than twenty-five, and he was built like the statue of a Greek athlete. He did not introduce himself, so Rick didn't ask his name.

"A quarter sounds reasonable," Rick said. "Do you think I could use one of the tea balls before paying my dues?"

"Help yourself," Solly said, waving a short, wide hand. "The Captain makes his living on this concession anyway."

Rick rose and went to the cupboard, found the cardboard container of tea balls, and was reaching for a cup when a voice behind him said, "That's mine."

The voice was mild. Rick turned and saw that it belonged to a thin man in a gray, pencil-stripe, rumpled suit. The man wore rimless glasses, and his eyes were sad behind them. He had thin brown hair and shaggy brown eyebrows, and he repeated, "That's mine," almost apologetically.

"I didn't know . . ." Rick started.

"Everything belongs to Lou," Solly said. "He's got a proprietor's complex."

"We have our initials on the cups," the thin man said. "So we can tell them apart. See the L.S.? That's me. Lou Savoldi."

"He thinks he owns everything," Solly said, grinning. "You talk to Lou, you find out he owns Manual Trades. He just leases it to the city during the season. In the summer, he runs a whore house here."

"You're one of my best customers," Savoldi said, unsmiling, his eyes sad.

"Not since your wife left for one of those fancy East Side places," Solly countered.

"That's all right," Savoldi answered, his eyes still sad. "I get more calls for your wife anyway."

"That's natural. She's a prettier woman."

"The kettle's boiling," Savoldi said. "Anybody want tea?"

"I'll have some," George Katz said, looking up from his history book. "Would you bring me a tea ball, Dadier?"

"Sure," Rick said.

"My cup is in there, too," Katz went on. "G.K. Be careful, the initials may still be wet."

"I see it," Rick said. He took down Katz's cup as Savoldi left the room. "Can I use one of these without any initials on it?" Rick asked.

"Sure," Solly said. He walked to the cupboard and took down a cup marked with S.K. in bright blue letters. "Hell, we might as well all have some tea." He brought his cup to the table, putting it down next to Rick's sandwiches. "How about you, Manners?" he asked the Greek athlete at the end of the table.

"None for me," Manners replied. "I'm strictly a milk man. Two quarts a day."

"Sugar baby," Solly said. "I'll bet you don't drink, smoke, curse, or screw either."

"You've got me wrong," Manners said. "They call me Amoral Alan in my neighborhood."

"Where's that? In the Virgin Islands?"

"Bensonhurst," Manners said quickly, proudly.

"So why the hell did they give you a school in the Bronx?"

"I've got pull," Manners said dryly.

"Pull this a while," Solly said. He sat down abruptly, and Lou Savoldi came back into the room with the steaming tea kettle in his hand. Rick sat down with his cup, and Savoldi poured for himself, Solly, Rick, and Katz.

"I won't be here long, anyway," Manners said, smiling.

"How come?" Savoldi asked.

"I want an all-girls' school," Manners said honestly.

"They're worse than all-boys' schools," Savoldi told him.

"Yeah, but think of the pussy," Manners said honestly.

"Think of twenty-year jail sentences," Savoldi said sadly.

"I know a guy who's teaching science in a school in Harlem. All girls. He got propositioned six times his first day at the school. He was almost raped on the staircase."

"I'll stay here," Savoldi said sadly. "It's safer at my age." He finished pouring and left the room to put the kettle back on the stove.

"Well," Manners said, "that's for me. An all-girls' school."

"You're just a regular Lover Boy," Solly told him.

Savoldi came back into the room and said, "You're the original Lover Boy, Solly."

"Don't I know it?" Solly picked up his tea cup in both hands, sipped at it noisily, and then said, "This is too damn hot."

Rick bit into his ham sandwich and then sipped at his tea. The man lying on the couch had not moved a muscle since Rick had entered the room.

"You can go to an all-girls' school if you like, Lover Boy," Solly said, "but you won't find it any different than any other vocational school in the city."

"Girls are different from boys," Savoldi said. "Ain't you heard, Solly?"

"You always got your mind up some pussy," Solly said. "I'm telling you there's no difference. I know plenty of guys teaching in girls' vocational schools. It's no different. If anything, it's worse. You can't smack a girl around."

"You never smacked any boy around, either," Savoldi said.

"That's true. I don't want to get contaminated."

"What do you mean?" Rick asked, chewing on his sandwich.

"What do I mean?" Solly repeated. "I'll tell you something, Dadier. This is the garbage can of the educational system. Every vocational school in the city. You put them all together, and you got one big, fat, overflowing garbage can. And you want to know what our job is? Our job is to sit on the lid of the garbage can and see that none of the filth overflows into the streets. That's our job."

"You don't mean that," Rick said politely, incredulously.

"I don't, huh?" Solly shrugged. "You're new here, so you don't know. I'm telling you it's a garbage can, and you'll find out the minute you get a whiff of the stink. All the waste product, all the crap they can't fit into a general high school, all that stink goes into the garbage can that's the vocational high school system. That's why the system was invented.

"Sure, the books will tell you the vocational high school affords manual training for students who want to work with their hands. That's all so much horse manure. Believe me, there's only one thing these guys want to do with their hands. So some bright bastard figured a way to keep them off the streets. He thought of the vocational high school. Then he hired a bunch of guys with fat asses, a few with college degrees, to sit on the lid of the garbage can. That way, his wife and daughter can walk the streets without getting raped."

"No one would want to rape your wife, Solly," Savoldi said sadly.

"Except me," Solly said. "The point is, you got to keep them off the streets. And this is as good a place as any. We're just combinations of garbage men and cops, that's all."

"I don't think that's true," Rick said slowly. "I mean, there are surely boys here who really want to learn a trade."

"You find me one," Solly said. "Go ahead. Listen, I've been teaching here for twelve years, and only once did I find anything of worth in the garbage. People don't knowingly dump diamonds in with the garbage. They throw crap in the garbage, and that's what you'll find here."

"That's why I want an all-girls' school," Manners said.

"Yeah, sure," Solly said. "The only difference in an all-girls' school is that you'll find perfume along with the crap in the garbage."

"You're just bitter," Savoldi said.

"Sure," Solly said. "I should have been a teacher instead of a garbage man."

"Garbage men get good salaries," Savoldi put in.

"Which is more than teachers get," Solly answered.

"Me," Savoldi said sadly, "I'm very happy here."

"That's because you're stupid," Solly told him.

"No, I'm smart," Savoldi admitted. "I teach Electrical Wiring, and that gives me bread and butter. Outside, I do odd jobs, and that gives me little luxuries."

"I don't see you driving a Caddy."

"I don't want a Caddy. I'm not that ambitious."

"You're not ambitious at all," Solly told him.

"I have one ambition," Savoldi said, nodding his head. "Just one."

"What's that?"

"Someday I'm going to rig an electric chair and bring it to class with me. I'm going to tell the kids it's a circuit tester, and then I'm going to lead the little bastards in one by one and throw the switch on them. That's my ambition."

"And you're happy here," Solly said dryly.

"Sure. I'm happy. I'm like a man in a rainstorm. When the rain is coming down, I put on my raincoat. When I get home, I take off the coat and put it in the closet and forget all about it. That's what I do here. I become Mr. Savoldi the minute I step through the door to the school, and I'm Mr. Savoldi until 3:25 every day. Then I take off the Mr. Savoldi raincoat, and I go home, and I become Lou again until the next morning. No worries that way."

"Except one," Solly said.

"What's that?" Savoldi asked politely.

"That the kids will rig that goddamned electric chair before you do. Then they'll throw the switch and goodby Mr. Savoldi and Lou, too."

"These kids couldn't wire their way into a pay toilet, even if they had a nickel's head start," Savoldi said sadly. He sipped at his tea and added, "You made my tea get cold."

"Maybe the kids just need a chance," Rick said lamely. "Hell, they can't all be bad."

"All right," Solly said, "you give them their chance. But whatever you do, don't turn your back on them."

"I turned my back on them this morning," Rick said, a little proudly.

"And you didn't get stabbed?" Solly shrugged. "The first day of school. They probably left their hardware home."

"You're exaggerating," Rick said, smiling.

"I am, huh? All right, I'm exaggerating. Tell him how much I'm exaggerating, Lou."

"He's exaggerating," Savoldi said. "Solly is a big crap artist."

"I turned my back on a class just once," Solly said, "that's all, just once. I never turned my back again after that."

"What happened?" Rick asked.

"I was putting a diagram of a carburetor on the board. You have to illustrate things for these dumb bastards or they don't know what the hell you're talking about. I had my back turned for about forty seconds. I had hardly picked up the goddamned chalk and started the drawing."

"I heard this story already," Savoldi said sadly.

"Yeah, well it's true," Solly said defensively.

"What happened?" Rick prodded.

"A goddamn baseball came crashing into the blackboard about two inches away from my head. It knocked a piece of slate out of the board as big as a half dollar." Solly nodded, remembering the experience.

"What'd you do?" Rick asked.

"He wet his pants," Savoldi said.

"You would have, too," Solly said. "I did that, and then I got so goddamned mad I was ready to rip every one of those bastards into little pieces. I turned around, and they were all sitting there dead-panned, with that stupid, innocent look on their faces. And then I cooled down and played it smart. I picked up the baseball, dropped it in the wastebasket, smiled, and said, 'You'll never pitch for the Yanks, boy.' Just that. But I never turned my back again. Even writing on the board. I do it sideways."

"Like a Chink," Savoldi said. "Solly is part Mongolian."

"Thank God I'm not part wop."

"I'm all wop," Savoldi said.

"Solly's right," George Katz put in, laying down his history book for a moment. "You've got to realize what you're dealing with. You've got to understand the problem of most of these kids, and adjust your teaching accordingly."

"What teaching?" Solly wanted to know. "Who's kidding who? There's no teaching involved here, none at all. The sooner you realize that, the better off you'll be."

"Well," Katz said respectfully, "I think that's carrying it a little far."

"I'm understating it," Solly said flatly. "If you want to be a success at Manual Trades, or any other goddamn vocational high school, you've got to live by two simple rules. One: Forget any preconceived notions you may have had about adolescents wanting to learn. There's no truth in that when you apply it to the vocational high school. Two: Remember that self-preservation is the first law of life. Period. Amen."

"I told you," Savoldi said wistfully, "Solly's a philosopher."

"You *didn't* tell us," Solly said, "but who's paying attention anyway?"

"You should have been President of the United States," Savoldi said. "You're going to waste, Solly."

"Agh, who's the President?" Solly asked. "He sits when he goes to the can, doesn't he?"

George Katz laughed, and Manners said, "Anyway, I'm looking for an all-girls' school."

"All right, Lover Boy," Solly said. "Look. I hope you find it."

"Me too," Manners said, smiling.

"Me, I'm stuck in the Forbidden City. I tried to get out of it a long time ago. But once you're appointed here, it's like being made a guard on Devil's Island. There's no escape."

"I'm just a sub," Manners said. "I won't have any trouble."

"*Mazoltov,*" Solly said, bowing his head.

There was the sound of loud laughter in the kitchen outside, and Solly said, "Here comes the Captain." The laughing got louder, and then the red-headed gym teacher whom Rick had seen earlier burst into the dining room, slapping his thighs, tears rolling down his face.

"You're late, Captain," Solly said. "What happened? Kids didn't feel like the parallel bars today?"

"Oh God," the Captain said, roaring with laughter. "Oh my God!"

"What's so funny?" Savoldi asked sadly.

"Oh great holy mother of Moses," the Captain said,

slapping his thigh again. "I'll be goddamned to Samuel Gompers and back again. Oh my living ass!"

"What the hell is it?" Solly asked impatiently.

"I'll be a sonofabitch," the Captain said, the tears streaming down his ruddy cheeks. He shook his head, and the laughter subsided for a moment, and he said, "This beats it all. I'm standing there on the platform, you know, about fifteen minutes after the period started. Oh, my aching ass."

"You going to tell the story or you going to pee all over the floor?" Solly asked.

"I'm reading the kids the riot act, and the door pops open and who should walk in?"

"Governor Dewey," Solly said.

"Almost," the Captain said. "But not quite. Who walks in but Mr. Small, principal of North Manual Trades High School. Mr. Small, himself, the bastard. Inspecting my class on the first goddamned day of school. Oh, my bleeding piles."

"So?" Solly asked.

"I tell you, this is one for the books. I haven't seen anything like it since I was in the infantry." He began laughing again, and he continued laughing for a full minute before he was able to go on with his story. "He comes in, and the minute I see him, I shout, 'Boys! Mr. Small, the principal!' Like 'Gentlemen, the Queen!' you know? Well, he comes striding across the room, and the kids are standing there like limp rags, and he shouts in a commanding officer voice, 'All right, boys. At ease!'

"At ease!" the Captain shouted. "At ease, when half those kids had their asses dragging on the floor, anyway.

Well, he comes up to the platform, and he climbs up there, and he puts his hands on his hips and then he looks out over all the kids, and he doesn't say a goddamn word. He just keeps looking out at them for about five minutes, with me standing right behind him. Then he climbs down from the platform, walks to the door, turns and says, 'Carry on, Mr. Schaefer.' CARRY ON, MR. SCHAEFER! Carry on, mind you, carry on, and a pippip and a cheerio! I swear to God I thought he was General MacArthur. I couldn't stop laughing after he was gone. I picked up a towel and started wiping my face so the kids wouldn't see me.

"What the hell does he think this is, a military academy?"

"He's just showing them who's boss," Solly said, chuckling.

"Oh my back. I'm telling you, he convulsed me. That simple bastard. All he needed was a riding crop! Listen, I got to get back. I've got the idiots playing basketball, but the period's almost over."

He turned and left the dining room, striding across the kitchen, and laughing until he was out of earshot.

"He was a captain in the last war," Solly explained. "Hell of a nice guy."

"I didn't give him my dues," Rick said.

"Oh, he'll get you. The Captain never misses."

Lou Savoldi stood and began clearing the table before him. He took his cup out to the sink, washed it, and then hung it back on its hook. "I'm going down," he said.

"Back to the salt mines," Solly said. "You free the sixth?"

"No," Savoldi said sadly.

"I'll see you tomorrow then."

"I guess so," Savoldi said sadly.

Rick rose, cleared his place, and dumped the waxed paper and brown bag in the trash basket near the bulletin board. Then he washed the cup he'd used and put it back in the cupboard.

When the bell rang, he picked up his briefcase, and Solly said, "I'll walk down with you."

"Okay," Rick said.

"What've you got now?" Solly asked as they left the lunchroom.

"Fifth-termers," Rick said.

"Fifth-termers, you say?" Solly asked, his eyebrows raised.

"Yes."

"Mmm," Solly said. He didn't say another word as they walked down the steps and across the gymnasium.

Rick could have become a hero during that fifth period, fifth-term English class. He certainly had opportunity enough to become one if he'd wanted to. It's to his credit that he did not achieve heroic stature until later in the day.

The first thing he noticed when he entered the room was that the class was a small one, not more than twenty or so boys. He was happy about that because it's easier to teach a small group. He didn't know, of course, that there were thirty-five boys in 55–206, and that most of them had already begun cutting on this first day of the term.

The second thing he noticed was the well-built Negro boy with the white tee shirt and dungarees. The boy noticed him at the same moment, and the charming grin broke out on his handsome face.

"Well," he said, "hello, Chief."

"Gregory Miller," Rick said.

"You did remember the name, dintchoo, Chief?"

"Sit down, Miller," Rick said. "And *my* name is Mr. Dadier. I think you'd better start remembering that."

Miller took his seat, and Rick looked over to the other boys who were standing in clusters around the room, talking or laughing.

"All right," he said, "let's sit down. And let's make it fast."

The boys looked up at him, but they made no move toward their seats.

"You deaf back there? Let's break it up."

"Why?" one of the boys asked.

"What?" Rick said, surprised.

"I said, 'Why?' "

"I heard you, smart boy. Get to your seat before you find a seat in the principal's office."

"I'm petrified," the tall boy said. He had stringy blond hair, and the hair was matted against his forehead. His face was a field of ripe acne, and when he grinned his lips contorted crookedly in a smile that was boyishly innocent and mannishly sinister at the same time. He continued smiling as he walked to the middle of the room and took the seat alongside Miller. The other boys, taking his move as a cue, slowly drifted back to the seats and turned their attention to Rick.

"You may keep the seats you now have," Rick said, reaching into his briefcase for the Delaney cards. He distributed the cards as he'd done with his official class, and said, "I'm sure you know how to fill these out."

"We sure do," the blond boy said.

"I didn't get your name," Rick said pointedly.

"Maybe 'cause I didn't give it," the boy answered, the crooked smile on his mouth again.

"His name is Emmanuel, too," Miller said. He smiled at the private joke which only he and Rick shared.

"Is it?" Rick asked innocently.

"No," the blond boy said.

"Then what is it?"

"Guess," the blond boy said. "It begins with a W."

"I'd say 'Wiseguy' offhand, but I'm not good at guessing. What's your name, and make it snappy."

"West," the boy said. "Artie West."

Rick smiled, suddenly reversing his tactics, hoping to throw the boys off balance. They were expecting a hardman, so he'd wisecrack a little, show them that he could exchange a gag when there was time for gagging. "Any relation to Mae West?" he asked.

West answered so quickly that Rick was certain he'd heard the same question many times before. "Only between my eyes and her tits," he said, the crooked grin on his mouth.

His answer provided Rick with a choice. He could drop the banter immediately and clamp down with the mailed fist again, or he could show that he wasn't the kind of person who could be bested in a match of wits. For some obscure reason that probably had a smattering of pride attached to it, he chose to continue the match.

"Watch your language," he said, smiling. "My mother's picture is in my wallet."

"I didn't know you had one," West said.

Again there was the choice, only this time West had penetrated deeper. A warning buzzer sounded at the back of Rick's mind. He saw the grinning faces of the boys in 55–206, and he knew they wanted him to continue the battle of half-wits. He would have liked to continue it himself, despite the incessant warning that screamed inside his head now. The truth was, however, he could not think of a comeback, and rather than spout something inadequate, he fled behind the fortress of his desk and said, "All right, let's knock it off now, and fill out the Delaney cards."

West smiled knowingly, and winked at Miller. He was a sharp cookie, West, and Miller was just as sharp—and if the two were friends, there'd probably be trouble in 55–206, Rick figured.

Rick looked out over the boys as they filled out the Delaney cards. There was a handful of Negroes in the class, and the rest of the boys were white, including a few Puerto Ricans. They all appeared to be between sixteen and seventeen, and most of them wore the tee shirt and dungarees which Rick assumed to be the unofficial uniform of the school.

"As you know," he said, "this is English 55–206, and we're here to learn English. I know a lot of you will be wondering why on earth you have to learn English. Will English help you get a job as a mechanic, or an electrician? The answer is yes, English will. Besides, no matter what you've thought of English up to now, I think you'll enjoy this class, and you might be surprised to find English one of your favorite subjects before the term is finished."

"I'll be s'prised, all right," Miller said.

"I don't want any calling out in this classroom," Rick said sternly. "If you have anything to say, you raise your hand. Is that understood? My name, incidentally, is Mr. Dadier."

"We heard of you, Daddy-oh," a boy at the back of the room said.

"Pronunciation is an important part of English," Rick said coldly. "I'd hate to fail any boy because he couldn't learn to pronounce my name. It's Mr. Dadier. Learn it, and learn it now. Believe me, it won't break my heart to fail all of you." A small Negro boy wearing a porkpie hat suddenly got to his feet. He put his hands on his hips, and a sneer curled his mouth. "You ever try to fight thirty-five guys at once, teach?" he asked.

Rick heard the question, and it set off a trigger response in his mind which told him, *This is it, Dadier. This is it, my friend.* He narrowed his eyes and walked slowly and purposefully around his desk. The boy was seated in the middle of the room, and Rick walked up the aisle nearest his desk, realizing as he did so that he was placing himself in a surrounded-by-boys position. He walked directly to the boy, pushed his face close to his, and said, "Sit down, son, and take off that hat before I knock it off."

He said it tightly, said it the way he'd spoken the lines for Duke Mantee when he'd played *The Petrified Forest* at

Hunter. He did not know what the reaction would be, and he was vaguely aware of a persistent fear that crawled up his spine and into his cranium. He knew he could be jumped by all of them in this single instant, and the knowledge made him taut and tense, and in that short instant before the boy reacted, he found himself moving his toes inside his shoes to relieve the tension, to keep it from breaking out in the form of a trembling hand or a ticcing face.

The room was dead silent, and it seemed suddenly cold, despite the September sunshine streaming through the windows.

And even though the boy reacted almost instantly, it seemed forever to Rick.

The boy snatched the hat from his head, all his bravado gone, his eyes wide in what appeared to be fright. "I'm sorry, teach," he said, and then he instantly corrected it to "Mr. Dadier."

He sat immediately, and he avoided Rick's eyes, and Rick stood near his desk and continued to look down at the boy menacingly for a long while. Then he turned his back on the boy and walked back to the front of his room and his own desk. His face was set tightly, and he made his nostrils flare, the way he'd learned to do a long time ago in his first dramatics class.

He flipped open his Delaney book, stared down at it, and then raised his head slowly, the mock cold anger still in his eyes and the hard line of his mouth. "Pass the Delaney cards to the front of the room. Pass down your program cards, too, and I'll sign them. You there, in the first row, collect them all and bring them to my desk."

The boy in the first seat of the first row smiled at Rick vacuously, and he made no move to start collecting the cards which were already being passed down to the front of each row.

"Did you hear me?" Rick asked.

"Yes," the boy said, still smiling vacuously.

"Then let's move," Rick said tightly.

The boy rose, still smiling that stupid, empty smile. *Another wise guy,* Rick thought. *The room is full of wise guys.*

The stupidly smiling boy collected all the cards, and brought them to Rick. Rick inserted the Delaney cards into his book, and then began mechanically signing the program cards in the spaces provided, a system which made it impossible for a boy to miss being enrolled in the class to which he had been assigned. When the program cards were returned to the official teachers the next day, any delinquent would automatically be exposed. It was an effective system.

"We won't accomplish much today, other than getting acquainted. Tomorrow we'll get our books from the book room, and begin work."

He shifted his glance to the boy in the first seat of the first row. The boy was still smiling. The smile was plastered onto his thin face. He looked as if he were enjoying something immensely. Rick turned away from him, irritated, but not wanting another showdown so soon after his brush with the other boy.

"Our trip to the book room shouldn't take more than . . ."

"Is this trip necessary?" one of the boys called out.

Third seat, second row. Rick automatically tabulated the boy, and then fingered his card in the Delaney book. "What'd you say, Belazi?" he asked, reading the boy's name from the card.

"I said, is this trip necessary?"

"Yes, it is. Does that answer your question?"

"Yes, it does," the boy said.

"I'm glad it does, Belazi. Do you have any other important questions to ask?" He recalled something about sarcasm being a bad weapon to use against a class, but he shrugged the memory aside.

"Nope," Belazi answered.

"Well, good. May I go on with what I was saying then, with your kind permission?"

"Sure," Belazi said, smiling.

"Thank you. I appreciate your thoughtfulness."

"He the most thoughtful cat in this class," Miller said emphatically.

"Nobody asked you, Miller," Rick snapped.

"I ony just volunteerin' the information."

"I appreciate it," Rick said, unsmiling. "But I'll try to manage without your help."

"Think you'll make it, teach?" West asked.

"I'll tell you what, West," Rick said. "I'll be here until four this afternoon, planning tomorrow's lesson for this class. Since you're so worried, why don't you join me, and we'll plan it together."

"You can handle that case alone," West said.

"Aw, go on, help him," another boy called.

Rick located the card in the Delaney book. "Antoro? Is that your name?"

"Yeah," the boy said, proud to be in the act.

"Do you know what Toro means in Spanish?" Rick asked.

"My name ain't Toro," Antoro replied.

"Nonetheless, do you know what it means?"

"No. What?"

"Bull. Plain, old, ordinary, common BULL."

Antoro, plainly insulted, retreated behind a sullen visage. Rick turned away from him and looked directly at the boy in the first seat of the first row. The boy was still smiling that blank, stupid smile.

"What's so funny?" Rick asked.

The boy continued to smile.

"You," Rick snapped. He looked at the card in the Delaney book. "Santini. What's so funny?"

"Me?" Santini asked, smiling vacuously.

"Yes, you. What's so funny?"

"Nothin'," Santini said, smiling broadly.

"Then why are you . . ."

"He the smilinest cat in this whole school," Miller informed Rick. "He smile all the time. Thass 'cause he an idiot."

"What?" Rick asked, turning.

Miller tapped his temple with one brown forefinger. "Lotsa muscles," he said, "but no brains."

Rick looked at Santini. The boy was still smiling, and the smile *was* an idiotic one. There was no mirth behind it. It perched on his mouth like a plaster monkey. He felt suddenly embarrassed for having brought the smile to the attention of the class. Surely, the boy was not an idiot, but his intelligence was probably so low that . . .

"Well, try to pay attention here," Rick said awkwardly.

"I'm payin' attention," Santini said innocently, still smiling.

Rick cleared his throat and passed out the signed program cards. He hated these damned orientation classes. The beginning was bound to be difficult, and it was made doubly difficult by the fact that there was really nothing to do without books and without . . . without a plan, he reluctantly admitted, realizing he should have planned out these first, difficult, getting-acquainted periods.

"We'll cover a lot of interesting topics this term," he said. "We'll learn all about newspapers, and we'll read a lot of interesting short stories, and several good novels, and we'll cover some good plays, too, perhaps acting them out right here in class."

"Tha's for me," Miller said suddenly. Rick smiled, pleased because he thought he'd struck a responsive chord.

"The acting, you mean?" he asked.

"Man, man," Miller said. "I'm a real Ty-rone Power type. You watch me, Chief. I'll lay 'em in the aisles."

The boys all laughed suddenly, and for a moment Rick didn't know what the joke was. He understood suddenly and completely. Miller had used the word "lay" and that was always good for a yak. He wondered whether or not Miller had chosen the word purposely, or had simply blundered into the approving laughter of the boys. Whatever the case, Miller basked in his glory, soaking up the laughs like sunshine.

"Well, you'll get plenty of opportunity to act," Rick said, pretending he didn't understand what the laughter was about. "And we'll have all sorts of contests, too, for letter-writing, and for progress made. I'm thinking of awarding prizes to the boys who show me they're really working. Like tickets to football games and hockey games, things like that. Provided I get some co-operation from you."

"You ever hear of Juan Garza, teach?" one of the boys piped.

"No, I don't believe so," Rick said. "Who was Juan Garza?"

"He used to be in my class," the boy said. Rick had located his card now in the Delaney book. The boy's name was Maglin.

"What about Juan Garza, Maglin?" Rick asked.

Maglin smiled. "Nothing. He just used to be in my class, that's all."

"Why'd you ask if I knew him?"

"I just thought you might have heard about him. He used to be in my class."

"I gather he was a celebrity of some sort," Rick said dryly.

"He sure was," Maglin said, and all the boys laughed their approval.

"Well, it's a shame he's not in the class now," Rick said, and for some reason all the boys found this exceptionally funny. He was ready to pursue the subject further when the bell rang. He rose quickly and said, "I'll see you all tomorrow. Miller, I'd like to talk to you for a moment."

Miller's brow creased into a frown, and the frown vanished before a confident smile. He came to the front of the room, and while the rest of the boys sauntered out, he stood uneasily by the desk, shifting his weight from one foot to the other.

Rick waited until the other boys were all gone. He knew exactly what he was going to do, but he wanted to do it alone, with just him and Miller present. Its effectiveness would depend upon Miller's response, and he was sure the response would be a good one, once he separated Miller from the pack. When the other boys had all drifted out, he said, "Man-to-man talk, Miller. Okay?"

"Sure," Miller said uneasily, staring down at his shoelaces.

"I've checked your records," he lied. "You've got the makings of a leader, Miller. You're bright and quick, and the other boys like you."

"Me?" Miller asked, lifting his eyes, surprised. "Me?"

The flattery was beginning to work, and Rick pressed his advantage, smiling paternally now. "Yes, Miller, you. Come now, let's have no modesty here. You know you're head and shoulders above all of these boys."

Miller smiled shyly. "Well, I don't know. I mean . . ."

"Here's the point, Miller. We're going to have a damned fine class here." He used the word "damned" purposely, to show Miller he was not above swearing occasionally. "I can sense that. But I want it to be an outstanding class, and I can't make it that without your help."

"Me?" Miller asked again, really surprised now, and

Rick wondered if he hadn't carried the flattery angle too far.

"Yes, you," he pushed on. "Come on, boy, let's lay our cards on the table."

"I don't know what you want, Ch . . . Mr. Dadier," Miller said.

"I want you to be the leader in this class, the way you're entitled to be. I want you to set the example for the rest of the boys. I want you to give me all your co-operation, and the other boys will automatically follow suit. That's what I want, Miller. If you help me, we can make this class the best one in the school."

"Well, I don't know," Miller said dubiously.

"I do know," Rick insisted. "What do you say, boy?"

"Well . . . sure, I'll help all I can. Sure, if you think so."

"That's my boy," Rick said, rising and clapping Miller on the shoulder. "I'll see you tomorrow, Miller." He walked Miller to the doorway, his arm around the boy. "Now take it easy."

"Sure," Miller said, puzzled. His brow furrowed once, and then he smiled again. "Sure," he said. And then, almost arrogantly, "Sure!"

Rick watched him go down the corridor, and then he went back into the room and packed his briefcase. He had been smooth there, all right. Brother, he had pulled the wool clear down over Miller's eyes, clear down over his shoelaces, too. Once he put Miller in his pocket, he'd get West, too. And once he got the two troublemakers, the clowns, the class was his. He'd used flattery, the old-est of weapons, and Miller had taken the hook without once suspecting any trickery. A leader, indeed! *Rickie, he told himself, you are a bloody goddamned genius!* The class had been troublesome, true, but he'd put his finger on the trouble spot and immediately weeded it out. That was the way to do it, despite what Solly Klein preached. These kids *were* humans, and not animals to be penned up and ignored. All you had to do was hit the proper chord.

He zipped up his briefcase, and when he left the room for his Unassigned sixth period, he was pretty damned happy, unaware that he would be elevated to the pedestal marked Hero within a matter of ten minutes.

When he left the classroom, he had no idea where he was going. He knew he could go up to the teachers' lunchroom again, but he also knew Solly Klein was free during this sixth period, and he somehow did not feel like listening to more comments this day upon the imbecility of the students at Manual Trades. Especially after his *coup* with Miller. No, he was not anticipating any serious trouble with any of his classes, and Klein's bitter pronouncements would definitely clash with his present frame of mind.

Had he decided to go to the teachers' lunchroom, he'd have headed toward the short side of the L, and then climbed to the third floor where he would cut across the gymnasium. He might have avoided the laurel of Herohood had he done so. But he did not head for the teachers' lunchroom.

Instead, he decided to leave the building, take a brisk walk outside. He did not know that a teacher was not permitted to leave the building during an Unassigned period. A teacher could do what he wanted on his lunch hour, which was a God-given right, but he was expected to be around during an Unassigned period, should any emergency arise. Not knowing the technicality or legality involved, Rick decided to leave the building, returning in time for his seventh-period class. On a whim, and because he did not feel like walking, he stopped near the elevator and rang for it.

Had the elevator arrived when he summoned it, he might also have missed becoming a hero. Unfortunately, the elevator was parked on the fourth floor of the building, stacked with World History books. George Katz, the eager beaver that he was, was directing the unloading of those books, and he had thought far enough in advance to include books for his entire battery of classes. The elevator would be inactive on the fourth floor for the better part of the sixth period.

Rick pressed the button three more times, waiting patiently for the elevator. When he saw that the floor indicator refused to budge from the figure four set in its semicircular face, he shrugged and headed for the stairwell.

The stairwells at North Manual Trades High School were divided into *Up* and *Down* sections. He was ready to start down the open steps that confronted him when he stepped through the doors, and then he saw the *Up* sign. A strange sense of right and wrong suddenly possessed him, and he could not at that moment ever consider going down on a staircase plainly marked *Up*. He backed off, and began walking around the landing, toward the meshed window set in the wall, and toward the *Down* part of the stairwell.

It was then that he became a hero.

The sunshine streamed through the meshed window, blinding him for an instant. He saw a blur of movement to the right of the window, and he blinked his eyes against the sunlight, and then the blur became two figures.

He was still walking slowly, with his briefcase in one hand. He suddenly realized that the figures were struggling, and he instantly figured it for a fight between two of the boys. And then the figures took definite shape, and he dropped the briefcase, and started forward at a sprint.

One of the figures was a tall boy in tee shirt and dungarees, no more than seventeen years old. The other figure was Miss Hammond.

The boy had one hand clamped over Miss Hammond's mouth. The other hand was around her waist as he forced her backward against the wall.

"Hey!" Rick shouted.

The boy turned suddenly, moving to Miss Hammond's side. It was then that Rick saw the torn front of her suit jacket, and the ripped blouse and lingerie. *My God,* he thought wildly, *that's her breast,* and then he was clamping his hand on the boy's shoulder and spinning him around.

Fear and panic were mingled on the boy's face. He had gotten more than he'd bargained for, a hell of a lot more. He had planned on a quick piece on a deserted stairwell. He had planned it from the moment he'd caught a glimpse of Miss Hammond's legs in the auditorium that morning. He had also planned on scaring hell out of her, threatening her with violence if she told anyone what had happened. But this was different. He was caught, and there'd be no threats of violence now that this crew-cut bastard had stepped in and loused up the works.

Miss Hammond, her mouth free now, screamed. Rick probably wouldn't have hit the boy if Miss Hammond hadn't screamed, but the scream gave urgency to the situation, and he brought back his fist as he spun the boy around, and then he threw his arm forward, and when his fist collided with the boy's mouth, the shock rumbled all the way up to his shoulder socket.

The boy bounced back against the radiator, and Miss Hammond screamed again, holding her hand up to cover the purple nipple and roseate of her breast behind the torn slip and brassiere.

"You lousy bastard," the boy yelled, and Rick hit him again, and this time a smear of crimson spread on the boy's mouth, staining his teeth. Miss Hammond kept screaming, and the stairwell was suddenly flooded with teachers and monitors. Rick held the boy's arm tightly, twisting it up behind his back.

"What happened?" someone said, and Miss Hammond said, "A jacket, something, a jacket," blubbering incoherently. Another teacher grabbed the bleeding boy, and Rick stripped off his jacket, handing it to Miss Hammond. She slipped into it quickly, still sobbing, her hair disarranged, her hands trembling. The jacket was too large for her, but she clutched it to her exposed breast thankfully, her cheeks flushed with excitement. Rick looked at her again, at the delicate features, the full body thrusting against his jacket. He looked at her, and felt terribly embarrassed for her all at once. And feeling her embarrassment, he suddenly hated the boy who'd attacked her. He hated him intensely, and he thought of the innocent exposure of Miss Hammond's breast as he had seen it, full and rounded, the torn silk of her underwear framing it, providing a cushion for it. A youthful breast it had been, firm, with the nipple large and erect. He concentrated on the embarrassment he felt for her, and he concentrated on his hatred for the boy, and he seized the boy roughly and shouted, "Come on, mister. The principal wants to see you."

The quicker of the teachers had grasped the situation immediately, and they were shooing the monitors away from the scene of the attack. Martha Riley, whose math class happened to be on the second floor, arrived on the scene and began comforting Miss Hammond, putting her fat arm around her and clucking like a mother hen. She led her to the ladies' room, and Rick watched the pair depart, still feeling embarrassed for Miss Hammond.

The teachers began talking it up, and amid the babble of voices, Rick took the boy down to the principal's office. He listened to everything the principal said, listened to the principal say, "We're going to take care of you, smart guy. We're really going to take care of you." He filled out reports and signed them, and he told the story at least ten times before the bell sounded for the beginning of the seventh period.

It is accurate to say that Richard Dadier, even though he went through the paces of orientating his seventh- and eighth-period classes, did not really know what the hell was going on. He was excited now that it was all over. He had not had a chance for excitement while it was happening because it all happened too quickly. But the excitement bubbled inside him now, and as he spoke to the classes, he thought of the experience again and again, putting all the pieces in their proper order, reliving it again and again. He did not remember afterward what he had said to the classes. He was totally unaware of them throughout the last two periods of the day.

And he was certainly unaware of the fact that his heroism, tales of which had spread through the school like a brush fire, was regarded by the students of Manual Trades as nothing but the basest, most treacherous type of villainy.

4

It was not until Thursday of that first school week that Rick came down from outer space and tried to evaluate his new standing at the high school. It *was* a new standing, and even the most casual observer could not have denied that fact. The Richard Dadier who emerged from the sordid business of rape was not the same Richard Dadier who'd been headed for an illegal stroll outside the building in an Unassigned period.

When the initial excitement had worn off, when Small had already congratulated him, when Stanley had already congratulated him, when even George Katz had offered his congratulations, Rick began feeling a little embarrassed over his part in the drama.

He had never stopped a rape before, except by changing his mind, and he found his role of "protector of the virgin" a difficult one to assume. He was sensitively aware of the heads that turned when he walked through a corridor, of the hushed whispers that sprang up behind his back, of the curiously lifted eyebrows, the cupped hands. There was not a student on Tuesday morning—except those who'd been cutting since the term began—who had not heard of Rick's derring-do. He had been elevated to a celebrity's position on the first day of school, and he did not know whether or not he appreciated the sudden fame.

The fame, ignoring Rick's feelings completely, walked everywhere before him. Students parted in the corridors to let him through. Teachers he hadn't met stopped to pat him on the back or pass the time of day. The monitors at his Hall Patrol post seemed afraid of him, and the Students' Lavatory at that end of the corridor was conspicuously empty for long stretches of time.

He wore the fame the way he'd wear a Christmas tie from a wealthy aunt. The gaudy brilliance of it embarrassed him, but he simply couldn't throw it away now that he'd received it.

His classes on Tuesday beheld him with a mute curiosity. When he spoke, they listened. No one called him "teach." Everyone raised his hand before speaking. There was no calling out, and no buzzing, and no disorder of any kind. The curiosity was of the same kind that would have been afforded Rocky Marciano had he paid a visit to the school.

The kids all knew that Rick had stopped a rape, and they knew he'd stopped it by clobbering a fairly hefty boy square on the kisser. Hardly any of the students had seen the attacker after Rick split his lip. Some had, though, and the quantity of blood spilled had increased with each telling of the gruesome tale. By the time the story had made its rounds through the school, the kid who'd tried to rape Miss Hammond had been carted away to the hospital with half his teeth missing, a broken nose, and a possible concussion of the skull, with brain surgery a likelihood.

So Rick's classes watched him, and whereas their silence was appreciated, it was also a peculiar silence, a calculating silence. If Rick had been a reader of Westerns, he'd have been able to interpret the calculating silence. For he was, in actuality, the renowned gun-slick entering a strange town. His fame had spread before him, and the eyes were not so much admiring as they were appraising. The eyes were waiting, waiting for a chance to test the skill of this notorious fellow.

Rick was not of the bulging muscles variety of man. He was thin and sinewy, and the kids appraised his lanky length and wondered if perhaps he hadn't pulled a lead pipe on the rapist. His physical appearance whetted their curiosities further, and there were those who fondly recalled Juan Garza, remembering that he'd been a skinny little runt, much skinnier than Rick could ever be, and look at the hell he had raised.

Curiosity led to conjecture on the part of the kids. The lead pipe story was in vogue for about two hours, to be replaced immediately by a story which said Mr. Dadier carried a brass doorknob in his briefcase, and that he'd used the doorknob unmercifully on the rapist.

One of the kids in the schoolyard, watching a hand-ball game, ventured the possibility that Mr. Dadier had once had boxing lessons. The possibility became a real-ity within the next half-hour. Rick had not only had box-ing lessons, but he was contender for the Hawaiian championship, having left the army to teach only because he'd once blinded a man in the ring.

There were the jokers, too. The jokers spread the yarn that Rick hadn't really rescued Miss Hammond. On the contrary, it was Rick who'd been about to get raped, and Miss Hammond had saved *him* in the nick of time.

And, of course, there were the righteous protectors of student rights who felt that it was Rick who'd attempted to rape Miss Hammond. The unfortunate student had happened along, and Rick had slugged him and quickly shifted the blame.

But beneath all the stories and the raillery, the kids knew deep within them that Rick had indeed stopped the rape, and that he'd done it by slugging the attacker. And so they watched his every move silently, like vultures wheeling over a thirsty man on the desert. They devoted more intense concentration to Rick's footwork and the size of his clenched fist on that Tuesday than they'd devoted to the process of education in all their collective lives.

On Wednesday, the picture changed.

Up to that time, the rapist had remained a faceless nobody, a phallic symbol floating on a sea of rumors. Mr. Small changed all that on Wednesday, at his get-acquainted assembly with the students.

He was a big man, and the kids gave him almost as much attention as they'd given Rick's sudden rise to fame. Hell, this might be a new trend. First a goddamn English teacher who goes around batting kids on the staircase, and now a principal who looks like a wrestler. What the hell was North Manual Trades High School coming to anyway? The grapevine had already told them he'd come from Brooklyn Automotive, a fact they greeted without noticeable enthusiasm. The grapevine also added that the scar on his face had come from a knife fight, and that he'd taken the knife from its wielder and shoved it down the poor bastard's throat.

This was not good news.

It was always rough when a new man hopped in the principal's chair. It was like a woman marrying an alcoholic, gambling, lying, screwing drug addict. Right away came the reforms.

There had been reforms before. The kids were used to hot-shot principals who shot their loads in the first month and then settled down to letting the school run itself. These guys were always tough in the beginning. Until they knew what they were up against, and realized they were shoveling manure against the tide. You take a few shovelfuls of the stuff, and then you decide to go up on the boardwalk and watch nature. It's less smelly that way, and you expend less energy.

Small, however, looked like the kind of dim-witted jerk who would enjoy a little horse dung in his hair. Hell, he'd keep shoveling the stuff until he was covered with it, and then he'd order some for lunch. He'd probably done a lot of shoveling at Brooklyn Automotive. A job like that can get to be a habit. Like Charlie Chaplin tightening the bolts in *Modern Times*.

So they looked at Small, and they said, "*Small*, huh?" and they wondered whether or not they'd be asking for transfers to Bronx Vocational or Samuel Gompers before long. Nothing can screw up a good school like a hot-shot principal, especially one who pulls knives away from people.

Small crowded the microphone, as if he expected no back talk from it or anyone present. The kids disliked him instantly. Their worst fears were realized the minute he opened his big yap. He was, the bastard, a reformer, and they needed a reformer like they needed a hole in the head.

He gave them the usual reform pitch, the one all the new jerks gave, only he sounded as if he meant it. He sounded, in fact, as if he dared anyone to doubt that he meant it. This was not good at all. This was miserable. This was a bad way to start out. How were you supposed to enjoy school when you got a guy like this one for principal? How were you supposed to learn anything?

And then Small got around to the attempted rape. He lowered his voice, and the kids sitting up front saw that he also narrowed his eyes and tightened his lips.

"There was an unfortunate incident here on the first day of school," he said. The kids had all been silent before this, but the room seemed to grow even more hushed, as if all breathing had suddenly stopped. Sitting in the back of the auditorium with his official class, Rick sucked in a deep breath. The heads were beginning to turn already, a few at a time, spreading across rows, racing through the packed auditorium like a petroleum blaze. They turned in two directions, as if the blaze were fanned by cross-currents of wind, one half turning toward Rick where he sat, and the other half swiveling to catch a look at Miss Hammond.

"One of our boys decided he was out in the streets," Small said, ignoring the twisting heads and craning necks. "The boy's name was Douglas Murray."

It was out now. Douglas Murray. And there were kids who'd known Murray, and there were kids who'd liked Murray, and the entire rape had suddenly assumed a very personal aspect. If it happened to Murray, who was just one of the guys, why couldn't it happen to any one of them? You get bastards like Dadier fouling up the detail, and you get a hot-shot like Small who condones such horse manure, and next thing you knew they'd all be in reform school. The kids leaned forward eagerly, turning all their attention to Small again. This was no laughing matter. This was something of vital importance to all of them.

"One of our teachers stopped the incident from becoming a disastrous one," Small said, casually ignoring the fact that every kid in the auditorium knew the "incident" was an attempted rape. "Douglas Murray may be a little sorry he stepped out of line. Criminal assault charges have been pressed against him. I think you all know what that means."

They all knew, all right. They all knew that this didn't mean reform school. They mentally calculated Murray's age, and they figured this for a prison rap, if anything, and all because the poor bastard tried to cop a feel. And all because Dadier had stepped in and made like a goddamned hero.

"I'm telling you this story," Small went on, "to illustrate an important point." He paused, and then roared, "I WILL STAND FOR NO NONSENSE IN MY SCHOOL, IS THAT UNDERSTOOD?"

The kids caught their breaths collectively, and Small's voice dropped to almost a whisper.

"No nonsense at all. None. Never. We took care of Douglas Murray, and we'll take care of anyone who steps out of line. Remember that, boys, because we'll all be a whole lot happier if you do. And you'll be a whole lot sadder if you don't."

Rick's hands were trembling. He clenched them in his lap, and bit his lip, and then stopped biting his lip when he realized the boys in his official class were watching him. He sensed hostility from them, and he wondered if Small had done the right thing in calling attention to what had happened. Certainly, enough attention had been called to it before this.

Small's manner suddenly changed. He was no longer the tyrant addressing his peasant multitude. He was a nice guy now, a master of ceremonies at a stag smoker.

"Boys," he said, smiling, "we're going to get along fine. I've taught at schools before, plenty of them, but I've never felt so good as I do about being appointed principal here. This is going to be a fine term, and we're going to make it one of the best in the school's history." He shrugged sadly, his eyes becoming dolorous. "We've had a bad start, but the teams that win the pennants very often have bad starts." He clenched his right fist and leaned out over the microphone. "North Manual Trades High School is going to win a pennant, boys!" He chuckled and then said conspiratorially, "What's more, fellows, we'll probably win the Series."

The boys did not applaud. They did not move. This big bastard may think he's Milton Berle, they were thinking, but he's not fooling us, not one bit. We know he's a louse, and we've got him pegged, and we're going to watch him because he's liable to stick a knife in our backs while he's patting us there. And Dadier . . . well, we'll see about our good friend Daddy-oh, the tough guy.

So the colors were carried out, and the assembly was dismissed, and since the day was shot anyway, what with shortened periods in order to give *all* the boys a chance to meet Small at two separate assemblies, there wasn't much time left for teaching. The school term, for all practical purposes, did not start until Thursday morning, even though it had started with a considerable bang several days before that.

And it was on Thursday, at precisely 2:07 in the morning, that Rick started evaluating his position. He and Anne had talked until almost one-thirty, lying in bed and conversing in whispers, almost as if they were not the only two people in the apartment. She had seemed terribly distressed about the incident, and she had not liked Small's handling of it at all. She firmly pronounced that the new principal must be a very stupid man, and she hoped his little speech hadn't started *Rick* off on the wrong foot, together with the Series-winning school.

She had also exhibited a womanlike contempt for Miss Hammond, blaming her for not wearing sackcloth and ashes to a teaching job in a school like that. Even after Rick explained that Miss Hammond hadn't been dressed flashily at all, Anne still held to the theory that no woman gets raped or nearly raped unless she's looking for it.

Rick did not pause to analyze the psychology of the pregnant woman. It had not occurred to him that pregnancy was a complete paradox. It was paradoxical in that only the female of the species could perform the amazing feat, while perhaps being less psychologically prepared for it than a male would have been. No woman enjoys the sight of sagging breasts and a bulging stomach, no matter how maternal her urge. A woman's good looks are a woman's good looks, and there is little good-looking about a pregnant woman.

Rick did not know that his wife had stood before the full-length mirror in the bathroom, sometimes for half-hours on end, studying her profile and wagging her head in sad, amazed wonder. She could not be blamed, therefore, for feeling some contempt for the woman who had plunged Rick into his present predicament. Such contempt was only normal. This Miss Hammond was slim. This Miss Hammond's breasts were not tender to the touch, nor did they feel like heavy stones. This Miss Hammond did not have a constant backache, nor was the skin on her stomach stretching like a bloated balloon. This Miss Hammond did not have to stand before a full-length mirror and drape a towel from chin to toes over a mountainous fetus in order to remember what she'd once looked like.

No. Miss Hammond had been sufficiently attractive to provoke a rape. Anne had heard of pregnant women being raped, but she doubted very much if she could arouse any rampant male interest at this late stage of the motherhood game. So whereas she looked forward to the new addition with an almost childlike expectancy, she still possessed a woman's eye, and she could not trick that woman's eye into thinking all was well in the state of Denmark, or even in the state of her expanding middle.

That Rick had performed gallantly was another matter entirely. She'd have been surprised if he hadn't. But that a slender, attractive, rape-provoking woman had been the cause of his gallantry—well, this did not sit too happily in her lactating breast. Especially if it led to trouble for Rick, and it showed every indication of doing just that.

Rick had listened to everything she'd said, silently agreeing with her, but not wanting her to get upset about the whole thing. He even wondered if he should have told her about it at all. She did, after all, have a condition.

He smiled in the darkness. Anne was asleep already, her hands holding his own hand to her breast, clinging to it warmly. He thought again of the "condition" and the smile expanded. Ever since the beginning of her pregnancy, even when it had hardly shown at all, Anne had girlishly lowered her eyes whenever Rick raised his voice. And then, in a barely audible whisper, she would say, "Please, Rick. I have a condition."

She did indeed have a condition, and it looked as if he had one, too. Tomorrow was another day, of course. Maybe the kids would have forgotten Small's speech by that time. Rick doubted it. He would have to play his cards right tomorrow, because tomorrow might be a very important day. Tomorrow might be the day that made or broke him.

Thoughtfully, with the street noises far below him, with the shade rattling only slightly at the casement window, he evaluated his position.

He was still doing that on Thursday morning when he stopped in the Teachers' Lavatory at 8:22 A.M. He had barely closed the door behind him when the voice said, "Ah, the conquering hero."

He looked over to the urinal near the window, spotting Alan Manners.

"Hello, Manners," he said.

"Ready to do battle today?" Manners asked.

"Ready every day," Rick said, smiling. He had taken a lot of ribbing from the assembled teachers in the lunchroom on Tuesday and Wednesday. Oddly, Solly Klein had been the only one who hadn't joined in the good-natured sport. Solly had simply stated, "I knew that broad would get raped," and then let it drop. Not the other teachers. In fact, their humor had closely paralleled that of the students of Manual Trades. Rick had taken it all good-naturedly, smiling and parrying all their thrusts. But this was Thursday, and this was the day after Small had delivered his speech to the boys. Rick did not expect any kidding today, and when it came, he was a little surprised.

"You sure she didn't try to rape *both* of you?" Manners asked.

"I'm sure," Rick said, smiling.

"Some guys have all the luck," Manners said, wagging his head. "I'd have known how to take care of that situation, all right."

"That's because you're a Lover Boy," Rick said, borrowing Solly's terminology.

"I admit it," Manners answered, smiling. "Have you talked with Miss Hammond yet? Or has it reached the 'Lois' stage by this time?"

"Is that her name?" Rick asked.

"You mean you don't know? Brother," Manners said.

"I haven't spoken to her since Monday," Rick said.

"Hero," Manners said, "you are slipping. Now is the time to cement the friendship. Now is the time to gather in the lady's gratitude."

"Hell," Rick said kiddingly, "I'm a married man."

"But not a blind man, surely," Manners told him. "This Hammond woman is a lot of woman, Dadier. Or had you noticed?"

"I've been too busy to notice much of anything," he said honestly. He stepped back from the urinal and waited for Manners to leave the sink. Then he washed his hands and dried them on a paper towel.

"You ought to start noticing. It's not every day a man rescues a woman's purity."

"Me," Rick said, still kidding but a little annoyed by Manners' persistence, "I rescue them every day. I'm a regular Galahad." He paused. "You going upstairs?"

"In a minute. No sense rushing into the ring before the bell." He sighed deeply. "Brother, will I be glad to get out of this place."

"Even with Miss Hammond here?"

"Lois? My only regret. I can see I'm leaving her to swine."

"Well . . ." Rick started.

"Have you figured on how to handle this yet, Hero?" Manners said.

"Handle what?"

"The kettle of fish. It's a fine kettle, you will admit."

"The kids, you mean?"

Manners shrugged. "If you insist on calling them that, yes. The 'kids.' "

"I've done a little thinking," Rick said, grossly under-estimating the hours of lying-awake he'd put in the night before, and the concentration he had given the problem during breakfast, and on the way to school, and even now just before he'd entered the toilet.

"And what have you figured?"

Rick summed up the total of his earlier thought on the situation in a single sentence. "If I've got the name, I'll have the game," he said.

"You're going to make like a tough guy?"

"I think so. Yes. I think that's best."

"Maybe so, Hero. But maybe the kids won't like it."

"I can't be worrying about what they'll like," Rick said. "I didn't ask to get dumped into a rape scene."

"You think you can carry it?"

"Carry what?"

"The tough guy part. Maybe they'll want to test you."

"I can take care of myself," Rick said, not really certain that he could, but resenting Manners' intimation.

"Spoken like a true hero," Manners said, grinning. "I shall think of you when I'm far away in some all-girls' school."

"Suppose you don't . . ."

"I'll get out, don't worry," Manners said, examining his classic profile in the mirror over the sink. "And I'll think of you playing Humphrey Bogart back here."

"Come on," Rick said. "We'd better get upstairs."

"I can see why things happen to you," Manners said knowingly, lifting his briefcase from the window sill. "You're too damned eager."

"Me?" Rick said. "I'm not eager, I'm Humphrey Bogart."

He was Humphrey Bogart all through that day. He had no trouble at all during the first three periods, even though he could sense resentment on the other side of his desk. He tried to forget the resentment, and he kept the classes pinned down with an iron fist, never once forgetting he was Humphrey Bogart. He was beginning to feel good about his part in the little rape drama. He didn't care if every kid in the school feared him, and he didn't care if they hated him. He was there to teach them, and since the major problem in a vocational school was making yourself heard, he was thankful for the wall of silence that stretched out in front of him. The kids, he realized, were using a sort of passive resistance on him, but their Gandhi philosophy was playing right into his hands, and he conducted his classes in an efficient and orderly manner. Yes, that old rape might very well turn out to be the best thing that could have happened to him. He made a mental note to tell Anne to stop worrying as soon as he got home, and when the bell sounded at the end of his duty period, he dropped the Humphrey Bogart role and headed straight for the teachers' lunchroom.

Contrary to the way he'd felt in the lavatory with

Manners, he was a little disappointed when the teachers showed no signs of continuing the past few days' banter. Hell, the thing wasn't that serious. If anything, it was helping him. But Solly Klein was holding forth about a friend of his who taught shop in a junior high school, a real cream job from the way Solly described it, and all of the teachers—with the exception of the one who lay face down on the leather lounge, who'd been lying there every day now, whose face Rick had never seen, and whom Rick suspected of being dead—listened to Solly and paid very little attention to the hero of Manual Trades. He ate his sandwiches silently, almost morosely. He'd have liked to hear their opinions on the course he was taking, but Solly monopolized the floor until the bell sounded, and Rick disgustedly went to greet 55–206.

The boys were talking when he entered Room 206, but they took their seats immediately and stared at Rick as he went to his desk. Miller watched him with raised eyebrows. The room was dead silent.

Good, Rick thought. *That's the way it should be.*

He put his Delaney book on the desk, opened it, and quickly took the attendance. West, he noted with satisfaction, was absent. That was good, too. He'd be able to concentrate on Miller exclusively.

He reached into his briefcase and pulled out a blue-jacketed book titled *Graded Units in Vital English*. He opened the book on his desk, reading the stamped lettering on the title page:

NORTH MANUAL TRADES HIGH SCHOOL

This book is loaned to the pupil with the distinct understanding that he will not deface it in any way and that his responsibility for it will not cease until he has returned it to his teacher and received a receipt therefor.

Keep the Book Covered

He wondered if they understood any of the highfalutin' language therein, turned his attention therefrom, and said, "I'd like to pinpoint some of your most common grammatical faults today, so that I'll be able to plan the remedial work we'll need throughout the term."

He said it coldly, and the boys eyed him coldly, showing neither distaste nor enthusiasm for his project.

"Antoro," he said, "will you get these books from the closet back there and distribute them to the class?"

Antoro rose without a sound. He was a good-looking boy, with sandy-brown hair and brown eyes. He walked to the front of the room, extended his hand for the key Rick offered, and then walked back to the book closet and opened it.

"You'd better give him a hand, Belazi," Rick said. Belazi rose as soundlessly as Antoro had, walked quickly to the back of the room, and then began carrying the blue books through the aisles, dropping one on each desk top. Antoro started on the other end of the room, and the book distribution was accomplished neatly in a very few moments. Both boys returned to their seats after Antoro gave the key back to Rick.

"If you'll all turn to page one," Rick said, and he watched the boys move like automatons, heard the whispering pages as the boys flipped past the *Preface*, and the *To the Teacher* section, and the *Suggested Aids for Study* section, and the *Correction Chart*, and the *Bibliography*, and the *Table of Contents*.

"Page one," Rick repeated. "Have you all got that? It's an Achievement Test. If you'll all look at part A, now. It says, '*Select the correct word or words in each parenthesis.*' Have you all found that?"

No one in the class answered Rick. He frowned slightly, and then went on.

"There's an example there of what's to be done." He paused, and then read aloud: "EXAMPLE: He (done, did) what he was told. *Answer:* did." He paused again. "Do you all get the idea? There are thirty-five sentences in this first section, more than enough for all of us. I'll call on you, and you'll take the sentences in order. Don't be afraid of making mistakes. That's what I want to find out. When I discover your weak spots, I'll be able to fix them. Is that clear?"

The class remained silent. The boys looked up from their books expectantly, but no one said a word.

"All right," Rick said, "will you take the first one, Miller?"

He had chosen Miller purposely, hoping the boy would start things off right, especially after his chat with him the other day. A lot of things had happened since that chat, though, and Rick didn't know exactly where he stood with the colored boy. Miller made a motion to rise, and Rick quickly said, "We can do this seated, boys."

Miller made himself comfortable in his seat again, and then studied the first sentence. Rick wasn't really anticipating too much difficulty with the test. This was a fifth-term class, and they'd had most of this material pounded into their heads since they were freshmen. The first sentence read: *Henry hasn't written (no, any) answer to my letter.*

Rick read the sentence, and then looked out at Miller. "Well, Miller, what do you say?"

Miller hesitated for just a moment. "Henry hasn't written no answer to my letter," he said.

Rick stared at Miller, and then he looked out at the class. Something had come alive in their eyes, but there was still no sound. The silence was intense, pressurized almost. "No," Rick said. "It should be 'Henry hasn't written *any* answer.' Well, that's all right. I want to learn your mistakes. Will you take the next one, Carter?"

Carter, a big red-headed boy looked at the second sentence in the test.

If I were (he, him), I wouldn't say that.

"If I were him," he said rapidly, "I wouldn't say that."

Rick smiled. "Well," he said, "if I were you, I wouldn't say that, either. 'He' is correct."

Something was happening out there in the class, but Rick didn't know what it was yet. There was excitement showing in the eyes of the boys, an excitement they could hardly contain. Miller's face was impassive, expressionless.

"Antoro, will you take the next one, please?" Rick said. He had been making notes in his own book as he went along, truly intending to use this test as a guide for future grammar lessons. He looked at the third sentence now.

It was none other than (her, she).

"It was none other than her," Antoro said quickly.

"No," Rick said. "The answer is 'she.' Take the next one, Levy."

Levy spoke almost as soon as his name was called. "George threw the ball fast," he said.

"Throwed the ball?" Rick said, lifting his eyebrows. "*Throwed?* Come now, Levy. Surely you know 'threw' is correct."

Levy said nothing. He studied Rick with cold eyes.

"Belazi," Rick said tightly, "take the next one."

"It is them who spoke," Belazi said.

He knew the game now. He knew the game, and he was powerless to combat it. Miller had started it, of course, and the other kids had picked it up with an uncanny instinct for following his improvisation. Now Rick would never know if they were really making errors or were just purposely giving wrong answers even when they knew the right ones. The "he-him," "she-her" business may have thrown them, but nobody used "throwed" for "threw." No, he couldn't buy that.

He listened to scattered sentences throughout the test as he called on every boy in the class.

Won't anyone borrow you a pen?

The player stealed a base.

Last term the class choose Mary Wilson as president.

She speaks worst than her brother.

Where was you when the policeman came?

Where was I indeed, Rick thought, when the brains (was, were) passed out?

"We didn't do too well on that, did we?" he asked.

The class was silent.

Okay, Rick thought, we can play this game from both sides of the goddamn fence. If we're going to be little smart guys, let's all be little smart guys.

"Since we've gone over all the sentences in class now, and since I gave you the correct answer for each sentence, the homework for tonight should be fairly simple," he said.

"Home . . ." one of the boys started, and Miller turned in instant reproval. The word "Shut . . ." burst from his mouth before he could stop it, but he never finished the sentence, never added the "up," apparently realizing the completed sentence would be too incriminating.

But Rick knew the whole story now, and the class sensed it, and they kept their silence only with the greatest effort. A battle of wills raged before Rick's desk, and he watched it with amazement, because it was obviously Miller who was holding the minds of his classmates captive in a clenched fist. He had given Miller a leadership pitch on Monday, but he hadn't for a moment believed that Miller was really a leader. A troublemaker, yes, someone to laugh at, but not a person to follow seriously. He revised his thinking rapidly now, and he even wondered if he hadn't, like Frankenstein, helped create this monster. Damnit, had he established Miller as a leader in Miller's own mind?

He watched the battle out there, watched the students' protest, like sand held in the tightest fist, slowly seeping through Miller's closed fingers. It was one thing to play games with the new snot-nose teacher, but when that teacher began dropping homework on their skulls, the game wasn't so hilarious anymore. Rick smiled, sensing the conflict, wanting to bring the battle to a head.

"Yes, homework," he said, still smiling. "And since I don't want you to take these books home, you can begin copying all thirty-five questions into your notebooks right now."

"Hey, what the hell!" Carter shouted. Carter's outburst started it. His words were livid with outrage, and his carrot-topped head seemed to lend fiery pictorial support to his indignation.

De la Cruz, a pale, thin boy with a reedy voice shouted, "Homework? How come we have thees . . ."

"It ain't even the first week of school!"

"Goddamnit, talk about slave drivers . . ."

"I go to work after school, teach!"

"That's enough of that!" Rick shouted. He tightened his jaws and calmly said, "Start copying the sentences now. The homework will count as one of the tests the class receives during the term. It may very well decide whether you pass or fail this course."

The rebellion ended as suddenly as it had started. Miller smiled at his classmates coldly, his face telling them they were all jackasses for having protested in the first place. It all led to the same thing anyway, didn't it, and now the teacher had the satisfaction of having heard them whine. He flipped open his notebook with weary superiority, and the other boys followed suit while Rick watched them copying the sentences.

"Better get them all," he said, almost enjoying his

power now. "The test will be marked on the basis of thirty-five questions."

This time, the class was silent. They had apparently grasped the meaning of the Miller-Gandhi method of attack. They wouldn't give Rick any more satisfaction. They would be separate stones now, held together by a mute mortar that bound them into a wall as solid as any fortress. Rick sat at his desk and watched them laboriously transcribing the sentences. His victory, if considered such at all, had been a hollow one. And aside from the momentary elation he'd felt when they'd finally broken to his will, he felt no real joy.

The silence out there was an almost tangible thing. He wanted to reach out and probe it with his finger, push at it like some gelatinous mass. He could hear the scratching of pen on looseleaf paper, could see the tops of the boys' heads as they worked.

What the hell goes on inside those heads? he wondered.

Probably nothing. Zero. Perfect vacuum.

This is a job for a man with a vacuum cleaner, he mused.

How do you go about cleaning a vacuum? Do vacuums get dirty? How do you get inside a vacuum to begin with? Someday we'll discuss vacuums in class. And for the best ten-thousand-word thesis following our discussion, I'll award a hollow loving cup, the hollow symbolizing the vacuum, and the loving cup symbolizing the mutual love and affection the boys and I share.

That was fun, he thought wryly, *what'll we play next?*

Probably charades for the rest of the term if this goddamned silent treatment persisted. The silence, of course, could be broken easily enough. Just shock them out of it, that's all. Like using insulin on a schizophrenic. Steady now, sir, easy now. WHAM! I beg your pardon, doctor, but did you see the top of my skull? I'm sure I had one when I came in.

Shock always worked, one way or another. Cure them or kill them.

It had its definite setbacks, though, the way this sudden homework assignment did. The shock may have goosed them out of their silence, but once the shock wore off the silence returned, and with it the memory of the shock to increase the formidability of the silence. Vicious circle. Elementary, my dear Watson.

Well, my dear Watson, just what do you propose? Shall we allow the silence to smother activity, like a dense London fog? Or shall we pierce the fog occasionally, knowing it will return anyway? Well, my dear Watson, what the hell's wrong with you, old boy? No answers? No suggestions? Nothing? Hell of a help, all right, you are.

Or should we treat the disease rather than the symptoms? If so, just what was the disease? Resentment, of course. They didn't like his interference in the rape. Well, he didn't like it much either, so they were even. Nobody likes polio much, for that matter, but everyone recognizes it as a disease. You can't discount something simply because it doesn't appeal to you.

Well, there was nothing to be done about the rape intervention. That was history, dead and gone, and rightfully in the province of the Social Studies department, with George Katz perhaps teaching a sparkling course on The Rise and Fall of Richard Dadier.

But, as with any disease, you can isolate the germ— or at least the germ-carrier. He knew who the germ carrier was in this ward, by God. His finger unconsciously tapped the Delaney card in its slot in the book.

Miller, Gregory.

He sounds like a movie star, Rick thought.

Only you and I, Watson, know that he is in reality a germ-carrier.

Shall we operate?

We shall operate. Scalpel, please. Sponge. Suture. Scotch tape . . .

The bell sounded.

"That's all," Rick said. "Pass the books down to the front of your row. Belazi and Antoro, collect them please and take them to the closet. Your homework is due tomorrow when we meet again." He paused. "Miller, I'd like to talk to you. Would you mind waiting?"

The class began filing out silently as Belazi and Antoro picked up the grammar books. Rick gave Antoro the key, and Miller waited alongside Rick's desk until the books were back in the closet. When Antoro and Belazi left, Rick faced Miller squarely.

"What do you say, Miller?" he said.

Miller did not smile. His face was in complete repose. He eyed Rick levelly and asked, "About what, Chief?"

"I thought we had a little talk."

"So?"

"You led them today," Rick said earnestly, being completely honest with the boy, using the same hook he'd used on Monday, but really meaning it this time. "But you led them the wrong way. Why?"

"Maybe you should of ought to minded your own business, Chief," Miller said. "Ain't many guys who like whut happened to Douglas Murray."

"That wasn't my fault, Miller," Rick said seriously. "You should know that. You'd have done the same thing in my position."

"Would I of? You don't know me so good, Chief."

"You're angry because I intervened, is that it?"

"Murray's goan to jail, you know that?"

"I had nothing to do with pressing charges, Miller."

"No?"

"No."

"You jus' pure-white innocent, that's all," Miller said.

"But what about our talk the other day, Miller? I thought we . . ."

"Mr. Dad-yay," Miller said, "s'pose we jus' forget that li'l snowjob, okay?"

"I wasn't snowing you," Rick lied. All right, he had snowed Miller. That was before he knew. This was different now.

"Man," Miller said, "the snow was knee-deep."

Rick stared at the boy, feeling curiously like the fellow who'd cried wolf. He'd tried to capture Miller's loyalty on a false peg Monday. The peg had turned out to be a true enough one, and now Miller had turned the tables. He hadn't believed Rick then, and he wasn't buying anything Rick sold from now on.

"I mean it, Miller," Rick said fervently.

"Man, you know that li'l poem, don't choo?" Miller asked.

"What poem?"

Miller smiled. "The wind blew, and the crap flew, and for days the vision was bad." He paused and studied Rick's face, still smiling.

"I don't see the point," Rick said slowly.

"You don't, huh? Well, what I mean, Chief, the vision is jus' now beginnin' to clear up a little. I can see fine now."

"You *are* a leader," Rick said, almost desperately this time, the realization overwhelming.

"I got a class now," Miller said. "Mind if I go, Chief?"

He walked across the room and hesitated at the door, seemingly about to say something further. Then he smiled, shrugged, and left Rick sitting at his desk with an Unassigned period.

The remainder of Rick's teaching day was almost a repetition of what went on in his fifth-period English class. He could not, of course, know whether or not Miller had engineered the silences which persisted in both his seventh-term classes. Perhaps he had, or perhaps the boys had hit upon this method of treatment on their own initiative.

They *were* silent. They were as silent as Death. They volunteered nothing. When he called on an individual directly, the boy would answer tersely and sullenly. The ball was all his own, and they sure as hell weren't helping him carry it. Any interference they ran was all in the opposite direction.

He gave them all he could give them, and then went into some written drills in an attempt to crack the silence that way. The silence remained silent, and Rick

felt his anger rising, and he controlled himself only with
the greatest effort. He learned on that Thursday of his
first week at Manual Trades that there is a vast difference between an orderly classroom and an ostracizing
one.

By the end of the day, he was as jumpy as a toad. He
gathered up his books and papers and stuffed them
into his briefcase viciously. Then he went to his closet
at the back of the room, unlocked it, and took out his
topper, slinging it over his arm. He was leaving the
room when he noticed all the windows were open.
Angrily, he dumped his briefcase and topper on his
desk, and then went around closing each window, using
the long window pole and almost breaking a pane of
glass on one window. He put the pole back into its corner, gathered up his briefcase and topper again, locked
the door to Room 206, and headed down for the
General Office.

Lois Hammond was standing by the time clock when
he got there. She inserted her card, punched out, and
then slipped the card into its identically-numbered slot
in the rack near the clock. She turned then and spotted
Rick.

"Oh, hello," she said.

"Hello," Rick said briefly. He did not mean to be
intentionally rude, but his mind was occupied with
Miller and the treatment he'd received from his classes,
and he could not exactly discount Lois Hammond's role
in the sequence of events.

She was smiling now, her pale lipstick almost dark
against her delicate face. She had good teeth, Rick

noticed, the better to eat you with, Grandma. There were lines of weariness around her eyes and her sensuous mouth, and he suddenly wondered what kind of hell she'd been going through, and this softened his attitude a little.

"I've . . . I've been wanting to thank you," she said in a low voice. She lowered her eyes momentarily, and then lifted them suddenly in a turning-full-power-of-brown-eyes-on gesture. He noticed this, and he wondered if she were being artful or coy, and then he decided she was not. There seemed to be an aura of innocence about this one, a naïveté that gave the lie to the woman's body beneath the loosely tailored suit. He realized abruptly that she had no more desired the attempted rape than he had, and he smiled.

"I guess we've just been missing each other," he said. "It can get pretty busy the first week."

"Yes," she said. She took her lower lip between her teeth, nibbled at it, and then dropped it. "Well, now that I've cornered you . . . thanks."

"Now that you've cornered me," he said, "you're welcome."

Lois Hammond hesitated. "I hope . . . I hope this hasn't hindered you in any way. With your classes, I mean. I'd hate to think . . ."

"No," he lied hastily. "If anything, it's helped. Made me a notorious figure."

"Well, that's good," she said uneasily.

"And . . . you?"

"Oh, it's been fine," she said. "I teach two senior classes and two freshmen classes. My official class is a senior group. They all want to graduate, you know, and I think they're frightened by what happened to Murray. I haven't had any trouble with them at all. And the freshmen, of course . . . well, they're not too aware." She smiled knowingly, and said, "I mean, they're just little boys, really."

"I understand," Rick said.

"So it hasn't been bad at all. I was just worried that you might have suffered for it. It's been bothering me."

"Nope," Rick said with manufactured nonchalance, "no pain at all."

"Well, I'm truly happy about that. And thanks, really, I don't know what got into that boy. He just . . ." She shrugged her shoulders, as if she honestly could not understand what had provoked lust. But in shrugging, her breasts moved, and Rick wondered for the second time if she were being artful, exhibiting her femininity while denying it. She seemed unaware of her breasts, though, like a little girl visiting a mature woman's body, living in it for a while, but not really getting used to all the furniture.

Rick smiled and said, "Well, tomorrow is Friday. I think the hardest part will be over once this week is gone."

"I hope so," she said. She sighed. "I think I'll celebrate its passing."

"Have a good time," Rick said, still smiling.

"I've got to run now," she said. She extended her hand, and when Rick took it, she tightened her fingers. "Thanks again. Very much."

"Don't mention it," Rick said.

"Good-by."

He nodded and watched her leave the office. When she was gone, he took his card from the rack, inserted it into the clock, and punched out.

It was 4:05, and he was tired and anxious to get home.

5

At 3:45 the next day Rick was just as tired, and perhaps just as anxious to get home. With his last period class dismissed, he sat at his desk without budging, staring out over the empty seats, relaxing completely for the first time that day.

The silence had persisted. It had reached almost gruesome proportions. He had fought it tenaciously, but the battle was a one-sided one, a struggle in which he was forced to take the offensive while all of his classes sat behind their calm defenses and watched.

He savored this other silence now, this silence that was a normal one, the silence of an empty classroom. It was a good silence. He appreciated it. He sat at his desk and let it swirl around him, like the warm currents of a tropical lake. He rose finally, and lazily began stuffing his briefcase. This was Friday, the end of the week. There was no rush. Tomorrow was Saturday, and the next day was Sunday, and by Monday he'd have figured something out.

He moved slowly, not rushing, and not wanting to be rushed. He was like the classic man who stopped batting his head against the stone wall and was immensely grateful because the pain had stopped.

When Josh Edwards poked his head into the classroom, Rick did not mind the intrusion. Josh was an adult. Josh was someone to talk to.

"Come on in," he said.

Josh smiled, the lenses of his glasses catching the late afternoon sun that streamed through the windows, reflecting it wildly, giving him a fiery-eyed look. He came into the room and plunked himself down in the nearest seat, propping his feet up on a desk across the aisle. "Pal," he said, "I'm bushed."

"Rough day, huh?" Rick said, snapping shut his briefcase.

Josh sighed heavily. "As my sainted father oft remarked while cracking Brazil nuts: this ain't as simple as it appears."

"It ain't," Rick agreed, smiling. "It most decidedly, emphatically, definitely, goddamn well ain't."

"You feel like a beer?" Josh asked abruptly, swinging his feet off the desk and sitting upright, almost bouncing in his seat. His store of energy never failed to surprise Rick. In this past week, he had seen Josh after many a difficult session with the kids. They'd usually meet in the corridor, or in the teachers' lavatory where they went to catch a smoke between classes. They'd spend about three or four minutes together, and then rush back to their respective classrooms in time for the next assault wave. At the start of each of these brief meetings, Josh always seemed exhausted, just about ready to collapse. But before he went in to greet his next class, he had regained all his pep. He was like a handball that got slapped soundly, only to bounce back more strongly when it hit the wall.

"I don't know," Rick said. "Beer . . ."

"I'll buy," Josh offered. "Come on, boy, this is Friday." He paused and then sang, *"No more pencils, no more books, no more . . ."*

"Okay," Rick said, deciding suddenly. "Let me get my coat." He walked to the closet at the rear of the room, opened it, and called over his shoulder, "Have to phone my wife, tell her I'll be a little late."

Josh nodded solemnly. "Duty bound," he said. They left the room together, and when Rick had locked up, they went downstairs and punched out. A bunch of boys were standing in one corner of the schoolyard when they stepped out of the building, and Josh glanced at them casually and remarked, "They can't bear to leave the place. It's like home to them."

"Oh, yes," Rick said. "Oh my, yes."

"Oh, my ass too," Josh answered. They smiled and walked across the schoolyard and out past the Cyclone fence and onto the sidewalk. They did not look back at the knot of boys in the schoolyard.

Rick felt good. All at once, he felt good. There were no more kids to worry about until Monday. No more dead silences. No strategy to be planned, no offensives to be taken. The prospect of a few beers, even if he wasn't crazy about beer, seemed like the most delightful idea he'd heard in a long time. In a sudden glow of warmth, he clapped Josh on the shoulder and said, "Brother, am I glad this week is over!"

"Ditto, came the reply," Josh said.

"Are you familiar with the local bars?" Rick asked. The outing had become a thing of excitement to him. He looked forward to getting it started, anticipating the cool dimness of a bar in the afternoon, the bottles stacked before the mirror, the juke box glowing with bubbling reds and oranges and greens.

"Never been inside one," Josh said. "We'll pick the closest one, okay? Beer tastes the same all over."

"Fine," Rick said enthusiastically. He walked along beside Josh, feeling unaccountably happy as hell. There was a nice nip in the air, a nip that made him appreciate the rough tweed of his collar at the back of his neck. He wished he smoked a pipe. Autumn was the time for pipes, and he had always secretly envied those broad-shouldered, cleft-chinned characters who smoked pipes so nonchalantly, and who apparently enjoyed them. The tall apartment buildings stood out in firm, afternoon-shadowed relief against the clear sky. They made him feel comfortably hemmed-in, like a soldier walking sentry in the courtyard of a fortress. Damn, he was happy.

They stopped at the first bar they found. A few men sat at the bar, watching the television, sipping at their drinks. It was a quiet place, warm with the glow of a neighborhood drinking spot. He felt immediately at home, and he took off his coat and went to phone Anne, leaving Josh to order.

When he came back to his stool, he was surprised to see two martinis resting on the bar top.

"You go for martinis?" Josh asked.

"Yes, but I thought . . ."

"Beer is everyday stuff," Josh said. "Hell, we've just completed a week at Manual Trades, and we're still alive. It calls for more than beer."

"Suits me fine," Rick said happily. "But no treat if we're drinking . . ."

"I just got a dividend check on my GI insurance," Josh assured him. "Come on, drink up."

Rick shrugged and picked up the fragile stemmed glass. "Here's to our own North Manual Trades Reformatory," he toasted.

"And to its charming inmates," Josh added, nodding solemnly.

They tilted the glasses, almost draining them. The martini was dry, and it burned a hole clear down to Rick's stomach, but he enjoyed it, and he finished the drink with his second pull.

Josh put his own glass down on the bar top and said, "This has been a week, Rick. A mighty week."

"Are you disappointed?" Rick asked.

Josh seemed to consider this a moment. "Not really," he said. "No, not disappointed. I think the kids'll shape up. This is just an adjustment period, I suppose. Me to them, and them to me." He paused and added, "I hope."

"They're not exactly what I'd call ideal students."

"No, not exactly," Josh answered, smiling. He poked at his eyeglasses with the forefinger of one hand, lifting them, rubbing at his eye, and then letting them drop onto the bridge of his nose again. "But they'll come around. I'm not expecting any Einsteins."

"Another drink?" Rick asked. He remembered abruptly that Josh was paying, and he said, "Look, let me split this, won't you? Otherwise I'll be drinking guiltily."

"Drink all you want," Josh assured him. "I'm loaded, believe me."

"Well, all right," Rick said, signaling the bartender. "He mixes a good drink, this fellow."

"Does he?" Josh said. "I hadn't noticed."

"Yes, he does." The bartender came up, and Rick ordered two more of the same. They sat silently, waiting for the drinks, as if they could not manufacture any further conversation until Josh had commented on the quality of the drinks the fellow mixed. When the martinis came, Rick lifted his glass, but he did not drink until Josh had tasted the mixture.

"Yes," Josh said, "it is good. Very good."

"Dry, but good."

"We're lacking music," Josh said. "I like music when I drink. Shouldn't we have some?"

"Sure," Rick said. "Why not?"

"All right," Josh said. He rose and walked to the juke box, fishing a quarter out of his pocket and stabbing at five buttons. He came back to the bar, finished his drink standing, and then straddled the stool again. "I like music. Let's have another one, shall we?"

He signaled for the bartender, and they heard the whir of the juke as it dropped a record onto the turntable, and then the sudden blast of an orchestra erupted into the room.

"Kenton," Josh said. "Stan the Man. Terrific stuff. Very far advanced for this day and age."

"Like our students," Rick said.

"Everything gets back to our students," Josh said, almost sadly. "You want to know something, Rick?"

"What?"

"I *am* disappointed. I am goddamn disappointed. I didn't think it would be like this at all." He paused and listened, his brown eyes sparkling with sudden life behind their spectacles. "Here, listen to this passage." He swung his knees out toward the juke. "My God, what those trumpets are doing!"

"I like Kenton," Rick said.

"Mmm, yes. What a sound. God, what a sound!"

The fresh martinis came, and they listened to the record and sipped at their drinks. Rick hadn't eaten since the fourth period, and the first two drinks had already attacked his blood. He felt them working inside him, and he listened to the almost-cacophony of Kenton's music, feeling it pulse inside him, sensing the drive behind the band, a drive that was almost a physical thing. The alcohol felt warm within him, and he was aware of a vague hazy feeling in his head, but he did not give a damn.

"I've got no right to complain, I guess," Josh said. "I suppose I'm luckier than most." Josh had already finished his third drink, and he stared at Rick curiously, blinking his eyes as if he were trying to focus him properly.

"How so?" Rick asked.

"Well, this isn't really a *bad* school. Oh, it's no picnic, but there are some that are a lot worse."

"Name one," Rick said perversely. He lifted the martini, sipped at it once, and then drank it all down. He took the olive from the glass, popped it in his mouth, and waited for Josh to answer.

"Name one?" Josh repeated. He watched Rick chewing on his olive, seemed to be possessed of a sudden appetite, and reached into his own glass, popping the olive into his mouth. Around the olive, he said, "Hell, I can name a dozen."

"All right, name one."

"A worse school than North Manual Trades?" he asked, chewing.

"Yes. Go ahead, name it."

Josh chewed thoughtfully for a few moments, and then delicately removed the olive pit from his mouth and placed it in the glass. "You name it," he said. "I want another drink."

Rick laughed aloud, feeling better than he had all week, feeling free and light, and almost able to float. He looked up at the ceiling and wondered if he could float up there. He did not see or hear Josh order, but when he looked down a fresh drink was waiting for him.

"I wonder if there is a large percentage of alcoholics among trade school teachers," Josh said.

"Why?" Rick asked. "What makes you ask?"

"Seems like the most sensible thing to do every Friday is go out and get drunk. Don't you think so?"

"Possibly," Rick said, and the word twisted around his tongue, and he thought it sounded like "poss-iss-ossibly." He stared at the fresh martini dubiously for a moment, wondering if he should drink it. Josh had already lifted his glass and tilted it to his mouth. *Oh, what the hell*, Rick thought. He brought the drink to his lips.

"I tell you, Rick," Josh said a little thickly, "I feel kind of cheated. You know what I mean?"

"The martinis?" Rick asked innocently. "Not enough gin?"

"No, no, martinis is fine," Josh said, tasting what was in his glass, just to make sure. "No, not the martinis. The school."

"Oh, yes," Rick said. He intended to nod his head slightly in agreement, but it emerged as an exaggerated, slow-motion lifting and dropping of his chin and head.

"They shouldn't give us schools like this one, don't you think?"

"No."

"You don't think so?"

"No, I meant no, they shouldn't give us schools like . . ."

"Yes, that's what I said. It's not fair, you know? I mean, Rick, I *want* to teach. I really do. Do you want to teach?"

"I do indeed," Rick said firmly, finishing the drink and holding up two fingers to the bartender. The bartender was standing close to them now, apparently having realized these two boys were going to be drinking in earnest. Rick watched him mix the drinks, and then said to Josh, "These are really good, you know? I must have had three already."

"You had four," Josh said thickly, "but who's counting?"

Rick slapped the bar top in an outburst of laughter, and Josh laughed along with him. They were still laughing when the next round came, and the bartender eyed them curiously, shrugged, and wiped the bar top with a wet rag even though it was absolutely clean.

Josh stopped laughing abruptly, and he stared at Rick seriously. "I really want to teach, Rick, like you. So why won't they let me teach? That's what I do not understand. I get up there, and I try to teach, and they won't let me. A man who wants to teach should be allowed to teach."

"You're positively right," Rick said emphatically.

"Didn't the people allow Christ to teach?" Josh wanted to know, his indignation mounting as he started his drink. "Didn't they?"

"You are not Christ," Rick said with the air of a man who has made a remarkable discovery.

"In this school, even Christ would have a tough time being heard," Josh said. He raised his eyebrows. "Hey now, listen to this one. You like Sarah Vaughan?" He cocked his head at the juke box.

"I love Sarah Vaughan," Rick said.

"She does things," Josh agreed. "She certainly does things. Did I tell you I'm going to bring my record collection to class someday?"

"Yes, you did," Rick said thickly.

"Well, I am. I got a good collection, started it when I was in high school. All the old Miller stuff, and the early James records. Charlie Barnet, the Duke when he was really laying them down. You remember 'Concerto for Cootie'?"

"I remember," Rick said.

"*Do nothin' till you hear from me,*" Josh sang in a horrible voice. "*Pay no attention to wha's said . . .*"

"Tha's pretty," Rick told him.

"Yeah, nice tune. I got all those old records, all of them, the old records. Remember 'Trumpet Blues'? I got that one. 'Trumpet Blues,' I mean."

"Tha's a good one," Rick said.

"Fine," Josh said thickly. "An' 'Tuxedo Junction,' remember that? An' Shaw's 'Backbay Shuffle.' All of them."

"Hey," Rick said, "how 'bout 'Sing, Sing, Sing'?"

"Oh, why sure!" Josh said, spreading his hands wide. "Certainly. Of course. *Sinsinsin,* naturally."

"I used to go to the Paramount every time Miller came to it," Rick said. "I liked Miller."

"He was good," Josh agreed. "A clarinet on top of four saxes, you know. Tha's how he got that sweet sax section sound, that nice high reedy sound. Shame he died. He was really good."

"Bet the kids today don't even know who Glenn Miller is," Rick said sadly.

"They're missing out," Josh said, just as sadly.

"Remember 'The Make Believe Ballroom'?" Rick asked.

"Tha's still on the air," Josh reminded him.

"Yeah, sure, but didn't you used to listen to it always?"

"Oh, sure. Every night."

"Jus' close your eyes

"An' visualize

"In your solitude

"Your fav'rite bands

"Are on the stand

"An'

   "Mis-

      "ter

         "Mill-

            "er

               "puts you

                  " *'In the Mood,'* " Rick sang.

" '*In the Mood,*' " Josh said. "That was another great one."

"You like Harry James, Josh?"

"In the old days, yes. Oh, he really did some fine ones. 'Trumpet Rhapsody,' 'He's My Guy,' 'Sleepy Lagoon,' 'I Don't Wanna Walk without You.' There was a record. Remember that one?"

"Sure. Helen Forrest."

"That's right. I wonder what happened to her." Josh sipped at his drink, a happy thoughtful expression on his face.

"They vanish," Rick said thoughtfully. "Remember when Bob Eberle and Helen O'Connell were with the Jimmy Dorsey band? You hardly ever hear from them anymore."

"They're still around," Josh said. "Trouble is, bands are on the way out. You listen to the Ballroom now, and all you get is vocals. The day of the instrumental is dead and gone."

"Maybe the kids won't like your records, Josh," Rick said suddenly, surprising himself with the observation.

"My records?" Josh asked incredulously. "Oh, sure, why sure they will. It's good stuff, Rick, really. An' I always kept them fine. Hardly a scratch on any of them.

Oh, they'll like it." He grinned. "I'm jus' tryina figure how to tie it in with an English class, tha's all."

"Why bother?" Rick said. "Jus' tell 'em you're gonna have music that day, tha's all."

"Yeah, but I like to tie it in. Tha's the way they tell you to do it." He paused, sipped at his drink again, and said, "Tha's what gets me, you know?"

"What?" Rick asked, feeling really dizzy now, drinking the martini automatically now, and feeling dizzier with each additional sip. "What gets you, Josh?"

"The things we learned in school. The Ed courses. What a bunch of horse manure."

"Right," Rick said, nodding his head.

"Damn right," Josh agreed. He paused for a moment, studying the open rim of his glass. He scratched his head and then asked, "What was I saying?"

"Ed courses," Rick said, silently congratulating himself upon having remembered.

"Oh yes, Ed courses." Rick waited for more, but Josh had apparently said all he cared to say about the subject.

"A bunch of horse manure," Rick supplied. "Tell you to give difficult kids board erasers to clean. Well, I got a question for the bigshot Ed Psych experts."

"Wha's that?" Josh asked lazily.

"What do you do when you got thirty-five difficult kids? There ain't that many board erasers in the city of New York."

"Besides, what are we raising, a generation of board-eraser cleaners?"

"Damn right," Rick said, getting angry about nothing in particular.

"Tha's what I like about you," Josh said, wobbling unsteadily on his stool now. "You got a keen, analytical mind."

"Thank you," Rick said.

"Don't mensh it. Not at all."

"If it's true," Rick said staunchly, "I'll mention it."

"What'll you mention?"

"That you got a keen, analytical mind."

"Tha's jus' what I said," Josh said, nodding his head.

"Thank you," Rick told him.

"Don't mensh it," Josh said solemnly.

They sat silently, sipping at their drinks, listening to the silence of the bar now that Josh's quarter in the juke had been exhausted. A kid of about eighteen came into the room, and they watched him walk to the cigarette machine near the door and punch out a package for himself. He glanced briefly at Josh and Rick, and then left the bar. Josh watched him, and as if the sight of an adolescent had reminded him of something, he said, "I'm gonna teach them, you know. I really am, Rick."

"Good for you," Rick said.

"Oh yes, I'm gonna teach them. I waited too long for this, Rick, too damn long. I been wantin' to teach since I was knee-high to a grasshopper. They don't know how much I been wantin' to teach, Rick. Some kids wanted to be cops or firemen. Not me. I wanted to be a teacher. Long as I can remember. Tha's all, jus' a teacher. So now I'm a teacher, an' a teacher's job is to teach, ain't it? Of course. So I'm gonna . . . going to . . . teach. Even if they don't want me to. A man's got to do what a man wants to do, Rick. He's jus' got to."

"An' the best way he can," Rick said. "He's got to do a good job, Josh."

Josh nodded reflectively. "Am I a bad guy, Rick?"

"You a good guy, Josh. A damn fine guy."

"So why won't they let me teach?"

" 'Cause they're bad guys," Rick said.

"Oh no, don't say that."

"Yes," Rick said, "they're bad guys."

"No," Josh said with drunken dignity, "tha's a common error, fallacy. They ain't bad guys. They're jus' ignorant."

"Same thing," Rick said.

"No, no, Rickie, don't say that. Please don't say that. These kids ain't bad guys. I mean it. Now I mean it, so pay attention an' please don't say that again. They are not bad guys. They jus' don't know any better."

"They ain't good guys," Rick said, blinking his eyes, holding to the bar top. He tried to concentrate on what Josh was saying because he had a feeling this was very important to Josh, and he didn't want to appear rude and not pay attention to something that was obviously very important to somebody else.

"They're good guys," Josh said. "Yes. Jus' like me an' you. Good guys. Unless they don't get taught, then they'll be bad guys, Rick. Tha's why I got to teach them, you see? Can y'understan' that? It ain't fair that no one should want to teach them. Teachers got to teach, Rickie, an' especially these kids. Please unerstan' me, Rickie."

"I understan' you, Josh," Rick said, trying very hard to understand.

"Okay then. Okay. An' you promise you won't call them bad guys?"

"All right," Rick said, "they're just ignorant."

"That's right, ignorant."

"Bad guys can be ignorant, too," Rick persisted.

"But ignorant guys don't have to be bad. You're reversin' the syllog . . . you know."

"Sure," Rick said.

" 'Zactly. Le's finish this drink."

They lifted their glasses and Rick said, "Here's to all the good guys."

"Well spoke," Josh said. "Spoken."

"An' here's to Stan the Man, a real good guy."

"To Stan."

"An' the Duke."

"The Duke, Rick."

"An' you an' me, God bless our bleeding . . ."

"Wounds," Josh supplied.

"Asses, I was gonna say."

"All right, whatever you say."

"Wounds," Rick finished.

They drank solemnly.

"I got to go home," Rick said suddenly. "Wife's pregnant."

"Congratulations," Josh said, taking Rick's hand.

"Thanks," Rick answered.

"How does it feel, being a father?"

"Not yet. I'm not one yet."

"How soon, Rickie?"

Rick began counting on his fingers, and then shrugged. "Soon." He stood up, staggered to the coat rack, and struggled into his topper, with Josh awkwardly trying to help him.

"I got to pay," Josh said.

"Lemmee split it," Rick offered.

"No, no, this's on me."

"Okay. Me next time."

"Nex' time," Josh said. He put a large bill on the bar top, and then waited for his change, scooping it up without counting it. "How do you go home, Rickie?"

"Bus. Third Avenue," Rick said.

"I'll walk you down," Josh said.

"Good," Rick answered.

They went out of the bar and into the darkness of the street. The street lights had come on, casting a warm yellow glow on the concrete. The sky was a dense black, studded with stars, streaked with scudding purple clouds. Rick looked up at the sky, receiving an abstract impression of blackness and pinwheeling stars, and realizing it was probably later than he thought.

"Got to get home," he said. "Got to hurry."

"Okay," Josh agreed.

They staggered down the street together, arm in arm, their heels echoing on the pavement.

"Le's cut down to Third," Rick said.

"Okay," Josh answered agreeably.

They took a narrow side street behind the department stores that crowded Third Avenue. A street lamp burned at the far end of the block, but this end was in darkness. They started down the street, and heard the footsteps behind them almost instantly.

"Somebody comin'," Josh said without turning.

"Let 'em come," Rick answered, trying to concentrate on Anne, and worried lest she was worrying, but not able to focus his thoughts clearly through the alcoholic haze on his mind. They staggered down the street, sometimes on the sidewalk and sometimes in the gutter. Rick clung to his briefcase with one hand, the other slung around Josh's shoulder.

They heard the footsteps grow closer, and then move up on their left, and then pass them, and they glanced up disinterestedly.

"Bunch of kids," Josh said.

There were three of them, boys of about seventeen or so, and they walked past Josh and Rick without even looking at them. Their shoes clattered on the asphalt, and then the darkness swallowed them up. Josh and Rick kept walking, unsteady on their feet, the air sharpening the effect of the martinis.

"Tha's funny," Josh said abruptly.

"What? Wha's funny?"

"Still footsteps behin' us."

Rick listened, hearing the even cadence of footsteps behind them, like marching feet in a German parade, listening to them and wondering at the same time what had happened to the footsteps that had been in front of them.

Something came alive in his mind. He whispered, "Josh!" and he wished desperately that he were sober.

The boys struck at the same instant.

There were seven all told. The three who had gone ahead, passing Rick and Josh just a few moments before, suddenly came out of the darkness, blocking the path. Rick turned unsteadily and looked up the street, trying to focus on the other four boys who were closing fast.

The street lamp was a good way off, down at the other end of the block, and the area of ambush was in almost complete darkness, darkness enough to have effectively hidden the three boys who'd gone ahead and then doubled back. They were far enough from Third Avenue, too, to make any cries for help worthless. Rick shook his head, trying to clear it, wondering why the hell he had to feel so dizzy when he knew he was going to have a fight any minute. He found himself thinking of Bob Canning, good old "Bob" who'd been assaulted on his way to the subway.

Well, this was good old Rick and good old Josh, and they were on their way home, too, and God knows how long these kids had patiently waited outside the bar while they'd been drinking themselves silly. The gang in the schoolyard, when he and Josh had been leaving— were these those boys? That seemed so long ago, such a long time to wait.

What does such long waiting do to an appetite hungry for blood?

"Hello, Daddy-oh," the voice came out of the darkness, and if he'd had any doubt before, there was no doubt now, none at all. Josh stiffened beside him, and his voice came softly, still slurred with alcohol.

"Back to back, Rick," he said.

The boys were glad about how things had worked out.

The boys couldn't have been gladder, because this

was an ideal trap, worthy of guerillas, worthy of cut-throats anywhere. They'd have liked it better if Daddy-oh had been alone, but the shrimp with him was nothing to worry about, and if he didn't take off his glasses he was going to be picking glass slivers out of his nose.

The street was dark, nice and dark. They were seven, and there were only two of the enemy. With odds like that, you couldn't lose, not even if you tried, and they weren't going to be trying.

One of them shouted, "This is for Douglas Murray, you bastard," and he threw his fist and felt it connect with flesh and bone. He felt Daddy-oh's head lurch back, felt the teacher slam up against the shrimp's back and then bounce off swinging wildly.

The shrimp had taken off his glasses and he was yelling, "All right, you bastards, all right, you bastards," and swinging his fists like pistons. Daddy-oh wasn't saying anything. Daddy-oh had his feet planted wide, and his back up against the shrimp's, and Daddy-oh was taking this fight as if it was hard work.

Another boy slammed his fist on the back of Daddy-oh's neck, and Daddy-oh grunted and bent forward, and another of the attackers brought his knee up, connecting with his groin. Daddy-oh grunted again, and then swung out and one of the boys felt his fist and backed away respectfully. But Daddy-oh was facing the side with four boys on it, and Daddy-oh hadn't been in a street fight since that time in Panama when everyone on his ship had got drunk and turned on each other. That fight had been a good one, and a bloody one, but it had been a long time ago, when Daddy-oh had been twenty

and considered a good fight an exciting thing. He was
plainly not enjoying this one. He was plainly not enjoying it because any one of the attackers knew his blows
were scoring. Even if they hadn't seen the blood pouring from his nose, they'd have known they were scoring.
They'd have known because their knuckles were getting
sore from the pounding they were giving him. They felt
flesh ripping, and they felt the grind of knuckle against
bone, and they heard him grunt, and they knew his
blows were getting weaker.

The shrimp just kept yelling, "All right, you bastards,"
as if it was the only song he knew. Only the song was
beginning to fade, like a radio program does just before
an electrical storm.

The boys felt victory near. They felt it with the
instinct of all good street fighters, and they were glad
they hadn't used anything but their fists. There was a
certain pride attached to it this way. Hell, anybody can
use a knife or a zip gun. You don't have to be smart to
beat somebody that way. They'd used only their fists,
and they were still using those fists, climbing all over
Daddy-oh now, wedging themselves between him and
the shrimp, breaking the pair apart, and then really
going to town.

One of the boys grabbed Daddy-oh from behind,
struggled for a grip in his short hair, and then gave that
up as a sorry task. He looped his arm around Daddy-
oh's neck, tightening his forearm across the mother-
lover's Adam's apple, pulling his head all the way back.
Another boy brought back his foot and gave it to Daddy-
oh, right in the balls, and Daddy-oh yelled, and another

boy whacked him in the mouth, tickled pink when he felt the blood spurt onto his fist.

"All right, you bastards," the shrimp kept yelling, but the shrimp was on the ground now, and feet had taken over because it was easier to use feet when a guy was down. The feet connected with his rib case and his thighs and his groin and even his head. He kept yelling all the time, the same tune, over and over again like a goddamned broken record. And then somebody broke the record by kicking him under the chin, and the shrimp ended his song and his resistance, and he didn't even feel the ensuing kicks that rained on his body like horseshoes.

You had to hand it to Daddy-oh because he went down swinging all the way. He hadn't said a word all through this, one of those guys who take their fights seriously. He wasn't saying anything now either. He was spitting blood, and his clothes were all torn, and his nose was running off into the gutter, but he kept swinging until they dragged him down to the pavement and gave him four sharp blows to the stomach. He stopped swinging then, but he didn't stop struggling, and he didn't stop bleeding. He couldn't swing because his arms were pinned to his sides, but he could sure as hell struggle, even though he was bleeding like a whore on her legitimate day off.

This was getting sloppy as hell. Maybe Daddy-oh could afford dry cleaning bills, but the boys would rather spend the dough in a movie. They decided to end it fast. They ended it by resorting to feet, and this time there were six pairs of feet because the shrimp was already out and, except for one boy who was enjoying kicking the piss out of an unconscious man, the others were free to give their undivided attention to Daddy-oh.

They gave it to him. They gave it to him until they felt they'd squashed his scrotum flat, and then they gave it to him equally around the head. He stopped struggling at last, and they grabbed his briefcase and dumped everything into the gutter, tearing the papers and the notebook, and then ripping the stitching on the bag, and breaking the clasp, and finally working it over with a knife, until it looked like a holiday streamer hanging from the ceiling of a dance hall. The kid with the knife in his hands got ideas, but the sport was over now, and when the sport is over you get the hell out of the neighborhood before the cops show on the scene. The kid put the knife away reluctantly, and they all strolled off down the street, heading for the street lamp near Third Avenue.

They walked out of the darkened block in pairs, two, two, and a final group of three. They walked up Third Avenue and looked in the shop windows and whistled at a few girls in tight sweaters, and they laughed a little and joked a little and then met in one of the ice-cream parlors, where two of the boys shot the works on banana splits. The other boys had ice-cream sodas or malteds, and they were all very orderly even though they laughed a lot.

When they left, the proprietor couldn't help commenting to his wife that high school kids were much quieter than they were in his day.

The clock on the kitchen wall had become a leering face. She could almost see eyes on it, could almost twist the advancing black hands into a crookedly grinning mouth.

The steam had gone off at a quarter to eleven, and the apartment was cold now. She trembled slightly, holding her robe close to her, looking at the clock once more.

It was possible, of course, that Rick had begun enjoying himself, had possibly even gotten drunk, and had forgotten to call her again. Anything, of course, was possible. But when he'd called, he told her he was going to have a few beers with—what was his name?—and that she should plan on a later-than-usual supper. He'd also asked her if she minded, and she'd said no, not at all, even though she'd have preferred him to come directly home.

The later-than-usual supper had been ready by eight. She did not remember how many times she'd gone to the living room window and looked down to the street eleven stories below. She knew Rick's walk the way she knew the new contours of her body. She was able to spot him a good half-block away from the project, and generally when he saw her standing by the window, he'd wave at her, then look hastily in both directions before crossing 174th Street and heading for the door of the building, out of her line of vision.

The street tonight was unusually deserted. Perhaps it was the unseasonally strong wind that had driven everyone indoors, leaving the lamp posts solitary and forlorn-looking. The supper she'd prepared stood in its pots on the stove, cold now. The dishes set on the kitchen table looked up at her with open white faces.

She was worried, truly worried. The radio in the living room was tuned to WNEW, and the strains of "Music 'Till Midnight" wafted into the apartment, soft, lilting melodies that made the place seem more empty. She would wait until midnight, until the announcer with his honeyed tones gave the talk about another day having gone to rest, with a future day ready to burst on the horizon. Or maybe she'd wait for the opening theme of "The Milkman's Matinee," or perhaps until the theme had played and Art Ford came on the air. Yes, she'd wait until then, and if he wasn't home, she would phone the police.

Even the idea of phoning the police frightened her. It was as if by admitting the possibility of violence, she was openly acknowledging that violence had happened.

She felt tears spring to her eyes, and she held them back desperately, hating the way she cried so easily lately, knowing it was due to her condition, and hating even that word now.

If anything has happened to him, she thought. *If anything has happened to him.* She could not hold back the tears. They streamed down her cheeks, and she wiped at them with the sleeve of her robe, and her mind conjured a picture of her giving birth to her child, with Rick not there, sometime in the future, with Rick not there, not there.

No, nothing has happened, she told herself. *He's just having a good time. He's just forgotten to call.*

But doesn't he know I'm worried frantic? If that's all it is, I'll kill him, I really will, not calling when he knows I'm worried sick.

She smiled at the idea of killing him, because that was silly, because she was worried that . . . that something *had* happened to him, and she would certainly not kill him, and when the realization of her silliness struck her she laughed a little, and the laugh dissolved into rapid tears, and she wiped at them with her robe until the sleeve was all wet. She prayed desperately for the phone to ring, prayed for the doorbell to burst into sound. The tears kept flowing unchecked, as if all the worry inside was running down out of her eyes.

There was a rush of violins from the radio, gripping the cold air of the apartment, and then a crooner's voice flowed from the prolonged violin passage, as warm as copper, tender, soft.

"*Long ago and far away,*

"*I dreamed a dream one day . . .*"

She rose and walked far into the kitchen, walked right up to the clock, as if she were defying its hands to move while she watched them. It was eleven-fifty, ten minutes to the deadline she had set. She wrung her hands together, stopped it when she felt like the heroine of a cheap melodrama, and then began pacing the floor, walking back and forth before the set table.

"*And now, that dream*

"*Is here be-side me . . .*"

Rickie, Rick, come home, she pleaded silently.

She walked back into the living room again, stopping at the window and looking down at the deserted streets, watching a newspaper sidle up to the curb, flap wildly in the gutter for an instant, and then leap onto the sidewalk.

When she heard the key in the latch, her breath caught in her throat. She whirled from the window and shouted, "Rick? Rick?"

She listened to the rattling of the key for a second and then rushed into the foyer, reaching for the inside lock. He was twisting his key at the same time, and they worked at cross purposes, fumbling on either side of the door, each anxious to have the door open, each anxious to remove the metal barrier between them.

And then the door was open, and he stood there unsmiling, blood caked on his mouth and streaked on his face, his left eye almost closed, his cheek ripped wide in a flap of flesh. His suit was torn, his new suit, the tweed he looked so well in, and there was a rip in his shirt, and she saw the flesh of his chest beneath that tear, and it was the sight of that skin, exposed-looking, white against the soiled white shirt, vulnerable-looking, that brought the tears again.

"Rick," she said, "Rick," and she led him into the apartment, not bothering to lock the door, sensing that the danger had passed long ago. "Darling, oh my darling, my poor darling."

He didn't speak. He walked into the living room like a dead man, with his arm around her shoulder, his weight heavy on her. He flopped down onto the couch, still not speaking, lifting his legs as if the effort was an extremely painful one.

"I'll get a doctor," she said in a rush, and he shook his head, and she stood there undecided for a moment, not knowing quite what to do, knowing only that he was hurt badly, and wanting desperately to help him. She left him and ran to the bathroom, still crying wildly, unable to control the tears. She got iodine and peroxide, and gauze and adhesive tape, and she rushed back into the living room, helping him out of his jacket, kissing his hands when she saw the lacerated skin there. She undressed him, biting her lip when she saw the blue bruises on his body, almost screaming when the red welts on his crotch were exposed.

"Darling, darling," she kept repeating, soothingly through her tears, unable to think of anything else to say, working hastily with her medicines and her bandages.

"*When the world should all be sleeping,*" the radio sang, "*and a melody comes creeping, 'til you want to sway, it's the Milkman's Matinee . . .*"

"Midnight already," Rick said hoarsely.

"Yes, darling, yes," Anne answered, not knowing what to do about the flap of skin that hung from his cheek, with the criss-crossing red fibers under it. She splashed peroxide into the wound and Rick winced, and she said, "Oh, I'm sorry," and he said, "That's all right." She put the flap of skin back into place, wondering if that were the right thing to do, and then she covered it with gauze and adhesive tape and began treating the other cuts on his face.

"They didn't hurt your teeth," she said, really wanting to think it, and surprised when it found voice.

"No," he answered.

"Were they . . ."

"The boys, yes. Me and Josh. I took him home first. We got a cab. I'm sorry, honey, but he . . ."

"It's all right," she said.

"He's a good guy, Anne. I'm sorry he got dragged into it. Oh Christ, why did he have to get dragged into it?"

"It's all right, Rick," she repeated.

"We were high," he said. "We shouldn't have got high. We'd have stood a better chance . . ."

"How many were there?" she asked, not wanting to hear his answer, but having to know.

"Seven, I think. Big kids. We shouldn't have got high."

"You didn't know, Rick. Rick, shall I get a doctor?"

"No, I'll be all right."

"Did you recognize any of them?"

"It was dark," he said helplessly.

"That's all right. Come, Rick, come to bed. Come, darling. You'll be all right."

"Can't I just . . . just rest here a while?"

"Yes, whatever you want. Would you like some coffee? Did you eat anything, Rick?"

"No. Nothing, Anne. I'm not hungry."

She washed his face, and then got him into his pajamas and threw a robe around his shoulders. She got a pot of coffee going anyway, remembering something about hot drinks being good for shock. She almost started crying again as she measured out the coffee, but this time she held back the tears because she didn't want him to know what a sissy she was. When the coffee was ready, she poured two cupfuls and brought them into the living room, dragging over one of the end tables and placing them on it.

He drank the coffee gratefully, even though he'd said

he hadn't wanted anything. She saw a little color coming back into his face, and she watched him while he
sipped at the coffee, hardly touching her own, just
watching him and glad to have him home again, and
knowing he'd be all right, knowing she'd do everything
she could to make him all right.

"Shall I get a doctor?" she asked again, and he shook
his head and sipped at the coffee, the steam enveloping
his face.

"I must look like The Invisible Man," he said. "All
these bandages."

She smiled, feeling her eyes moist again. He began
telling her what had happened then, leaving nothing
out, telling her the whole story. She listened with her
hands clenched in her lap, feeling unaccountably proud
of him, not knowing why, knowing you're not supposed
to be proud of the side that loses, but feeling this pride
bursting inside her anyway. When he finished his story
and his coffee, she sat beside him on the couch and held
him close to her breast, stroking his face.

They sat silently and listened to Art Ford and his
records, and after a long while, Rick said, "I think I'll survive, don't you?"

"You'd damn well better," she said. "I'm too young to
be a widow."

He laughed, and she laughed with him, and she knew
that everything was really going to be all right. Their
laughter broke the solemn mood that had been upon
them. As if they were both anxious to forget what had
happened, they began talking of other things, of what
she'd done all day, avoiding any talk of the school and

the attack and what was to happen when he went back to his classes on Monday.

"Jerry called," she said.

"Jerry Lefkowitz?"

"Yes. He got a job."

"Really?" he asked. "Where?"

"Central Commercial."

"I'll be damned," Rick said. "And I was worrying about *him!*"

"Is it a good school?" Anne asked, smiling because Rick was smiling, but not really knowing what was funny.

"Is it a good school?" He began laughing. "Oh, Anne, baby, and I felt guilty about taking *this* job from him. Oh, honey!" He started laughing again, really laughing this time, the laughter that is produced sometimes after tears, the laughter that is spontaneous and often completely humorless, the laughter that is more a release of sorrow than an expression of joy. He laughed boomingly, shaking his head continually, and because the laughter was so spontaneous, and because he looked so pathetic in his bandages, she laughed with him. They sat there on the couch and laughed like two idiots, shook with laughter until the tears were streaming down their faces, laughed until the man upstairs banged on the floor with a broom handle, and even then they couldn't stop.

PART TWO

PART TWO

6

The first snowfall came on Monday, October 19th, a little more than a month after Rick and Josh were attacked.

It started in the early hours of the morning, while the city slept. The snowflakes filtered down from a cast-iron sky, lazily at first, large wet flakes that melted the instant they touched the pavement. The darkened, empty streets took on a glistening, wet, polished look, black asphalt slickly shining in the wan light of the street lamps. And then the snow began in earnest. The big, sloppy, wet flakes fled before an onslaught of smaller, sharper white. The wind swept the snow over the pavements and gutters, and the snow clung and whirled and clung again. The street lamps stood like sentries at attention, their yellow-capped heads erect, the snow lashing at them, swirling about them. The snow covered. Slowly, patiently, it devoured black patches of asphalt, smothered the gray concrete, lodged in the brown earth of open lots, caked on the chipped paint of window sills, heaped against the curbs and the bases of the lamp posts, dropped a clinging downy-wet blanket on the metal-beetle tops of the parked automobiles.

And still it fell, silently, covering, muting, hushing the world and disguising the filth of a city, thick underfoot, a fleecy cold robe of crowded white flakes.

He sat at his desk and waited for the boys in 55–206 to arrive. The classroom felt warm, and he watched the falling snow outside the wide windows, and he felt peculiarly cozy, even though he was waiting for 55–206. The world outside was very white and very quiet. He studied it from the warmth of his wood and glass and concrete cocoon, watching the flurry of snow, seeing the white flakes lap soundlessly at the windowpanes, cling there for a moment, and then fall away.

His face bore no marks now. The wounds had healed very rapidly. They were nothing serious to begin with, if you like your face looking like hamburger, and time has a wonderful way of clotting blood and forming scabs, and then dropping the scabs to leave a fresh new layer of epidermis. Time was nice that way, and a month is a long time. The torn cheek had taken longest, of course, but even that had healed after the flap of skin had peeled and withered. He had looked like hell in the beginning, and all during that Saturday and Sunday after the beating, he had winced every time he looked into the mirror.

He had taken beatings before. He had taken a lot of beatings in his day. He had taken beatings when he'd lived in a tenement on 120th Street between First and Second avenues. He'd taken plenty of beatings there, all right, because his mother had insisted on dressing him neatly in a neighborhood that was all filth. And later, when they'd moved up to the Bronx, he'd taken beatings again, but only in the beginning, only when he was the newest kid in the neighborhood and every other kid felt it was his duty to test the boxing skill of the newcomer. And in the Navy, there had been beatings, but by that time fist-fighting was habit to him and he had given as much as he'd taken.

So he had seen cuts on his face before, cuts far more serious than those he studied in the mirror that week end. He still bore a scar under his chin where he'd been clobbered with the wooden orange-crate handle of a rubber-band gun when he was twelve. That had been a cut, all right, and they'd taken three stitches in his chin before that episode was over. No, it wasn't the appearance of his face that made him wince. It was the knowledge that he'd have to present that face to the assembled multitude of North Manual Trades High School on Monday.

He was not afraid of facing the boys again. That did not enter his mind at all. He had, after all, taken the beating already. He hoped that would be the end of it. If it wasn't, he wouldn't be drunk next time, and next time there'd be a few broken heads to account for his bruises.

But there was something shameful about the appearance of his face, and whereas he couldn't pinpoint the origin of the shamed feeling, he was guiltily aware of it. He felt like a pregnant woman wearing the badge of a bulging belly, the badge that proclaims to the world at large, "I've been layed." His face shouted, "I've been beaten," and he didn't want his face to advertise that slogan because it wasn't a true one. He had not really been beaten. He'd been ambushed and kicked around, but he hadn't been beaten, and there was a vast difference between getting beat up and being beaten. And so he was ashamed of this face which told such flagrant lies, this face that said, "Look at me. I am a beaten man." He studied it in the mirror, and he thought *I am not a beaten man.*

He was surprised, on Sunday night, when Anne asked, "Are you going back, Rick?"

He looked at her curiously, as if he did not quite understand what she'd said. "Of course," he said, his voice incredulous. "Why, of course I'm going back." He had cursed his face again in that moment because it had lied even to Anne, had led *her* to believe he was beaten, too. Anne had stared at him silently, and then simply nodded, and he knew she'd been pleased over his decision.

He tried to forget about his lying face on that Monday after the beating. And when Stanley asked what happened, and of course Stanley knew damn well what had happened, Rick had made some inane remark about having run into a belligerent doorknob. And when Small asked what happened, and of course Small knew damn well what had happened because he saw what Josh Edwards looked like on that Monday morning and he knew two belligerent doorknobs in the same week end was stretching coincidence just a bit too far, Rick had simply answered, "A little trouble," and that had been the end of that.

Except for the kids.

The kids knew what had happened, too. The kids knew it better than anyone else in the school. The kids got the story straight from the horse's mouth, all seven horses in fact, and the kids knew that Daddy-oh and Edwards had been worked over but good on Friday night. The kids knew it, and they liked it. This sort of evened the score. If Daddy-oh wanted to go around messing up some guy's life, okay, fine. But there were other guys who could go around messing up Daddy-oh's life just as well. And they'd done just that. They'd beat the living hell out of him, and damn if his face didn't look nice with all that plaster on it. The score, as far as they were concerned, had been evened. Daddy-oh had been paid in full.

And so the silent treatment, which had begun abruptly on the day after Small's delightful little speech, ended just as abruptly on the Monday after Rick's beating. Rick was surprised by the sudden change, and he spent a good part of his day trying to figure out the reason for it. He did not once mention the chopped-meat appearance of his face. He knew the kids knew what had happened, and he also knew that any show of leniency on his part would lead them to believe he'd been cowed into it. He did not show any leniency. Instead, he reversed the silent treatment. He played it hard as nails, Silent Sam himself, trying to show the kids that his face was a liar. The kids settled down to normal, for a vocational school, behavior. They called out, and they shouted, and they laughed, and they cursed, and they were disobedient and disorderly and plain goddamn ornery. And Rick settled down to trying to teach them in this normal, for a vocational school, atmosphere. There was no silence to cope with now, nothing like that, and Rick surmised that the street fight had miraculously removed that bloc.

He played it hard for a week, practically ignoring his classes, treating them with cold disdain. His attitude plainly told them what he thought of ambushes. He loaded them with written exercises and tests, and he was severely strict in his grading of papers and answers in the classroom. The kids remained unfazed. This was normal. The Douglas Murray score had been settled, and now they could relax and be just plain bastards rather than super grade-A bastards. The distinction, to them, was a fine one.

The second week after the attack, Rick changed his tactics. He realized he'd get nowhere with his sullen, unapproachable attitude. He also sensed that the kids knew exactly how he felt by this time, despite the appearance of his face. He was here to teach these kids, and he sure as hell couldn't teach them if he pretended they didn't exist. So he put the attack out of his mind. He stacked it in a dark corner under what he considered *Finished Business,* and he started with a clean slate, not realizing that almost every slate in a trade school is a dirty one.

He got the idea the day the machine shop upstairs went into operation. He'd brought an adventure magazine to school, figuring he'd start a new regime by showing some friendship toward the boys, by reading them a story from a popular publication rather than a textbook. The story was a good one, if not a classic masterpiece, and he read it well, injecting life into the descriptive passages, giving the dialogue real meaning. He had reached the climax when the machine shop erupted.

It started as a dull whine, and he barely glanced up from the printed page. The whine increased in volume until it sounded like a runaway buzzsaw. Rick looked up with honest bewilderment on his face, and he saw the boys in the classroom begin to smile. He lifted his eyebrows, shrugged, and started to read again.

The buzzsaw began to click, and then it began to clank, as if someone had thrown a monkey wrench into the gears and the gears were pounding hell out of it. The entire room seemed to vibrate from the sound. The windows rattled, and the pencils lying on his desk began doing an impromptu jig.

Rick opened his eyes wide in astonishment. The boys laughed, and something inside him responded to the laughter. For the moment, even though his astonishment had been real at first, he had become a showman. He opened his eyes wider in mock astonishment this time, and then let his jaw fall open, and he lifted his eyebrows until they were almost touching his hairline.

The class waited, and he felt the way he had back at college when the group had done *Room Service*. He felt that waiting for a gag line, sensed the anticipation, and he seized upon the interest and very slowly and very precisely said, "Now-what-the-hell-is-that?"

The class laughed, and then one of the kids said, "Machine shop upstairs, teach."

Rick had slapped his forehead and pretended to swoon. "Brother," he answered, "that's all we need."

He'd laughed aloud, a half-sincere, half-phony laugh, and the kids had laughed with him. He knew they were not laughing *at* him. He knew they were, just for the moment, sympathetic with his problems, looking at themselves from where he stood at the front of the room, realizing they were not exactly angels, and laughing because this added sound barrier was making a tough job tougher. They laughed with him because, just for the moment, they saw things as he saw them, and perhaps as they actually were.

"Read the story, anyway," one of the kids had called out. "It's a good one."

Rick had looked up at the ceiling and regarded the noise suspiciously, like a man about to dip his toes into an icy pool. Then he'd sighed, smiled, nodded his head in resignation, and gone on with the story, finishing it before the bell sounded. A feeling of good spirit had prevailed during that class, and Rick correctly attributed it to his impromptu dramatic reaction to the situation. He began to give this dramatization business deep consideration.

He'd been fairly good in college dramatics, and he knew that no one liked anything better than a show, especially if the show were free. And if he could hold the kids' attention by putting on a show, why not do it? There was no doubt that he had held their attention during the machine-shop episode. They had listened to him attentively, and he had felt something like rapport for the first time at Manual Trades. If the single problem was in reaching them, and if he had successfully reached them by becoming an actor, why not carry the thing further? After all, he didn't care how he reached them, so long as he did. And if dramatics was the answer, dramatics he would try.

He tried it. A little at a time at first, a few hammy gestures, a few mugging expressions. They ate it up, so he expanded on it. He tried illustrating a grammatical point by doing a little skit. They loved it. So he revised his lesson plans, organizing them so that everything he taught revolved about some piece of dramatics. He dramatized everything he did in class, whether it was reading a story or explaining the structure of a newspaper. He found himself exhausted at the end of each day, but the exhaustion was worth it, he reasoned, if he was accomplishing something.

He recognized the fallacy of his reasoning after he'd been acting for two weeks. He should have recognized it sooner, but he was so enthusiastic over the idea that its shortcomings went unnoticed. He made a common mistake, a mistake Solly Klein had repeatedly warned against. He assumed the intelligence level was higher than it actually was.

He greeted his seventh period, seventh-term English class with the news that he wanted them to write a composition in class. There was the usual grunting and groaning, and when the class had settled down, Rick explained exactly what he wanted done.

"The title of the composition," he said, "will be *Something Lost*." He paused and looked out at the vacant faces before him. "Lost," he said, spreading his hands wide, "you know, lost. Now there are a million things that get lost every day. I simply want you to write a composition about something you've lost, either recently, or a long time ago, or anytime, for that matter."

He saw the faces out there, and he hoped the gears

were beginning to click behind the expressionless eyes.

"You mean jus' somethin' we lost?" one of the boys asked.

"That's right," Rick said. "Tell me how you lost it, where you lost it, how you tried to find it, and how you finally did find it, if you did. For example . . ." he said, rubbing his hands together and preparing himself for his dramatic stint. He saw the smiles appear magically on the boys' faces, saw the anticipation in their eyes. He was going to put on a show again, and they liked his shows. Hell, let the bastard knock himself out. Didn't cost them nothin'.

Rick walked to the door of the room.

"You come home from school," he said. He opened the door, stepped out into the corridor briefly, and then entered the room again. He was no longer Richard Dadier, English teacher. He had rolled up the cuffs of his trousers, and he strolled into the room whistling, mugging broadly, giving his interpretation of what a seventeen-year-old kid looks like entering his home when the school day is over.

"You drop your books on the kitchen table," he said, reliving the way he'd done it every day when he came home from high school. He pantomimed the dropping of the books, and then he pantomimed taking something from his pocket. "You take your fountain pen from your pocket," he said, "and you put it down on the table, *right next to the books.*" He patted his desk alongside the imaginary books there. "Right here now. Right here alongside the books. That's where you put the fountain pen."

The kids nodded, really enjoying this. He was driving

at something, Daddy-oh was, something about that fountain pen, right there near the books.

"Okay," Rick said, smiling idiotically, rubbing his hands together and looking down at the imaginary fountain pen, "time for a little refreshment. Hard day today, English a pain in the neck, as usual." He paused and waited for his laugh, pleased when it came, timing it the way he'd done on the stage, waiting for it to reach its crest, and then speaking again when the laugh had almost but not quite subsided. "Think I'll have a little milk."

The kids nodded at each other, liking this goddamned show. What was he gonna do with that fountain pen?

"Off to the refrigerator!" Rick shouted, pointing his finger up at the ceiling like a kid getting an inspired idea. He raced across the room, paused at the door, and said, "Ahhhhh," opening the door and pretending it was a refrigerator door. He reached out into the corridor, shoving around some imaginary items in the refrigerator.

"Pickles, mm, cream cheese, mm, lasagna, bagels and lox, the cat, mm——" He did a take, reached in for the imaginary cat, and yelled, "What's the cat doing in there?" gingerly depositing the animal on the floor while the class howled. "Ahhh," he said when the laugh had died, "the milk." He held up the imaginary bottle, beamed, and then went to the sink for a glass.

"So you've got the milk and the glass, and you go into the living room and relax," and here he walked to the opposite side of the room, toward the windows. "And you forget all about the kitchen, and the books, and . . . the fountain pen!"

He nodded his head to emphasize the point, pursing

his lips. The kids watched him, realizing it was a mistake to forget about that fountain pen because something was sure as hell going to happen to it.

"You're drinking your milk in the living room, minding your own business," Rick said. He pointed toward the windows, indicating someone drinking over there, out of sight of the kitchen. "So who should come into the kitchen?"

He paused, waiting, listening.

"Your kid sister!" he announced, and here he became a prancing ten-year-old brat, sticking his tongue out at the class, skipping up to the kitchen table and looking for trouble.

"Ooooh," he squealed, "a great, big, fat, old fow-tin pen!" He picked up the pen with childlike delight, hugged it to his chest, and then began scribbling on an imaginary sheet of paper, doodling wildly, his tongue caught between his teeth as he leaned over in a grotesque position. Then he skipped across the room, held up the fountain pen, and said, "But the kid gets tired of it, so she finally puts it down. But where? *Where?* On top of the refrigerator!"

The class howled, and Rick let them howl, and then he carried the sequence to its end, dragging in mama and papa, and even the refrigerated cat, moving the fountain pen from spot to spot until its original owner couldn't possibly find it in a million years.

"Do you get the idea?" he asked when the class had stopped laughing. "*Something Lost.* I just gave you an example of how something can get lost. Now you tell me about your own experiences."

He passed out the lined composition paper, said,

"Don't forget the heading at the top of the paper," and then watched the class get to work. He was rather pleased with himself. He'd held their interest all the way, and he'd graphically explained the type of composition he wanted them to write. The class worked until the bell rang, and then he collected the papers.

The surprise and realization didn't come until later, when he was correcting them. He did not expect decent English. He had long since stopped expecting good spelling, organization, or grammar from any of his classes, even the seventh-termers. So he was not disappointed on this count. But he was almost floored when he read the contents of the compositions.

Jackson, a seventeen-year-old boy, a seventh-termer, wrote:

> *Come home from school. Opin door an get mik from rifridgator. Putt books and fontin pen on table. Go drinck mik. Kid sister comes in the kichen, took pen from table, putts it on top refrigater. Father took pen from rifijerater, takes up to bedroom on burow top. My mother fines the pen up there and . . .*

Conrad, eighteen years old, a term away from graduation:

> *Wass I suprise when I put down my fountain pen on the kidgen table, when I get home, from school, and then latter I can't. I wass drin a glass of milk in the room so I don't know my sister takes the pen*

*and moves it around the house while I am. Latter
my father also moves this pen, and wass I suprise.
Thats how my pen got lost, and I have'nt found it
to this day. Its sure funny how things can get move
around a house when you not looking or drink
your milk. It can come like a shock if you not careful and leave with your things to lay around and
get. Even my mother move the pen, so I cant find it.
Careful with things means they don't get lost.*

Rick read the compositions slowly and carefully, the
fear growing within him. He kept thinking of the little
skit he'd performed, kept seeing that same skit performed over and over again in composition after composition. A little imagination, yes, but just a little. Not
what he'd wanted at all. A few embellishments on what
he'd done, but basically all the same, all poured from the
same master mold.

From Di Luca:

*Even my cat; shes a angora with a bell on her
neck; took the pen in her mout and carryed it
down her baskit.*

From Perez:

*This pen move the house all around like a chicken
head. I never fine him cause everybody stick they
fingers in the soup. Pretty soon my fader come
home fine the pen and take it upsters with himself. I drink my milk this time wile the pen go.*

Rick stared at the compositions, feeling completely defeated, wondering how this thing could have happened. Hadn't he made it clear? Didn't they know he wasn't asking for a simple repetition of what he'd given them? God Almighty, didn't they know that? Could they be that stupid? Had all his goddamn work been for nothing?

He checked on their records the next day during his Unassigned period. He found the I.Q. of every boy in every one of his classes listed on their permanent record cards. He knew that intelligence tests weren't truly accurate gauges of intelligence, especially with people whose manual skills were better than their language skills. He had never fully trusted such tests, but the evidence presented on the record cards—especially in the light of what had happened the day before—seemed overwhelming.

Like the low-numbered jerseys on the backs of a football team, the intelligence quotients spread across his field of vision.

72 85 83 86 84 89 77 81 85 93 82 87 80

He checked all the cards, and then he went through them again, making a rough computation and coming up with an average intelligence of 85. He was familiar enough with the Stanford-Binet test to know that an I.Q. between 80 and 90 was considered Low Normal. He sighed and looked through the cards again, studying each one carefully, trying to identify each boy as he read off the intelligence quotients.

He was not surprised to find that Santini, the smiling, first-row-first-seat boy in 55–206, had an I.Q. of 66, and he knew the Stanford-Binet test classified anyone within the 50 to 70 range as a moron.

There was one boy in all of his classes with the surprisingly high I.Q. of 113. In Rick's mind, the Stanford-Binet table took photographic shape and form:

Normal 90–110
Superior 110–120

He looked at the figure on the record card again—113. And then he looked at the boy's name.

MILLER, GREGORY

On impulse, he turned to the card headed WEST, ARTHUR FRANCIS, almost relieved when he saw an I.Q. listing of 86. He left the records with a new knowledge within him, and he wondered why a teacher in a vocational school wasn't told about little unimportant things like average I.Q.'s before he started teaching. Or was it policy to let a teacher find out for himself? Was it policy to let him blunder around on his own until he happened to hit the right combination? And if he never hit the right combination? Well hell, vocational school teachers were expendable.

But he could not dismiss the seeming injustice of the system. He had taken enough education courses at college to qualify him for licenses in both the high school and the junior high school. He had taken the junior high school examination and had passed it. The license, in fact, was home in his dresser drawer, under his socks. He had tried to get a job in a junior high, and failing in that, had taken the emergency license examination when it was announced. The exam had not been an easy one, in spite of the need for teachers in vocational high schools. He had taken a good many exams throughout his years of schooling, and this one had definitely not been a snap.

Nor had the education courses at Hunter College been lacking. Dry, yes; but lacking, never. At least, not lacking by current standards. He was taught exactly what he was supposed to learn. Hunter was a good teachers' college. He knew that, and was secretly proud of the fact. He had no doubt that the education courses offered there were equal, if not superior, to those offered at any other teachers' college in the country.

But he could not remember any emphasis being placed on the vocational school. Passing mention, yes. But emphasis, no. And perhaps passing mention was sufficient for the fellow who wound up teaching at Christopher Columbus, but it was definitely not sufficient for someone who now found himself in a vocational high school. The topic had, of course, come up during his conferences with Professor Kraal, the college instructor who'd supervised his student teaching. When Rick had been assigned to Machine and Metal Trades, even though he'd asked for an academic high school, he'd been none too pleased about it. He'd voiced his displeasure, and Kraal, a mild-mannered man who preferred discussing the days of the nickel glass of beer to education, had shrugged and simply replied, "Someone's got to get the trade schools. It'll be good experience for you."

Rick supposed it had been good experience, although he still wasn't quite sure. He'd had no trouble with the boys there, mainly because Miss Daniels, the teacher to whose class he'd been assigned, never left the room when he taught a lesson. He taught exactly eight lessons during the semester. The rest of his mornings spent at the high school were devoted to work in the English office—typing up tests, running the mimeograph, little chores that helped the department chairman—and observation at the back of Miss Daniels' room. The observation had been enlightening, in that he'd learned a good deal about Miss Daniels' technique. He did not, unfortunately, get much opportunity to develop his own technique.

Nor had his conferences with Professor Kraal helped, and those conferences could have contributed a great deal toward his understanding of the vocational high school. He invariably left a conference feeling bored, tired, and unrewarded.

"Someone's got to get the trade schools," Kraal had said, and that seemed to sum up the attitude of everyone concerned. That plus the always-thought but never-voiced addition: "And no one *wants* the trade schools."

All right, no one wanted the trade schools. No one wants leprosy, either, but . . .

But what? Rick wondered. Suppose the college had given elective courses titled *Teaching the Trade School Student*. Sure, let's suppose that. Would there have been a mad scramble to elect those courses? Doubtless, oh yes. Ohmyyes.

Everyone was just dying to learn how to teach the trade-school student. Everyone was just itching for the opportunity to get out there in the system and land smack in the middle of a trade school.

Sure. He knew at least twenty people who'd yelled bloody murder and threatened mayhem when they'd been assigned to vocational high schools for their student teaching. Picture anyone actually counting on the trade school as his career. Picture that.

"What are you going to be when you grow up, Johnny?"

And proudly: "A vocational high school teacher."

But . . . but there *were* teachers who ended up in the trade schools, and goddamnit, their job was to teach kids who happened to be in those schools. The system was there. It existed. There were kids enmeshed in that system and some of them, surely *some* of them, really wanted to learn, were really counting on the system to teach them a trade, something from which they could earn their daily bread. You can't condemn a kid because he's not a mental giant. There's a poetry in repairing the carburetor of an automobile, too, even if the kid repairing it can't spell carburetor. Then why ignore the system? Why give birth to it and then flush it down the toilet?

Why pretend it's not there?

Why prepare a teacher for an altogether different type of student, an ideal student, and then throw him into a jungle hemmed in by blackboards and hope he can avoid the claws and the teeth? If the teacher survives, well all fine and dandy. If he doesn't, the wild animals will surely survive, won't they? But who wants wild animals in the street?

Or was that why the system had been invented? Was Solly Klein right? Was it just to keep the kids off the streets, just to keep them out of trouble for the major part of the day?

No, Rick couldn't believe that. Maybe Solly Klein had been in the racket for a good long time, and maybe Solly had seen things Rick would never see, but Rick could not believe the system was a sham. A lot of thought had gone into its conception, a lot of careful thought, a lot of consideration for the kids who were at a total loss groping with the subjects taught in the academic high school. When had the system come into being? Rick wondered.

He did not know.

He did not know, and he felt a deep shame for not knowing, the same shame he'd felt about not knowing the average I.Q. of his students. Why hadn't anyone told him? Wasn't that something he should know? Goddamnit, wasn't that one of his tools? Would they send a soldier onto a battlefield without a goddamn rifle? Would they send a surgeon to an operating table without a scalpel? Not when a human life depended on it.

Well, a great many human lives depended on what he did at North Manual Trades High School. He taught a lot of kids every day, and every day he went into the blackboard jungle without even knowing how many teeth there were in a lion's mouth. Or how many claws on a lion's paw. Or anything about a lion at all. They'd taught him how to milk cows, and now they expected him to tame lions.

Perhaps they expected him to behave like all good lion tamers. Use a whip and a chair. But what happens to the best lion tamer when he puts down his whip and his chair?

Goddamnit, it was wrong! He felt cheated, he felt almost violated. He felt cheated for himself, and he felt cheated for guys like Joshua Edwards who wanted to teach and who didn't know how to teach because he'd been pumped full of manure and theoretical hogwash. Why hadn't anyone told them, in plain, frank English, just what to do? Couldn't someone, somewhere along the line, have told them? Not one single college instructor? Not someone from the Board of Ed, someone to orientate them after they'd passed the emergency exam? Not anyone? Not one sonofabitch somewhere who gave a good goddamn? Not even Stanley? Not even Small? Did they have to figure it out for themselves, sink or swim, kill or be killed?

Rick had never been told how to stop a fight in his class. He'd never been told what to do with a second-term student who doesn't know how to write his own goddamn name on a sheet of paper. He didn't know, and he'd never been advised on the proper tactics for dealing with a boy whose I.Q. was 66, a big, fat, round, moronic 66. He hadn't been taught about kids' yelling out in class, not one kid, not the occasional "difficult child" the ed courses had loftily philosophized about, not him. But a whole goddamn, shouting, screaming class-load of them, all yelling their sonofabitching heads off.

What do you do with a kid who can't read, even though he's fifteen years old? Recommend him for special reading classes, sure. And what do you do when those special reading classes are loaded to the asshole, packed because there are kids who can't read in abundance, and you have to take only those who can't read the worst, dumping them onto a teacher who's already overloaded and who doesn't want to teach a remedial class to begin with?

What do you do with that poor ignorant jerk? Do you call on him in class, knowing damn well he hasn't read the assignment because he doesn't know how to read? Or do you ignore him? Or do you ask him to stop by after school, knowing he would prefer playing stickball to learning how to read, and knowing he considers himself liberated the moment that bell sounds at the end of the eighth period?

What do you do when you've explained something patiently and fully, explained it just the way you were taught to explain it in your education courses, explained it in minute detail, and you look out at your class and see that stretching, vacant wall of blank, blank faces, and you know nothing has penetrated, not a goddamn thing has sunk in? What do you do then?

Give them all board erasers to clean.

What do you do when you call on a kid and ask, "What did that last passage mean?" and the kid stands there without any idea of what the passage meant, and you know he's not alone, you know every other kid in the class hasn't the faintest idea either? What the hell do you do? Do you go home and browse through the philosophy of education books the G.I. bill generously provided? Do you scratch your ugly head and seek enlightenment from the educational psychology texts? Do you consult Dewey?

And who the hell do you condemn, just who?

Do you condemn the elementary schools for sending a kid on to high school without knowing how to read, without knowing how to write his own name on a piece of paper? Do you condemn the masterminds who plot the educational systems of a nation, or a state, or a city?

Do you condemn the kids for not having been blessed with I.Q.'s of 120? *Can* you condemn the kids? Can you condemn anyone? Can you condemn the colleges that give you all you need to pass a board of education examination? Do you condemn the board of education for not making the exams stiffer, for not boosting the requirements, for not raising salaries, for not trying to attract better teachers, for not making sure their teachers are better equipped to teach?

Or do you condemn the meatheads all over the world who drift into the teaching profession, drift into it because it offers a certain amount of paycheck-every-month security, vacation-every-summer luxury, or a certain amount of power, or a certain easy road when the other more difficult roads are so full of ruts?

Oh, he'd seen the meatheads, all right, he'd seen them in every education class he'd ever attended. The simpering female idiots who smiled and agreed with the instructor, who imparted vast knowledge gleaned from profound observations made while sitting at the back of the classroom in some ideal high school in some ideal neighborhood while an ideal teacher taught ideal students.

Or the men, who were perhaps the worst, the men who sometimes seemed a little embarrassed over having chosen the easy road, the road to security, the men who sometimes made a joke about the women, not realizing they themselves were poured from the same steaming cauldron of horse manure. Had Rick been one of these men? He did not believe so.

He had wanted to teach, had honestly wanted to teach. He had not considered the security, or the two-month vacation, or the short hours. He had simply wanted to teach, and he had considered teaching a worth-while profession. He had, in fact, considered it the worthiest profession. He had held no illusions about his own capabilities. He could not paint, or write, or compose, or sculpt, or philosophize deeply, or design tall buildings. He could contribute nothing to the world creatively, and this had been a disappointment to him until he'd realized he could be a big creator by teaching. For here were minds to be sculptured, here were ideas to be painted, here were lives to shape. To spend his allotted time on earth as a bank teller or an insurance salesman would have seemed an utter waste to Rick. Women, he had reflected, had no such problem. Creation had been given to them as a gift, and a woman was self-sufficient within her own creative shell. A man needed more, which perhaps was one reason why a woman could never understand a man's concern for the job he had to do. So Rick had seized upon teaching, had seized upon it fervently, feeling that if he could take the clay of undeveloped minds, if he could feel this clay in his hands, could shape this clay into thinking, reacting, responsible citizens, he would be creating. He had given it all his enthusiasm, and he had sometimes felt deeply ashamed of his classmates, often visualizing them in teaching positions, and the thought had made his flesh crawl.

These will teach my children, he had mused. *These.*

And these had sent kids to his classes without knowing how to read. These had taught a total of nothing, but who was to be condemned?

Who, who was to be condemned?

He had a tool now, one tool. A magnificently powerful, overwhelmingly miraculous tool, a tool no one in all his years of preparation had ever thought to tell him about. And worse, his preparation had not even instilled in him the curiosity or common sense to ask about this fantastic tool.

He now knew the average I.Q. of his students.

He spent the next week observing his classes. He taught, or tried to teach, while he was observing, but he was really stalling for time, trying to learn in one week all the things he'd never been taught. On this Monday of October 19th, he did not know if he was any closer to reaching the kids. But he had some ideas now, just a few ideas, and he sat at his desk and waited for 55–206 to put in its appearance, waited and watched the snow nuzzling the windowpanes.

He sensed that the beginning of the teaching process had to come from the kids themselves. He knew, in fact, that there could be no beginning in this school unless the kids desired it. Standing up there in front of the room and throwing facts at them was a waste of time, until they realized that there could be no teaching and no learning unless there was a give and take. And rather than spend all his time giving, and hoping they would be taking, he'd decided to let them do a little giving, let them do all the giving in fact, until this sense of mutual exchange became a habit.

The boys were beginning to trickle into the room now, one at a time, breezing by his desk and looking at the leather box there. Rick looked at the box and smiled. The box was part of his plan, and he was anxious to see how 55–206 reacted to that plan. He had reached the conclusion that 55–206 was the worst of his classes, a deduction he'd cleverly made after learning about Juan Garza from Solly Klein. He knew that if he licked 55–206, he had them all licked, and so he'd chosen this class as the first for his experiment. He would not let them know there was anything extraordinary about today's lesson, of course. He would handle the class the way he always did, letting them believe nothing had changed. He spotted Miller in the doorway, and then the colored boy entered the room smiling.

He walked directly to Rick's desk, indicated the leather box with a slight movement of his head, and asked, "You bring your cosmetics t'school, Chief?"

"Take your seat, Miller," Rick said.

Miller opened his eyes wide in innocence. "Don't be touchy, Chief," he said, smiling. "I know lotsa guys use makeup."

"Sit down," Rick said patiently. "Come on, Miller."

"Why, sure, Chief," Miller said, delighted. "Why, sure."

He slouched up the aisle and collapsed into his seat, and Rick looked at the leather box and thought, *He knows damn well what it is. He never saw a cosmetics case that big.*

The boys drifted into the room, walking to the windows and looking out at the snow, lingering there a while and finally taking their seats before the bell sounded. West, his blond hair plastered against his forehead, rushed into the room just as Rick was closing the door. He grinned, said "Thank you" as though Rick were a doorman, and then went to his seat beside Miller.

Rick closed the door, walked back to his desk, took the attendance rapidly, and then rapped on his desk for silence. The boys went right on chatting, ignoring him completely.

"Okay," he said, "let's knock it off."

The kids modulated into silence, and Rick said, "Let's keep it quiet for now, anyway. You'll have plenty opportunity to talk later during today's class."

"We goan make speeches, teach?" Miller called out.

"No," Rick said, "we're just going to talk."

The other kids were already considering what Miller had said. So that's what was on deck for today. A goddamn speech period. Give a three-minute speech on *How I Spent My Summer Vacation.* This was going to be real jazzy.

"Any of you fellows plan on becoming President of the United States?" Rick asked, hoping they would see the absurdity of this, and hoping it would provide the peg he needed.

"Yeah," West said, "I'm planning on that."

"You are?" Rick asked. "Well, I didn't know that."

"Lots of things you don't know about me, teach," West said, grinning.

"I didn't think we had any future presidents here," Rick said. "I was going to say that . . ."

"But we do have a future president," Miller put in. "You jus' heard West there, dintchoo?"

"You gonna vote for me, Greg?" West asked.

"Why, sure, man," Miller answered. "I goan lead the campaign."

"Well," Rick said, wanting to recapture the class before it got too far away from him, "those of us who *aren't* going to become President will never have to make any speeches in my class. Of course . . ."

"I changed my mind," West said, getting a laugh from the class. "I think I'll be a mechanic instead."

"Do mechanics got to make speeches, teach?" Miller asked.

"No," Rick said. "No speeches." He looked out at the class to see how all this was registering. 55–206, like all his other classes, had been disappointed during his past week of observation when his play-acting had come to an abrupt halt. They couldn't understand why he'd stopped putting on shows, and they were disgruntled over this good thing having come to an end. The fact that they hadn't learned a single thing from all his play-acting didn't matter to them at all. The period had at least been an entertaining one, and that's the most anyone could ever expect from an English class.

"Politicians make speeches," Rick said. "I don't think

any one of you will ever be called upon to make a speech, so let's forget speeches. You'll never have to make a speech in one of my classes."

"Oh yeah," Corrente called out. "Yeah, sure."

"I'm not kidding," Rick said. "If there was anything I hated in high school, it was . . ."

"You go to high school, teach?" Miller asked innocently.

"Yes," Rick said. "Of course."

"That right? Which one, teach? You go to a vocational high school?"

"No," Rick said. "I went to . . ."

"This your first teaching job?" West asked.

"No," Rick lied.

"Where'd you teach before?" West asked.

"Brooklyn Automotive," Rick said impulsively.

"Then you must've known Mr. Small there, huh? Is that right, teach?"

"Let's knock the small talk off," Rick said, unintentionally presenting a pun on the principal's name.

Miller slapped the top of his desk and threw his head back. "Hey now," he shouted, "that's real clever! We talkin' 'bout Mr. Small, and Daddy-oh here say we should knock off the small talk! That's real clever, by God, that is."

The class began laughing, and Rick said, "All right, cut it out. And you just keep your mouth shut, Miller."

"How's that, teach?" Miller asked, the smile dropping from his face.

"I said keep your mouth shut. We can't all talk at the same time, and I happen to be doing the talking right now."

"I thought you said we'd all get plenty opp'tunity to talk today, teach," Miller said.

"If you'll let me get on with the lesson," Rick said, exasperated, "maybe we will."

"Gee, teach," Miller said innocently, "I had no idee I was detainin' you. Go right ahead."

Rick sighed, wondering why he'd lied about having taught before. Was he hoping to gain their respect that way? And had he really hoped to fool them?

"We don't have to make speeches," Rick said, going back to the lesson he'd prepared, "but we do have to *talk* in life. If you want a glass of water, you have to say, 'Let me have a glass of water.' You can't say, 'Og migga zoo nod' and expect a glass of water. Am I right?"

"Was that French, teach?" West asked.

"No, it wasn't French. I was just . . ."

"Rooshian, Chief? You speak Rooshian?"

"No, it wasn't Russian, either. It was just nonsense, something I made . . ."

"You talkin' nonsense, Chief?" Miller asked.

"I thought I asked you to shut up, Miller," Rick snapped.

"Did you?"

"I did! Now keep your mouth closed or you'll find yourself sitting in Mr. Stanley's office for the rest of the day."

"That Stan man, boy he scare me," Miller said.

"Did you hear me, Miller?"

"When you say, 'Ig mogga re-bop'? Why sure I heerd you. That was nonsense, wunt it?"

"I was just trying to illustrate a point, Miller. You see,

we all talk. All day long, we talk. Right now, you're talking too damned much, Miller, and . . ."

"Watch the language, teach," Levy shouted. "Watch the language."

"Thank you, Levy," Rick said coldly. "What I'm trying to say is that in spite of all this talking that's going on, we very rarely stop to listen."

"I don' follow," De la Cruz said.

"I mean just what I said," Rick answered. "We never really listen."

"How cou' that be?" Kruger said belligerently, his jaw thrust forward. "You got to listen if you 'spect to hear."

"Oh, we listen, sure," Rick said. "With half an ear, and a little part of the mind maybe. But we're not really listening. We don't really know what we sound like. And believe me, some of us sound as if we're saying, 'Og migga zoo nod.' "

"Hey, bobba ree bop!" Miller shouted.

"There's that Russian again," West added.

"Keep quiet, Miller," Rick said. "Now just keep quiet, do you hear me? Just shut up!"

"Other guys talkin'," Miller said sullenly. "Why you pickin' on me?"

"Because you're talking altogether too much. And because I don't happen to like your attitude. Now shut up."

Miller folded his arms across his chest and tightened his mouth. Rick stared at him for a few seconds, and then said, "You've all seen this leather box on my desk, and perhaps you've been wondering what it is."

"I *know* what it is," Miller said.

"It's not a cosmetics case, Miller."

"No kiddin'?" Miller said pointedly. "No kiddin'? It couldn't be a li'l ol' wire recorder, could it, teach? It couldn't be that, could it?"

"Yes," Rick said, the wind taken out of his sails, the careful preparation all shot to hell. "Yes, Miller, that's what it is."

"Well, well," Miller said happily, "what do you know?"

"The idea is this," Rick said. "The reason you can't hear what you sound like is because you're usually too busy talking to listen. Well, I'm going to give you the chance to talk first and listen later."

"You mean we gonna make records?" Carter asked, lifting his red head for a better look at the recorder.

"Yes," Rick said, unsnapping the lid and then plugging the cord into an outlet. He fiddled with the spools, giving the boys a little opportunity to talk it up out there. He was fairly certain most of them hadn't used a recorder before, and they seemed to be fairly enthusiastic about the project now that it had finally got rolling. He had not been able to introduce the lesson the way he'd wanted to, thanks to his good friend Miller, but he'd still been able to generate enough interest among the kids, and that was what counted. If he could get them to loosen up, get them to give a little . . .

"So we gonna make speeches after all," Miller said knowingly.

"No," Rick contradicted, "we are not. I've said it before, and I'll say it again. We're just going to talk. And then we're going to listen."

"That's doubletalk for sayin' we gonna make speeches," Miller said.

"How'd you like to bring your mother to school, Miller?" Rick asked.

"I wunt," Miller said.

"Then please keep quiet." He paused and stared at Miller, hoping to strengthen his threat that way. Even the most difficult kid usually flinched at the thought of his mother coming to school. A mother coming to school usually preceded a beating from the father that night, no matter how uninterested the parents were in their son's learning process. There was something terribly embarrassing about being called to school and chastised about a delinquent son.

"We'll all talk a little," Rick said, "and the recorder will take down everything we say. Then I'll play it back, and we'll have the chance to hear what we really sound like. If we don't get to everyone today, I'll borrow the recorder again. Now I want you all to speak the way you normally speak. Don't try to sound like Gabriel Heatter. Just talk naturally. That's the idea of this."

"Why don't we sing a little?" West suggested.

"We'll save that for your Music Appreciation class," Rick answered.

"All we get in Music Appreciation is 'Marche Slave' and 'To A Rose,' " West said.

"To a rose, to rose, to a lovely wild rose," Miller sang.

"Knock it off, Miller."

"We learn lots of those," Miller said, smiling. He nodded his head in self-agreement and sang, *"Narcissus was, a very good-looking boy. His im-mage in the brook, would fi-ill him up with joy . . ."*

"You got the recorder going, teach?" West asked.

"No. Now, let's cut out this . . ."

"He looked, and looked, and looked, and looked, un-til he turned, into, a lovely flow-er," Miller concluded. "You got that machine takin' down this marv' lous voice, Chief?"

"No. Listen, Miller, I . . ."

"I know lots of them, Chief. I could go on all day."

"Don't bother. We want to . . ."

"You know *'Amaryllis,'* Chief? Tha's a good one. *Amaryllis written by Ghys,"* he sang, *"Use to sell oranges, fi' cents apiece.* Hey, Chief, you takin' all this down? Man, this shunt go to waste, I mean it."

"Miller, I don't want to warn you a—"

"Man, I a musical genius. You hum any ol' tune, an' I'll name it for you. Go 'head, Chief, try me. Go 'head."

Rick was half tempted to take Miller's challenge. Give the wise guy a passage from Shostakovich and see how quickly he identified it. He was ready to do so, but he couldn't remember any passages from Shostakovich, and he was also a little afraid that Miller *might* be able to identify one, even if he could remember it. Besides, he'd be playing right into Miller's hands if he went on with the repartee, so he let it drop and said, "We'd better start recording before the period runs out."

"Dawn," Miller sang, *"over mountain, and Dawn, ov-er valley, and Dawn, while the shep-herd is play-a-a-ing his fluuute—"*

"Shut up, Miller."

"That's from the *William Tell Overture*, Chief. That's by—"

"SHUT UP, MILLER!" Rick shouted.

"Rossini," Miller said softly.

"Now let's get this machine going before . . ."

"These periods sure do seem short, don' they?" Miller asked.

"All right, Miller," Rick said, really angry now. "All right, wise guy. I warned you. Now we'll see how you like . . ."

"I'll be quiet, Chief," Miller said, a serious look on his face. "I'm sorry."

"You'd *better* be quiet. I'm not kidding around anymore."

"I'll be quiet," Miller promised. He folded his hands before him on the desk top, striking an angelic pose, a pose which got a laugh from the class. Rick felt his jaws tighten, and he waited a moment while he gained control of himself.

"All right," he said, "who will we start with?"

"How 'bout Morales?" Miller piped.

"No, I think . . ."

"What's wrong with Morales?" West said.

"Sure, Morales he like to talk," Miller said.

"I don' want to make no speech," Morales said from the back of the room. He was a Puerto Rican boy with a thick accent, and Rick didn't want to subject the boy to any class ridicule. He looked at Miller, trying to understand why the boy was insisting on Morales. An accent might be good for a laugh, but it seemed like a cruel way to strike at the teacher.

"No," Rick said, "let's start with—"

"I know why you don't want Morales," Miller said. " 'Cause he can't talk English good."

"That's got nothing to do with it," Rick said, annoyed.

"Then why? It's 'cause he speak Spanish, tha's why."

"Look," Rick protested, "that has nothing to do with it." He glanced at his watch, cursing Miller silently, and cursing the way the time had all but vanished.

"Come on, Morales," West shouted, "get up there. Let's hear you talk."

"No, no," Morales said thickly. "No' me."

"Agh, you jus' chicken," Miller said. "Tha's all."

"Come on, Morales," Erin shouted.

"Let's go, boy," Pietro said.

"We want Morales," Vandermeer chanted.

"We-want-Morales," the class began chanting. "We-want-Morales. We-want-Morales. We-want-Morales."

"Come on, chicken," Miller said.

"I no chicken," Morales said angrily.

"Then le's hear you talk, man. What's wrong, cat got yo' tongue?"

"Let's cut this out," Rick said wildly, but his voice was drowned beneath the "We-want-Morales" chant. He watched as the thin Puerto Rican got to his feet and reluctantly slouched to the front of the room. He had a surly look on his face, a look that told the class he was not chicken and not afraid of any goddamned machine in the world. He walked right up to Rick's desk, looped his thumbs in his dungarees and spread his legs wide, waiting.

"All right, Morales," Rick said, resignedly. "All I want you to do is talk, that's all. Nothing fancy. You just talk."

He started the spools, and then walked to the back of the room. Miller was silent, listening now, waiting for Morales to begin his talk. West leaned forward in his seat eagerly, and the class waited with smiles on their faces while Morales fidgeted at the front of the room.

"All right," Rick said, "start talking. And remember, I want to hear you all the way back here."

"What I gon' talk about?" Morales asked, looking down at the revolving spools of the machine.

"Tell me how you got ready for school this morning, what you did, where you took the train, all that. Go ahead, Morales."

Morales glanced at the machine again, casting it a dirty look. "I get up at se'n-thirty," he said, "an' I go the bat'room to wash." He paused and looked at the recorder. "My sist', she in the bat'room, so I can' get in, so I ha' to wait outsi'. I wait there, an' she singin' insi', so I keep waitin', an' then she come out." He looked at the machine again, apparently beginning to realize that the silently revolving spools were not going to bite him.

"That's fine, boy," Rick said. "Go on, keep talking."

Morales smiled, complete master of the machine and the situation now. He visibly relaxed, and Rick said encouragingly, "Go on, Morales, go on."

"I go in the fuckin' bat'room an' I wash my fuckin' face an' hans," Morales said, smiling. "Then I come out an' eat some fuckin' corn flakes."

The boys were beginning to snicker. The first *fuckin'* had shocked them, and they'd glanced toward the back of the room at Rick. It had shocked Rick, too, but he'd let it pass, unaware that a series of profanities would follow it. He didn't know quite what to do now. Morales had finally relaxed. Morales had forgotten all about the recording machine, had forgotten that his words were being captured for posterity. He'd relaxed, and in relaxing he'd begun to speak the way he normally spoke, and the word *fuck* in all its various uses was a normal part of his normal speech. Rick looked at the smiling faces, and then he spotted Miller, and he saw the look in Miller's eyes and knew then why Miller had insisted on Morales being the first to record.

"So I go don' the fuckin' street," Morales continued, smiling happily, "wit' my fuckin' books under my arm, an' I meet this fuck he lives in the same buildin' wit' me. He say, 'You go to school, Pete?' an' I say you fuckin' A right. So we walk together the fuckin' subway."

The class was laughing now, laughing loudly. Miller clutched his middle and rocked in his seat. West jabbed Miller in the ribs with his elbow, guffawing wildly. Rick stood at the back of the room and watched the class disintegrate. He could stop it now, sure, but what difference would it make? The damage was done now. Miller had successfully fouled up the lesson. Miller had—

"So wat the fuck you think?" Morales asked seriously. "Fuckin' train, she late, an' they a big fuckin' crowd on the station. My frien', he say, 'Those fucks at school, they mark us late, jus' 'cause this fuckin' train.' So tha's how come I so fuckin' late to school today, teach."

"All right," Rick said tightly, "that's fine, Morales.

Take your seat now, won't you?" He walked toward the front of the room and Morales, a gold tooth shining in the front of his mouth, beamed happily.

"I wass all right, teach?"

"You were fine," Rick said. He snapped the recorder off, and the class continued to laugh, the laughter rising and ebbing, rising again, and then falling as Rick stood silently by his desk.

A hush fell over the classroom as the kids watched Rick, wondering what was coming next. That was, after all, a recorder on his desk, and a recorder made records, and now when he played it back at them, there'd be a few more good laughs.

Rick glanced at his watch. "I think that's enough for today," he said. "Time's running short."

"Ain't you goan play back that li'l talk, Chief?" Miller asked, smiling.

"There isn't time," Rick said flatly.

Miller looked at his own watch. "Hell, we got least five minutes yet. Tha's plenty time."

"I'm running this class, Miller."

West looked up suddenly. "And some fuckin' class it is," he mumbled.

"*What?*" Rick asked, turning to West.

The class was very quiet now. It was one thing for Morales to curse all over the place; he just didn't know any better. And it was okay for Miller to ride the teacher 'cause he was a card that way. But this with West, this was something else.

"*What* what?" West asked, smirking.

"Your mouth is filthy," Rick said. "Just watch it."

Miller stepped in quickly, smiling. "No filthier'n Morales," he said. "An' he a recordin' star."

"Never mind Morales," Rick said, turning to Miller again.

"Wha's the matter?" Morales asked from the back of the room.

"Nothin'," Miller answered. "Teach don't like the way we talk, tha's all. Guess he won't make no more records now."

"You guessed right, Miller," Rick said, speaking impulsively. "It's too bad you had to foul it up for everybody."

"Me?" Miller asked innocently. "What I do, Chief? Morales who made the speech."

"Wha's the matter?" Morales asked again, perturbed.

"Yes, you, Miller," Rick said. "It's a shame. I think the class could have really enjoyed this recorder."

"I doan see what I done," Miller said, shrugging.

"Ain't we gonna make no more records?" Maglin called out.

"No," Rick said, wondering if that was what Miller wanted, and wondering if he wasn't behaving like a spoiled brat by denying them the privilege of the machine.

"Why not?" Antoro asked.

"Ask your friend Miller," Rick answered. "You might all ask Miller," he added. "He'll tell you."

Miller shrugged again. "I doan know what you talkin' 'bout, Chief."

"*Don't* you. Well, you think about it. And if you all get a test tomorrow, in place of a lesson with the recorder, you've got Miller to thank for it."

"Hey, what the hell!" Parsons bellowed.

"A test! Man, why . . ."

"What the hell did Miller do?"

"Knock it off," Rick shouted. "Just knock it off or you'll find yourselves with a homework assignment to boot."

55–206 did not knock it off. They continued complaining and protesting, and Rick stood at the front of the room and said nothing for the remaining two minutes of class time. When the bell rang, he locked the recorder in his coat closet, scooped up his things, and left the room without even looking at the kids. He was disappointed and hurt. Disappointed because he'd really hoped the recorder would be the beginning of something, the origin of a new teacher-student relationship. And hurt because the class had missed the significance entirely, had chosen to follow Miller instead and make a complete mockery of his attempt to reach them.

And now, he surmised, things were worse. The class really did not know why he had picked on Miller, or why he was punishing them for this imaginary thing Miller had done. What the hell *had* Miller done? Nothing you could put your finger on, surely. Could you accuse the kid of having known Morales' speech pattern? Could you say, "Miller, you bastard, you knew Morales would talk that way?"

Supposing Miller hadn't known? Supposing Miller just didn't like Morales and wanted to see him suffer up there in front of the class? Or supposing Miller thought it would be amusing to hear Morales' accent-thick voice coming from a recorder?

No, Miller had known all right. He knew Morales, and he knew Morales used profanity with every breath, and he knew damn well what would happen once Morales loosened up. Miller had spotted the recorder the instant he'd stepped into the classroom. He'd spotted it, and he was intelligent enough to know what was coming, and intelligent enough to know that Morales' language would break up the class completely.

What the hell is this, Rick wondered, a war? Do I have to plan a campaign against Miller every day of the week? Is that how I'll finally get to teach?

Sure, except Miller isn't the only one. West is another, and West may not be as smart, but he's just as dangerous.

Dangerous? *Dangerous?* Come on, boy, let's not exaggerate the situation. They're just kids, you know.

Sure, but mighty big kids.

Yes, but the biggest kid . . .

"You ever try to fight thirty-five guys at once, teach?"

No, Rick thought, I never did. And I never want to. Miller is no shrimp. He's only about two inches shorter than I, and he probably weighs just as much as I do, and he looks like a strong kid, if you can call him a kid at all. And West may look thin, but that thinness is deceptive, and I knew a lot of thin, lanky guys who would kill you as soon as look at you.

So now we're down to the killing stage, something in his mind said. *A bit melodramatic, no, Richie?*

Miller and West aren't my only problems, Rick thought, ignoring the other part of his mind. There's Sullivan in my official class, and Marchetti in the seventh period and Harris in the eighth period. No, Miller and West aren't all by a long shot. They just . . .

But what you said about killing? What about that?

Why don't you take a walk? Rick thought. Go on, take a walk, Bud.

Are you afraid of these kids? They're just kids, you know.

No, I'm not afraid of them.

What then?

Nothing. Who asked you, anyway?

You're getting touchy, boy. The kids are making you touchy. I think you're afraid of them.

I'm not afraid of them, damnit. I'm just trying to do a job. Can't you see that?

Well, you're not doing too well, boy. I'd say you're not doing too well at all.

You're an observant sonofabitch, Rick thought. Go take a walk.

He told Solly Klein and the assembled teachers about the wire recorder the next day. They sat around the wooden table in the lunchroom, with the exception of the man lying face down on the couch, and Rick related the incident, telling them about Miller's part in it, and explaining the apparent innocence of Morales, who hadn't known what happened from start to finish.

"That's why I want an all-girls' school," Alan Manners said.

"I don't get you," Rick answered.

"You take this kid Morales. He uses *fuck* all over the place, and he doesn't even know what he's saying. If a girl uses that word, she knows damn well what she's saying, and you can chalk up another roll in the hay."

"It's guys like you who get in trouble," Solly Klein said. "I wouldn't let my daughter come within ten feet of you."

"What's wrong with a normal sex urge?" Manners wanted to know.

"On you already," Solly said, "it's an urge beyond normal. It's super-normal."

Manners smiled shyly. "I'm just a red-blooded American boy," he said.

"Then you should be happy here in the Forbidden City. You're surrounded by a lot of red-blooded American boys."

"I won't be here long," Manners said, nodding his head for emphasis. "Believe me."

"Famous last words," Savoldi said wisely.

"I'm pulling strings," Manners told them. "I want to be surrounded by underprivileged eighteen-year-old girls. I can't help it, it's my calling."

"They'll be calling your name at Quentin," George Katz said, munching on his sandwich. "Why'd you become a teacher, Manners? Why didn't you get a job backstage at a burlesque house?"

"I'll do that during the summer vacation," Manners answered, smiling.

"He's got all the angles figured," Savoldi said. "Those are the guys who wonder later why they were there when the crap hit the fan."

"Anyway," Manners said, "there won't be any kids like Morales in an all-girls' school."

"Or any troublemakers like Miller," Rick added.

"No," Solly said, wagging his head.

"No what?" Rick asked, chewing on his sandwich. Solly rose and walked to the windows, looking out, not facing Rick.

"You're making a mistake, Dadier. You always make a mistake when you isolate one kid in the class as a troublemaker."

"I don't follow," Rick said.

Solly cocked his head and seemed to meditate for a second, still staring through the window. "There's no such thing as a single troublemaker in this school."

"Solly's going to philosophize again," Lou Savoldi said sadly.

"In a dump like this," Solly answered, "it's only the philosopher who survives."

"I'm no philosopher," Savoldi said, his eyes sad over the steaming teacup he held close to his mouth.

"That's why you haven't survived. You're just dead and too stupid to lay down." Solly nodded his head in sour reflection and turned away from the window. "Look, Dadier, learn to accept these kids as a big rotten whole. Like an apple with worms in it. The apple is rotten to the core, and it's the worms that make it rotten, but if you take out the worms you're still left with the rotten apple. I know this kid Miller. I taught him last term. He's a smart kid, Dadier, I'm telling you."

"I know he is," Rick said. "That's what puzzles me. Why's he doing all this? What's he got against me?"

"You see," Solly said, shaking his stubby forefinger, "there's the mistake in your reasoning again. You think

Miller has something against you personally. Forget it, 'cause he hasn't."

"But . . ."

"He gave me trouble, too. Look, every goddamn kid in that class will give you trouble. They take turns, that's all. Today it's Miller, tomorrow it's some other bastard. You're giving Miller too much credit." Solly paused, searching for a clincher to his point. "Look, Dadier, in this school . . ."

"Miller's got a high I.Q.," Rick interrupted.

"For this school, maybe."

"For any school," Rick said. "What's the average, something like a hundred?"

"More or less," Solly said, shrugging. "So what's Miller got? 110, 120, 130 even? Who cares? Don't you see, Dadier, that makes it worse. He stands out because he's in with a pack of morons. The morons can give you a lot of trouble, but it's the bright ones who become the leaders. That's why . . ."

"You're contradicting yourself," Rick said.

"No," Solly answered, "I am not. I'm just saying that these bright ones need an outlet for their leadership qualities. In a normal setup, those qualities would find normal outlets. But in this dump, there are no normal outlets. Does a kid become a leader here by kissing the teacher's ass? Hell, no. He becomes a leader by making things rough for the teacher. That's how he's recognized. The bigger the bastard, the better the leader. But he hasn't anything against you personally, believe me. He'd be insulted if you accused him of carrying a grudge, I mean it. You understand, Dadier?"

"I understand, but I can't believe it. I'm sorry, but . . ."

"Solly's right," Savoldi said sadly. "You listen to him, Dadier. He knows."

"They all stink," Solly said emphatically. "You'll learn that, Dadier. They all stink to high heaven. For you, Miller happens to stink the worst right now. For me, it's a kid named Grandioso who stinks the worst. You start grading the stinks according to intensity and you'll go nuts."

"It's tough on the nose," Savoldi agreed.

"I think you're too preoccupied with odors and aromas," George Katz said in an attempt at wit. "That's what's wrong with you, Klein."

"Solly is a professional smeller," Savoldi said.

"In a girls' school," Manners said, "you get perfume. That's what I want: perfume."

"Yeah, perfume," Savoldi said dolorously. "Some perfume."

"I'm just trying to say that you've got to recognize these bastards as one big machine," Solly persisted. "You start picking it apart and looking for individual cogs and wheels, and you get no place. The machine is labeled North Manual Trades High School. It's manufactured in New York City, and it happens to have defective parts. It doesn't do a damn thing right, and it wasn't made to do anything in the first place. It just stands there and makes a hell of a lot of noise and it takes a hell of a lot of trained mechanics to keep it running. But it's no goddamn good, and it never will be any good."

"Solly," Savoldi said wistfully, "that was beautiful. You should have been a poet."

"Miller," Solly went on, "is just a part of the machine. For all you know, he may be a doll outside school." Rick raised his eyebrows and Solly said, "You don't think so, huh, Dadier? Well, you don't know yet. That little jerk may be supporting his blind grandmother, and he may be the nicest kid in his neighborhood. He gets inside the machine, and he becomes a part of the machine." Solly paused and tweaked his nose with his thumb and forefinger. "Don't worry about Miller, Dadier. That's how you go buggy in this joint. Just consider the picture as a whole. You're like a general worried about one stinking private in the front lines."

"Solly has a point," George Katz admitted. "After all, Dadier, it's the over-all results that count."

"You won't get any results here, anyway," Solly said. "You missed my point completely, Katz."

"Isn't that what you were saying, Klein?" he asked.

"No, it's not what I was saying. Who the hell is talking about results? You think I'm a goddamned dreamer? I'm talking about survival. I'm talking about stomachs without ulcers. Wake up, Katz."

"I'm sorry I misunderstood you," Katz said, his face taking on an offended look.

"Miller provoked that profanity exhibition," Rick said doggedly. "You can't tell me he didn't."

"You should have done what Ironman Clancy does," Savoldi said.

"Agh, Clancy is a bedbug," Solly said.

"Still, they don't curse in his classes."

"When's the last time you visited any of his classes?

They curse in everybody's class, even the women's. Clancy can't control it any more than the rest of us," Solly said.

"Clancy controls it," Savoldi insisted. "I know he does."

"You mean he has some method?" Rick asked.

"I suppose you could call it that," Savoldi said. "It works, anyway."

George Katz leaned forward curiously. "What does he do, Savoldi?"

"You mean you haven't heard about Clancy?" Solly asked. "He's a bedbug."

"He's got this box of candies on his desk," Savoldi said, sipping at his tea. "Only they're not all candies."

"What are they?" Rick asked.

"Some of them are candies," Savoldi said, "but not all of them. He's got them wrapped like bonbons. You know, the paper twisted on each end."

"If they're not candies," Katz asked, "what . . ."

"Well, some of them are. But some of them are just little hunks of soap, wrapped up exactly like the candies. The idea is, the kids can't tell which are the candies and which are the pieces of soap. They're all wrapped the same, you see. And, take it from me, there's more soap than there is candy in that box."

"So what does he do?" Rick persisted.

"When he hears a kid cursing, he brings him up to the desk and offers him a piece of candy. This is established routine, you understand. I mean, he's got those kids so trained now that they'll rat on their best friend if they hear him curse. The kid reaches into the box, and then unwraps what he pulled out. If it's candy, all well and good. Nine times of ten, though, it's soap. Clancy forces the kid to chew that soap and blow three bubbles before he can spit it out. It works, believe me."

"But suppose the boy gets candy?" Katz asked. "It seems to me he'd be getting rewarded for swearing."

"There's not much candy in the box," Savoldi said.

"There's probably no candy at all in the box," Solly put in. "Maybe Clancy used to have candy in there to start with, and maybe he throws in a hunk every now and then to keep things looking legitimate."

"They think it's a big game," Savoldi said sadly astonished. "They love to watch the guy who's caught. Three bubbles, the kid has to blow."

"Wouldn't it be easier to simply establish discipline?" Katz inquired. "This seems like a rather roundabout method."

"There you go again," Solly said, pointing at Katz. "You and Dadier, and this other guy, what's his name? The one with the glasses."

"Josh Edwards," Rick supplied.

"Yeah, him. You've all got ideas about teaching these kids discipline and manners and whatever the hell. You're all crazy."

"I'd like to teach them," Rick said softly.

"Forget about it. Just oil the machine and let it run in its own fouled-up fashion. Don't try to get it to produce anything. It wasn't built for that."

"I'd still like to teach them," Rick said, more softly.

If Solly heard him the second time, he showed no indication of it. He walked over to the windows again and hooked his thumbs in his suspenders, looking out.

"Look at that project go up, will you?" he said in amazement.

"They work fast," Savoldi said, not looking up from his sandwich.

"They've got these molds," Solly expanded, "and they just pour the concrete right into them. They can put up a building in no time."

"These projects are very good for the city," George Katz said.

Solly shrugged. "The people who live in them have them looking like craphouses inside of a month."

"That's not true," George Katz said suddenly. "I have some friends in middle-income projects."

"That's a different story already," Solly said. "I'm talking about these low-income jobs. You take most of those, and you'll see what I mean. They put them up in slum areas, and they expect the project to defeat the surrounding area. It can't be done."

Rick said nothing, even though he lived in a low-income project which was in a good neighborhood, and which did not look like a craphouse though it had been standing for more than a year. But he began to wonder about the accuracy of Solly's observations.

"Some are in good neighborhoods," Katz said.

"Yeah, some," Solly agreed. "Some vocational schools are in good neighborhoods, too, but I can't think of any offhand." He stared at the construction work in the distance again and said, "That's a job, all right. Outside all the time. Fresh air."

"You're maladjusted," Savoldi said wearily. "On a day

like this, with snow on the ground, I'm damn glad I've got an inside job."

"You talk like a bank teller," Solly said.

"I wish I was," Savoldi answered sadly. "All that money."

"Fresh air," Solly said, "that's what a man needs." He looked down to the snow-covered street, placid and white now that the snow had stopped. "Not the stink that's in this place." He sighed and turned away from the window.

"Fresh air," he said again.

At ten minutes to four that day, when Rick was leaving the building, he met Josh Edwards and Lois Hammond. He studied Josh's face carefully for a moment, repeating the habit he'd fallen into lately. He forced his eyes away at last and said, "Another day, another dollar."

"Ah," Lois said, smiling pertly, "but this has been a very special day, Rick."

"Oh really? I wasn't aware. What happened?"

"I've been put in charge of the newspaper," Lois said.

"Well, well. Are congratulations or condolences in order?"

"It's a very important job," Lois said primly, sucking in a deep breath and throwing her shoulders back, seemingly completely unaware of what her breasts did whenever she went through such a simple maneuver.

"Well then, congratulations," Rick said, his eyes lingering on her expanding chest a moment longer than they should have. He turned to Josh and asked, "How were *your* monsters today, boy?"

"So-so," Josh answered dully. "I'm getting there."

"Well, fine," Rick said with false enthusiasm, looking at Josh's face again. *You may be getting there,* he thought, *but where the hell are you getting, Josh?* He turned his eyes from Josh's face, wondering if his concern had shown. The beating that night had done something to Josh. He'd come to school the following Monday, of course, but something seemed to have gone out of him. Not his desire to teach the kids, certainly, because that was still obviously there. The energy, perhaps, the restless, nervous energy that had been so much a part of him before. Or perhaps his optimistic viewpoint. Perhaps that had fled.

Whatever it was, he was not looking well lately. There were heavy pockets of shadow beneath his eyes, and his cheekbones stood out too prominently, and Rick didn't like the tight way he carried his mouth. There was such a thing as trying too hard, even in a vocational school, and Josh was apparently doing just that.

"Unless you like walking in the snow," Josh said softly, "I can give you a lift to the bus stop. I've got my brother's car today."

"Nothing I like better than a walk in the snow," Rick said, attempting to get a smile out of Josh. "Unless it's a ride in the snow. Lead me to it, boy."

"I'm dropping Lois off, too," Josh said, unsmiling. "You don't mind, do you?"

"He'd better not mind," Lois said, looking at Rick in a surprisingly warningly way.

"No, not at all," Rick said, puzzled, wondering what had prompted the almost possessive, proprietary look she'd given him. Hell, he thought, it's my imagination.

They walked down the corridor and then out of the building, and Lois took his arm as they went down the steps. She looked at the slushy snow underfoot and said, "I hate snow. I'm scared to death of slipping."

"Careful," Rick said, aware of the pressure of her hand on his arm, feeling uncomfortable because he was used to Anne's hand on his arm, and this hand did not belong to Anne.

They began crossing the schoolyard, and Rick spotted Miller leaning against the Cyclone fence, and then he noticed West beside him with a cigarette dangling from his mouth. Rick glanced at Miller, and the boy looked back and then smiled disarmingly.

"Hello, Mr. Dadier," he said politely. "Nice day, ain't it?"

"If you like snow," Rick said, smiling back.

"Oh, yes, I like snow," Miller said. West's eyes traveled the length of Lois Hammond's body, and then a smirk filled his mouth.

"Good-night, boys," Rick said.

" 'Night," Miller said. West did not answer.

Rick coughed uneasily. He turned his eyes from Miller, increasingly aware of Lois's hand on his arm. He wanted to shake the hand off, but he knew he couldn't do that, and at the same time he felt guilty as hell, and he thought of Anne and wondered how she'd react to a glimpse of this scene.

"It's this way," Josh said, turning right as they left the schoolyard. They walked in silence, the snow squeaking underfoot, a cold nip in the air. When they reached the car, Josh unlocked the door and then walked around to the driver's side. Rick helped Lois in as Josh waited for his door to be opened. She slid onto the seat, and her coat caught for an instant, pulling back over her nylons. She reached down and adjusted the coat almost immediately, but not before Rick had seen the taut tops of her stockings and a little of the white flesh beyond that. He turned away as she pulled down the coat, and then he slid onto the seat beside her.

Josh rapped on the window, and Lois giggled suddenly. "Oh my goodness, we've forgotten Josh," she said. She looked at Rick curiously, and he wondered about her choice of language, including him in the "we've forgotten Josh," as if they'd been so involved in something else, so completely unaware, that they'd forgotten Josh completely. She reached over for the inside handle near the driver's seat, straightening one nyloned leg, and Rick unconsciously looked down at her leg, averting his gaze when she turned back suddenly, glanced at her leg, and then smiled.

He felt very warm all at once. His face was very warm even though Josh let in a blast of cold air when he opened his door. Josh crowded onto the seat, and Lois moved closer to Rick, her thigh tight against his. He felt the warmth of her body, and he thought again of Anne, and he said to himself, *Hey Dadier, am I imagining all this? Am I crazy?* and Lois moved her leg at that moment, and her foot brushed his lightly, and he knew goddamn well he wasn't imagining anything.

"It's crowded," Lois said, smiling. "I like crowded cars in the winter. They're so cozy."

Rick remained silent. He did not like this warm feeling within him, and he did not like the feeling of guilt that accompanied it. He knew that Lois Hammond was a woman, and it had been a long time since he'd looked at any woman as a woman, at least any woman other than Anne. He wondered if Anne's pregnancy had anything to do with this strange new awareness, and he tried to recall the last time he and Anne had enjoyed bed together, and then he told himself that was foolish, that had nothing to do with it. But the pressure of Lois's thigh against his own was disconcerting, and he wished Josh would hurry up and start the car and take him to the goddamned bus stop and hurry up about it because he felt uncomfortable, and he felt uncomfortable because he was feeling like a man reacting to a desirable woman, and he sure as hell did not want to be reacting to any woman, least of all Lois Hammond, when Anne was home and waiting for him and probably feeling as big as a balloon.

Josh started the car, and Lois wiggled on the seat, wiggled so gently that it could hardly be classed as a wiggle at all unless someone was waiting for it, unless someone was anticipating it, and then it felt very much like a wiggle, almost like a suggestive tautening of flesh on the thigh, almost like the seductive nuzzling of a woman curling up for the night.

He could smell her perfume very close to him, and he was exceptionally warm now, with the blood all clotted up there in his face. He wanted to loosen his tie, but he knew that would seem foolish. He wanted to get away from her, too, and yet there was something else inside him that enjoyed the soft feel of her thigh against his, and the light movement of her foot brushing his own.

He sat unmoving because he didn't want her to think he knew what was going on, didn't want her to know he was enjoying and disliking this at the same time. He sat scarcely breathing, but he saw the tiny smile on her flawless face, and he knew damn well he wasn't fooling her a bit, not one goddamn bit.

The car was in motion now, and when Josh rounded a corner she was hurled against Rick, and she seemed to move sideways when the car turned, so that her breast touched his arm as she was thrown toward him. She lingered there for an instant, and he thought back to that day she was about to be raped. He could feel her breast against his arm now, and he wanted to take his arm away, but he didn't, until finally she moved and he was grateful for that, but sorry at the same time. She turned sideways on the seat, and her knees touched his gently, nylon-sleek, touched his for the fraction of a second and then pulled away.

He thought of Anne. He thought of Anne, and he remembered the touch of her hair, and the color of her eyes, and the way she used to look, and he remembered her sweetness above all, the sweetness of her that he had never found in another woman, the thing he loved most about her. He thought of Anne, and he forgot the pressure of Lois's thigh against his, forgot Lois completely.

"I'm going to bring my records in next week," Josh said tiredly. "Remember I told you about them, Rick?"

"Yes," Rick said.

"Going to bring them in," Josh said, as if he were trying to convince himself to do just that. "Give the kids a lesson on jazz."

"Sounds good," Lois said, wriggling on the seat, and then turning to Rick for his comment.

"Yes," Rick said, "it sounds very good. I think they'll like it."

"I hope so," Josh said. He sighed heavily and then said, "You get off here, don't you, Rick?"

"This is it," Rick said.

"Oh, so soon?" Lois said. She faced Rick and smiled, and Rick smiled back wearily. Josh pulled the car over to the curb and Rick opened the door and stepped out into the snow.

"Someday we ought to all go for a drink together," Lois said, looking at Rick steadily. "All three of us."

"Sure," Rick said. "Someday." He smiled, waved, and said, "See you all tomorrow." And then he closed the door. Lois waved at him, but he spotted the bus and turned his back on her, running to catch it because Anne was waiting and he didn't want to be late.

7

The day Rick had his brief encounter with Arthur
Francis West was, coincidentally, the same day that
Joshua Edwards brought his record collection to school.
It started like any ordinary day starts, except that Rick
had grown wary of ordinary days, knowing that the students of North Manual Trades had a peculiar knack for
turning the ordinary into the extraordinary within a
matter of minutes. It was this peculiar ability to twist
the mundane into the grotesque that made the job so
difficult, Rick thought. You could never really plan
because you never knew exactly how your plans were
going to work out.

It wasn't like working in an office somewhere. It
wasn't like consulting a rigid schedule: call Andrews at
11:00 to close deal, lunch with Mrs. Mahaffey at 12:30 to
discuss Bigelow account, interview prospective stenogs
at 3:00, get memo off to Frisco office re delinquent pay-
ments. Nothing like that. Because, barring the small
office annoyances that came up, it was usually possible to
call Andrews at eleven, or wine and dine Mrs. Mahaffey
at 12:30, or hire the stenogs, or get off your memos.

It wasn't like that at Manual Trades. Rick spent a good part of every evening planning his lessons. The lessons all looked good on paper. They were the same kind of lessons which had garnered A after A in his education courses at Hunter. There was only one hitch: they didn't work. Because if he started out to show the difference between "shall" and "will," he invariably wound up trying to make himself heard over the roar of a class that preferred discussing the coming Election Day holiday, or the damage they would wreak on Hallowe'en. And if he started out to teach the correct form for a friendly letter, he almost always wound up giving the class a test to keep them quiet and busy. Or sometimes he just gave up and sat there, telling them they'd get a test the next day on the material they should have covered today, and then watching the kids complain and fuss and fidget into silence, only to burst into disorder again when they discovered he'd really meant what he'd said.

So on this very ordinary day, with its very ordinary beginning, the loins of Richard Dadier were girded for whatever surprises the students of North Manual Trades had up their collective sleeves.

The first surprise came in 55–206, and that was no surprise because 55–206 was just full of surprises. It would, in fact, have been surprising if 55–206 had come up with no surprise.

There was something peculiar about the class on that day. Rick noticed it when he was taking the attendance, flipping over the Delaney cards of those boys who were absent. He didn't know quite what the difference was until he came to Miller's seat, and then he realized what had changed.

Miller was absent.

"Well," Rick said aloud. He was truly surprised because Miller had attended his class religiously, even when the other boys were indulging in wholesale cutting. Miller's appearance at each class had in itself been a surprise, and Rick couldn't quite understand the boy's motivation. If someone disliked something so intensely, you'd imagine he'd want to avoid it as much as possible. It was almost as though Miller had formulated a strict set of rules for the playing of the game, though. Those rules included strict attendance at each and every class Rick taught. He had also seemed to have drawn an arbitrary line over which he would not step. It was true that the line seemed to advance a few inches each day, with Miller growing bolder and bolder, but it seemed that once the line had been set for any particular day, Miller observed it as the law, and would not tread beyond it no matter how far he was provoked. His observance of the line extended to holding back anyone else who attempted to cross it. It was as if he said, "This is as far as we'll go today, and don't you forget it."

His absence, therefore, was almost shocking in that Rick had come to understand the rules that governed the game they played, and this was a distinct breach of the rules. When he looked at Miller's vacant seat and exclaimed, "Well," there was honest surprise on his face, and West promptly supplied, "Greg ain't here today."

"I gathered," Rick said dryly.

"He ain't cutting neither," West said.

"We'll find out about that when I send a list of absentees down to the office," Rick answered.

"Go ahead," West said. "He ain't cutting. His sister's in the hospital."

"Oh?" Rick said. "Nothing serious, I hope."

"Naw," West answered. "She got knocked up, that's all." He smiled and stared at Rick. "You know what 'knocked up' means, teach?"

"I, ah, think I've heard the expression before," Rick said, a bored look on his face.

"Yeah, well she got knocked up. At a grind session." West smiled again. "You know what a grind session is, teach?"

"You know what a jam session is, West?" he asked, suddenly annoyed with all this nonsense. The boys automatically assumed that an English teacher was some sort of sexless, neuter, unthinking, unfeeling, unaware person who knew only his textbooks. He had upheld this misconception up to now, but he was all at once disturbed by it. He didn't like West's intimation that expressions like "knocked up" and "grind session" were foreign to him. He'd been a kid, too, and he'd flopped in whore houses from Panama to Tokyo, and his manhood was somehow offended by West's implication. He realized this was all a matter of masculine pride, but he could not control the urge to show West that he knew a few things about life, too, perhaps a little more than West with his goddamned wise-guy smirk would ever know.

"A jam session ain't a grind session, teach," West said knowingly.

"No kidding? Is that right, West? Tell me, West, do you know what a dream session is? You ever been inside a shooting gallery, West? You know what mootah is, West? You dig a monkey scratching at your back, West? You know what a twist is? You ever flop into some cat's pad, West? You know what screech trumpet is? Are you hip or from nowhere? What do you say, West?"

West stared at Rick, plainly confused. "You don't fool me," he said. "You're a square."

"Like a bear," Rick snapped. "But tell me, West, do you know what H is? Or C? Or M? Do you know what a fix means? Have you ever met The Man, West? Tell me, West, has your experience included names like Cat Andrews or Thelonious Sphere Monk or Vido Musso or Cozy Cole? Come on, West, talk. You want to talk, don't you?"

"I heard of them guys," West said, frowning.

"Well good, boy. Fine. Then you know what smoke is, huh, West? You dig a high on smoke, boy? You hip to the art of a water mix? You ever dance fish, West? You ever swap spit? Or are you just all talk and no *cojones*? You ever read Hemingway, West?"

"Who's he?" West asked.

"He plays drums with Gillespie, West. He beats a wild skin. He beats a wine skin, too. But you've been to Spain, haven't you, West? A man of your wide experience. A man who knows what 'knocked up' means, and 'grind session.' You also know what planked means, don't you? You know what a dry run is, huh boy? Or do you go for crime jargon, West? Is that your speed? You a heel and toe boy? A grifter? A fish? What are you, West? A con man? Come on, West."

"You don't fool me," West said.

"You got it wrong, boy. You mean I'm not snowing you, don't you? That's what you mean, isn't it? Well, I don't think you're any of those things, West. You're not a paper hanger, and you're not a small fry pusher, and you're not even a booster. I dig your MO, West, and here's what you are, man, here's just what you are. You're a lot of noise, West, and that's all. You're an empty barrel. You're a lot of sound and fury, if you'll pardon my quoting Willie, who beats the bass for Kenton, and you signify nothing, West. Absolutely nothing.

"So don't come expanding your chest and spouting 'grind sessions' as if I'm a half-wit who was weaned on the other udder. Just keep your smart-guy language to yourself, and remember that I know just what you're talking about, everytime you talk, whenever you talk. Remember that, and then remember that I don't want to hear what you have to say, anyway. That way we'll get along fine, West, just dandy. Is that clear?"

"You don't fool me," West said. "You picked that up in books."

"I'm a book man from 'way back, West. But you can't get everything from books. Now let's stow the talk and go on with the lesson. We've had enough nonsense for one day."

"Yeah, you don't fool me," West said, determined to have the last word.

Rick let him have the last word. He felt immensely

pleased with himself, felt almost purged of something that had been bothering him since the term began. He knew it was not good policy to put yourself on the same level as the kids, but there had been something ecstatically satisfying about his outburst. He had spouted choice expressions culled from a variety of things: his own experience, stories and novels he'd read, plays he'd seen, even radio shows he'd listened to. Why, he hadn't even been sure of the meanings of some of the words that had spilled from his mouth. He'd simply tossed them all at West, a potpourri of bop, a mélange of underworld slang, a real boilermaker.

Boilermaker. There was a good one. He should have used that, too. Had he mentioned smoke? Yes, he had. What the hell was smoke, anyway? Something alcoholics did with wood alcohol, or denatured alcohol, or something. If the alcohol turned smoky after a few drops of water were added, it was good to drink. Or maybe it wasn't good to drink. What the hell difference did it make? West hadn't known what he was talking about anyway.

That *cojones* business. He shouldn't have used that. No, there were a good many Puerto Ricans in the class, and they sure as hell knew what *cojones* were. Well, let it pass. He had done well. He was pleased, and he felt damned good.

He went on with the lesson, convinced he would have no more trouble from West, pleased that Miller was absent, wondering if his sister were indeed pregnant. *Knocked up.* "You know what 'knocked up' means, teach?" He couldn't get over it. He went on with the lesson, a satisfied smirk on his face. He gave the boys a written assignment to do in class, and then he went over the test papers from his second-termers. He was grading the papers when he became aware of someone standing near his desk.

He looked up.

West slouched there with his thumbs looped in his dungarees.

"What is it, West?" Rick asked.

West smiled. "Give me the pass, Handsome," he said.

Rick blinked up at him. "What?"

"I said give me the pass, Handsome."

"What?" He kept staring at West, blinking his eyes at him. He almost couldn't believe what he was hearing. After the tongue-lashing he'd given the boy . . .

"I got to go to the john," West said. "Give me the pass."

"Sit down, West," Rick said tightly.

"I said I got to go to the john. Give me the pass."

"I heard you, West. Sit down."

The boys had stopped writing now, and they were looking to the front of the room, anticipating trouble, perhaps hoping for it.

"All right," West said, "keep the pass. I'll go without it."

He started to move around the desk behind Rick, and Rick shoved his chair back suddenly, blocking the narrow passage behind his desk, ramming the chair up against the blackboard, and standing quickly.

"You're not going anywhere, West. Get back to your seat."

"I got to go to the john," West said, his voice louder. "You want me to piss all over the floor?"

"Shut your filthy mouth, West," Rick said. "Shut up and sit down, do you understand?"

"I understand I got to take a piss, that's all."

"Sit down, West," Rick said warningly, his lips tight against his teeth. "Sit down or I'll knock you down."

West stood there with his thumbs looped in his dungarees, silently appraising Rick. "You can't stop somebody from going to the john," he said softly.

"Try me," Rick said, angry as hell now, a strange sense of power inside him, a sense of power generated by his previous outburst, fanned now by West's rebellion.

They stood glaring at each other for a few moments, and then West backed off, slouching up the aisle to his seat. He sat down reluctantly, his expression sour, his eyes glowing.

"You can't stop me from going to the john," he called out ineffectually.

"You can go the second you learn how to ask for the pass properly," Rick said. "Not until."

"I *did* ask for the goddamn pass," West shouted. His face was flushed, and he seemed on the verge of tears, and Rick wondered if he hadn't carried the episode a bit too far.

"But not properly," he said curtly.

West suddenly bounced out of his seat and started for the front of the room, his fists balled. "You want me to get down on my knees? You want me to beg for the goddamn pass?"

"Get back to your seat, West," Rick said, his own fists clenching unconsciously. He felt anticipation out there, waiting like a poised tiger.

"I'll piss all over the goddamn floor," West shouted. "You think I won't? You think I give a damn? You gonna give me that pass, or do I piss all over the floor?"

"You're putting yourself in bad trouble, West," Rick said. "Ask for the pass properly."

"I'll piss on trouble, too," West shouted. He unzipped his fly, and moved toward Rick's desk, and Rick took a step forward, and the bell sounded at that instant.

West froze with his hand on his fly, listening to the bell, listening to the silence that followed its insistent ring. He smiled then, a superior smile that told Rick he didn't need the pass now anyway.

He zipped up his fly, and the rasp of the zipper was harsh in the silent room.

"Saved by the bell," he said, and then he turned his back on Rick, gathered up his books, and left the classroom. The other boys lingered a while, watching Rick where he stood near the desk with his fists clenched. His mouth was tight, his eyes were gleaming hotly. They looked at him for a few seconds, and then they drifted out of the room.

You sonofabitch, Rick thought. *You rotten, lousy, filthy sonofabitch.*

Viciously, he packed his briefcase and headed out of the room, thankful for the Unassigned period ahead of him.

There was no Unassigned period ahead of the kids in 66–201. None at all. There was another English drag with Mr. Edwards, little ol' Josh-wah fittin' the battle of Jericho. Man, these guys could think of more ways to bore a guy. Like all they had to do was sit around and think up new ways of torture. That lesson he had preached yesterday, that garbage about a business letter. Nuts, who'd ever have to write a business letter in his life? Edwards maybe, but not them. No, this stuff was all for the birds, and even the birds wouldn't swallow it unless you covered it with chocolate sprinkles.

They walked into the room slowly, like prisoners being forced into the cell block after their afternoon meal. They looked at Edwards sitting at his desk, looked at the flutter of his hands, looked at his goddamn goggles perched on his nose, looked at the intense, serious eyes behind those goggles. Man, they thought, why was you born such a ugly child? And such a boring one in the bargain. Didn't no one ever teach you how to be interesting, Edwards? Josh-wah, old boy, didn't no one ever tell you you was a boring sonofabitch? It's a shame, Josh-wah, because somebody should sure as hell have told you. Someday, you're gonna get reported to the Society for the Prevention of Cruelty to Children, Josh-wah, and then you will lose your gold-plated license, and then you will have to go out and dig ditches or climb flag-poles or sit around with your thumb up your backside, which is a good job for you, Josh-wah, because you are really a boring sonofabitch.

They drifted into the classroom, and they took their seats, resigned to their fate, waiting for Edwards to begin blabbing again. Balls, Josh-wah, don't you never learn? You need another beating to wake you up? That was a fine beating, wasn't it, Josh-wah? Boy, you looked jazzy on that Monday morning, like a steam roller had tried to flatten your head, only better because your head was flat to begin with. Still, some guys never learn. What's it gonna be today, Josh-wah? A letter to Grandma in Oshkosh? How you feeling, Grandma? Your rheumatiz bothering you, girlie? You keeping your legs crossed, Grandma? Come on, Josh-wah, get through with the attendance and let's start. We can hardly wait for this ball to begin.

Edwards closed his Delaney book and smiled at the boys. "I've got a surprise for you today," he said.

Well now, Josh-wah has a surprise. Ain't that great? Let's all stand up and clap our hands. What kind of surprise, Josh? Little test maybe? Little homework? Something pleasant like that? Something you thought up last night in your torture chamber?

"What kind of surprise?" Vallera asked.

"A surprise I think you'll like," Edwards said, still smiling.

"Not a test?" Jones asked suspiciously.

"No, not a test," Edwards answered, smiling secretly. "Something you'll like."

Yeah, something we'll like. This boy's ideas are always pips. Like the time he asked us to bring newspapers in. Yeah, we were gonna like that, too. So he spends the next week telling us to read the *New York Times*. That's his idea of a big ball, a real snappy time. Sit on your ass and wade through all that fine print. Boy, what a ball! Man, it gassed us, the happiest time, the most. Now he's got another peachy idea. He's got a million of them, this boy. Why don't he just throw in his jock?

Edwards was not throwing in any of his underwear. He was, instead, walking to his coat closet at the rear of the room. Maybe that's his surprise. Maybe he's gonna put on his coat and go home? Now that would be a surprise. That was something to look forward to.

"As you know," Edwards said, "literature is not the only form of expression. We'll be studying a lot of literature this term in class, but there are other means of expression, too. A lot of other means of expression."

He sounds nervous, Josh-wah does. Repeating himself all over the place. What's he got in that closet, a naked girl? Never saw a guy as nervous as this one. Jumpy as two skeletons screwing on a moving freight car.

"Art is one form of expression," Edwards said. "Painting, sculpture . . . uh . . . art, in general. And music is another form."

He had the closet open now, and he was taking out something that looked like . . . well, how do you like that? A record player! A phonograph. And what was that little case with the lock on it? Records? Dig that! Old Josh-wah was turning into a disc jockey.

"Today we're going to listen to some music," Edwards said. He was walking back to his desk now, the phonograph under one arm, the leather case of records dangling at the end of his other arm.

"What kind of music?" Pasco asked suspiciously.

"No longhair stuff," Edwards said. "Today, we're going to hear swing, and jazz, and even a little bop."

Bop? From you, Josh-wah? Oh, come down, man.

Climb off that cloud, boy. Bop? Bop this a while, Josh-wah.

"I think you'll like these records," Edwards said. "I've been a collector for a long time now, and there's some exciting stuff here."

Like the *Times,* huh, Josh-wah? Exciting like the *Times* is exciting. Man, that was really exciting.

He was setting up the player now, plugging it into the outlet. He tested the needle with his forefinger, and a scratching sound flooded the classroom. He smiled and said, "The player's not my own, but it'll do. Let's see now." He fiddled around in his record case, and came up with a shining black disc. He looked at the disc like a guy sick over a girl, and then brushed at it with his sleeve.

"We'll play this one first," he said. " 'I Can't Get Started' is the title. It's one of Bunny Berigan's best records."

Bunny Berigan? Who the hell is Bunny Berigan? What kind of crap is this, anyway?

He put the record onto the turntable, dropped the arm into place, and then stepped back with his arms folded across his chest, a broad smile on his face.

So this is Bunny Berigan. What's so special?

"I've flown around the world in a plane

"Settled revolutions in Spain . . ."

So it's a guy singing. Does he stack up against Como? Where does he shine to Tony Bennett? Guys singing are a dime a dozen. Who does Josh-wah think he's fooling? This is exciting stuff, huh? Like the old maid said when she kissed the cow, "It's all a matter of taste." Ain't he got no stuff by The Hilltoppers?

"Listen to this fine trumpet work," Edwards said. "This man is the predecessor of James and Spivak and Elman. Just listen."

James? He mean Harry James? But who's Spivak? And who the hell is Elman? Man, this guy lives in another world. All right, so we hear a trumpet player. Bunny Berigan. Sounds like a strip queen in Union City. What else you got, Josh-wah? Come on, this one is almost over.

The needle raced through the record, clicked in the retaining grooves. Edwards stood with a stupid grin on his face, and finally he picked up the arm, lifted the record from the turntable, and returned it to the case like a guy tucking his daughter into bed. He picked up another record and said, "This is the old Will Bradley combo. A fine record, and it's called 'Celery Stalks at Midnight.' "

How's that again? *Celery* stalks? Come on, Josh-wah, we ain't that dumb. Celery stalks? Jesus Christ! Ain't you got nothing good in that goddamn box? How about Julius LaRosa? Now he's got something on the ball. Or how about Joni James? Nothing from her?

"What else you got, teach?" Brothers shouted.

"This is a good one," Edwards said, engrossed. "Listen to it."

"You got any recent stuff?" Magruder asked.

"Listen, listen," Edwards said, his head cocked toward the player.

That simple jerk, watch the look on his face. He really digs this crap. A band playing around with a tune. This is his surprise, his big jazzy surprise. Hell, he must have *something* good in that box. What's he got in that box?

"Hey, come on, teach," Kramer said. "What else you got?"

"I've got plenty more," Edwards said. "Don't worry. Here, listen to the trombones."

"Ain't you got nobody singin'?"

"Well, you just heard Bunny . . ."

"Yeah, I mean somebody who knows *how* to sing."

"Well, yes, I have. As soon as this one is over, I'll . . . I'll see what else I have."

"Aw, take it off now," Liggett shouted.

"This is really a classic," Edwards said lamely. "Will Bradley. Have you ever heard of Ray McKinley?"

"Who?"

"Ray Mc—— he got his start with Bradley. He was . . . a . . . the drummer with the Bradley . . . combo. He . . ."

"Any relation to President McKinley?"

"Well, well no, I don't think so. That is . . ."

"What the hell is this, a history lesson? Come on, let's have some music."

Edwards lifted the arm near the end of the record and quickly took the disc from the turntable.

"I've got a lot of vocals," he said. "Some of them, I'm sure will . . . a lot of vocals. Here's . . . here's one by Ella Mae Morse. It's called 'Cow-Cow Boo——'"

"More history!" Falanzo shouted. "Finley Breeze Morse, we're gettin'."

"Come on, Josh-wah!" Alexander shouted. "What the hell you hidin' in that goddamned box?"

"Watch your language, Alexander," Edwards warned.

"Agh, let's see what the hell he's hiding," Alexander shouted to the class. Vallera leaped to his feet and started for the record case. Edwards had already put the Morse disc on the turntable, and he dropped the arm now, whirled, and shouted, "Sit down, Vallera."

"What you got in the box, teach?" Vallera yelled.

"Out on the range . . .

"Down-a near Santa Fe . . ."

"Keep away from those records!" Edwards yelled. He rushed to the record case and stood before it, his arms widespread, like a cop trying to hold back a throng of parade watchers. "Keep away!" he yelled.

Well, dig the little bastard! Damn if those records ain't like a woman to him. Look at the little sonofabitch! You'd think he was protecting some pussy.

"We want some good stuff," Vallera insisted, reaching for the records. Edwards shoved him away, and then backed up against the case again, his arms still widespread.

"I'll choose the records!" he yelled. "You keep away!"

"It was a ditty . . .

"Born in the city . . .

"Come-a cai-yai-yai-yay,

"Come-a cai-yippy-yai-yay . . ."

"So choose some good ones!" Jones shouted.

"Oh, get the hell out of the way," Vallera yelled. He shoved Edwards, and Edwards staggered and then went flying back against the blackboard.

"Keep away from that case!" he screamed, but Vallera already had a record in his hands, and he held it up and shouted, " 'Clap Hands, Here Comes Charlie!' "

"Put that record——" Edwards started.

"You want to hear that one?" Vallera roared.

"No!" the class shouted in unison, rising out of their seats now, ready to join in the fun. Edwards flung himself off the blackboard, rushing toward Vallera, but the record had already left Vallera's hands, was spinning through the air in a dizzying black arc.

Edwards stopped short and made a grab for the record, but it was beyond his reach, and it hit the wooden floor, and the crash was lost in the din that had suddenly sprung up in the classroom.

" 'Cherokee'!" Vallera shouted. "You want to hear this crap?"

"NO!" the class bellowed. "Throw it out!"

Edwards was down on his hands and knees, scrambling for the broken record. He saw the second record leave Vallera's hands, sail across the room, and smack into the wall alongside the light switch and the bulletin board. Black shards showered from the wall, and Edwards turned to the second record, dropping the pieces of the first record, and then whirling and rushing over to Vallera.

Jones grabbed his arm and spun him back across the room, and Liggett shoved Vallera away from the record case and yelled, "Here's 'Kalamazoo.' What am I bid for 'Kalamazoo'?"

"Smash the friggin' thing!" someone shouted.

"No!" Edwards yelled. "No, don't! Stop it, stop it! You don't know what you're . . ."

The record hit the wall, splashed off it in a dozen flying black pieces. Someone else was at the record case now, and Edwards was rushing across the room, trying to stop him. A boy in the first row stuck out his foot, and Edwards fell forward on his face, his glasses shattering on the bridge of his nose.

"Stop it!" he yelled. "Please, you don't know what . . ."

He tried to get to his feet, the bridge of his nose bleeding. He struggled about blindly, searching for the elusive record case now, trying to push past the knot of boys swarming around his desk.

Sonofabitch, this had turned into a real party after all! Goddamn, if those records weren't smashing all over the joint like hand grenades! Man alive, this was a surprise all right, the best damn class they'd had all term!

"Here's 'B-19'!" And then the crash as the record hit the wall and exploded.

" 'Concerto for Cootie'!" And another crash, and then the crashes came one after the other, like machine-gun fire, because everybody had his hands in the record case, and everybody was yelling all at once and throwing records, and the floor was covered with shining black shards.

" 'Sophisticated Lady'!"

"Not that one," Edwards shouted. "Please, that's my . . ."

And then the crash and then another voice yelling, " 'Harlem Nocturne,' " and the crash, and then " 'Sing, Sing, Sing'!" and Edwards blindly tore at the backs of the boys as the record splattered against the ceiling and showered black slivers on them.

" 'Tippin' In'!" and Edwards was screaming wildly

now like a woman, just screaming and saying nothing, and when the crash came, he slugged the boy nearest him, slugged him with all the power of his arm, slugged him blindly because his glasses were on the floor with the broken records, trampled under the feet of the milling boys, crushed into the wooden floor.

And then one of the boys grabbed the case, and shouted, "Here it goes!" and he held it in both hands, swung it down beneath his knees, holding it tightly, holding it the way a basketball player holds the ball when he's taking a foul shot. He brought his arms up straight and stiff, just the way Captain Schaefer had taught him to do. The case left his hands, sailed upward toward the ceiling, hung at the apogee of its orbit like a square rocket in flight, and then plunged toward the floor, upside down, the records tumbling from their slots, falling like black rain, crashing against the floor, shattering, singly, spattering, the case thudding to the floor, too.

"You bastards!" Edwards screamed. "You dirty bastards!"

The boys kicked around the records that had miraculously escaped damage, and then they realized all this screaming and yelling and crashing around was going to bring somebody damned soon, so they cut out for the door, leaving Edwards on the floor with his broken records and dented case, leaving Edwards mumbling "You bastards," over and over again. The machine shop upstairs was in operation, and so the boys were lucky because the racket all but drowned out the good fun they were having. Christie Paulson was teaching a

Science class next door, but it was a well-known fact that Christie was a deaf old crumb who wouldn't hear a ton of nitro if it exploded in one of his own test tubes. So the boys were lucky, and they ran like bastards, away from the room, each one ready to swear they'd had no part in the mess there, each one ready to swear Edwards had dismissed them early, and they sure as hell didn't know what had happened after that.

It wasn't until Rick came up from his Unassigned sixth period, a little before the seventh period started, that he found Joshua Edwards.

He walked into the room and saw Josh sitting in the middle of the floor, his fingers idly running over the dented case, the broken records scattered around him like a dead army.

"Josh!" he said. "What the hell . . ."

"My records," Josh mumbled. "They . . . they broke my records, Rick." He looked up, and his face looked pathetically young without glasses perched on his nose, and there were thin streams of blood running down his nose, and he suddenly began to cry bitterly, tears that welled up from deep inside him. He was ashamed of the tears, but he couldn't stop them, and they streamed down his face together with the blood, and Rick put his arm around Josh's shoulders and held him in a firm grip, and Josh kept crying and saying, "Why'd they want to do that, Rick? Why'd they want to do that? What'd I do wrong? Rick, they broke my records."

The tears kept coming because the records *were* broken, and each time he said it he was reminded of the fact. And the tears kept coming because the records were a part of Josh Edwards, and if the beating that night so long ago had taken something out of him, this breaking of the records had taken a little more, only this time it was a little more that was really a part of the man, and you can't dissect a man slowly and expect him to survive.

And so Rick crouched alongside Josh on the floor of the classroom, and he kept his arm around Josh's shoulders, and he listened to the sobs that wracked his friend's body, and he wanted to cry himself, but he didn't.

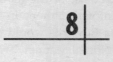

8

The first note came on November 4th, the day after the Election Day holiday. It was not in the mailbox when Rick left for school that morning, and it was not placed in the mailbox until 10:44 when an overburdened mailman pulled down the row of boxes in the hallway of 1935 East 174th Street and methodically began dumping letters into the open metal mouths. He was busy, and he gave only a cursory glance to the small envelope typed MRS. RICHARD DADIER, and then he dumped it into the box for 11C.

The delivery of the note was preceded by an important flow of events at North Manual Trades, a tide in fact which left no doubt about Mr. Small's reformative policy. The incident in Joshua Edwards' classroom had disturbed him deeply. The records, of course, had meant little or nothing to him. Hell, you could buy records anywhere. The record player, on the other hand, had belonged to the school, and the record player had been damaged in the disorderly fracas, and Small could not let such an incident go unnoticed or unpunished.

The parents of every boy in Josh's sixth-period

English class had been summoned to school, and an itemized list of the damages presented to them. Small had informed them in firm, principal-like tones, that Joshua Edwards would be reimbursed for his loss, and that North Manual Trades would be likewise reimbursed for the damaged record player. There had been twenty-six boys present that day, and the sum total of the damages had been divided by twenty-six, and Small advised the parents that payment should be made promptly. He would not like to call in the police on a matter such as this, but he was sure they all knew that willful destruction of private or public property was a criminal offense. He was quite willing to forget the police; he knew that no one liked trouble with the police. On the other hand, he could not ignore the damage that had been done, hence his suggestion that payment be made promptly or he would be forced, in spite of his distaste for such a course of action, to inform the police of the incident. The collected, collective parents got the point. They got the point, and they forked over the cash, and there were many raw, red behinds that week, and a few battered heads. Money did not grow on trees, and being called to school was humiliating even when it didn't cost anything.

Nor were the red and aching behinds the only punishment the boys in Josh's class suffered. They were brought in a group to Mr. Small's office, whereupon Mr. Small delivered a shouting, ranting, biting, vituperative ten-minute speech on the conduct he expected from the students of Manual Trades. He concluded his dissertation by telling the boys they would spend their next week at school in the auditorium, all day, every day. They would come supplied with fountain pens, paper, and bottles of ink. They would sit three seats apart from each other all day long, and there would be three Unassigned teachers watching them during each period of the day, a task which did not appeal to the faculty of the school, who enjoyed their Unassigned periods fully as much as they did their God-given lunch periods.

The boys would not be idle during their week of incarceration. They would use the pens, the ink, and the paper. They would write. They would write all day long. They would write, *"I shall learn to respect the property of others."* They would fill page after page of lined paper with these words. The teachers watching them would make sure that none of the boys shirked their literary efforts. The boys would write until their fingers were ready to fall off, and then they would write some more. So did William Small, Principal and Chief Executioner of North Manual Trades High School, decree.

Rick, perhaps prompted by the Boss' decisive action in The Edwards Affair, inflicted his own punitive program upon Arthur Francis West. He exiled the Urinating Unicorn to the English Office during the fifth period every day. There, under the watchful eyes of Mr. Stanley, Department Chairman and Executioner in Charge of English Department Violations, West practiced his own penmanship to the tune of *"I shall learn to ask for the pass properly."* West did not like the tune. He also did not like Stanley. He cared even less for the English Office, and his lack of affection spread rapidly to include North Manual Trades High School, Bronx

County, and even the entire City of New York. Most of all, he definitely did not like Daddy-oh. Not at all. Not in the least.

And while his cramped right hand struggled with *"I shall learn to ask for the pass properly,"* a punitive technique which allegedly went out of practice with the coming of the horseless carriage, his mind silently avowed *"I shall piss all over Daddy-oh."*

Anne Dadier, on that morning after Election Day, was not aware of West's urinating aspirations. She had given Rick his breakfast that morning and then gone back to bed, rising finally at 9:10 and beginning another day, a day which loomed large on the horizon, and which loomed large in the area beneath her breasts and above her legs.

She went into the bathroom in her shorty nightgown, and when she spotted herself in the full-length mirror behind the bathroom door, she put her hands on her hips and thought, *Gad, you sexy creature, you.*

She turned sideways and examined her profile, studying the insistent bulge with fascination. She placed both hands on her belly, holding it like a medicine ball, and then she turned again, looked at herself fullface, and thought, *You can hardly tell this way. Except that my hips have gone.*

She turned her back to the mirror, looking back over her shoulder, her eyes traveling over her good, long legs where they jutted out from beneath the end of the gown. *This is the best view,* she thought. *All expectant mothers should be forced to walk backwards.* She shrugged, walked to the mirror over the sink, and unbuttoned the top part of her gown. She cupped one breast and studied it in the mirror, amazed at the way the nipple had darkened, had become somehow more mature, had become a woman's nipple. She dropped the breast and her thoughts about pregnancy and then brushed her teeth, washed her face, and brushed out her hair.

She enjoyed the new shine of her hair, the only improvement her pregnancy had brought to her. *Well, that's not true,* she thought. *My face has filled out a little, and I look better this way. Less gaunt.* She counted out the brush strokes, and when she'd finished she took a last look at herself in the full-length mirror.

She put one hand on her hip and the other at the back of her head, like a prostitute lounging in a dimly-lit doorway. She lowered her head, and her blond hair fell over one eye. She wet her lips, narrowed her eyes, and then rotated her hips in mock lewdness, tossing a burlesque grind and bump at the mirror.

"Baby," she said aloud, "you should be in the movies."

She burst out laughing suddenly, covering her mouth and almost looking over her shoulder to see if anyone had been watching her. She was still laughing when she left the bathroom and went into the bedroom to dress. She put on the three-sizes-too-large girdle she'd bought over Rick's protests. Rick hated girdles. "Who wants a stuffed sausage?" he was fond of repeating. When she explained that her doctor felt a girdle would take some of the strain of carrying away from her stomach muscles, he'd grudgingly allowed her to buy one, but his attitude plainly stated that this had better be only a temporary thing.

She struggled with her stockings, stooping to roll them up over her calves. The stockings and shoes were always the hardest part. What did people who were fat all the time do? Pregnant women should have eunuchs to help them on with their stockings, she thought. And then she wondered, *Eunuchs?* Why in heaven's name would a pregnant woman need a eunuch?

Poor Rick, she thought. He's a technical eunuch. I wonder if it's difficult for a man? I mean, it doesn't really matter to me because I haven't any desire anymore. Isn't it terrible how this takes away desire? I wonder if you have to feel desirable in order to feel desire? The only thing I desire right now is to have this over and done with. Nine months is such an awfully long time. It seems to me that Whoever planned all this should have taken that into consideration. But Whoever planned it was probably a man. Or a manlike God. Why is God always presented as a manlike figure? Something there to consider, all right.

I'll make it up to Rick, of course. Afterward. They tell me the afterward is the worst part, the six weeks' wait after the baby is born. Because desire returns then, and you can't do anything because it's dangerous. That's what they say, anyway. Freida finally took to sleeping on the living room couch during those six weeks, but Freida's a nymphomaniac, I'm sure.

I'll make it up to you, darling, she promised. *And I won't sleep on the living room couch, either.*

And it won't be too long, either. The middle of December, Dr. Bradley said. Wouldn't it be nice if the baby were born on Christmas day? Or would it? It would be nice for Rick, I suppose, a sort of super Christmas present. It wouldn't be very nice for the baby, though, because he'd miss out on either a birthday present or a Christmas present. It wouldn't be fair to cheat him of . . .

Him.

I always think of him as *him.* I suppose I subconsciously want a boy. Rick wants a boy, I know. Oh, he'd love a boy.

I love you, Rick, do you know? she thought, and she smiled and reached for the slip her mother had given her. She pulled the slip over her head, and then thwacked the elastic around her waist. She put on a blouse and the skirt with the hole in it, the one that allowed her stomach to pop out through the big hole, with the blouse covering it, so that the skirt fell straight and no one could tell you were carrying.

No one except everyone you met, she thought.

She smiled, dabbed on some lipstick, and then went into the kitchen where she started the coffee going. She drank a little orange juice, put up the toast, and then had two cups of coffee, leaving half a slice of toast on her plate. She lighted a cigarette, smoked it down, and then reluctantly rose and washed the dishes. She dusted around a little, and then decided she'd better get downstairs and do some shopping if anyone expected supper that night.

Eating, as far as she was concerned, was something that had to be done now. There was no longer any enjoyment attached to it. Like the bed, she supposed, except that you couldn't do anything there in the eighth month, no this was the ninth month, well not really but soon, even if you did enjoy it, and even if you had the desire to do anything, which she certainly did not have, not now in the eighth-nearly-ninth month.

She put on her coat and locked up the apartment, walking down the hall to the elevator. Viola Jackson, her colored neighbor, was standing in front of the red elevator door, waiting for the car to come.

"Hello, Anne," she said warmly. Viola had a rich voice that started deep down within her someplace. She was a plump woman with a ready smile, and Anne never failed to feel a warm sort of happiness in her presence.

"Hello, Viola," she answered, smiling.

"I think the kids are holding the elevator downstairs," Viola said. She shook her head. "It's a shame." She smiled suddenly and asked, "How do you feel?"

"Fine," Anne said.

Viola laughed a hearty, booming laugh. "It's the first ten are the hardest," she said. She sobered instantly and said, "Now, listen, you haven't been taking your laundry down to those washing machines all by yourself, have you?"

"Well, yes, I have," Anne said.

"Well, you can stop that right now, do you hear me? You in your eighth month. My daughter will take it down for you, do you hear me?"

"That's awfully nice," Anne said, surprised, "but—"

"Never you mind your buts," Viola bullied. "She has to take mine down, and she can just as soon throw yours in, too. Now do you hear me?"

"All right," Anne said, smiling. She had first met Viola Jackson two days after Rick and she had moved into the project. Her husband, Fred, had been out sweeping up the corridor, and when they'd stepped off the elevator he'd explained, "If you got a nice place to live in, you got to keep it nice." He'd introduced himself, then, and Viola—hearing the conversation through the open door to her apartment—had come out and joined them. Fred had been in his undershirt, and he'd seemed embarrassed over having been found in this state of undress. He'd put down his broom and gone into the apartment, to emerge a few moments later wearing a shirt. That had been the beginning of their friendship.

"Here it is now," Viola said, wagging her head. "Darn kids."

The car stopped and they got in and punched the ground floor button. They got off in the wide entrance foyer and Anne walked directly to the mailboxes, taking the key out of her purse, and unlocking the box.

There was a phone bill, and a handbill from the local supermarket, and also a letter. She glanced at the brown telephone company envelope without opening it, stuffed the handbill into her purse for later when she made out her shopping list, and then looked at the letter.

The envelope was neatly typed and it read simply:

> MRS. RICHARD DADIER
> 1935 East 174 Street
> Bronx, New York

She looked in the upper lefthand corner for a return address, but there was none. She turned the envelope over, looking at the flap, hoping for some clue as to the identity of the sender. There was nothing on the flap.

"Bills, bills, bills," Viola said. "Not a day goes by without another bill. Sometimes I wish the mailman would never come."

Anne smiled and ripped open the flap of the envelope.

"Today is my rent day," Viola said. "Are you going to the office?"

"No," Anne said, reaching into the envelope. "I've got some shopping to do."

"Nothing heavy," Viola said suspiciously.

"No, just a few things for tonight."

"All right," Viola said. "You get that husband of yours to do the heavy shopping."

"He does," Anne said, holding the folded contents of the envelope in her hand now, wondering who had written them a letter.

"Well, I'm going. I'll see you later, Anne."

"All right, Viola."

Viola waddled out of the building, bundling her coat around her. Anne walked to the windows near the radiator, and unfolded the letter. It was a plain white sheet of paper. There was no date on it and no salutation. In the exact center of the page, neatly typed, were the words:

WATCH RICHARD.
THERE'S ANOTHER WOMAN!

The note was unsigned.

9

"Oh, Mr. Dadier!" Lois Hammond called, poking her head out of the doorway and waving to him in the corridor. She'd addressed him formally because there were students in the corridor, rushing to their sixth-period classes, and teachers never used first names before the students.

Rick smiled and waved back, and then started for the stairwell. He'd planned on going down to the auditorium and grading his seventh-term test papers, a time-saving device which would afford him a free evening when he got home.

"Would you come in a moment, Mr. Dadier?" Lois said. "I want to show you something."

Rick hesitated, and then swerved away from the moving stream of students and headed for the open doorway. A lettered sign hung on the door, and the sign boldly stated that the room beyond the door was the office of *The Trades Trumpet*, if office it could be called. Rick had been inside the room only once before, when he'd used the mimeograph machine to run off some material for his classes. The room was small and square, and it possessed a desk, two windows that looked out on the courtyard enclosed by the school's L shape, a bulletin board, three chairs, a metal bookcase, and the mimeograph machine. It now also possessed Lois Hammond, and she held the door wide and said, "Come on in."

He entered the room, and she closed the door behind him.

"It's not the *New York Times*," she said, "but it'll have to do."

"*The Trades Trumpet*, huh?" he asked. "Whose brainstorm was that?"

"Mine," she said proudly. "Do you like it?"

"It's alliterative, at any rate."

"Do you know what they used to call the paper?" Lois asked.

"No. What?"

"The North Manual Trades High School Monthly." She smiled and lowered her lashes. "Sounds like a woman's complaint, doesn't it?"

Rick chuckled a little and said, "Yes, I suppose so."

"*The Trades Trumpet*," Lois said. "I like that. *The Trades Trumpet*. Don't you like it?"

"How about *The North Nickelodeon*?" Rick asked.

"Oh, Rick," Lois said, delighted.

"Or *The Manual Mandolin*?" He paused and laughed. "There's a good one."

"You're joking, but don't you really like the name?"

"It's a dandy," Rick said. "What'd you want to show me?"

"Oh, yes," she said, excitedly reminding herself. "Lock the door, will you, Rick?"

Rick raised his eyebrows, and Lois, seeing his surprise, quickly said, "Oh that has nothing to do with what I've got to show you. I feel like a smoke, and I'm also hot as hell, and I don't want any of our students popping in."

"I thought you had some French postcards," Rick said jokingly.

"You would," Lois replied, and Rick wondered just what she'd meant by that, and he didn't know whether or not he enjoyed the implication. He locked the door, and Lois fished a package of Chesterfields out of her purse, promptly tucking one between her lips and waiting for Rick to light it. Rick, who was the kind of smoker who had to smoke whenever anyone else smoked, took a single cigarette from the package in his jacket pocket, and then struck a match, holding it first to Lois's cigarette and then his own.

Lois exhaled a deep cloud of smoke and then said, "This is the stuffiest room in the building. Do you mind?"

He didn't know what she meant at first, and then she began unbuttoning her suit jacket, and he remembered what she'd said about being hot as hell. The jacket was a long gray one with a tight waist and it flared out over her hips with a straight black skirt sheathing her thighs and legs. She unbuttoned the jacket quickly and then slipped out of it, throwing it over a chair.

"After my first-day escapade," she said, "you won't find me anywhere in this school without my armor on. Unless there are no students present."

She had turned to face him now, and the blouse she

wore was sheer and frothy, a nothing-thing of transparent silk, a blouse similar to the one she'd worn to the
Friday Organizational Meeting so very long ago. But
there was something different about this blouse, and
Rick stared at her for a few moments before he realized
what it was, and then he self-consciously averted his
eyes lest she realize that he had realized what it was.

For whereas the blouse worn to the Organizational
Meeting had been worn with only a skirt and no jacket,
this blouse had been put on beneath a jacket, and by
Lois Hammond's own testimony, she would not be
found anywhere in the school without her armor on,
and the armor she referred to was her jacket. Indeed,
when she had been inside the jacket and the jacket
around her, there was no telling she wore a blouse
under it. With the jacket off, and it was off now, and
Rick knew it was off, and he wanted to leave the office
of *The Trades Trumpet* and get the hell down to the auditorium and grade his seventh-term papers, there was no
doubt that Lois Hammond wore a blouse beneath the
jacket.

And because the blouse was of the sheerest stuff,
there was also no doubting that Lois Hammond was not
wearing a slip, or if she was, it was a half-slip that began
at her waist and did nothing to conceal the firm, abun-
dant cones of her breasts caught tight in a white cotton
bra. As he had noticed about her so many times before,
she did not even seem aware of the fact that rounded
white shoulders and a firm white solar plexus were
showing above and beneath the thrust of her brassière.

"There," she said, "that's better," and Rick did not

entirely agree with her, because this was not better but worse. He was aware of her again as a woman, and he did not want this awareness which sneaked up on him like a cutthroat and slashed his stomach to ribbons. He did not want the awareness, and because it was unbidden, it produced the guilty feeling again, and he wet his lips nervously.

"What did you want to show me?" he asked, anxious to get this over with, wanting to get out of this office and away from her. His palms were wet, and his eyes strayed back to the front of the blouse, and he again visualized the exposed white breast on that day of the attempted rape. The brassière now cupped her breasts firmly, and there was a deep shadow of warmth between the breasts, and he longed to touch that softly pocketed valley, longed for just an instant, and then turned his eyes away and felt the guilt spread into his face.

"I've got the first page for the Thanksgiving issue," Lois said, turning and walking to the desk. "It's a honey."

He watched her walk, and he realized that the removal of the jacket had revealed more than her transparent blouse and what lay beneath it. For whereas the jacket had successfully hidden her hips and buttocks, its removal just as successfully exposed them. The black skirt was very tight, and he could see the firm, rolled edge of her panties beneath the skirt. She walked, and her buttocks rolled, and the panty line rolled with the movement, a slow, insinuating movement. He watched the slender lines of her skirt, and the roundness of her buttocks and the tapering fullness of her legs and he knew very well what he was thinking but he thought anyway, *What the hell am I thinking?*

Lois turned suddenly, and he lifted his eyes too late, knowing he was too late, and knowing she found him watching her, but knowing at the same time she'd wanted him to watch her.

She held a sheet of paper in her hands, and her eyes met his, and she said, "It looks good, doesn't it?" and she could have been talking about the first page of the Thanksgiving issue, but Rick knew damn well she wasn't. It was all about as subtle as a rivet, and he knew that, and he resented her obvious tactics, but at the same time he enjoyed them in a strange, forbidden-cookie-jar manner. Except that the cookie jar was not forbidden, the cookie jar was indeed within easy reach, and the only thing that stopped him from reaching was something like an unwritten law, despite his appetite at the moment.

He did have an appetite, a very strong appetite, and Anne's pregnancy was not helping that appetite in the least. If anything, it was making things worse because Anne's flesh was still warm and soft and her breasts had become larger and fuller with nipples that hardened the instant his hands found them. And Anne still curled against him each night, curled in the arc of his body, and she was there but not there because she was *really* the forbidden cookie jar, with no ifs, ands, or buts about it.

And so he walked the tightrope of the celibate, with desire on one side, and here, now, temptation on the other side. He would be lying to himself if he did not admit that Lois Hammond was temptation. One of the things Rick had never done was lie to himself. He admitted this, and in admitting it he acknowledged the guilt that accompanied his sudden, unbidden desire for her, and he resolved to get the hell away from her damned fast because he did not like walking a tightrope.

"It's a little early for Thanksgiving, isn't it?" he asked, and he realized his voice was trembling, and then he wondered if his body were trembling, too. Lois studied him with a small smile on her face, a smile that told him she knew just what she was doing to him, and she was enjoying it immensely. But a smile that said she wasn't kidding, and this enjoyment was just a small enjoyment, because she was not kidding and because she knew what she was doing.

And because he knew she was aware of all this, he was pleased deep within his masculine self, pleased that she was making an obvious effort, even though he disliked the obviousness of her effort, to display herself as a woman, even though she knew he was a married man. He was pleased because the smile on her face had not a damn thing to do with Thanksgiving issues, but with issues which might call for thanksgiving. He was pleased because her unashamed advances were telling him just what she wanted, and she wanted him, and he was married, and that combination appealed to his ego immensely.

But he was ashamed of himself for catering so to his ego, and ashamed of himself for even thinking what he was thinking because he knew he could never—in a million years—not if she ripped off the blouse and the bra, too, not if she slipped out of the skirt, and then he realized he was hoping she would do just that, and this time his hands did begin to tremble and he was even more deeply ashamed of himself.

She held out the first page to him, the ink still wet on it. He looked at the large turkey there, drawn by one of the students no doubt, and at the pumpkins decorating the page, and at the banner and then at the lettering which told everyone this was the Thanksgiving Issue. And above the page she extended, holding it just below her breasts, holding it so that his eyes took in a panorama of mimeographed page and white cotton bra, above the page was the soft shadow, and the rounded mounds of white flesh on either side of the shadow. His eyes strayed from the page, and Lois said, "Do you like it?" and again her voice was low and insinuating, and he knew she was not talking about the first page but about what rested just above the first page, and he answered, "Yes, I like it very much," and he knew, too, that he was talking about just what she was talking about.

"This is just the beginning, you know," she said, skillfully twisting the knife of *double entendre,* her eyes on Rick's face, the smile on her lips. "The ground work, so to speak. The rest will come later." She paused and suddenly withdrew the extended page, reaching behind her to put it on the desk. She kept her arms behind her, the palms flat on the desk. "The rest will come later," she repeated. And then she turned the full power of her gaze on him, and her lashes almost touched, and she wet her lips and added, "Before Thanksgiving."

She pushed herself off the desk, standing erect,

standing so close to Rick that her breasts almost touched his chest. He smelled the perfume of her hair, and for a wild moment he almost reached out and clasped her to him. But he stood there unmoving, a muscle in his jaw twitching, his eyelids blinking.

"I don't want to keep you," Lois said softly. She walked around him, her shoulder brushing his arm, and he turned and watched her walk across the room, watched the exaggerated swing of her hips, watched the rolled edge of panties, the straight seams of stockings, the high-heeled pumps. She walked to the chair and picked up her jacket, snuffing out her cigarette and then slipping into the jacket quickly, buttoning it with slender, red-tipped fingers, covering the blouse slowly, starting with the bottom button and working her way upward, closing the V over her breasts, hiding the bra, hiding the blouse, buttoning the jacket to her throat like a strip teaser working in reverse.

"I'll see you," Rick said tightly, and he walked to the door without turning to look at her again, angry at himself all at once, angry because he was behaving like a goddamned adolescent ogling a cheesecake magazine. He tried to put her out of his mind, but the anger mounted, a frustrated sort of self-incriminating anger which finally spread to include Lois Hammond and then focused on her alone.

He thought of her rich body, and then he thought of what she was trying to do, and he hated her intensely in that moment. He slammed the door behind him, and in his anger he almost missed Gregory Miller walking past the stairwell.

"Hello, Mr. Dadier," Miller said, his eyes taking in the flush on Rick's face.

"Hello, Miller," Rick said briefly. "You cutting a class?"

"Why no, Chief," Miller said. "I was just goan to the john." He held up the large wooden room pass and said, "See?" And then he glanced curiously at the closed door of *The Trades Trumpet* and asked, "You . . . uh . . . cuttin' a class, teach?"

"What do you mean by that?" Rick asked touchily.

"Why nothin'. Nothin' at all, teach."

"Mr. Dadier," Rick snapped.

"Why, sure. Mr. Dadier. That's what I said, wunt it?"

"No, it wasn't what you said. And you know damn well it wasn't."

"You got somethin' against me?" Miller asked suddenly.

"I might ask the same of you," Rick answered, his anger forcing the words out of him.

"Me?" Miller asked, seemingly surprised.

"There aren't but two of us here," Rick said nastily, "and I'm not talking to myself."

"You *ha'* got somethin' against me, hant you?" Miller said.

"Oh, go to hell, Miller," Rick answered. He turned his back and started away from the boy, heading into the stairwell.

"Hey, Mr. Dadier," Miller called, "wait up, will you?"

Rick stopped and whirled. "What is it now, Miller?"

Miller caught up with Rick, standing very close to him, his eyes almost level with Rick's. " 'Bout that class of yours I missed."

"What about it?"

"I wunt cuttin'."

"No one said you were."

"I jus' wanted you to know."

"All right, so now I know."

"My sister had a baby," Miller said, a proud smile forming on his face, a gleaming white smile against the brown of his skin.

"Congratulations," Rick said briefly.

"A boy," Miller said, and Rick wondered what the hell all this was about. He looked at Miller curiously for a moment and then said, "That's very nice, Miller."

"My brother-in-law's overseas," Miller explained. "He in the ahmy. Tha's why I took my sister to the hospital. Tha's why I wunt to school that day."

"I see," Rick said, still wondering why Miller was telling him all this. They stood close to each other for a few seconds, neither speaking, the silence closing in around them. Rick was aware of the silence, and he felt enormously awkward.

"My wife's expecting a baby, too," he said suddenly, wondering what had provoked him to tell this to Miller.

"That *right?*" Miller asked, seeming truly interested.

"Yes," Rick said. And then like a fighter who has momentarily lowered his guard and suddenly realizes he's liable to get punched, he said, "I'm busy, Miller." The guard was up again.

The smile disappeared from Miller's face. "What is it, Chief?" he asked.

"What's what, Miller?"

"You an' me, Chief? Why you got the knife out for me?"

"I haven't got a knife out for anyone, Miller. You're imagining things."

"You do, Chief. You sure as hell do. Why, tha's what I like to know. Why?"

Rick stared at Miller. "Are you serious?" he asked, his voice rising.

Miller looked confused. "Why, sure I am."

All of the contained anger seemed to suddenly spill out of Rick's mouth. "You've got the nerve to ask that! After all the trouble you've caused in my classroom? After all you've done? After your goddamn wise-guy remarks, and after the way you fouled up that lesson with the recorder, and after the way you're thick as thieves with your buddy West? Goddamnit, Miller, you've got the nerve to ask that?"

"Steady, Chief," Miller said, the smile reappearing, but somehow a defensive smile now. "Jus' take it easy."

"Oh, just get the hell out of here, Miller," Rick said. "You make me sick."

"I still doan see . . ."

"Don't hand me any of that, Miller," Rick said, his anger gaining new momentum. "You're not stupid, and you know damn well what's been happening." He paused and then blurted, "I wouldn't be surprised if you were in on that beating I got a while ago." He was instantly sorry for his accusation because his anger seemed to burn out with it, but there was nothing to help it now.

Miller's eyes tightened, and he looked at Rick soberly. "You doan mean that, Chief," he said softly.

"I do mean it," Rick said, refusing to budge an inch, refusing to eradicate his mistake now that he'd committed himself to it. "I damn well do mean it."

"You really got it bad, huh boy?" Miller said. He shook his head and glanced into the corridor, and Rick, still feeling the guilt of his reactions to Lois Hammond's body, mistook the gesture, understood Miller to be looking at the closed door of *The Trades Trumpet*.

"What the hell do you mean by that?" he shouted.

Miller's eyes popped wide in surprise. "What? I . . ."

"You heard me! What'd you mean by that? What'd you mean, you little . . ." He took a step toward Miller, and the boy backed off, and his eyes narrowed and his lips pulled back over his teeth.

"You gonna hit me, Mr. Dadier?" he said.

"What . . ."

"I'd like that, Mr. Dadier. Tha's all you need, boy. Tha's all you need to wash you up. Go on, hit me."

Rick gained instant control of himself, and now that he was calm again, he could not understand Miller's anger. Nor could he understand how a seemingly innocuous conversation had led to this explosive point.

"I'm sorr——" he started, and Miller backed off another pace and crouched over low, as if he were ready to deliver a punch from the floor.

"Go ahead, Mr. Dadier," he shouted, "go ahead and hit me. I doan know what the hell's eatin' you, but I'd sure like to see you hit me. Come on, hit me. Come on, come on, COME ON!" he shouted, his voice rising in hysteria.

Rick turned his back to Miller. "I'll see you in class tomorrow," he said coldly.

"And maybe you won't!" Miller shouted, as if that were the worst threat he could hurl. He turned his back and started off down the hallway, and Rick walked down the steps, his own anger slowly returning.

The little bastard, he thought. *The little black . . .*

He stopped abruptly.

Hey now. Hey now, what the hell was that? Now just what the hell was that?

Nothing, it just . . .

No now, no now don't "nothing" me. Now just what the hell was that, and just what the hell did you mean by that, and just who the hell are you anyway? Now just who the hell are you anyway? Now just what the hell were you about to say?

It's not because he's black, Rick thought. *That has nothing to do with it.*

Then why did you think that? Come on, you prejudiced sonofabitch, start making your alibis. Why the hell . . .

I'M NOT. *Goddamnit, you know that. If you know me at all, you know I'm not that way. You know that never once entered my mind.*

Until now.

Not now either. Look, that has nothing to do with it.

Then don't think it again. Not ever again. You understand that, you bastard? Never again.

I didn't even think it this time. I was angry, I . . .

Don't give me any horse manure. Just promise, that's all. Just redeem yourself, you chauvinistic sonofabitch. Just . . .

Don't say that. For Christ's sake, you know it isn't true. Fred and Viola are . . .

Some of my best friends are niggers.

All right, if you're going to get flippant about it, the hell with it. But inside you know it isn't true. Either that, or you don't know me at all, and then I don't give a damn what you think, anyway. You know I'm not that way. Don't you?

Yes, I know.

Then why accuse me of thinking . . .

What you think isn't important. What does Miller think?

Miller?

Miller, Miller, the boy you almost called a little black bastard. What does he think, stupid? What does he think about you? What does he think about what you think, and does he think you think of him as a little black bastard? Had that ever occurred to you? Had that ever occurred to your brilliant, all-seeing, all-powerful intelligence? Had it ever occurred to you, or were you too goddamned busy observing the udders on that goddamn Trades Trumpeting cow?

It . . . it never occurred to me. No. No, it never did. And Lois means nothing. You know that. You know I'd never . . .

I know. I know you damn well better never.

I don't need threats. I know what's right and wrong.

Then start thinking about Miller, and start thinking about how you've wronged him.

But I haven't . . .

Unless he thinks you have, and then you have. And I'm going to forget all about what you almost said, did in fact say, I'll forget all about that and pretend it never happened, but you'd better start thinking about it, you'd better start thinking about it damned hard.

He started thinking about it.

It had never occurred to him that Miller might feel that way, and he cursed himself for his own blind stupidity. That would be ironic, he thought, that would be really ironic. If Miller thought that about me. If that were the nub of all the trouble. It would be something like the story he'd heard about the white man married to a Negress, the white man who'd been going home to his Negress wife when the race riots broke out in Harlem, the white man who'd had his throat slit for being a white man in black territory on that night when color was the all-important factor in deciding the behavior of human beings. Color or the lack of color.

It would be something like that because Rick had never consciously thought of Miller as a Negro. Miller was another boy in his classes, and Miller happened to be a troublemaker, but Miller was never a Negro. Rick knew he was colored, of course. He knew that, but he knew it the way he knew that Carter had red hair. He had no grudge against red hair, and he certainly had no grudge against Miller's pigmentation. That had never once entered into his thoughts about the boy.

But if *Miller* thought that . . .

Rick had been in a similar situation once before. It had caused him an uncomfortable two weeks, but he'd finally straightened it out. It had happened while he was in the Navy, and it had nothing whatever to do with color, or the lack of color, but it had a lot to do with misunderstanding. If Miller believed this about him now, it was clearly a case of misunderstanding, and the only way to combat that was with understanding. If anything, the time in the Navy had been more difficult because Rick had been on a destroyer, and a destroyer is a small ship, and you've got to live with a lot of different guys, and the living is cramped. You can't step on anyone's toes without getting your own toes crushed.

They'd been coming back from liberty in the town of Kagoshima, with the twin volcanos steaming in the distance, with the ash-covered slopes leading down to the beach and the LCVP that would take them back to the ship. He'd been sitting on the metal deck aft of the ramp, chatting in a group of guys from the radar gang, when Mr. Goldin walked over to the circle, leaned down into it like a man ready to roll in a floating crap game.

"This gunner's mate," Mr. Goldin had said. "A blond guy, thin, with a sort of hooked nose. What's his name again?"

The guys had been talking about the town, and the women in the town, and they looked up uninterestedly when Mr. Goldin asked his question. They all knew the gunner's mate's name, and any one of them could have supplied it and probably would have because Mr. Goldin's question had been innocent enough. Rick just happened to be the first one to speak.

"Bowden," he said. "Is that the one you mean?"

"Yes," Mr. Goldin said, smiling. "That's him."

"What about him?" Rick asked.

"Oh, nothing," Mr. Goldin said, and then he strolled

away from the group. The guys went back to talking about the town and the women in the town, and suddenly the LCVP's squawk box burst into static, and a gravelly voice said, "Now hear this, now hear this. Bowden, Gunner's Mate Third Class, report to the bridge on the double. Bowden, Gunner's Mate Third Class, report to the bridge on the double."

The radarmen in the circle stopped talking and looked at Rick, and then looked over to the port side of the landing craft where the gunner's mate, Bowden, pushed himself to his feet with a curious smile on his face. He walked forward and mounted the ladder to the bridge, and Mr. Goldin went up that ladder a few seconds afterward.

The whole thing couldn't have taken more than five minutes. Goldin came down from the bridge first, and then Bowden followed after him, that same curious smile on his face. He walked back to where he'd been sitting on the port side of the landing craft, and then he looked across to where Rick was sitting on the starboard side. His eyes met Rick's, and the smile dropped from his face, and that was the beginning of it.

At first, Rick wasn't even aware of what was happening. It started with all the gunner's mates, of course, but it spread rapidly to people on the ship he didn't even know, and people he was sure did not know him. The first indication came that time in the head when he'd been waiting for a sink. Arbuster, a gunner's mate first whom he'd always exchanged a friendly word with, was shaving, and Rick slouched near the sink, watching him, waiting for his turn.

"You make me nervous," Arbuster had said suddenly, irritably.

Rick looked into the mirror and at Arbuster's reflection there. He smiled and said, "That's okay, take your time. I'm in no hurry."

"Then why the hell don't you take a walk someplace, 'stead of watching me like an eagle?"

Rick was surprised by Arbuster's outburst, but he attributed it to a hair across the ass, something that happened to everyone sooner or later. He'd shrugged, and been saved any further conversation by the appearance of a suddenly vacated sink. He hadn't thought further about the incident until he'd noticed that none of the gunner's mates returned his greetings when he passed them on the ship. That struck him as being peculiar, and then the sickness spread to the radar gang, and everyone began treating him like some sort of leper. He finally cornered Frank Port, a radarman and his closest buddy aboard ship.

"What's the scoop, Frank?" he'd asked. "Did I do something?"

"You know," Frank said, avoiding Rick's eyes.

"No, I don't know. What is it?"

Frank lifted his eyes like a man with four aces about to call a pair-of-deuces bluff. "You ratted on Bowden," he said.

"I *what*?" Rick asked, astonished.

"You told Goldin he swiped that bottle of Coke," Frank said.

"What bottle of Coke? What the hell is this?"

"On the LCVP," Frank said patiently. "Come on,

Rick, you don't have to snow me." He'd turned to go, but Rick caught at his sleeve and forced Frank to face him again.

"No, wait a minute, Frank. I don't know what it's all about, I mean it."

Frank had hesitated a moment, and then given Rick the whole story. There'd been a Coca-Cola case aboard the LCVP, one of these red metal jobs with the doors on top. The crew apparently chipped in each month for the Coke and they were allowed the privilege of dipping into the ice-filled case whenever they were thirsty. This privilege, however, did not extend to include the crews of every ship in the Pacific Fleet. Bowden, probably thirsty after his bout with the dust-filled streets of Kagoshima, had dipped into the metal case, swiped a bottle of Coke, and drunk it hastily and apparently unseen.

Except that someone had seen him, and someone had supplied Goldin with the information, and that someone had been Rick Dadier.

"Me?" Rick asked. "Hell, I only answered Goldin's question. I didn't know Bowden swiped anything."

"Yeah," Frank had said, and then dismissed the subject.

It was really an amazing thing. He'd been accused and tried and convicted without ever once opening his mouth in defense. The funniest part was that everyone believed it, even the guys who'd been sitting in the circle when Goldin had come over, the guys who knew damn well what was asked and damn well what was answered, the guys who probably would have supplied the same information had not Rick spoken first.

He let it ride for two weeks, bearing the ostracizing looks, the accusing glares. And finally he took a stand, and he took it in the mess hall. He got his food and carried the tray into the mess hall, and he spotted Bowden sitting at the far end of one table. He walked down the aisle on the opposite side of the table, climbed over the bench, and sat down directly opposite Bowden.

Bowden did not look up. His blond head was bent over his tray, and he ate studiously, even though this was Sunday night and horse's cock was being dished out.

"Bowden," Rick said softly.

Bowden looked up, his eyes a pale gray, his nose hooked, his mouth tight. "Yeah?"

"I want to get something straight between us," Rick said.

"Yeah, what's that, Dadier?"

"I didn't rat on you. I didn't even know you swiped the Coke. Goldin came over and gave us a description of you, and then casually asked what your name was. I told him, but I didn't know why he wanted you or what you'd done. Hell, I figured he was just looking for you."

"Yeah?" Bowden said.

"You don't have to believe me," Rick said, "but it's the truth. Why should I get you in hot water?"

"There was no hot water," Bowden said. "I just had to pay for the Coke, that's all."

"Well, I wouldn't even have wanted you to do that. I don't give a damn what you swipe. I'd have swiped a bottle myself if I'd known it was there."

"Yeah?" Bowden said again.

"Okay, don't believe me if you don't want to. I'm

telling the truth, though. I don't care what these other guys think about me, but I wanted you to know the truth. Okay, Bowden?"

Bowden looked at him levelly, studying him for a few seconds. "Sure," he said finally. He rose, picked up his empty tray with his left hand, and then extended his right across the table. "Forget it, Dadier."

Rick had taken his hand firmly, and that had been the end of that—as far as Bowden was concerned, anyway. It took a while for the rest of the crew to catch on to the idea that Rick and Bowden had squared it all away, but even that came eventually. It had simply been a question of substituting understanding for misunderstanding.

But could he do that with Miller?

Could he go over to the boy and say, "Look, Miller. You've got me all wrong. I don't care what color your skin is."

Could he do that?

He himself was always wary of people who said, "I don't care what color his skin is. He can be purple for all I care." A kind of *Methinks the lady doth protest* suspicion always possessed him whenever someone made such a statement. So wouldn't Miller feel the same way?

And how could he make an issue of the color of Miller's skin and at the same time state that the color of that skin was a thing of no importance? And would Miller believe him?

And suppose he was wrong, suppose Miller never once considered that as the source of the trouble between them? Suppose he brought it to Miller's attention, and by so doing created a problem that had not previously existed?

No, he could not take the direct approach. If color was a sore spot with him, Miller would not want to discuss it openly and frankly. And if it wasn't, there was no sense making an issue of it, and risking a fresh breach.

As it turned out, the whole thing was simpler than he ever imagined it could be.

The corridor run-in with Miller seemed almost to have never happened. Miller, apparently forgetting his parting threat, diligently appeared at each fifth-period English class, and it was during one of those classes that the opportunity presented itself.

Antoro and Taglio provided the opening.

The class was discussing, after a fashion, a story Rick had just read aloud to them. Rick had asked Antoro a question, and Antoro had got to his feet, and then fumbled haltingly with his thoughts on the subject.

Taglio, bored with Antoro's ideas, shouted, "Oh, sit down, you crazy wop. You don't know what you're talking about."

"You're a bigger wop," Antoro had answered, smiling, and Rick had stepped in instantly, a serious look on his face even though he knew the boys were joking good-naturedly.

"That's enough of that," he said sternly.

Antoro sat down immediately, relieved to be off the hook, but not knowing what Rick was talking about. Miller sat placidly in his seat, and West sat beside him, both boys unusually quiet.

"I don't like name-calling in my classes," Rick said, a bit too pompously perhaps.

"I wasn't calling no names," Taglio said. "I was just kiddin'."

"That's the way it starts," Rick said. "Just kidding. Like a fist-fight in the streets. You shove a guy jokingly, and he shoves you back, and the next thing you know you're at each other's throats. Name-calling is the same way."

The class regarded him silently. He had their complete attention, and he sensed that he was broaching a subject in which they were interested.

"All right, Antoro, you're of Italian descent. So's Taglio. You call Taglio a wop, and he calls you a wop, and everything's okay. But suppose Levy calls you both wops? Is it okay then?"

Rick paused and waited.

"No, it's not okay," he provided. "It's not okay, and you'll snap right back and call Levy a kike or a mockie. But you were the ones who gave Levy the idea in the first place, don't you see? Because you used the expression yourselves, just kidding around."

"Aw, I didn't mean nothin'," Taglio said, a little embarrassed.

"I know you didn't. That's just my point. You shouldn't use vicious expressions, whether you're joking or serious. Look, my parents are French. Do you know how many times I've been called a frog? Do you think I like it? Well, no, I don't.

"Do you think Morales or De la Cruz or Rodriguez here like being called spics? Well, I can tell you they don't."

He looked out at the class, saw the three Puerto Rican boys smile in embarrassment.

"Do you think Kruger or Vandermeer like being called krauts? Do you think O'Brien or Erin like being called micks or donkeys?" Rick paused and then focused his gaze on Miller. "Do you think Miller or Parsons or Baker like being called niggers?"

The class stirred a little, and Rick knew damned well they'd all used every one of these expressions at one time or another.

"No one likes fun poked at his color, creed, or nationality," Rick went on, "and I won't tolerate it in my class. So don't tell me you're kidding or not kidding or whatever. I'm not interested. Just don't use derogatory expressions in my classroom. Is that clear?"

The kids remained silent. Some of them nodded, and some of them fidgeted in their seats. Miller smiled. He smiled broadly, and Rick could not read the smile, but he felt that his little lecture had made a point, and most of all, he felt he had delivered his message to Miller.

He met Miller's smile with his own, and said, "Let's get on with the lesson now, shall we?"

Miller continued smiling, and now West was smiling, too.

10

The executive ax began falling the day before Armistice Day, and it dropped finally just before the Thanksgiving vacation. Rick had no idea the ax would fall, nor did he even know it was poised over his head. He considered Stanley's first visit to his classroom a part of normal procedure. He did not know it was the whetting of the ax-blade.

The Department Chairman arrived at Room 206 just before the fifth period began. He entered the room smiling, walked to Rick's desk and said, "Hope you don't mind a little observation, Dadier?"

"Why . . . why not at all," Rick answered, wishing at the same time that Stanley had not chosen this particular class to observe. But then, Stanley undoubtedly knew all about Juan Garza, knew that 55–206 was a class full of his disciples, and had purposely chosen it.

"I'll just sit at the back of the room," he said, his lips moving below his now-full mustache. He was dressed impeccably, as always. His not-quite-blond hair was brushed neatly, and his gray eyes had been ordered to attention by a strict drillmaster. There was no doubt that he was the chairman of the English Department. "I'll be very quiet," he added, smiling, assuming the role of a mildly interested observer, giving the lie to his regal bearing and his cold eyes. He walked familiarly to the back of the room, took the last seat in the first row, crossed his legs after lifting the trouser to preserve its crease, and then opened a black notebook on the desk before him.

The class filed in, spotting Stanley instantly, and behaving like choir boys before the Christmas Mass. There'd be no trouble today, Rick knew. It was one thing to badger a teacher, but not when it led to a knockdown-dragout with the Department Chairman. No one liked sitting in the English office under the cold stare of that Stan man.

The cold stare showed no signs of heating up during the lesson. Rick gave it all he had, glad he'd prepared a good plan the night before, able for the first time to actually follow the plan because the kids kept their peace in Stanley's presence. He called primarily on his best students, throwing in a few of the duller kids to show Stanley he was impartial, but he steered away from Miller and West, not wanting to risk any entanglements while Stanley was observing.

At the end of the period, Stanley came to the desk and smiled briefly. "You might watch the distribution of your questions," he said, a bored expression in his eyes. "You seem to favor several students."

"Oh, do I?" Rick asked innocently, cursing Stanley for having seen through his scheme. "I'll watch that."

"Yes, do." He paused and consulted his notes. "Ever call on Morales?"

"Yes," Rick said, a little flustered now. "Yes, I do."

"Nice boy."

"Yes."

"Ever call on Rodriguez?"

"Why, certainly. Yes. Yes, I do."

"Like him?"

Rick shrugged and smiled. "He's all right. Not too bright, but not a bad kid."

"Uh-huh. What about Miller? Notice you didn't call on him once."

"Didn't I? No, I guess I didn't. Oh, he's quite active in the class usually." Rick smiled a fraternal smile. "Oh yes, quite active," hoping Stanley would understand what he meant. Stanley did not return the smile.

"I'll have a report typed up for your guidance, Dadier. I may drop in again sometime."

"Please do," Rick answered politely.

Stanley did not drop in the next day because the next day was Armistice Day and there were no teachers or students present at the high school. But he did drop in on November 12th, this time during Rick's eighth-period class. He took his seat at the back of the room, observed Rick while he taught, made several notes, and then left when the bell rang, not stopping to chat with Rick this time.

Nor was that the last visit. Stanley began stopping by frequently, sometimes remaining for the full period, and sometimes visiting for ten- or fifteen-minute stretches, and then departing silently.

In the beginning, Rick resented the intrusions. He would watch Stanley scribbling at the back of the room, and he wondered what Stanley was writing, and he felt something like a bug on the microscope slide of a noted entomologist. Why all the secrecy? What the hell was this, the Gestapo?

He began to realize, after a while, that Stanley's visits were probably just what he needed, and he found himself looking forward to the unannounced appearances of the Department Chairman. With painful honesty, he admitted to himself that his students were not entirely to blame for the lack of teaching that went on in his classes. He was not prepared to cope with them, and unless someone told him what he was doing wrong, he'd probably never be prepared to cope with them. Perhaps Stanley's visits were the answer to his problem. Perhaps Stanley would eventually make known the results of his observations, would say, "See here, Dadier, this and this is your trouble. Such and such is fine, but you've got to concentrate more on that and that."

Rick would have appreciated that immensely, and so he was quite pleased with the sudden attention Stanley devoted to him. For the first time in his educational career, he honestly felt that someone was interested in what he did, and in whether or not he was doing it correctly. So where he had made lesson plans carefully before, he now devoted more time to them, enlarged on them, outlined his lessons in the minutest detail. And when Stanley asked to see his plan during one of his visits, Rick felt amply rewarded, even though Stanley made no comment on the outline.

He was grateful, too, for the obedience of his classes whenever Stanley was present. One of his greatest problems had been discipline. With these kids, it was almost impossible to get a word in edgewise and—especially in the beginning—his teaching efforts usually disintegrated into a contest to determine who could shout the loudest. He had never fully licked the discipline problem, and he doubted if he ever would. He had succeeded, though, in forcing some sort of obedience out of the kids, usually by threats of homework or tests or after-school confinement, or visits from parents. There were times when no threat would work, times when the kids were just feeling bastardly and presented a solid, unyielding front that could not be cracked no matter how much he ranted or raved. These times were not infrequent. They were a part of vocational school teaching, a part acknowledged by any teacher who'd ever served in the system.

There were formulas for establishing discipline, Rick learned, and one of these formulas had been succinctly stated by Captain Schaefer during one of his periodic visits to the lunchroom.

"Clobber the bastards," he'd said. "It's the only thing that works. What do you think happens at home when they open their yaps? Pow, right on the noggin. That's the only language they understand."

Perhaps they understood that language in Captain Schaefer's domain, a domain devoted to the physical, a domain of sweating, athletic bodies, a man's world of physical strength. Perhaps they accepted a cuff on the mouth from a man in a tee shirt, a man who was sweating just as they were, a man who was king of this writhing land of bodies unadorned. Perhaps so.

But Rick could not picture Josh Edwards clobbering a kid. Nor could he, in all honesty, picture himself doing that. The urge to do so was always present, of course. You can push someone just so far, and when he finds he can't strike back verbally his first instinct is to inflict some sort of damage, and his only remaining weapons are physical. Especially when these kids did not seem to be kids. The second-termers, yes. They were kids. He could look upon them as kids, and he could feel the superiority of adulthood. There was a difference between his body and their bodies, and a difference between the basic mechanism of his mind and their minds.

Not so with the fifth-termers and certainly not so with the seventh-termers. Perhaps they weren't old enough to vote, and perhaps some of them weren't old enough to be drafted. But their bodies were mature, strong bodies, and they thought—in their own twisted manner—the way adults think, and it was extremely difficult to consider them "kids" when a good many of them outreached you, and outweighed you, and sometimes (only sometimes) outthought you.

So the temptation to clobber was always there, and it was sometimes more difficult not to strike than it would have been *to* strike, and the consequences be damned. Because, despite any edicts about corporal punishment, there were a good many vocational school kids who got clobbered every day, and when the heavy hand of someone like Captain Max Schaefer clobbers, the clobberee knows he's been clobbered, but good.

Clobbering, then, was one accepted means of establishing discipline in a trade school.

Another method was Slobbering, and this worked most efficiently when a female teacher—scarce as such creatures were—used it.

The Slobbering method appealed to the sympathy of the boys, and it took various forms. The most common form (and this is why the method worked best when employed by females) was the one which turned on a touched-to-the-quick expression, and then dolefully complained about the ingratitude of the class.

"After all I've done for you," the Slobberer whined. "You give me this treatment."

When a female used this tactic, unattractive though she might be, there was usually something inside the boys which responded. Perhaps it was their innate chivalry, their desire to come to the rescue of the damsel in distress. Whatever it was, in the hands of a good female Slobberer (and Martha Riley was one of the best at Manual Trades, if not *the* best in the City of New York) an assorted collection of hoodlums could be made to feel like heels, and would indeed hold a respectful silence throughout the remainder of the period, showing their gratitude for all the teacher had done for them, which was usually nothing.

A male Slobberer performed a variation on the theme, and the variations were multiple and many-faceted. The most common form of male Slobbering was the one which appealed to the boys' sense of fraternal spirit. Treating them all like Alpha Beta Tau boys, the male Slobberer would say, "Come on, fellows, give me a break. I'm just a poor slob trying to do a job, that's all."

And the fellows, knowing all about poor slobs trying to do jobs, might or might not respond to the teacher's plea, depending upon how they felt about the proletariat on that particular day.

The Veteran Hook was another variation on the male Slobberer's pitch. The Veteran Hook was not a direct plea; in fact, its effectiveness lay primarily in its quality for understatement. It entailed a dramatic reconstruction of several isolated war experiences, with a few descriptions of the Germans, Italians, or Japanese who had met death at the hands of the male Slobberer. The more dead enemies, the better. The boys loved tales of bashed skulls. But this was not where the Slobbering ended. In fact, had it ended here, it would have accomplished nothing. The Slobberer then went on to tell about the Purple Heart he received, or the steel plate he carried in his head, or the cork leg beneath his trouser, or the way his balls were shot off—none of which things ever happened to him. He then went on to describe the rough time he had rehabilitating, and the rough time he had in college, and the rough time he had finding a teaching job. And now, now that he *is* teaching, he's grateful to the United States and the wonderful people who made all this possible, and he only hoped he could keep his job and continue to teach all these swell kids who helped make all this possible.

And the kids, weaned on the hero legend, unable to tell a cork leg from a cork-tipped cigarette, usually accepted this type of Slobbering and made it a little easier for the teacher to keep this job he fought for, provided they did not kick his leg out from under him some day to see if it really was cork.

Another type of male Slobbering, akin to the fraternal pitch, but different in a degree, was the type Halloran used. Halloran, as he exhibited on the first day of school while introducing the assorted teachers to the assorted students, was "just one of the boys." He'd never been to college. He fulfilled the Board's requirements for becoming a shop teacher in a trade school by:

1) Graduating from Junior High School, and having nine years of trade experience. Or . . .
2) Graduating from Senior High School, and having seven years of trade experience. Or . . .
3) Graduating from a technical or vocational high school, and having five years of trade experience.

He was, as any fool could plainly see, just one of the boys. And so he spoke like the boys, and he joked like the boys, and he even borrowed from the Clobbering approach and sometimes batted the boys around, but all the time just being one of the boys and basing his Slobbering technique upon that single peg.

Oh, the ways of the Slobbering technique were many and varied, and Rick heard about all of them, but he somehow felt all of them were a little degrading, like sucking up to an officer to get a weekend liberty, except that these kids weren't even officers, and there were a good many of them.

If you didn't choose to Clobber or Slobber, you could

Slumber. Slumbering, as apart from Slobbering, was an art in itself, and Solly Klein was one of its most ardent practitioners. The Slumberer treated discipline as a non-existent problem. For him, indeed, the problem *was* a non-existent one. He chose to ignore it. He taught, and if no one heard what he was teaching, it was just tough. He taught like a man talking in his sleep. He rattled on and on, and the noises and sounds of the outside world meant nothing to him. If, as occasionally happened, the noises broke into his slumber, the Slumberer would simply step outside the room for a moment, waiting for the class to knock itself out, and keeping an eye open for The Boss at the same time. The Slumberer's philosophy was a simple one: *Let the bastards kill themselves. So long as I'm not hurt.*

So if a fist-fight started in the Slumberer's classroom, the Slumberer allowed the two protagonists to beat themselves silly while he stood by and watched. He then stepped over the pool of blood on the floor and went on with his lesson, not caring if anyone was listening, and having long since realized that no one was listening anyway. No one ever failed a course the Slumberer taught. There were a lot of Slumberers in the New York City system.

The Rumbler was a fellow exactly like the Slumberer, except for one thing. The Slumberer knew there was no discipline in his classes, but he slept soundly at night as well as during the day. The Rumbler, on the other hand, did exactly what the Slumberer did all day long, but then he went home and complained to his wife about the lack of discipline, or he complained to his Department

Chairman, or even to the principal. Or when no one else was around to listen, he would rumble silently to himself, cursing everyone responsible, including God, and especially cursing people like the Slumberers who had allowed such a shocking disciplinary problem to develop.

The Fumbler, and Rick classified himself in this broad group of teachers, simply didn't know what the hell to do. The Fumbler kept trying. He tried this way, and he tried that way, and he hoped that some day he would hit upon the miraculous cure-all for the disciplinary problem. Most Fumblers eventually became proponents of one of the other methods of establishing discipline. Some Fumblers really did lick the problem eventually, but they never divulged their secrets—learned after many years of batting their heads against the wall—to the lesser mortals who shared the teaching profession.

So Rick fumbled, and he was immensely grateful for Stanley's visits because there was no disciplinary problem whenever Stanley was present. On those occasions, he was allowed to teach, and he discovered then that there was something other than a lack of discipline to fight at North Manual Trades. The discovery left him feeling a bit defeated, like a man who's purchased an AC television set only to discover that his apartment is wired for DC.

He discovered that the kids simply did not care.

It was as basic as that. They did not want to learn.

He did not know what had planted this attitude inside them, but he suspected it was the vocational

school system itself. He was surprised to find out that
the kids *knew* they were in a bad school. He'd mentioned something in class about North Manual Trades
being a damned fine trade school, and the kids had all
but laughed at him. He wasn't kidding them one bit.
They knew the school was lousy, and they knew they
were here because they'd flunk out of an academic high
school within a week. What's more, they knew that
most vocational high schools were lousy, and they
seemed to feel that the lousier the school was, the more
desirable it was.

Now that was a strange manner of thinking, Rick
felt, and he wondered who was to blame for it. Certainly
not the guidance counselors who recommended vocational high schools to students. Certainly not them.
They explained patiently and fully that perhaps a vocational school, since you *are* so good in shop, and since
your academic grades haven't been so good lately, might
be best for you after all. The picture painted *was* a pleasant one, there was no denying that. A school where
someone could learn a bread-and-butter trade. A school
like that, imagine! The answer to the working-man's
prayer. Are there really schools like that? Golly!

But somehow, the secret had leaked, or maybe it just
leaked after the kid was in the middle of a trade school
for a few days. The picture wasn't as pretty as it had
been painted. In fact, the canvas had been slashed with a
knife. And if a kid really wanted to learn a trade, see
how long he kept his ideals when he was surrounded by
other kids who'd have liked to blow up every school in
the city.

And the worst part was that when you were in the middle of a bad school, when you were surrounded by kids who were acknowledged problem students, you began to feel bad yourself. The man who goes to a whore house because he likes the magazines in the waiting room is not considered a bibliophile. He's spotted coming out of the red-lanterned doorway, and he's considered a man who has just had a piece of tail. *The Saturday Evening Post* doesn't enter into the observation at all.

So a kid who goes to a vocational school, even if he's going there to learn a trade, is not considered a hardworking, earnest student. He's considered a kid who didn't fit anywhere else in the educational system. He's considered that, and he senses it, and if he's got the name, he'll have the game, and so he becomes part of the waste product, and he considers the school itself a garbage can.

There are kids who survive, kids who learn trades, kids who maintain their individual goals despite the corrupting stench that surrounds them. Those kids are few and far between.

Those kids were not the problems. Rick had a few of those kids in each of his classes, kids who seemed to want him to say something, who were annoyed when his lesson was interrupted, who did their homework whenever it was assigned, who turned in book reports, who were excellent in the shops of their choice, who wanted to learn, who were eager to learn, and who somehow managed to learn in spite of the opposition.

Those kids were the easy ones to reach. They wanted

to be reached, they longed to be reached. It was the others. Those who didn't care, those who were content to
wallow in the filth, those who not only didn't want to
learn but consciously wanted *not* to learn.

It was those he could not reach, and it was those he
tried desperately to reach. It was almost fantastic, and
he doubted if he could have explained his problem to
anyone but Anne. It was like a man standing on a street
corner giving out fifty-dollar bills, and having a tough
time finding takers. Why wouldn't they take what he
had to give them? He did have something to give them,
so much to give them if they would only accept it.

So he tried to reach them, and he tried harder when
Stanley was present because he did not have to fight the
shouting and the ranting then. Time and again, he
found himself remembering Solly Klein's garbage can
metaphor, and more and more he began to see himself
as the fellow with the fat behind who sat on the lid of
the can. He fought against thinking that way because he
knew the thought preceded the action, and the instant
he conceded the kids were filth and he was a garbage
man, he would stop trying to reach them, and he didn't
want that to happen.

There were times when he wanted to shout, "Can't
you see that I'm trying to help you? Can't you see that?"

There were times when they irritated him so much
that he felt like chucking the whole goddamned mess
and taking a job as a shoe clerk.

And there were times when he simply did not understand. Like the afternoon four of his seventh-term,
eighth-period students stayed after school voluntarily,

helping him erase the boards and stack the books away in the closet. They'd asked him if he had a car, said they'd be happy to fix anything that was wrong with it. When he'd told them he didn't own a car, they'd seemed disappointed. They'd chatted with him about their own jalopies, and he'd found himself talking about Anne, and the baby to come, talking to these kids the way he'd talk to anyone else, treating them like the adults he felt they were. When they left him, they all waved and said, "So long, Mr. Dadier. See you tomorrow."

He'd felt a strange inner peace when they'd gone, a feeling of having made some inroad, a feeling of having taken a first wavering step toward breaking through the shell that surrounded them. He'd liked the kids that afternoon, and he couldn't wait to get home and tell Anne about how nice they'd been.

And then the very next day, those same four kids had raised all kinds of hell during the eighth period, creating a havoc he'd never had before in that seventh-term class. The same four kids, the same kids who'd listened sympathetically while he told them about his expected baby, the same kids who'd offered to repair his car if he had one, those same four were the worst bastards imaginable, shouting, yelling, disobedient, not caring for anything he said, not listening to any of his threats.

He could not understand.

He simply could not understand. They didn't even seem like the same boys. What could you do when they ran hot and cold like that? Why even *try* to reach them? Why not throw in the towel and sit with your fat ass tight to the cover of the garbage can? Why not fool the system and fool the kids and fool yourself in the bargain? Why not collect a teacher's salary, and tuck the good vacations into your hip pocket, and all the while be an employee of the DSC?

And you could forget all about being a man in addition.

Oh, so what the hell? Are you supposed to keep banging your head against a stone wall?

Yes.

Are you supposed to try to teach kids who don't want to learn, who aren't interested in learning at all?

Yes.

All right, how? How?

And he had no answer.

He had no answer to why Stanley dropped in so often, either, but he enjoyed the visits, and so he did not probe too deeply into the reasons behind them. He kept teaching in his own fashion, hoping for some miraculous thing to happen, hoping the kids would suddenly realize he was the man with the fifty-dollar bills, hoping he'd break through if he simply kept at it, hoping he'd find the way.

He did not find the way, but he did find Stanley's reasons for lavishing so much individual attention upon him.

It was two days before Thanksgiving. Stanley had dropped in on 55–206 again, taken his seat at the rear of the room, and watched, his gray eyes cold, his pencil moving. Rick had taught as well as he knew how to teach, calling primarily on his best students to impress the Department Chairman. At the end of the period,

Stanley came to him and said, "You're unassigned now, aren't you, Dadier?"

"Yes, I am," Rick said.

"I think Mr. Small would like to talk to you. Mind going down to his office?"

"Mr. Small?" Rick asked, surprised.

"Yes," Stanley said dryly. "Drop down there, won't you?"

"Is . . . is anything wrong?" Rick asked, suddenly suspicious of Stanley's frequent visits, suddenly wondering why The Boss wanted to see him.

"Mr. Small will discuss it with you," Stanley said noncommittally. "Get down there as soon as you can, Dadier."

"Yes, sir," Rick said. He watched Stanley leave the classroom, and then he packed his briefcase slowly, a perplexed frown knotting his forehead.

What could Small want? And wasn't it a little unusual for the message to be transmitted through the Department Chairman? Surely, it had something to do with Stanley's visits. But was this customary procedure?

He found himself becoming angry. Did they always send the Department Chairman around to snoop? like a member of the Gestapo? like a goddamned secret policeman? Was that how they worked it? And was Small going to fire him? Is that how they fired people? Just a few visits from the Department Chairman and then *blooie*?

Goddamnit, he'd tried his best. If they were so concerned over the teaching job he was doing, why hadn't someone offered advice? Instead, they sent around a storm trooper with a little black notebook. Damnit, how was he going to tell Anne? How do you tell a woman in her ninth month that you've lost your goddamned job? Sonofabitches, the least they could have done would . . .

Now, hold it, he told himself, just hold it. You're behaving like the guy going to borrow the lawn mower. Maybe Harry won't lend me the lawn mower, after all I've done for Harry, after all the things I've loaned Harry, after the way we've been neighbors for ten years, imagine that louse not wanting to lend me the mower. So when you get to Harry's door and knock on it, and Harry opens it with a friendly smile, you look at him coldly and shout, "Keep your goddamn lawn mower!"

You're doing the same thing here, he told himself. Maybe Small isn't going to fire you at all. Maybe Small is going to commend you for your excellent work!

But deep down inside him, he knew he was going to be fired, and his anger suddenly dissipated to be replaced by a sort of fear. He'd have to start looking for another job, and November wasn't a good time for getting a teaching job, and Anne was in her ninth month, and goddamnit, this was a hell of a way to fire a person.

He picked up his briefcase and then looked around the room, as if he were looking at it for the last time, as if he did not expect to be back. Then he went down to Small's office, and told Miss Brady, the Boss' secretary, that Stanley had asked him to stop in.

"Oh, yes," Miss Brady said haughtily, and Rick felt the fear expanding inside him. Even she knows, he thought. Good-by, Dadier. It's been fun, Dadier, but have you ever thought of becoming a toy salesman? Very nice racket, toys. Miss Brady entered the inner sanctum, was out of sight for a few moments, and then returned to say, "Mr. Small will see you now."

Rick left his briefcase on the bench outside, walked to Small's frosted glass door, and knocked on it tremulously, his heart in his mouth.

"Come in, Dadier," Small called from behind the door, and Rick felt another twinge of panic because the principal had not used a *Mister*, as was customary, before his name. He twisted the brass doorknob and entered the room. He had not been in this room since the day of the Organizational Meeting, when Stanley had taken his new teachers to meet the principal. There were bookcases on two walls of the room, and windows on the other two walls. Small's large desk sat catty-corner in the right angle provided by the banks of windows. He sat behind the desk, and the afternoon sun struck the side of his face, illuminating the scar that curled there like a withered banana peel.

He indicated a chair before his desk, said "Sit down, Dadier," and then picked up his pen to sign something on his desk. He capped the pen without looking at Rick who had already taken the seat, shoved aside the papers, and then lifted his head.

"Now, then, Dadier," he said.

He paused and stared at Rick, and the stare was a frigid one, and Rick felt certain he would be fired, and he could only hope that Small would make it clean and quick.

"Do you like Negroes?" Small asked.

Rick blinked, surprised. "Sir?"

"Do you like Negroes?" He frowned at Rick belligerently. "Can you hear me all right, Dadier?"

"Yes. Yes, it's just . . . I . . . your question surprised me."

"Why? *Don't* you like them?"

"Yes, I do. That is, as much as I like or dislike anyone else." Rick's brow furrowed. "I . . . I don't understand, sir."

"What about Puerto Ricans? What about spics, Dadier?"

"Spics, sir?" Rick asked, immensely surprised by Small's choice of language. "*Spics?*"

"Yes, spics. Do you like them?"

"Why do you ask, sir?"

"I'll ask the questions, Dadier. Do you or don't you like spics?"

"Sir, I like them or dislike them as they are people."

"And just what does that mean, Dadier?" Small asked, his voice a little louder now.

"It means there are Puerto Ricans I like and Puerto Ricans I dislike. That's what it means, Mr. Small."

"And how many do you like as against those you dislike, Dadier?"

"I never counted, sir," Rick said, tightly respectful, but beginning to be annoyed and confused by Small's questions. Was this the customary firing procedure? All this cross-examination? And why these questions about . . .

"What about wops?"

"Wops?" Rick asked, really amazed now by Small's vocabulary. "Italians, sir?"

"You know what I mean, Dadier. What about them?"

"Is this some sort of joke, sir?" Rick asked, smiling and thinking he'd found the answer at last.

"No, damnit, it is not a joke," Small shouted, "and I'll thank you to remember that I am asking the questions and that I happen to be the principal of this high school and the man to whom you are directly responsible. Remember that, Dadier, and answer my question."

The smile dropped from Rick's face. "You . . . you want to know if I like Italians?" he asked, really puzzled now, not able to understand Small's anger. "The same applies to what I said about Puerto Ricans, sir. I judge a person by whether or not I like him, and not whether or not he's Italian or . . ."

"Don't give me any double-talk, Dadier. Don't tell me . . ."

"I'm sorry, sir, but I wasn't trying to . . ."

"Don't tell me," Small shouted, "that you like someone because you like someone. I wasn't born yesterday, Dadier."

They were both silent for a moment, Small to catch his breath, and Rick to consider a course of action.

"Sir, may I ask what this is all about?" Rick asked politely, assuming Small was driving at something, and assuming he'd done something to really irritate The Boss.

"No, you may not ask what it is all about," Small shouted. "I'll damn well tell you what it's all about when I'm good and ready, and besides you know damn well what it's all about."

"I'm afraid I don't, sir," Rick said, his teeth clenched, his hands beginning to clench and unclench.

"Tell me, Dadier, what do you think of kikes and mockies and micks and donkeys and frogs and niggers, Dadier. Niggers, isn't it, Dadier? Isn't that it?"

"I'm afraid I . . ."

"Isn't it niggers, Dadier? And spics? And krauts, Dadier? Isn't it?"

"No," Rick said angrily, "it isn't. What are you insinuating?"

"I never insinuate, Dadier. I say or I don't say, but I never hint. Did you or did you not use these derogatory terms in your classroom, did you or did you not use these expressions before your students, did you or did you not malign racial, religious and national groups, Dadier, did you or did you not?"

"I certainly did not!" Rick said, rising. "Where the devil did you . . ."

"Sit down, Dadier," Small said menacingly.

"Where'd you get all this filth?" Rick asked. "Who . . ."

"DID YOU USE THE EXPRESSION 'NIGGER' IN YOUR CLASSROOM?" Small shouted.

"Yes, I did. But only to explain . . ."

"DID YOU USE THE EXPRESSION 'SPIC'?"

"Yes, in the same lesson. To show the kids . . ."

"AND KIKE AND MOCKIE, and goddamnit, Dadier, where the hell do you come off spouting such crap at my students, in my school? Are you a goddamned Fascist? A COMMUNIST? WHAT THE HELL ARE YOU, DADIER?"

"What the hell are *you?*" Rick shouted. "A Grand Inquisitor?"

"What?" Small sputtered.

"I used those expressions to teach a lesson on democracy. I used . . ."

"Do you realize . . ."

"I used them as examples of what should not be said. I used them as negative examples, goddamnit!"

"*You did not!*" Small roared.

"Are you calling me a liar, Mr. Small," Rick asked, his voice cold white.

"I am telling you exactly what was reported to me by one of your own students, one of the boys forced to listen to your maligning talk, and I am basing my conclusions upon what that student told me and upon reports from Mr. Stanley as to the prejudiced teaching practices employed by you in your . . ."

"That's enough!" Rick shouted. "That's just about enough, Mr. Small. I've heard enough!"

"What?" Small said.

"I don't care if you're the mayor. I don't care. I don't care if you fire me right this minute, do you understand? I don't want to hear any more of that, not another word, not if it costs me my job. I don't have to listen to it, do you hear me? So just stop it, that's all. Just stop it, Mr. Small."

He was trembling now, and his face was white, and he stood before Small's desk clenching and unclenching his fists, unable to control the anger within him.

"I told you I used those expressions as negative examples. I never once, not in my classroom, and not *anywhere,* ever referred to a minority group . . ."

"This boy said you did," Small answered, his voice somewhat on the defensive now.

"Which boy?" Rick snapped.

"A boy in one of your classes."

"Who? What's his name?"

"I prefer not to divulge that," Small said, quietly pompous.

"He was lying," Rick said tightly. "He was lying, and you took his word over mine."

"Mr. Stanley substantiated . . ."

"I called on my best students whenever Mr. Stanley was observing. I can't help it if he drew the wrong conclusions. If he'd visited my second-period class, I'd have called almost exclusively on Simpson, who happens to be the brightest kid in the class, and who also happens to be a Negro."

"Gregory Miller is in your fifth-term class," Small said. "He has an I.Q. of 113. I consider that bright, Dadier. Yet Mr. Stanley visited that class four times, and you called upon Miller only once during those four visits. Why, Dadier?"

"Because Miller is a troublemaker, and I didn't want to risk trouble while being observed by the Department Chairman. Is that difficult to understand?"

"I see," Small said.

"I didn't call on Harris in my eighth-period class either, and Harris is pure white Protestant. But Harris is a goddamned troublemaker, too, and I wasn't going to put my worst foot forward while the Department Chairman was taking notes."

"I see," Small said quietly.

"Do you?"

"Yes, I see. You can understand, Dadier . . ."

"Was Miller the one who put this idea into your head? Did he make the complaint?"

"I prefer not to divulge the boy's name, Dadier."

"Why not? Don't you think I have a right to know?"

"No, I do not think so. You can understand, Dadier, that a complaint of this type demanded immediate action. I won't stand for nonsense of that sort in my school. I don't care if someone's skin is purple, Dadier, he gets taught the same as the white boy does."

"Is it policy to accuse someone before he . . ."

"Perhaps I was a bit hasty, Dadier, but you can't blame me for misinterpreting the facts, especially in the light of the complaint. A thing like that makes my blood boil, Dadier." He paused and fingered the scar on his face. "If I was wrong, I apologize." He stared at Rick fixedly.

"You were wrong, sir," Rick said, not able to resist the twisting of the knife, "but I shouldn't have lost my temper, either."

"In that case," Small said, smiling benevolently, "shall we let bygones be bygones?"

He extended his beefy palm across the desk, and Rick took it, thinking back to that time in the mess hall when Bowden had extended his hand, and thinking about how he'd felt taking Bowden's hand then, and realizing he did not feel at all like that now.

"There," Small said, "that's better. I don't like tiffs in my school family, Mr. Dadier."

Rick heard the added *Mister*, and knew that he had regained his position in the principal's esteem, or at least he felt he had.

"No, sir, Mr. Dadier, no tiffs in the school family," Small repeated.

"Yes, sir," Rick said.

"We're here to do a job, and the only way we can do it is by presenting a solid front to these kids. Isn't that right?"

"Yes, sir," Rick said, very weary now that it was all over. "I suppose so, sir."

"Well," Small said, reaching for the pile of papers on his desk again, "don't let me cut into your unassigned time, Mr. Dadier. A little relaxation is important to a teacher."

"Yes, sir," Rick said.

"And . . ." Small smiled in a fatherly manner and cocked his head to one side, ". . . let's just forget about this little incident, eh? I've already forgotten it, believe me, and I have a memory like an elephant."

"Yes, sir," Rick said, backing to the door. He opened the door, and Small waved in farewell, and then Rick closed the door gently. Miss Brady, who'd apparently heard every word of the argument, stared at Rick in wonder when he picked up his briefcase. He stared back at her until she averted her eyes, and then he walked out into the corridor, his anger returning.

That's a hell of a way to do things, he thought. Drag a man in on the carpet and accuse him of being a prejudiced sonofabitch without even having heard his side of the story. That's a dandy democratic way of handling things, all right. And why hadn't he realized Small was a meathead long before this? How could he have been so blind? Anne had been right after all. She'd pronounced

Small a very stupid man, and he was just that, and he was also principal of North Manual Trades.

Oh the sonofabitch, Rick thought. The unmitigated gall of that dictatorial sonofabitch! I should have thrown him through his own window, the way Juan Garza had tried to do with Ginzer, who must have been another goddamned meathead. What do I have to do, fight the kids *and* the teachers? Am I getting a taste of school politics? Is this why Andy Jacobson kisses his principal's ass at the elementary school where he teaches?

Oh that dirty bastard! That simple goddamned birdbrained Mongolian idiot, the principal of a high school! He couldn't be the principal on a $2.00 mortgage. I should have told him to shove his job where his hemorrhoids are. No wonder the bastard carries a scar. Some teacher probably stabbed him with a razor-sharp Delaney card.

Rick smiled at the absurdity of his own observation, a little ashamed over his I-should-have-said behavior.

He's not the real bastard, he realized suddenly. The real bastard is whoever dumped the idea into his empty head. Miller, of course. Miller. Goddamn Miller to Hell! Goddamn Miller and his tricky goddamned handsome smile! The little bastard is like a snake; every time he bites, he spreads more venom. I wish I were Max Schaefer. I'd clobber the little bastard until he couldn't do a pushup if he had four arms.

The hell with them, he thought viciously. The hell with 'em all. All but six. Save them for pallbearers, and the hell with all the rest of them.

And, of course, he knew he didn't mean this at all.

He made his way up to the second floor after glancing at his wrist watch. It was 1:40, and the seventh period began at 1:50, and he could thank William Small, protector of the minority, for having swiped his free time. It was a good thing he'd eaten his lunch during the fourth period. Suppose he'd waited until the sixth, as he frequently did? Oh, what difference did it make? He wouldn't have felt like eating anyway, not after that stomach-turning exhibition. This isn't a school, he reflected, it's a police state. We ought to wear swastikas on our arms, and we ought to give Small the upraised finger salute whenever we see him. Here's to Small, long live Small, a damned fine guy, a stupid bastard who doesn't know his brass from his oboe, a clever chap whose brains leaked out that time they stabbed him in the head. Assuming there were any brains there to begin with. Assuming he'd been stabbed and hadn't cut himself while shaving and wasn't just using a fine variation of the slobbering technique, the variation that was similar to the veteran hook. Here's to Small, who had been appropriately named by a most wise Providence, despite his physical height. Here's to small Small, and here's to Miller, the Sorcerer's Apprentice, the sonofabitch who started it all. And here's to Eagle-eye Stanley, whose observations were right on the button, who wouldn't know prejudice if it came up and hit him on the head with an African war club.

He reached the second floor and started down the corridor, and that was when he heard the din coming from Josh Edwards' room, and he forgot his own troubles immediately. He walked rapidly to Josh's room, remembering that this was the sixth period, and remembering that this was the class that'd smashed Josh's records, now liberated from their penmanship exercises in the auditorium. He remembered all this, and he rushed to the door and looked through the glass panels. Josh sat calmly at his desk, and the kids were romping all over the room, shouting, yelling at the tops of their voices. Rick rapped on one glass panel, and Josh looked at him, and then waved.

Rick motioned for him to come outside a moment, and Josh stood, smiled out at the hell-raising kids in his class, and then walked nonchalantly to the door, opening it and stepping outside.

"Hello, Rick," he said, smiling. He'd got a new pair of glasses, and they changed the appearance of his face, but the sadness in his eyes, behind the new glasses, despite the smile on his mouth, changed the appearance of his face even more.

Rick looked through the glass panels again, anxiously this time, observing the disorderly conduct of the class. "Any trouble, Josh?" he asked, concerned.

"Trouble?" Josh's eyebrows climbed onto his forehead. "No, no trouble." He glanced over his shoulder. "You mean the way the bastards are acting up? That's not trouble."

"Well, I thought . . ."

"You thought I should quiet them down, Rick? That it? I would ordinarily. Not today, pal."

"What do you mean? What's so special about today?"

"Today . . . November 24th, isn't it . . . today is a very special day, Rick. Mark the date well."

"What happened, Josh? What is it?"

"Mr. Stanley and I had a delightful little chat earlier today, Rick. Charming. Really quite touching, too, if you look at it a certain way. Tragic, almost."

"What kind of a chat?" Rick asked.

"A fairly one-sided one, I'm afraid. I did most of the talking. Do you want a blow-by-blow report, or can I sum it up for you?"

"Sum it up," Rick said.

"It can be summed up in two words, clearly and concisely. I quit."

"You *what?*"

"I quit. I tendered my resignation. I am dropping from the roll call. I'm fading into the sunset. I'm leaving. Going, going, gone. I quit."

"No. No, you didn't."

"Ah, but I did. Verily, truthfully. I did indeed quit. So, you see, I don't give a damn what these little bastards do for the next two days. I'm through then. Off for Thanksgiving, and that's the last I'll see of Manual Trades. By God, it'll be a good Thanksgiving this year."

"Look, Josh . . ."

"I really did quit, Rick, I mean it. Stanley was terribly sorry to see me go, but that's the way it is, and all that sort of crap, you know. It's the first few months that separate the men from the boys, Rick. I'm just a boy, I guess." The smile dropped from his mouth, leaving only the sadness in his eyes, and Rick remembered what he'd said about wanting to teach ever since he'd been a kid. He rested his hand on Josh's arm and said, "Look, let's talk about this a little more, okay? After school."

"Sure," Josh said, "if you want to."

"Yes, I'd like to. I'll see you after the eighth, okay?"

"Fine," Josh said, nodding. The bell sounded, hanging in the empty corridor like the strident shriek of an eagle. "There it is," Josh said. "Beginning of the seventh period. That cuts it down to one day and two periods. Then liberation."

The boys were already piling out of Josh's room, and doors were opening all along the corridor, spewing kids who joined the departmental stream.

"I'll see you later," Rick said.

He started down the corridor, and Josh stood in the doorway of his room, smiling at the moving stream, nodding his head at the boys, his eyes never joining in the fun. Like a man on a high rock overlooking a river. From behind him someplace, Rick heard the shouted word "Daddy-oh!" but he did not turn. He was thinking about Josh, and he thought about him all through the seventh and eighth periods, and he almost forgot completely about his brush with Small. And finally it was 3:25, and his day was over. He packed his briefcase, hastily window-poled the windows shut, picked up his coat, and locked the door to 206. Josh was waiting in his room across the hall.

He was sitting at his desk, leaning back in his chair, looking up at the ceiling. He did not notice Rick when he entered the room, did not turn until Rick was standing beside his desk.

"Oh, hello, boy," he said. He looked down at Rick's feet and asked, "You wearing sneakers?"

"You seemed lost," Rick said. "Didn't want to startle you."

"Nothing can startle me anymore," Josh said. "You ready to go?"

"Well, I wanted to talk a little."

"Do we have to do it here? I've got my brother's car with me. I'll drive you home, and we can talk then."

"Well, gee, that's awfully nice of you," Rick said.

"My last magnanimous gesture," Josh said. "Come, let's go. I get claustrophobia sitting here."

They punched out, and when they reached the car, Josh asked, "Are you in a hurry to get home?"

"Why?"

"Well, I thought we'd take a little ride. Westchester, maybe. Unless you're in a rush."

"No, it's okay," Rick said.

"Good."

Josh unlocked the car and then walked around to the driver's side. Rick opened the door for him, and when he'd settled himself behind the wheel, he fitted the key into the ignition and started the car. He drove uptown, and Rick leaned back against the seat cushion, his legs stretched out in front of him. They hardly spoke until Josh turned onto the Bronx River Parkway, and then Josh said, "Well?"

"Well what, Josh?"

"Say what you think, Rick."

"About your quitting?"

"Sure. Start cursing me out."

"What do you mean?"

"You know, Rick. Quitter, coward, turncoat, I don't know. All of them, I suppose. They all fit, don't they?"

"I wasn't thinking anything like that," Rick said.

"No? Well, Stanley was thinking it. I could read it in those cold eyes of his. That superior smirk, you know? The commanding officer watching the green private turn and run under fire. That's me, Rick. Running under fire."

"Stanley's a jackass," Rick said, remembering the reports the Department Chairman had given to Small.

"Admittedly. But he's not a quitter. That's the difference. A jackass commands more respect than a quitter, doesn't he?"

"If you feel that way about it," Rick said, "why are you quitting?"

"That's a good question," Josh said. "I asked myself that question a lot of times, Rick. It's a very good question."

"Well, why?"

"Why? Not the beating, Rick. Hell, what's a beating? You took the beating, too, and you're not quitting. The records? Smashing my records? No, not that either. I loved those records, but you don't live with a phonograph. So it wasn't the beating, and it wasn't the records, though both helped in my decision. It was something bigger than both, Rick." Josh smiled at his own unintentional cliché. "This is bigger than both of us, baby," he said.

"What, Josh?"

"A feeling of failure."

"Hell, Josh . . ."

"Oh, I know what you're going to say. You're going to tell me the term started in September, and it's only November now, and why don't I give it a little time? I gave myself the same argument, Rick, and I always came up with the same answer."

"And what was that?"

"That I'm no damn good. I'm not a teacher."

"Don't be silly. You . . ."

"No, it's the truth. It's not my fault, Christ knows, because I certainly want to be a teacher, you know that. But I'm not one. I'm not teaching. I'm standing up there and doing a lot of talking and waving my hands a lot, but I'm not teaching anything. Sure, the license says I'm a teacher, but the license is full of crap. You're only a teacher if somebody learns from what you say or do. Nobody is getting anything from me, believe me."

"Josh, you've hardly given it a fair chance. It's a matter of breaking through to the kids, and once you've done that . . ."

Josh turned his eyes from the road momentarily, and then shifted his attention back to driving again. "No. I'll never break through. I'm the square peg in the round hole. I could teach for fifty years, and the kids still wouldn't learn anything. I'd stand up there and pour my heart out at them, and nothing would sink in. I know there are teachers like that, but I'm not of a mind to cheat the City of New York. If they pay for a teacher, they should get one, and I sure as hell am not one."

"Josh, you're as good as I am. I haven't reached the kids yet, either. But I'm not quitting. Why should I quit? How can I ever get to them if I quit?"

"Nobody's asking you to quit," Josh said. "I'm doing it because I have to do it."

"I don't understand that," Rick said.

"You don't? Maybe it's a little difficult, Rick. Maybe you don't know me well enough. Maybe it's just my makeup, I don't know."

"Explain it to me."

"I'm disappointed, but I've been disappointed before, too, and it never seemed to matter this much. I was disappointed in the service because I expected glamour and I got drudgery. I was disappointed when I was discharged because the apple pie and coffee dream wasn't that at all. I came home to a not-too-pleasant apartment and a lot of changes, and it didn't add up to my dreams of home while I was away. But I let that disappointment ride, and I enrolled in college, and college wasn't the way I'd seen it in the movies or in *Life* magazine. I didn't steal anyone's panties, and I didn't paint a cannon blue, and I wasn't a football hero, nor did I ever steal a girl's virginity in the chemistry lab after hours. I let all these disappointments ride because I knew what I wanted to do, and I'd known it for a long time. I wanted to teach. So I studied to be a teacher. I studied hard, and I swallowed all the junk they handed out because I thought that junk would really make me a good teacher. Well, I'm not a good teacher, and this time I'm not going to ride out the disappointment. This time I'm going to be goddamned good and disappointed, and I'm going to chuck it all and do something else, and maybe I'll find a niche someplace for myself. And if I don't, the hell with it, because I'm not going to teach when I know I can't teach."

"Josh, it's the kids. It's . . ."

"Sure it's the kids, because the little sons-of-bitches

don't want to learn. But a good teacher should *make* them want to learn. There *are* good teachers in the vocational schools, Rick, you know that, don't you?"

"Well . . ."

"There are, and maybe we're surrounded by lemons, but we've got some good ones at Manual Trades, too. Do you know Sokoloff? He's really good, and a grade advisor to boot, and there's Jamison and . . ."

"Then why don't you stick with it?"

"Because I'm no goddamned good, Rick, don't you see? Rick, what's the sense of kidding myself? Could I live with myself if I did that? Could I come to school all day and fake being a teacher, fake it all the way through, just blab all day long, and then go home and look at myself in the mirror and try to think I'm not a fake. Could I do that?"

"I don't know, Josh. I suppose . . ."

"Well, I know I couldn't. So I'm running out, and that may seem cowardly to Stanley and to Small who has a scar down his face and who probably took a lot of crap climbing the ladder in the system, and it may even seem cowardly to you. For all I know, it may be cowardly. I don't feel like a coward, though, so maybe I'm not being one. I don't know."

"Can't you stick it a while longer? To the end of the term? Josh, the term is almost over."

"Rick, I knew the first week. Rick, I just knew, that's all. When I got the beating, I began thinking about it seriously, and I tried harder to get at the kids, but they weren't having any. Why? How the hell do I know? Maybe it's the system. Maybe the vocational high school stinks completely, and maybe it isn't the wonderful idea they thought it was. Except that some teachers *do* teach, and I'm not one of them. What the hell am I supposed to do, Rick? Take a complaint back to my college? Tell them, 'Look, you stupid bastards, you didn't teach me how to teach! What have you got to say for yourselves?' Hell, are they to blame? They went to college, too, and someone who'd never learned to teach taught them how to teach me so that I never learned to teach. What came first, the chicken or the egg?"

"If you'd only give it a chance," Rick persisted. "Come on, Josh, don't throw it over so soon."

"Soon? I should have chucked it the first week. I should have chucked it the day my records were smashed. A real teacher never gets into a setup like that, Rick. Never."

"Real teachers . . ."

"They don't, Rick. The kids respect them. Me? They've got no respect for me, but that's because I'm not a teacher. Rick, I can be a fake teacher or a real man, and I think I'd rather be a real man right now."

"But all your training, all the years . . ."

Josh smiled wistfully. "All the years," he said, "the training, and the years before that when I just wanted. All those years. So, they go down the drain, Rick. But at least I don't go down the drain with them. Isn't that important, Rick? That I don't go down the drain? That I keep some self-respect? That I leave a job when I know I'm not doing it well? Is that being a coward?"

"No," Rick said seriously, "it's not."

"All right. So that's what I'm doing."

They drove on in silence, passing *Thwaite's* on the parkway, the evening shadows lengthening across the winding road. Josh held the wheel tightly, and Rick relaxed on the seat beside him, thinking of what he'd said, wondering if he should quit, too. No, he could never quit, not now anyway. Not until he knew for sure. And once he knew, then what? Would he hang onto the security? Would he have a kid then, two kids? Would he keep the job even if he learned he wasn't a teacher?

"I think we'd better start back," Josh said.

"Sure," Rick answered.

Josh pulled to the side of the road and waited for a car to pass. There was no heater in the car, and their breaths fogged the windshield, and Josh reached over to clear it with a gloved hand before making his U-turn.

"Am I doing the right thing, Rick?" he asked.

"I don't know, Josh. If you feel right about it, I guess it's right."

"That's what *I* figured," Josh said.

"But what will you do now?"

Josh was silent for a few seconds, and his voice sounded uncertain when he spoke again, almost sad. "I don't know. Get another job, I suppose. A bank teller, or something. I'm a college grad, Rick, lots of jobs for college grads."

"Sure," Rick said.

They drove to the project, and Rick glanced at his watch and saw how late it was. He hadn't called Anne, and he knew she'd be worried, especially after that night long ago. He got out of the car hastily, and then leaned over when Josh opened the window.

"So you've got one more day," Rick said.

"Yes."

He had a sudden feeling that he would not see much of Josh tomorrow, and so he took off his glove and held out his hand, and when Josh took it, he said, "Lots of luck, boy."

"Thanks, Rick," Josh said.

He retrieved his hand and rolled up the window, and Rick saw his troubled face behind the breath-fogged glass. It was the last good look he would have of Josh Edwards because tomorrow would be a busy day for Josh, and he would only get a chance to talk to him briefly in the teachers' lavatory before Josh passed out of his life completely. So he looked at Josh's face, and then Josh turned the car out into the stream of traffic and Rick watched until the car was out of sight, and then he walked to the entrance door of his building.

There were three notes, and she had placed them on the kitchen table, and she stared down at them for a long time, thinking perhaps they would change, thinking perhaps they weren't so, and concentration would change them.

The first note had come a long time ago, and the first note had said WATCH RICHARD. THERE'S ANOTHER WOMAN! and she had held that note in trembling fingers, standing in the lobby of the building with the sun streaming through the windows over the radiators. She had stared at the neat typescript, and then looked at the envelope again, finding nothing but a Bronx postmark smudged over a picture of George Washington. She had finally slipped the note back into its envelope and buried it at the bottom of her purse.

It had rested there like a hot coal, singeing her memory at irregular intervals while she shopped.

WATCH RICHARD. THERE'S ANOTHER WOMAN!

Boldly shrieking its message in upper case. Firm black letters on a white page.

She had thought about it all that day, wondering first who had sent it, and then wondering why it had been sent. She was not simple-minded, nor was she old-fashioned, but the mysterious informant could not have chosen a better subject than Anne Dadier. For Anne was the type of person who felt uneasy all day long if the phone rang and then stopped ringing before she had a chance to answer it. When she'd been sixteen, a prankster began sending her *Secret Pal* cards, and she received them regularly, starting with one on Hallowe'en, a card which wished her all the deviltry and merriment befitting the occasion, a card which boasted a printed inkblot over the alleged signature, a card that finally signed itself "Your Secret Pal." Another had come on Christmas, and then one arrived for no occasion at all, one which just inquired about her health, letting her know her Secret Pal had not forgotten her. On St. Valentine's Day, her Secret Pal had still not forgotten her, and by this time the receipt of a new card filled her with terror, even though the cards were innocently innocuous. The last card she received was on her birthday. She did not know it would be the last card, and she had almost begun crying when she opened the envelope and recognized the familiar format. She couldn't understand how anyone could be so mean, how anyone could cause her so much torment, even on her birthday, which should have been a happy day, and which was spoiled by receipt of the probably well-meaning card.

Not knowing it was the last card, she had waited for the next one to arrive, dreading any envelope which bore her name. But her Secret Pal had apparently lost interest, most likely because Anne had never mentioned the cards to anyone. There was no sport in mystery cards unless the recipient fervently sought to discover the identity of the sender. The flow of mysterious correspondence ended, and Anne grew older and perhaps wiser—until this note.

She did not for a moment attribute any truth to the message. There was not another woman, and there was no reason to watch Rick. *Richard,* as the informant had called him. Richard, which probably indicated that the informant didn't know Rick very well, or at least did not know him well enough to call him by the name everyone else used.

Watch Richard, indeed. And shall I begin searching his shirts for lipstick stains? Shall I search his pockets? Shall I test his virility, his . . . well, I can't very well do that, not at this stage of the game.

The note remained in the bottom of her purse, but it smoldered there like the hot coal it was, and she thought about it further, and she wondered WHO? and she wondered WHY? and she found herself thinking that maybe, but that was ridiculous, yet just maybe, no Rick would never, but perhaps, possibly, maybe, who knows, maybe there was just a smidgin, just a tiny bit, just an infinitesimal bit of truth . . . no, there wasn't.

Yet why would anyone.

No, there wasn't.

Still, why would anyone send a note, a malicious thing like that unless . . .

That's all it is, just a malicious thing, just someone who wants to cause trouble, that's all. But who? And why?

To cause trouble, that's all. That's why.

But WHO? WHO?

And *why*, her mind persisted, unless there was some truth to it, oh maybe not a lot of truth, but maybe just a little truth, maybe someone saw something that could be misconstrued, or maybe Rick had been a little indiscreet once, or maybe even twice, and he couldn't very well be blamed for that, not the way things were now, and you could certainly forgive a man for that, I suppose, you could forgive a man if you really loved him, and if there were any truth to the silly note at all, which there wasn't.

No, he could not be blamed, if the note were true, because he definitely did not have an attractive, provocative wife to come home to these days, and Lord knows there are plenty of attractive, provocative women running around all over the place, without bulging bellies and without complaints about backaches. I must stop complaining about backaches.

He *could* be blamed, if you wanted to look at it another way, and if there was any truth at all in that stupid note, he could be blamed, but I'm not blaming him if it's true, and I certainly won't make an issue of it, but goddamnit, why didn't whoever sent the note just shut up about it, I mean who cares? I mean who wants to know about such a thing, not now certainly, not now when I don't even *feel* like a woman. God, how could I hold him now if such a thing were true, if that note were telling the truth, how could I hold him when I don't look like a woman, don't act like a woman, don't even FEEL like a woman. I'm just some sort of growing parasite, just a big blob of, of protoplasm, a nothing, a thing, he could be blamed for not standing by now, of all times, he could be blamed, but I won't blame him if there is another woman, the way the note says, provided the other woman is just a temporary thing, provided she's another woman only as long as I'm *not* a woman.

But I can't believe it, she thought, not Rick.

Although in my fifth month he did dance a lot with Helen that night of the alumni gathering, though he was a bit high that night, and God knows I didn't feel very much like dancing, still he did dance with her a lot, and she seemed to be enjoying it immensely, but she's probably to blame there and not him, if a man feels like dancing and his wife just feels like vegetating. Still she seemed to be enjoying it a good deal more than she should have been, I've never really liked Helen anyway, and I don't remember if Rick enjoyed it or not, he was drinking, anyway, no, not Rick, and especially not now. Rick is, well yes he is, Rick is honorable.

But, damnit, why would anyone send me a note like that? Oh damnit, why would anyone have to do that?

Now start crying, sissy, that's all we need, right here on the street, go ahead, start crying like a damned fool over a stupid note which was maliciously sent and which doesn't mean a damned thing, and which can't be true, which certainly cannot be true.

She didn't start crying, nor did she forget the smoldering coal which was the note. Nor did she mention it to Rick.

The second note came a week later. She fished it out of the mailbox, and when she saw the neatly typed MRS. RICHARD DADIER, she felt a twinge of panic, felt the same dread she'd experienced a long while ago when her Secret Pal was at work. Only this was a Secret Enemy, and she studied the flap of the envelope and found no return address, and she knew this would be another note, and she was tempted to throw it away without opening it. But she did open it, and when she'd unfolded the sheet of white paper, she looked at the neatly centered, neatly typed message, and it read:

AT SCHOOL
ALL DAY, EVERY DAY

That was all, just that, but it started a new train of thought. She had never considered this before, never visualized the school itself as a trysting place. She always looked upon it as a place of labor, but now she began remembering stories about places of labor, stories about men and their secretaries, and she also began remembering Rick's part in an attempted rape long ago, and she began thinking about the woman who had provoked that rape, and Lois Hammond began taking shape in her mind.

She put her out of her mind, and she told herself this was all nonsense and probably a joke one of their friends was playing, but she could not think of any of their friends who would indulge in such morbid humor when she was in her ninth month. She toyed with the idea of Rick himself sending the notes, building to some kind of misunderstood surprise, the kind of surprise where he could say, "Why sure there's another woman! The baby, honey! It's going to be a girl, don't you know?" But Rick wanted a boy, and he wouldn't joke about something he wanted, and he wouldn't make a joke like that anyway when she was in her ninth month, and besides the second note wouldn't make any sense if that were the explanation, unless the surprise he'd planned was too intricate for her to comprehend, but still he wouldn't make a joke like that, not Rick.

Nor would Rick play around with another woman.

Unless the other woman were at fault, the way Helen had been that night at the alumni gathering, in which case you couldn't do anything but hope your man was strong enough to resist, and Rick was that, if nothing else, though he hadn't resisted very damned hard that night with Helen. Dancing is only dancing, though, for God's sake. Let's not make a federal case out of a few waltzes. And a few fox trots. And a few polkas and even a few lindys, even though he doesn't like to lindy, he lindied that night, but he was high remember.

AT SCHOOL. ALL DAY, EVERY DAY the note said, all in nice, simple language, but after all what *could* a man do at school, all day, every day, even every other day? There wasn't even a co-ed teachers' lunchroom, unless Rick were lying about the talks with Solly Klein and Lou Savoldi and all the other men teachers, and all his other time was occupied with classes and duty periods and whatnot. Of course, no one said you *had* to eat in the teachers' lunchroom. Oh, nonsense! Picture Rick in some quiet, out of the way place, holding hands with that Hammond woman. I don't even know what she looks like.

And I'm sure Rick doesn't either.

And I can't see him holding hands with her. And even if he were holding hands, what's so terrible about that?

Well, maybe it is terrible. After all, there's nothing wrong with my *hands*. You can sell the rest of me for scrap, but there's nothing wrong with my hands, or has it gone farther than hands, and if that's the case I'm out of the competition. What *does* Lois Hammond look like? What does the other woman usually look like?

A slinky bitch (you mustn't call her bitch, you don't even know the girl), a slinky bitch in a slinky black nightgown with a cigarette holder in her long, tapering fingers. That's the way it is in the *Ladies' Home Journal* serials. Her kisses are like . . .

Stop it, just stop it. You're hanging him without even telling him about the notes, without even discussing it with him, and you've always discussed everything else in your married life together, everything, even when you had to ask him what to do, because you didn't know what to do, not with your hands and not with anything, even though the anything was worth something then and not worth a damn now. Well, you *did* discuss it, and it was harder to discuss that, surely, than it would be to discuss these stupid notes. And you've leapt from hand-holding to kissing to God knows in the space of three minutes. And you know what to do with your hands now, that's a cinch.

And that makes me competition for a slinky bitch in a slinky black nightgown (and stop calling her bitch because you don't even know her and she's probably a girl who goes to church every Sunday—Helen goes to church every Sunday, too—and who wouldn't want your husband if you offered him on a silver platter), and besides there is no truth whatever to these damned silly notes, and I think I'll burn them.

She did not burn them.

She sat now in the kitchen of her housing project apartment, and she stared at the kitchen clock on the beige wall (the walls you were not allowed to paint or paper unless you wanted to lose the deposit you placed with the Authority when you took the apartment), and the notes were before her on the kitchen table, three notes now, and the third note read:

LOIS HAMMOND

And the clock read 8:22.

And Rick was usually home at 4:30, the latest.

But the clock read 8:22, and the notes read WATCH RICHARD. THERE'S ANOTHER WOMAN. AT SCHOOL. ALL DAY, EVERY DAY. LOIS HAMMOND. And she couldn't change what the notes read, nor could she change what the clock read, and she was dangerously close to tears, but she did not cry.

She looked at the notes again, and then she looked at the clock again, and she vowed to discuss it with him that night, because if it were true, she wanted to know, and if it were not true, she wanted Rick to know. She vowed to discuss it, and she picked up the notes tenderly, as if they were old friends, and she put them into their individual envelopes, and then she put the three envelopes into the bottom of her purse, under the disorderly array of junk she kept there.

She went into the living room where she could not watch the clock, and she turned on the radio, annoyed when an announcer gave her the time.

She was not frightened this time. She did not for a moment believe that Rick had met with another ambush. She did not know what to think, and she tried not to think that he was with Lois Hammond, but she could not forget the notes, and she did think he was with Lois Hammond, and that was why she wanted to discuss it with him, because it would certainly be better to bring this thing out into the open. She cursed the note sender again, thinking it would be better if she'd never known, and the notes ate at her mind, ate there like a disease, gnawed and ate until the disease showed on her face and in the clasping and unclasping of her hands in her lap.

He came into the apartment at 8:40.

She heard his key in the lock, and she bit her lip and stayed where she was in the living room, until she realized it would look strange, her not going to the door. She rose too hastily then, awkwardly, almost slipping, and

cursing the mountain of flesh which she partially blamed
for Rick's behavior, if the notes were true. She rushed
into the foyer, hoping all this didn't show on her face.

He was closing the door, and then he turned and she
went to him and kissed him tenderly, but he didn't seem
terribly interested. His face was very tired and somehow
sad looking, but she'd got used to sad faces when he
came home, faces that reflected the trouble he'd had
with the kids all day long.

"How was it today?" she asked, trying to keep her
voice light, but realizing at the same time that she had
made no mention of his coming in at 8:40, and wondering if she shouldn't make some mention because that
would be the normal thing to do.

"Lousy," Rick said. He shrugged out of his coat and
dropped it onto the sofa. "I had a fight with Small."

"Rick, you didn't!"

"Yes, I did," he said. "And Josh is quitting and . . . oh
the whole goddamned setup stinks!"

"What did you fight about?" she asked, momentarily
forgetting her resolve to discuss the notes with him,
feeling that this was important, too, and if she had nothing else to offer him she could certainly offer sympathy
and understanding.

Rick cupped the bridge of his nose with one hand,
and sighed heavily. "Oh, we fought," he said. "What difference does it make?"

"Well . . ." She paused, wondering if he hadn't
already discussed this with someone, wondering if that
someone weren't Lois Hammond. "I meant . . . don't
you *want* to talk about it, Rick?"

"He said I'd been intolerant in my classroom. He said . . ."

"What!"

"Honey, please don't have me repeat everything a dozen times. I'm . . ."

"I'm sorry, Rick. I just . . ."

"I'm tired, and it only makes me more tired to have to remember what that bastard . . ."

"If you don't want to talk about it . . ."

"I didn't say I didn't want to talk about it. Anne, for God's sake . . ."

"I'm sorry, Rick," she said.

They were both silent for a moment, and then Rick sighed again.

"Someone made a complaint to him. You remember that little lecture I gave? My bright idea? Well, someone misconstrued it. Accidentally on purpose."

"Who?"

"He wouldn't tell me."

"Miller?"

"He wouldn't tell me, Anne," Rick said, trying to hide his exasperation, but not succeeding.

"How did it happen? I mean . . ."

"Stanley told me Small wanted to see me. I went down to his office and he started throwing rocks. 'Did you use the expression nigger in your classroom?'" Rick mimicked. "'Did you use the expression kike and mockie?'" He slammed a clenched fist into the open palm of his other hand. "Oh, the hell with him!" he said. "The hell with them all."

"What did *you* say, Rick?"

"I told him he was wrong. I told him . . . what difference does it make, Anne? We kissed and made up, but
he's still a sonofabitch!"

Anne nodded, troubled by what Rick had told her,
and then abruptly remembering the notes again.

"Have you . . . have you had supper yet?" she asked.

"No," he said. "Where would I have supper?"

"I don't know. I just thought . . . well, it's rather late. I
thought . . ."

"Oh. Josh and I went for a ride."

"Oh."

"Did I tell you he's quitting?"

"Yes. Yes, you did."

"Well, he is. He told me this afternoon, right after my
wrestling match with Small. I thought I might be able to
talk him out of it, so we went for a ride in his car."

"You and Josh?"

"Yes, me and Josh. Anne, what's wrong with you? I
just told you it was Josh and me, and now you ask . . ."

"I'm sorry, it's . . . the chops got overdone waiting for
you, and now everything is cold. I just . . ."

"Oh, the hell with supper. I'm not hungry, anyway."

She stood there awkwardly, wondering whether he
had already eaten, afraid to ask him again, afraid
because she loved him terribly and did not want to lose
him, and afraid he would tell her the truth, and then she
would know everything, and she would be forced to
fight back, having none of the weapons a woman must
use against another woman.

"Should I . . . some eggs, maybe? Or a cup of coffee?"

"Coffee," Rick said.

She went into the kitchen and started getting the coffee ready, thinking, *I'll talk to him about the notes when I go back into the living room. I'll do it then.* She puttered with the coffee pot for a long time, not admitting to herself that she was stalling, and then she dried the palms of her hands on her skirt and walked into the living room. Rick was sitting at one end of the couch, his head resting on his cupped hand. He did not look up when she entered the room.

"Rick," she started, hoping her voice was not trembling.

"Coffee ready?" he asked.

"No, not yet. Rick . . ." She didn't know how to say it because she'd never done anything like this before. How do you accuse your husband of infidelity? Or do you accuse him? Maybe she should just casually mention the notes, just casually say, "Oh, Rick, I meant to tell you about these silly little notes I've been getting, someone's idea of a joke, I guess." Except it wasn't a joke to her, and she couldn't joke about them, not if she tried with all her being. She realized that she was standing there after having started to say something, and she frowned, and Rick asked, "What is it, hon?"

"You're . . . you're awfully late," she said.

"Yeah, we got to talking. Josh and I."

"Did you drive very far?"

"Upstate a little ways. Westchester. Not too far."

"Oh." She paused, biting her lip. *Now,* she thought. *Now is the time.* "Are you sure . . ."

"He's quitting, you know. I couldn't change his mind, and maybe he has the right idea, after all. Why bang your head against the wall?"

"Yes," she said. "Rick . . ."

"Yes?"

I can't do it, she thought. *I can't just come out and* . . .

"Are you sorry he's leaving? Josh, I mean?" she said lamely.

"Yes, I am. I like him, Anne. He's a hell of a nice guy, and . . ."

"But there are other teachers, aren't there? Others you like?"

"I suppose so. Josh and I, though . . ."

"Teachers you can talk to, I mean. You know."

Rick shrugged. "I talk to them all. They're all right. But Josh is most like me, I think. A new teacher, a guy who wanted to teach . . . you know what I mean, Anne?"

"Yes. Yes, of course." She was extremely nervous now because she was leading gradually to what she wanted to really talk about, and she hoped Rick didn't suspect. "Solly Klein, do you talk to him much?"

"When Solly's talking," Rick said, "it's pretty difficult to get a word in. We talk, though. Sure, we do."

"And the others? George Katz? And Savoldi? And Manners?" She paused. "And Lois Hammond?" She swallowed hard and watched him, her hands clenched.

"Sure, all of them," Rick said. "But I'll still miss Josh."

"I see." She paused again. "I don't suppose you get much chance to talk to Lois Hammond. I mean, there are no women in the lunchroom are there?"

"No. But I see her around. You know, in the halls, here and there. The school isn't very big."

"I suppose not."

"Honey, maybe I can eat something after all. Are those chops burned or what?"

"No, but they're pretty dried out, I think. Shall I heat them?"

"Would you?"

"Sure. Shall I heat the spinach, too?"

"If you will. Honey, you don't mind if I just sit here, do you? I'm really bushed."

"That's all right," she said. She went into the kitchen again and put the chops into the double boiler, not wanting them to get any drier than they already were. She put a flame under the spinach, and then called from the stove, "Does Miss Hammond know Josh is quitting?"

"What?" Rick called back.

"Miss Hammond. Does she know about . . ."

"Oh. I don't know."

"Didn't he tell her?"

"I don't know, hon."

She stood at the stove, her back to the foyer and the living room. "Did . . . did you tell her, Rick?"

"Me? Why, no. Why should I?"

"I . . . I thought you might have run into her, you know. In the halls, here and there."

"No, I didn't tell her," Rick said, and Anne suddenly wished she was in the living room, where she could see his face.

"Is she very pretty, Rick?"

"Who?"

"Lois Hammond."

"I suppose so. If you go for that type."

"What type?"

"Dark. Busty."

"She's dark?"

"Yes."

"And . . . busty?"

"Very."

"Oh."

She took a tablespoon from one of the cabinet drawers and began stirring the spinach so it wouldn't stick to the bottom of the pot.

"I like blondes," Rick said from the living room, and again she wished she was there to see his face.

"Do you now?" she asked, trying to make her voice sound light.

"Indeed I do. And your bust is fine, thank you."

"Thank *you,*" she said, automatically smiling.

"Don't thank me," Rick said. "I had nothing to do with it."

"You had a lot to do with the rest of my figure," Anne said. *I'm being unfair,* she thought. *I'm using the home and family hook. I'm trying to keep him that way. I'm giving him a motherhood idol to worship. Damnit, why can't I keep him as a woman?*

He was suddenly behind her, his arms encircling her waist. He'd entered the kitchen so softly that she hadn't heard him, and she wondered for a moment if she'd thought out loud. His hands rested lightly on her stomach, and he said, "You do have a bit of a pot, don't you?"

"A bit," she said lightly. "But only so you'll appreciate me more afterward."

"I appreciate you right now," he said.

"Well, you don't sound like it," she answered, busying herself with the spinach.

He spun her around, holding her by the shoulders. "What kind of talk is that?" he asked, smiling.

"Snapping like a . . . like a turtle or something the minute you come in the house," she said, pouting prettily.

"Did I snap?"

"Yes, you did."

"I apologize," he said. He kissed her on the tip of her nose. "There."

"Is that the best you can do?"

"I wasn't half trying," he said, still smiling.

"Well, half-try."

He pulled her closer to him and kissed her on the mouth this time, lingeringly. She felt his mouth on hers, and she clung to him tightly, thinking, *The notes are crazy, this is my Rick, he was with Josh, the notes are crazy.* And then she pulled her lips away and pressed her cheek to his tightly, her arms moving up around his neck, her fingers spreading, holding him close.

"Hey!" he said, surprised.

"Do you love me, Rick?" she asked, her lips close to his neck.

"Why, of course I love you."

"No, I don't mean 'of course,' darling. I know 'of course.' I mean . . ." She shook her head, her cheek still against his, not knowing what she meant. "I mean, do you *love* me, Rick?"

"Yes, darling."

"Even though I look like a horse?"

"You do not look like a horse."

"I do, Rick, really, darling, please don't deny it. But do you love me anyway?"

"Honey, what's got into you. Of course, I . . ."

"No, Rick, please don't say 'of course.' Just tell me you love me, darling. Just hold me close and tell me you love me."

"Honey, honey," he said, stroking her hair, closing his eyes, smiling. "Honey, I love you more than anything in this world."

"Really, Rick?"

"Of . . ." He cut himself short. "I love you, Anne," he said gently.

"I love you, too, Rick. I mean, I'm really crazy about you, Rick. Does that sound too high school girlish?"

"No, darling."

"I can't help it if it does, because that's the way I feel. I'm just crazy in love with you, Rick. That's why when you come home and snap at me, I think . . ."

"I didn't mean to snap at you, hon. It was just Small, and then Josh, and I guess I *was* hungry, in spite of . . ."

"I know, but I begin thinking all sorts of things, Rick, and I don't want to think those things. Darling, hold me. Please hold me very close."

He tightened his arms around her, and she clung to him desperately.

"Rick," she said, "Rick, Rick."

He kissed her again, and she thought, *I was silly, everything is all right, he likes blondes, and I'm as busty as most, everything is all right, and I'll burn those damn silly notes, I'll really burn them this time, oh Rick, I love you so much.*

"I think the spinach is burning," he said.

"Oh, my goodness!" She tore herself from him and turned off the gas, and then she began setting the table. He sat at the table and watched her, not helping because he was tired, and she didn't mind his not helping at all. They began talking about other things, not the school, and not Small, and not Josh. Things about family, and friends outside the school.

And while they talked, she thought about the notes again, and she realized she hadn't discussed the notes with him, hadn't even come near discussing the notes. She told herself it didn't matter because she knew Rick loved her now, but she couldn't forget the notes in spite of what she told herself. And so she thought of Lois Hammond again, dark and busty and there at Manual Trades all day long, and she condemned herself for not discussing the notes when she should have, but she listened to him talk and she nodded and she smiled and she thought, *How could I have doubted him,* doubting him all the while.

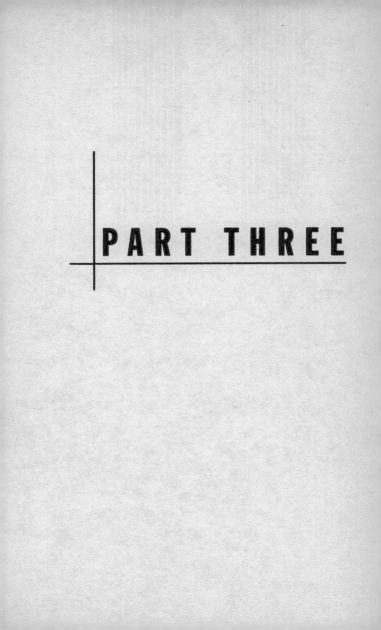

PART THREE

PART THREE

11

William Small, in his own words, and through his own voluntary admission, had "the memory of an elephant." And since William Small had fondly clasped the hand of Richard Dadier in a warm let's-forget-it-all handshake, he could not really be blamed for the persistence of his memory, or for the unconscious power it held over his alleged mind.

That memory, elephantine as it was, could not ignore the fact that Richard Dadier, a snotnose barely out of college, had in effect told Small to shut up. In reality, he had simply shouted, "That's enough!" but this was the equivalent of "Shut up" and snotnoses barely out of college don't go around telling principals to shut up, not when principals have memories as enduring as that of William Small's.

So when the yearly chore of producing the Christmas Assembly rolled around, a task which any teacher at North Manual Trades would have happily shirked, Small was not to be condemned for choosing Richard Dadier as the man best suited for the job. Did he not have Stanley's word that Dadier had done a lot of college dramatics, could indeed reel off obscure passages of Shakespeare at the drop of a leek?

And was not Dadier a young man, and did not students respond most eagerly to teachers who were not too far removed from them in age? Especially in something like a Christmas Assembly, where brotherhood prevailed?

This is what William Small told himself. This is what William Small told Stanley. And this is what Stanley told Rick at a meeting in the English Office. It is doubtful that Small ever realized the important role his memory played in deciding to choose Rick as the unlucky producer. For in truth, Small had completely forgotten the incident in his office, had forgotten that a snotnose barely out of college had told him, William Small, to shut up. Nor did William Small have an analyst with whom he could discuss that tricky dog of a memory. He was just a hard-working slob, William Small was, and Richard Dadier was obviously the best man for this particular dirty detail, and so Rick inherited it and—simple soul that he was—considered it a plum rather than a crumb.

Of course, Small could have relieved Rick from his third-period Hall Patrol, or even from one or two of his classes, was he of a mind to be magnanimous. He was not of a mind to be that, and so Rick carried a full program, and he was left to his own devious means in the matter of the Christmas Assembly. These devious means meant that he would have to devote his Unassigned sixth to the preparation of the assembly, as well as a good many after-school hours. Considering the fact that he would never even get to see the results of his labor, a fact of which he was not aware during his feverish preparation for the event, a more suitable punishment could not have been contrived—even if Small had consciously remembered Rick's outburst, which he hadn't.

Rick was truly happy about the job, and he got to work at once. He knew he could use the mimeograph in *The Trades Trumpet* office whenever he wanted to, whereas he might have to wait for a free opportunity to use the one in the English Office. However, he waited for that opportunity, rather than willingly bring himself into Lois Hammond's presence. He ran off notices for every teacher in the high school, notices which heralded the approaching assembly and announced that a search for talent was on. Any interested students could contact Mr. Dadier at once. After the notices had been distributed and, he hoped, read to the classes, he then spoke to the teachers he knew, asking them to plug the assembly and generate some sort of interest among the boys. He needed talent badly. As a matter of fact, he would settle for no talent, just so long as he got some boys to turn out. Without the boys, he couldn't very well put on a show, and he wanted very badly to put on a decent show.

He spoke to all his classes about the assembly, and at night—forsaking his lesson plans—he wrote a show. It was not intended for Broadway or Brooks Atkinson. It was intended for the enjoyment of the students and teachers of North Manual Trades High School. As such, it wasn't a bad little thing. It dealt with Santa's visit to North Manual Trades, accompanied by a host of angels.

Rick didn't know where the angels logically entered into the show, but he figured he'd get some of the senior boys into sheets and halos, and the costumes alone should be good for a laugh. He broached Solly Klein on the possibility of his playing Santa Claus, but Solly flatly refused.

He had to soft-pedal the play because the tendency to write what he really thought was overwhelming. He had Santa visiting various classes throughout the school, always accompanied by the angels of course, and finally deciding that North Manual Trades was a damned fine school, and leaving presents all over the place. The presents varied from the strictly cornball (like "And for all of you, all of you wonderful kids, a high school diploma, and the wish that you'll use it wisely and well") to the humorous (like "And to Mr. Clancy, of Carpentry and Woodworking, a great, big economy-size box of bonbons!"). He'd have liked to do a real satire, but he knew Small would be present at the assembly, and it wasn't nice to stab a man on the Wednesday before Christmas. So he portrayed the school as an earnest beehive of learning and activity, portrayed the kids as wonderful little adolescents who wanted to learn a trade, portrayed the teachers as part of the "little family" Small thought existed.

He told his classes about the show as soon as he'd completed writing it, hoping he'd get additional interest that way. His notices had brought paltry results. Aside from a handful of kids who'd have turned out for anything from a chess competition to a discussion of nuclear energy—and there were such kids at Manual Trades—he had nothing to work with. And so he plugged harder in every one of his classes, and he rode the teachers harder, and he told Solly Klein that if he wouldn't be Santa Claus, he could at least see that some of his kids turned out for the show.

His first break came when George Katz volunteered for the Santa Claus role. Rick accepted his services gratefully, and gave him a carbon copy of the script. The Santa Claus role was, naturally, the most difficult one in the show, and Rick had planned it with a teacher in mind all along. Katz's arrival was a godsend, and when Katz came to the teachers' lunchroom the next day and announced that he'd memorized the part overnight, Rick could have kissed him.

The second break came in 55–206, and that was a real surprise. It came from Miller.

The boy remained in class after most of the other boys had left, and then he walked to the front of the room and stood near Rick's desk. Rick was inking in the absences on his Delaney cards, and he looked up, saw Miller there, and asked, "What is it, Miller?"

"Got a few minutes, Chief?" Miller asked.

"What is it, Miller?" Rick asked again, annoyed. He still felt that Miller was the boy who'd complained to Small, and he had still not forgotten that day in the principal's office.

"I was thinkin' 'bout your Christmas 'sembly, Mr. Dadier," Miller said.

"What about it?"

"Well, them angels you tole us about in class. 'Member?"

"I remember."

Miller shifted his feet, and succeeded in looking very embarrassed. "They got a lot of lines to say? I mean, will they be a lot of memorizin' to do?"

"No, not too much," Rick said. He looked at Miller curiously. "Why do you ask?"

"Well, I had a idea, Mr. Dadier. You sure you got a few minutes?"

"Yes, yes. Go ahead."

"Whutchoo think of the idea of colored angels?"

Rick looked at Miller warily. "Colored angels?" he asked slowly.

Miller seemed to be just as wary of Rick. He looked at him levelly and said, "Black fellers. You know?"

"Well, what do you mean?"

"I figured maybe they'd look kind of . . . well . . . I figured it'd maybe be good for a few laughs, you know? Like four or five of us in them white sheets, with halos. You follow me, Mr. Dadier?"

"Yes, Miller," Rick said, surprised, wondering what was up the boy's sleeve.

"You want the angels for laughs, don'tchoo? You said you was gonna get seniors, if you could, 'cause they big." Miller smiled engagingly. "I got some friends, Mr. Dadier, an' they not ony big, they black."

"I . . . I don't know," Rick said, undecided, wondering whether the idea would work or not, seeing it in his mind's eye, and visualizing it as being good pictorially, but not wanting anyone to think he was poking fun at the Negro.

"These friends of mine," Miller went on, really trying to sell the idea now, "they got talent. They sort of sing aroun', you know, and maybe they could do a Christmus carol, if you wanted. They good on 'Silunt Night,' and they know 'God Rest Ye' an' all the others. They good, I mean it." Miller paused, seemingly more embarrassed, and then asked, "You . . . you was plannin' on colored boys in the show, wunt you?"

"Yes, yes, of course," Rick said. "I just don't know . . ."

"I think it might be good," Miller said softly, lowering his head, apparently feeling his idea had not met with Rick's approval.

"Would . . . would your friends be willing to work hard, Miller?"

"Oh, sure," Miller said, a spark returning to his eyes.

"After school?"

"Well, I don' know 'bout that. I mean, most of these fellers got jobs after school. But we'll come any time durin' school, I mean on our lunch hours or any time. An' we all know each other outside, so we could go over the stuff at night, you know? On our own time, I mean. I mean, if you like the idea."

Rick hesitated and then said, "How do you think the other . . . colored boys would react to it? The ones in the audience." He looked at Miller cautiously, surprised to find himself discussing the topic with the boy, and yet glad he was. "You see . . ."

"You mean you think somebody goan take offense?" Miller smiled confidently. "Naw, you got no worries there. They'll jus' think it's a big laugh, tha's all."

"I don't know," Rick said, really not knowing.

"Mr. Dadier," Miller said, possessed of a sudden idea, "you know *Green Pastures?*"

"Why, yes," Rick said, surprised that Miller was familiar with the play.

"They colored angels in that one, Mr. Dadier. They
even a colored God, and nobody took offense there, did
they? They did that play up at the Y in Harlem, and
everybody watchin' was colored, and nobody got mad
about it. It'll be all right, you'll see."

"Yes," Rick said, nodding his head, "maybe it would.
Look, Miller, let me check this with Mr. Small today. If
he likes the idea . . . well, you see, I don't want to offend
anyone. If he likes it, you can tell your friends okay." He
paused and tried a smile. "I hope, Miller, that . . . that
you were planning on coming out for the show, too."

"Why, sure I was," Miller said, surprised. "Hell, man,
I'm the bass in the group."

"Well, good," Rick said. "I'll let you know in class
tomorrow, Miller."

Rick checked with Mr. Small that afternoon, and
Small was in favor of the idea. He was especially pleased
that the idea had come from one of the students, and
when Rick had left him he congratulated himself upon
having made an excellent choice for the producer of the
all-important Christmas Assembly. At the end of the
fifth period the next day, Rick passed the information on
to Miller. He asked the boy to wait after class, and he
was annoyed when West waited with him.

"I want to talk to Miller alone," he said to West.
"Would you mind waiting outside?"

West shot Rick a disgusted glance and then walked to
the doorway, lounging against the door jamb.

"I spoke to Mr. Small, Miller," Rick said, keeping his

voice low so that West would not hear the conversation. "He thinks it'll be fine."

"Tha's good," Miller said, smiling and nodding. "I'll tell the boys. When do we start?"

"Well, can you get me a copy of the boys' programs, so I can arrange some sort of schedule? We'll probably rehearse Santa and the angels separately in the beginning. Maybe later we can work out something about night rehearsals."

"I'll get the programs," Miller said. He started for the door, turned, and added, "An' thanks, Mr. Dadier."

West, standing in the doorway, said, "What're you doin', Greg, suckin' up?"

The two boys passed out into the corridor, and Rick did not hear Miller's answer. He stared at the empty door frame for a long time, wondering why Miller had volunteered for the show, wondering if he weren't making a mistake. Was Miller plotting some trick? If Miller had been the one who'd complained to Small, couldn't this be some sort of extension of his complaint? Was it possible he'd try to foul up the show, try to present the Negro in a bad light, so that it would reflect upon Rick's taste and judgment?

Rick didn't know, but he made up his mind to watch Miller and the other angels very carefully, and to drop them from the show at the first sign of trouble.

As it turned out, his fears were ungrounded.

There were six angels in all, counting Miller. They were, as Miller had promised, all big boys, with one member of the sextet standing at six-two. Miller, in fact, was the shortest boy in the group, and Rick arranged

them according to height, pleased with the ocarina effect
he achieved. The first rehearsal was held during the
fourth period on December 2nd. Rick knew that Katz
was free during that period, and the programs Miller
provided showed that three boys in the sextet had lunch
during that period. He was forced to yank the remaining
three out of classes, and for a moment he wondered if
this wasn't what Miller had had in mind all along. Could
the boy have realized no rehearsal schedule was possible
unless some boys were taken out of classes? Since Miller
turned out to be one of those lucky boys, the supposition was not an unlikely one. But Rick passed no judgment. He promised to treat the thing fairly and squarely,
and he was surprised and pleased with the final results—
or at least the results he saw at the first dress rehearsal.
He never did get to see the actual show.

The angels were surprisingly co-operative. Surprisingly, because Rick had had experience with specialty
acts before. In college, whenever someone could dance
or sing or juggle, that someone became a specialty act, a
featured performer. Having become a member of this
elevated caste, the person usually felt the show should
revolve around himself, plot be damned, continuity be
damned, everything else be damned. The angels had
apparently sung together before, and Rick expected trouble on that account. He expected another specialty act,
and specialty acts don't like being squeezed into the
framework of a show, don't like being reduced to
ciphers. But the angels showed no signs of *specialty acti-
tis*. They listened to everything Rick had to say, and they
seemed delighted with their speaking roles.

The speaking roles, as Rick had written them, were not really individual parts. He surmised correctly that the success or failure of the angels would depend upon their actions and reactions as a group. Everything they said, therefore, was said in chorus. All of their actions were performed simultaneously. If one angel blew his nose, the other five angels blew their noses at the same instant. If one angel said, "Oh, yes," he could be certain that five other angels were mouthing those same words at the same time.

But rather than simplifying the individual roles, the chorus setup made it more difficult. If all six angels had to shout, "Hi, Santa!" together, they simply had to shout it together. If one angel were a beat behind and another a beat ahead, the resultant chorus would become a hodgepodge of incomprehensible sound.

Rick knew there would be difficulty on this score during that first fourth-period rehearsal. There were eight people at the rehearsal: George Katz, the six angels, and Rick. The rehearsal took place on the auditorium stage, with the curtains closed, and with a pile of lunch-eating students sitting in the auditorium seats, most of them unaware of what was going on behind the curtains.

Rick introduced Mr. Katz to the boys and told them he'd be playing Santa Claus, and that the angels and St. Nick would have to work very closely together because they'd really be carrying the largest burden of the show between them. The boys were respectful in acknowledging the introduction, as if being introduced to a teacher was something they were not used to. Rick handed out copies of the angels' parts, and then they all sat around on chairs in the center of the stage and began reading the parts, with Rick filling in by reading the minor roles in the script.

They'd read a few paragraphs when Rick noticed that one of the angels was silent. He called a halt and asked, "Is there any trouble there? I'm sorry, I don't remember your name."

"He Brown," Miller said. "He can't read so hot, Mr. Dadier."

"Oh, I see," Rick said, disappointed.

"We'll teach him his part," Miller assured him. "Don' worry. He can't read so hot, but he'll be all right. He got a good memory."

"Well, all right," Rick said reluctantly. "Let's take it from Santa's second speech."

George Katz had memorized the role, and he gave it all the stiffness of the Magna Charta. Rick let that pass because he was sure the stiffness would work out once he began walking the show through. Besides, the choral speaking was presenting more of a problem than George Katz's interpretation of St. Nick. The boys weren't together. Some were behind, and some were ahead, and the result was chaos, without a word being understood.

They went over one passage several times, with Rick trying in vain to synchronize them. He was saved, finally, by Miller's intrusion, and by the boys' innate sense of rhythm.

"We tacklin' this all wrong," Miller said. "We not givin' what Mr. Dadier wants. You want this together, don' you, Chief?" Miller asked.

"Yes, I do," Rick said, convinced already that the angels simply would not work out.

"Yeah, well we ain't doin' that." He looked at the script in his hand and said, "Look, fellers, you see there where Santa Claus he say, 'How're all my heavenly messengers today?' You see that spot there on the paper, where he say that?"

The boys nodded and mumbled, and Miller said, "Okay, so his last word there is 'today.' Now, here's the beat. One-and-two-and. You got that? One-and-two-and. Then we suppose to say, 'Oh, we jus' fine, Santa.' Okay, so we speed up that one-and-two-and, an' then we come in on the down beat. We say 'Oh' on the downbeat, an' then we stop a beat, an' then we say, 'we jus' fine, Santa.' Now, you got that?" The boys talked it up a little more, nodding and studying the script, while Rick watched in amazement.

"You want to give us that speech, Mr. Katz?" Miller asked.

George Katz dug into his memory and stiffly said, "How're all my heavenly messengers today?"

Miller said, "One-and-two-and Oh, beat, we jus' fine, Santa." He paused and looked at the boys again. "Okay, you got that? I'll give you the beat one more time, then we'll try it in our heads. Could we have that line again, Mr. Katz?"

"How're all my heavenly messengers today?" George Katz asked stiffly.

"One-and-two-and," Miller whispered.

"Oh," the boys said in chorus together—and Miller whispered, "beat"—"we jus' fine, Santa."

"That was very good," Rick said, grinning broadly, surprised and pleased, amazed that Miller had recognized the boys' talent for rhythm and utilized it so effectively. "Let's mark that down on the scripts. The one-and-two-and, and then the beat. We'll do that for every speech you boys have."

"Could we try it silent, Mr. Dadier?" Miller asked. "Doin' the countin' inside our heads?"

"Why, certainly," Rick said. "Sure. Geor——, Mr. Katz, would you give them their cue again, please?"

George Katz dutifully said, "How're all my heavenly messengers today?"

"Oh," the boys said in chorus, "we jus' fine, Santa."

"Very good," Rick said, excited now. "Very good. That was excellent. Now if we can do that for all of your speeches . . ."

"We can do it," Miller said confidently. "It's jus' like singin', Chief, 'cept there's no melody."

They went through as much of the script as they could during that fourth period, marking out the rhythm of the speeches, Rick deciding where the pauses should be, where the emphasis should come, tailoring the lines for their maximum effect. When the bell rang at the end of the fourth period, he reluctantly walked up to Room 206 to greet 55–206. Miller was in the room already when he got there, having left the auditorium while Rick stayed behind to exchange a few words with Katz.

"Hey, teach," Miller shouted. "You better watch that stuff."

Rick, still happy over the first rehearsal, pleased by

Miller's behavior and co-operation, smiled and asked, "What stuff, Miller?"

"Draggin' yo' ass in after the late bell, Chief. You settin' a bad 'zample for the pupils here."

The class laughed, and Rick stared at Miller, surprised.

"Well, ain'tchoo, Chief?" Miller asked, his eyes roguishly innocent. "Wunt you draggin' ass, man?"

Rick, still a little stunned, said, "I suppose so, Miller."

"You s'pose so? Hell, man, don't you know?" Miller asked. "You can't be that stupid!" and the class roared its approval.

"He's confused," West sneered. "He's gettin' nervous in the service."

"That's enough of that," Rick said tightly, suddenly shocked into reaction. "Let's just knock it off."

"Knock it off!" West shouted. "You heard the man."

"He say 'Knock it off,' " Miller put in. "An' when he say 'Knock it off,' by God . . ."

"He *means* knock it off," West concluded happily, clapping Miller on the shoulder in glee.

Rick blinked at Miller, not able to understand the change in the boy. Was this the same helpful co-operative kid who'd worked out the speech rhythms in the auditorium just a period ago? Could this be the same kid? This wiseacre who had just now initiated a new series of jibes against the teacher? He couldn't believe it, and so he let it pass because he couldn't understand it. But in the days that followed he learned a basic fact, and he also learned to live by it.

He learned that Miller formulated all the rules of this

game, and that the rules were complex and unbending. And just as Miller drew an arbitrary line before the start of each fifth-period English class—a line over which he would not step—he also drew a line which separated the show from anything academic.

It was a confusing situation. It was confusing because Rick really did get along well with Miller at rehearsals. The student-teacher relationship seemed to vanish completely. They were just two people working for a common goal, and Miller took direction and offered helpful suggestions, and stood by shamefacedly whenever Rick blew his top about a bit of stage business or a fluffed line. Rick valued the boy's participation in the show, and most of all he valued the way Miller led the sextet, helped Rick mold it into a unified, smoothly-functioning acting and singing machine.

And then rehearsal would be over, and 55–206 loomed on the horizon, and Miller drew his line again, and he pushed right up to that line, never stepping over it, always baiting Rick just so far, always annoying him until Rick trespassed onto Miller's side of the line and Miller was faced with the choice of retreating or shoving over onto Rick's side of the line, and that he would never do.

Rick tried to understand it, and the only conclusion he could draw was that the show provided a normal outlet for Miller's leadership qualities—and there was no doubt he possessed these qualities—whereas the classroom (as Solly Klein had said) provided no such outlet; it was instead an abnormal situation in which bad behavior was the criterion.

Miller didn't have to be bad during rehearsals. He had something to do, something which challenged his active mind. He had boys to lead, and he had a cause in which to lead them.

The English class was another matter. The other boys in the class considered English a senseless waste of time, a headless chicken, a blob without a goal. Miller may have felt the same way, though it was impossible to know just what he felt. But he sensed that approval lay in disorder, that leadership lay in misbehavior. And so he drew his line, and he drew his second line, the line that told Rick, "The show's one thing, Chief, but English is another. So don't 'spect me to go kissin' your ass in class."

Rick faced his two-headed gorgon squarely. He learned to accept the good Miller and the bad Miller, and he felt something like a psychoanalyst treating a schizophrenic. And all the while he wondered which was the real personality, hoping it was the good and not the bad.

The good certainly prevailed during rehearsals, and the show traveled along at top speed. By December 10th, the angels and Santa Claus were a working unit, and George Katz had lost most of the stiff regularity with which he'd initially interpreted the role. It was almost beautiful to watch the team in action. Katz, unable to completely disguise the pomposity and formality which was an intricate part of his own personality, was a perfect straight man for the six colored angels.

The angels, apparently putting in a lot of rehearsal time on their own at night, delivered their punch lines as one man. They breathed together, and they moved together, and they paused together, and they spoke together. They were like six marionettes governed by one set of strings. They were perfect, and Rick burst out laughing every time they performed, even though he'd heard the gags a hundred times, even though he knew exactly what was coming next. The boys developed a sort of deadpan delivery. The delivery held until the line had been uttered and until the laugh exploded from the audience, the audience being Rick at this rehearsal stage of the game. And then the deadpan vanished, and six mouths opened simultaneously over six sets of gleaming white teeth. False, burlesque smiles burst onto six black faces in a gesture that brought a double laugh following each punch line, one laugh for the deadpan delivery and the meaning of the line, and the second laugh for the simultaneous phony grins that followed the delivery. It couldn't have been better, and Rick thanked God that Miller had popped in with his angel sextet.

And the boys *could* sing! With remarkable versatility, they dropped their comic approach when attacking the carols Rick chose. They gave their renditions warmth and sincerity, singing in a harmony they'd obviously developed over a good many years of close friendship. They did "God Rest Ye Merry Gentlemen," "Deck the Halls," "Noël," and "Silent Night," and they gave each carol a separate interpretation. Rick saved "Silent Night" as the last number in the show, using the six-foot-two boy—who had the best voice in the sextet—as a soloist on the second chorus, and then hoping the audience would join in on a repeat of the first chorus. As it turned out, the audience did join in on the day of the Christmas Assembly, but Rick didn't know that until long after the show was over.

He began working harder. He contacted "Ironman" Clancy of carpentry and woodworking, and he told him what he needed in the way of sets. Clancy, having been secretly tipped off about mention of his name in the show, was only too willing to help, especially when his boys would be doing all the work. He designed the sets with the help of Scanlon in Blueprint Reading and Anuzzi in Related Drawing, and his classes dutifully put them together in a matter of days.

It was Lois Hammond who volunteered to make the costumes for the show. Rick's rehearsals had gradually grown to include the remainder of the cast. The remainder, as it was, consisted of a stock group of twenty-five boys who composed the students in each class Santa and the angels visited, and seven teachers who had volunteered their services, most of them portraying themselves in the show. Rick took a small part because he couldn't round up any other teachers as volunteers, and that part was played by Alan "Lover Boy" Manners on the day of the show, Rick's absence making the substitution necessary. Rick's absence was perhaps fortunate in that "Lover Boy" scored a personal triumph that momentarily caused him to forget his longing for an all-girls' educational paradise, complete with hot and cold running, willing legs.

As the cast grew, the problems grew because Rick was in charge of scheduling rehearsals, and it was

damned near impossible to get everyone together at the
same time. He finally resorted to night rehearsals, finding that most of the angels were through with their outside jobs at seven or eight, and scheduling the rehearsals
for them at eight-thirty or thereabouts. He had to get
parents' permission for this, and he also ran into trouble
with the night school. They themselves had programs
planned for the auditorium, but his need was more desperate and so they relinquished the stage to him. It was
during one of these late rehearsals, rehearsals which
caused Anne Dadier a good deal of torment, torment of
which Rick was totally unaware, that Lois Hammond
showed up.

She sat out front watching Rick put the cast
through its paces, laughing in obvious enjoyment
every time the angels opened their unified mouths.
Rick was a hard taskmaster, and he stopped the show
whenever something wasn't just right. Lois watched
him, watched the way he moved around the stage,
watched the way he ran to the back of the auditorium,
dashed to the side aisle, ran up onto the stage again,
shouted, "Louder, angels!" or "Dip from the knees,
George" or "Watch your back, Angostino. We don't
want your back." She watched him, and she watched
the show, but mostly she watched him, and it is difficult to imagine what she thought because her eyes
were very careful and hardly anyone detected the
heave of her breasts. When it was all over, she waited
until the auditorium had cleared, sitting in her seat up
front, watching Rick, and watching the boys and
teachers depart.

Rick remained onstage, penciling something on his script, checking the lights which one of Lou Savoldi's classes had thoughtfully rigged for him. Lois watched him, and one corner of her eye watched the auditorium doors whispering shut behind the departing cast, and finally the doors whispered shut after the last member of the cast, and the large auditorium was empty save for Rick on the stage and Lois Hammond sitting down front with her legs crossed.

"It was very good," she called from her seat, resting her arm on the seat back beside her, sucking in a deep breath, the better to project across the distance that separated them.

Rick, his shirtsleeves rolled up, his tie pulled down, and his collar unbuttoned, looked up, surprised that anyone had remained in the auditorium, more surprised that the anyone was Lois Hammond.

"Oh, thank you," he said.

"Really very good, Rick," Lois answered. "You should be quite proud of yourself."

Rick walked onto the apron and smiled. "Did you really like it?"

"Yes," Lois said, smiling back. "Wherever did you get those angels? They're magnificent!"

"Aren't they though?" he said, very pleased. He closed his script and began rolling down his sleeves.

"Is it all right to smoke?" Lois asked.

"I suppose so," he said.

"Or don't you like breaking rules?" she asked. She lifted her eyebrow, cocking it inquisitively, and Rick remembered back to when he'd have considered such a

gesture an innocent facial expression. He did not consider it that now. He recognized it for what it was, a not-
too-subtle strengthening of the *double entendre* of her
words.

"No," he said, smiling, "I don't particularly like breaking rules."

"Rules were made to be broken," Lois said softly.

"In that case," Rick answered, "enjoy your cigarette." He fastened the buttons on his sleeves, buttoned
his collar, and slipped up the knot on his tie. He found
his jacket draped over a chair onstage, slipped into it,
and then started down the steps.

"Sit down," Lois said. "Have a cigarette with me."

"It's really very late," Rick said.

"It's later than you think," Lois answered, studying
him with a penetrating gaze. "Why, Thanksgiving has
come and gone already," she said pointedly.

"Yes, it has," Rick answered, knowing what she
meant, but not playing the game this time.

"I'm trying to figure out my Christmas list now," she
said. "Trying to decide what presents I should give."

"Oh?" Rick said, lighting a cigarette and leaning
against the piano, the piano Martha Riley would pound
in accompaniment during the Christmas Assembly.

"I've got a really big present to give," she said, blowing
out a cloud of smoke. "A really big one. Do you know,
Rick?"

"Did you really like the angels?" he asked, trying to
change the subject, not wanting her present, and not
wanting to talk about it.

"Very much," Lois said quickly. "I've been wondering

when and where I can deliver this present. I've got it all wrapped up and ready to go. I just need a time and a place."

"Why not try Railway Express?" Rick said quietly. "They deliver anything."

Lois giggled and then dropped her cigarette to the auditorium floor, reaching out for it with a sleek leg in a black pump, crushing it underfoot.

"Do you think I should set the time and place, Rick?" Lois asked, leaning forward, her hands clasped in her lap. "Would that be proper?"

Rick was silent for a moment. He shoved back the sleeve on his jacket then, looked at his watch, and said, "I've got to get home. My wife is waiting."

"Ah, yes, the married man," Lois said sweetly.

"Ah, yes, the married man," Rick repeated, smiling.

"Does the married man need a wardrobe mistress?" Lois asked, and Rick wasn't sure whether or not a double meaning was intended this time.

"You mean someone to make costumes?" he asked.

Lois shrugged. "Yes. What else?"

"He sure does," Rick answered. "Are you volunteering?"

Lois smiled, but her eyes did not join in the fun. "Seems I've been volunteering all night," she said.

Rick chose to ignore her meaning. "The job is yours," he said, happily.

"Thanks."

"I mean, if you want it."

"I want it," Lois answered. "Oh yes, I want it."

"The only real costumes to worry about are the

angels," Rick said. "We can rent the Santa Claus costume, you know."

"And there's the root of all the trouble," Lois said.

"Huh?"

"Angel," Lois replied, smiling. She stood abruptly, smoothing her skirt over her hips. "Isn't that it, Rick? Wouldn't you say so?"

"I don't know what you're talking about, Lois," Rick said slowly.

"Don't you?" She stepped closer to him and patted his cheek. "Don't you, Rick? Don't you really?"

"I'm afraid I don't," he said, feeling the warmth of her palm on his face, feeling her closeness.

"Well," she said. "Well."

"I've got to get home," Rick answered. He picked up his briefcase from the piano top. "Are you coming?" he asked, and Lois burst out laughing.

He stared at her for a moment, not realizing what was so funny.

"Oh, Rick," she said. "Rick, you are an absolute doll."

"Well, thanks," he said, shrugging.

"Oh, you're a real doll, a real angel doll. Go home, Rick, for God's sake, go home." She laughed again and then said, "Go home to your wife, Rick."

"That's just where I was going," he said, annoyed by her laughter.

"I'll make your costumes for you, angel doll," she said. "Six white costumes for your six little angels. I'll do a very nice job for you, Rick. A very nice job."

"Well, thanks a lot, Lois. I was . . ."

"But tell me, Rick, doesn't this goddamned place

sometimes bore you to tears? Don't you get sick up to here of teaching these stinking little brats all day long, Rick? Don't you sometimes want to throw that stuffy little briefcase of yours up into the air and not care where the hell it comes down? Don't you, Rick?"

"I think you've got me wrong, Lois," Rick said, shaking his head. "I'm not . . ."

"I know you're not. Brother, do I know you're not. Okay, Rick, let it go. Just let it go. But will you mind if I'm bored?"

"I can't . . ."

"Will you mind if I consider the first day of school the only true piece of excitement we've had since I've been here? Will you mind that?"

"You mean . . ."

"Yes, I mean. I mean the time that stupid slob tried to rape me, Rick. That's exactly what I mean. My God, sometimes I wish he'd succeeded." She paused and said, "Oh, not really, but damnit, I'm bored. I'm bored silly. I'm so bored . . . oh, the hell with it."

"I had no idea you felt that way," Rick said. "Why'd you go into teaching, Lois?"

"That's right, steer us back to the academic train of thought. Play the absent-minded professor, Rick. Pretend we're discussing John Dewey. How the hell do I know why I went into teaching? What else does a girl go into? Biochemistry? Zoology? Geology? Typing and stenography? Why not teaching? Two months' vacation every summer, and a sabbatical in Italy with the rest of the teachers, cruising down a canal and ogling Venice. Oh, how the hell do I know why I became a teacher?" She paused and turned, leaning over to take a cigarette from her purse, her skirt tightening across her buttocks. She fired the cigarette and said, "But I'm bored, Rick, I know that. I'm bored silly, so now you've got a costume mistress, if that's what you want. That is what you wanted, isn't it, Rick?"

"It's what I wanted," he said.

"The Christmas Assembly is on Wednesday the 23rd," Lois said. She took the cigarette from her mouth. "Most places have a drink around Christmastime, sort of usher in the holidays. You think we'll have a drink here?"

"I doubt it," Rick said.

"I didn't think we would. So I've got an idea, angel. Try it for size, Rick, if it'll squeeze in under your halo. My idea is that we go out after the assembly and have a drink in a local bar. You can bring a friend along, if you like. How about Solly Klein? We'll have a drink, and we'll toast your wardrobe mistress, Rick, okay? We'll toast her and boredom, and all the angels in the world, and all the sweet wives waiting for those angels to come home to them. We'll toast everything, Rick. And we'll toast the present I told you about, and maybe we'll exchange gifts." She paused. "How does the idea sound to you, Rick? Flutter your wings a little and let me know." She paused again. "A sign, yes? Something I can read. Flash a light, angel doll."

"I took a beating the last time I toasted anything," Rick said dryly.

"You and Mr. Edwards. The Quitter. Where is the Quitter now, Rick?"

"I don't know. I suppose he . . ."

"Or am I offending you? He was your friend, I must remember. But didn't my invitation include a friend? I'm being a very good little girl, Rick, providing a chaperone and everything. No wife could object to Solly Klein, could she, Rick?"

"Let's cut it out, Lois," Rick said suddenly.

"Ah, the sign. There it is, the sign I asked for. Red light. Stop. The mistress remains in the wardrobe."

"Lois, you're assuming a hell of . . ."

"I'm not assuming a damned thing, Rick, not one damned thing, remember that. I read the signs and I obey them if I want to, like smoking a cigarette in this inviolate territory called the auditorium." She sucked in a long drag, blowing out the smoke in a swift, emphatic stream. "Just like that. I've got the sign now, Rick, but it's not the sign I wanted."

"Then why the hell don't we . . ."

"December 23rd," Lois said. "What's today, the 14th? 15th? Well, what difference does it make? It gives you a little time, Rick. A few drinks, a few toasts, a few gifts. A big present. An end to boredom. Oh, for an end to boredom. Oh, but this place is one big cancerous bore!"

"I'm going home," Rick said.

"Me, too," Lois agreed. "Me, too. Homeward bound." She smiled and touched Rick's arm. "Look Homeward, Angel."

"Come on," Rick said roughly.

They started up the aisle together, neither speaking. At the back of the auditorium, Rick snapped off the lights, and Lois was suddenly very close to him, standing so close that he could feel the brush of her thigh against his leg, could feel her breath when she spoke. "December 23rd, Rick," she whispered. "An early Christmas this year, and maybe a happy New Year, who knows?"

She leaned forward, expelling her breath, the rush of warm air caressing his face. She tilted her mouth up toward his, and her hand closed on his arm, and in that instant he pushed the auditorium door open and stepped into the brilliantly lighted corridor.

"I've got to hurry, Lois," he said conversationally. "Let me know how you make out with the costumes, won't you?"

He avoided her as much as possible after that. The cards were all on the table now, face up, and Lois Hammond was not of a mind to play footsie. Lois Hammond was bored with North Manual Trades, and there was nothing like an adventuresome little bout with a married man to relieve boredom. Except that Anne was bored, too, and Anne wasn't complaining much lately, but he could read her face and he knew damn well she wasn't enjoying this final stretch of her pregnancy. And whereas it would have been a simple matter to accept Lois Hammond's present—he had no doubt it would be an interesting package indeed—he would not have been able to live with Anne after that, and worse, he would not have been able to live with himself.

So he avoided her except for brief discussions about the costumes, discussions in which Lois never failed to mention December 23rd and the promise of that future day. She dangled the promise before him like an extended carrot, but he did not nibble at it. There was something confident about her manner, and he wondered how he could have ever considered her a shy, naïve little thing. It was almost as if she felt suggestion would accomplish whatever she wanted to accomplish. She used her voice, and she used her words, and she used her body, all bunched together into one powerful suggestive machine, all holding the promise, the glittering promise, a few drinks, a few toasts, a few gifts. A big present.

Rick ignored the promise. He ignored it, but it remained at the back of his mind, and he sometimes examined it secretly. It was like a satchel of bank loot which he'd stored beneath the floorboards of his mind. He knew it was there, but he couldn't spend it—nor did he particularly want to spend it. And the knowledge that it was there illegally filled him with guilt, even though he had not robbed the bank or placed the satchel under the floorboards to begin with.

Lois Hammond was a master—or a mistress—at the art of insinuation, and she plied that art well until December 23rd became a date to remember, like a birthday or an anniversary. Before she began working on Rick in earnest, December 23rd meant only one thing to him: the day of the Christmas Assembly. It meant more than that now, and he honestly didn't know whether he was really undecided about accepting her proposition, or whether he was undecided only because she constantly suggested that he was undecided. He'd thought that his mind was made up, made up from that day in *The Trades Trumpet* office when she'd done a modified strip for him. His resolve had strengthened the night in the auditorium when she'd offered her services as wardrobe mistress. He would have nothing further to do with Lois Hammond. He'd begun avoiding her, but it was difficult to avoid someone like Lois, and now he found himself doubting his own judgment.

She had an annoying knack of making him feel somehow unmanly. Sterile was the word, he supposed. As if he were behaving contrary to all the laws governing the sexual behavior of the human male as reported by, thank you, Dr. Kinsey. As if *not* accepting the gratuity were abnormal. As if a man with a wife in her ninth month should snatch at this opportunity. As if he were some sort of blind thing that had crawled from under a slimy rock. What's wrong with you, Rick? No blood? No hormones? No *cojones*?

Maybe not, he reflected. Maybe the boys in the locker room at the golf club would snicker behind their palms at this creep who passed up a good thing when it was offered up rare and not under glass. Maybe they would shake their shaggy heads and murmur, "Losing his grip, Dadier is. Shame. Nice chap otherwise."

Maybe so, and maybe he was being a creep and maybe he had no blood, or hormones, or anything. He doubted that because he heard his blood every night when Anne curled up against him. He heard the blood loud and strong, and his hands passed over her flesh, lingeringly, gently, until he had to stop himself because he knew he was being foolish, and besides it wouldn't be much longer.

And Anne? He knew she felt nothing now, and he could not blame her for that. And when she soothed him, and when she murmured, "Oh, my poor darling," he felt somewhat ashamed of himself, as if he should not be feeling desire, not now when she was feeling nothing. She understood, and she helped him, but it was not the same because she was not a participant, and he felt more shamed because sex becomes an empty hollow thing when it is not shared.

But he had blood, all right, and Lois' intimations that he was a neuter gender textbook insulted his masculinity. He knew that was part of her approach, a buildup which should normally lead to an "All right, you bitch, you're asking for it!" attack. He saw completely through her, but he still reacted to her approach, and his masculinity was greatly offended whenever she used "angel" as synonymous with "eunuch."

And at the same time, "angel"—as far as the show went—became more and more synonymous with Gregory Miller.

Miller was the picture of helpfulness. There was nothing he would not do for the show, and his co-operative spirit delighted Rick. The boy did anything that was asked of him, and frequently many things Rick wouldn't have thought to ask. Like the night Rick stayed over to repaint one of the flats which showed to bad advantage under the amber jells. He'd brought his Navy dungarees and denims to school, changed backstage, and sprawled out on the floor with his paint buckets and brushes, anxious to get the job over with.

Miller drifted in and stood over Rick, watching him

for a little while without saying anything. Then, at last, he asked, "You got an extra brush, Mr. Dadier?"

"Why, yes," Rick said.

"I thought maybe you could use a hand. Otherwise, you be here all night."

"Help yourself," Rick said, smiling. "That brush is a little hard, but I think it'll work."

Miller picked up the brush and tested the bristles on the palm of his hand. "Be all right," he said, and then he sprawled out beside Rick and got to work. The job was a tedious one at best. There was no detail work on the flat, and it was simply a matter of spreading a new color in place of the old one. They worked in silence for some time, and then, perhaps because painting is a task which normally encourages conversation, they began talking.

They talked about the show at first, maintaining the stiff formality of a student-teacher relationship. And then, perhaps because they were both in dungarees, and perhaps because they were both working and engrossed in what they were doing, the formality dropped, and they began talking about other things, movies they had seen, teachers and students around the school, the "characters" they both knew, the way Christmas was a special time of the year for both of them, and even— surprisingly—the books Miller had read outside of school, pocket-size editions for the most part, but many of them excellent books.

It was at this point that Rick asked, "How'd you happen to come to a vocational school, Miller?"

"Oh, I dunno," Miller answered, dipping his brush and slapping the paint onto the canvas. He worked the paint into the material in long strokes and then looked up. "Jus' like that, I s'pose."

"Had you considered an academic high school?"

"Yeah, I gave it some thought."

"I mean . . ." Rick hesitated, wondering if he should mention the boy's I.Q., and then deciding against it. "What are you majoring in, Miller?"

"Automotive," Miller said.

"You want to be a mechanic?"

"I s'pose," Miller said. He seemed suddenly embarrassed.

"Don't you?"

"Well, way I look at it, Mr. Dadier, there ain't much choice."

"How do you mean, Miller?"

Miller looked up, and there was no malice in his voice when he spoke. "I colored, Mr. Dadier."

"I don't understand you," Rick said.

Miller smiled. "You figure me for a lawyer or a doctor or somethin'? Can't fool myself like that, Mr. Dadier."

"Would you like to be a doctor?"

"No, no, nothin' like that. Don't misunderstand me. I jus' don't . . . well, you know. I mean, I rather be a mechanic than a elevator op'rator, or a bootblack, or a porter. You follow me? I figure a mechanic always got somethin' to do, like a skill, and maybe it won't matter he black or white. Tha's what I figure."

"But you'd like to be something . . . more than a mechanic?"

"Ain't nothin' wrong with bein' a mechanic, I s'pose."

Rick did not dip his brush. He held it in his hand and

stared at Miller. "But you'd rather be something else?" he asked.

"I s'pose."

"What, Miller?"

"I dunno."

"But something else?"

"I s'pose." Miller grinned embarrassedly. "I figured one time I could maybe be a singer, but I ain't good 'nough for that. Lots of colored folks drift into singin', you know. Nat Cole, Pearl Bailey, you know."

"Yes," Rick said.

"But I ain't good 'nough for that. I figured on maybe fightin', too, but I don't like hittin' somebody less'n I'm hit first."

"Well, what would you like to be?"

"I dunno," Miller said again.

"But not a mechanic?" Rick persisted.

Miller looked up and suddenly asked, "You think this is a good school, Mr. Dadier?"

"Sure I do," Rick lied.

"Yeah?" Miller said, his brow wrinkled. "You really think that?"

"Yes, I do," Rick lied again.

"You see, I wunt mind bein' a mechanic, I mean, if I felt like . . . like I was learnin' somethin'. But . . ." He let his sentence trail off.

"You feel you're not learning anything here, is that it?"

"I guess so," Miller said. He thought for a moment and then added, "You don't hafta be a mechanic all your life, you know. You could branch out, maybe have your own place, a little shop, maybe. You could use bein' a mechanic like a start, you know."

"Yes, I know," Rick said.

"I guess maybe I really did want to be a mechanic when I first come here. History an' English an' language an' all those don't 'peal to me. Tha's why I d'in take the tech course. I guess I'm good with my hands."

"But what you said about being . . ."

"Well, that too. You got to be sensible 'bout it, and I know a black man got a rough road. It's easier to be a mechanic, you know."

"You can't always take the easy road, Miller," Rick said.

Miller lifted his eyes. "You ain't black, Mr. Dadier."

"I know. And I understand what you're up against. But black men *have* . . ."

"Oh sure, I know. But you got to make your choice, an' I ain't no crusader or nothin'. I'm jus' a guy figurin' on how he can make a livin' the best way. An' I figured I could learn to be a good mechanic here, and a man don't care if black hands or white hands fixes his brake linin', so long as the car run. An', like I said, the mechanic angle can jus' be a start. A black man could be somethin' by startin' his own shop, I mean without havin' to battle his way all the time."

"All right, Miller, that sounds sensible. But what's the trouble? You sound as if you don't like the idea of being a mechanic, as if . . ."

"Well, I thought it was a good idea when I first come here, but now I ain't so sure. You see, if I got to be a mechanic, an' a black one to boot, I got to be a *good* mechanic. They plenty white mechanics, an' a white man goan get preference over a black man less'n the black man's *real* good. An' I jus' ain't learnin' to be a good mechanic here, tha's all."

"Why not, Miller?"

"I dunno," Miller said.

"Aren't your teachers good?"

"Oh, they okay, I guess."

"Well, what is it then?"

"I dunno," Miller said.

"Do you *want* to learn?"

"Oh, sure," Miller replied.

"Then what is it?"

"I guess . . ." Miller shook his head. "No, that ain't it."

"What, Miller?"

"Well, nobody else seems to give a damn, you know, Mr. Dadier? In the beginnin', I tried real hard, but what's the sense? This ain't no real school, not like a academic school. This jus' . . . jus' . . . I dunno. This jus' like a . . . like a big dump heap, tha's all."

A garbage can, Rick thought. *What chance have we got? Miller believes that, too.*

"That's not true," he said. "You shouldn't say that, Miller."

"Aw, it's true," Miller said. "You don't know, you jus' here a short while. You'll fine out, you'll see."

This isn't Miller, Rick thought, *this is Solly Klein.*

"You mustn't believe that," Rick said fervently. "You really mustn't, Miller."

"How can you b'lieve no different? You see it, doan you? Hell, I ain't learnin' nothin' here, nothin' at all."

"But there are boys who do learn here, Miller," Rick said, thinking, *This is crazy, this is an argument with Solly, this is all wrong.*

"Yeah, maybe, but I ain't seen none. All you see is a big screwed-up mess, tha's all. Nobody even know what's goin' on here. Ever'body thinks ever'thin's jus' fine, but it ain't. I'll never be a mechanic in this place, Mr. Dadier. Ever'body jus' fools aroun' here."

"Including you, Miller," Rick said.

Miller stared at him for a moment, and Rick thought he would lose contact with the boy right then, thought the conversation would come to a complete halt.

"I s'pose," Miller said.

"Why, Miller?"

"What else you goan do?" He looked at Rick with honest puzzlement on his face, and Rick wished he could say something immediately to take away the confusion. "You s'pose to work hard when ever'body else jus' friggin' aroun'? You s'pose to make a goddamn fool of yourse'f?" He shook his head, and his shoulders seemed to slump. "No, you jus' go 'long with it, tha's all. You forget 'bout learnin', tha's all. You fool aroun' an' have a good time."

"That's the easy way, Miller."

"Tha's the only way," Miller said firmly, softly.

"No, Miller, it's not the only way. You can't always take the soft way out. Sometimes you've got to do whatever's best, even if it makes things harder. Can't you understand that, Miller?"

"No," Miller said, shaking his head, forgetting completely that he was talking to a teacher, "no, I can't see that. I can't see anybody takin' the hard way when the easy way's open. You got to prove that to me, man. You got to show that to me."

"I wish I could, Miller. I wish there were some way to show you."

"There ain't, man, I'm tellin' you. You take the easy way, an' you get along, and you fool aroun' jus' like ever'body else, and tha's it."

"And you forget about being a mechanic," Rick said.

"I guess so," Miller said sadly.

"And what will you be?"

"Somethin'll turn up," Miller said. "Things always turn up."

"And meantime, you'll just drift with the tide."

"I s'pose," Miller said.

Rick wanted to mention the English class, wanted to say something about Miller's behavior there as contrasted with his behavior connected with the show, as contrasted with his behavior right now, right this minute. He sensed, however, that anything about the English class would be an intrusion here, and so he held his tongue, and they turned back to painting, and he wished he could think of something to say that would show Miller he was wrong about the easy road.

At the same time, he wondered if this talk would change Miller's conduct in class the next day, and he had a sneaking dread that it would not. He knew that Miller's line was drawn in indelible ink, and he didn't think anything as slight as a heart-to-heart talk could hope to erase that line. So they painted in silence, and he tried to think of the correct example, but he couldn't.

They left the school about nine-thirty, both lighting up cigarettes when they were outside the building. They walked together to Third Avenue, Rick in his street clothes now, Miller still in the dungarees which were his street clothes, his leather jacket pulled up high on his neck.

"I get a train here, Chief," he said.

"G'night, Miller," Rick answered. "I'll see you tomorrow."

"G'night," Miller said.

"And thanks for the help. I appreciated it."

"Don't mention it, Chief," Miller said, and they parted.

The next day, in English 55–206, there was no change in the behavior of Gregory Miller. Gregory Miller took the easy road, and the easy road was the road that raised hell and clowned and didn't give a damn about learning. And Rick was not disappointed because he was not surprised.

On Friday the 18th, Rick held his first dress rehearsal, and it went off without a hitch. George Katz, his stomach padded, his face bewhiskered, seemed really to acquire the St. Nick personality once he got into the costume, but he never lost his pompous interpretation of the role, so that the character became a cross between a jolly laugh and a request for two lumps of sugar, please. Rick couldn't have been more delighted with the interpretation. The angels, in costume, were— as Lois Hammond put it—"adorable." And whereas Rick disliked that particular word, he had to admit it fit them to a T. They wore brass halos, rakishly atilt, held aloft over their heads by a slender brass rod that jutted up from the harness attaching their downy yellow wings to their backs. Lois had done wonders with ordinary household sheets, cutting yoke necks into them, lining the necks with gleaming gold braid, fashioning the sheets into tunics. The tunics had short sleeves, each sleeve edged in gold braid. The skirts of the tunics were edged in the same fashion. The skirts reached to the boys' knees, and Lois had rounded out the costumes with golden sandals, each sandal sporting a pair of golden wings at the heel.

The picture was humorous as well as pleasing to the eye. The colors blended into a soft harmony: the warm brown of the boys' skin, the crisp white of the tunics, the metallic yellow of the halos, sandals and gold braid, the softer yellow of the feathered wings. The boys loved the costumes, and Miller beamed broadly and said, "Bet you never thought you'd see me in a angel's getup, did you, Chief?"

Rick looked at the angel Miller and laughed. "I'll admit I pictured you in the other place," he said, reflecting that Miller was always in the other place except during rehearsals.

They ran through the show without interruptions, while Rick took notes. He held the cast for about fifteen minutes after rehearsal, reading from his notes, making general comments about the caliber of the performances, correcting minor points. He told them there'd be two more rehearsals, one on Monday night in street clothes, and a final dress rehearsal on Tuesday night, the

22d. He also added that the show was a humdinger, and they'd all probably receive Broadway offers once it was presented.

Lois Hammond was waiting for him when he dismissed the cast, but he said good-night to her curtly, and then walked out of the auditorium with George Katz and Alan Manners who'd dropped in to see what was going on.

"You've really done a wonderful job with this, Dadier," Katz said as they crossed the schoolyard.

"I had a lot of help," Rick said modestly, feeling very pleased about the show, hoping it would go over well on the day of the assembly.

"Yes," Katz admitted, "but you were the guiding force." He paused, as if he were embarrassed by what he was about to say next. "I imagine you're a very good teacher, Dadier. The kids seem to like you."

"Me?" Rick asked, unconsciously using the standard Manual Trades reply. He chuckled in the darkness, wishing Katz's supposition were true.

"I enjoyed the show a lot, Dadier," Manners said. "I also enjoyed watching Lois Hammond." He grinned in the darkness. "You getting some of that, boy?"

"Oh, sure," Rick said lightly.

"How about seconds?" Manners asked.

"Seconds?" Rick said. "Hell, Manners, firsts are still free."

"You won't mind then? If I try?"

"You're joking," Rick said.

"I never joke where it concerns a piece of tail," Manners answered seriously.

"Go ahead," Rick said. "Hell, go ahead. I . . ."

"Manners is joking," Katz said diplomatically. "He knows you're married."

"Yeah," Manners said, "but does Lois know it?"

"Oh, come on," Katz said, a bit irritably. "I don't think this is something to joke about. I don't think so at all, Manners."

"Agreed," Manners said. "I notice the lady was sitting alone, so if you'll excuse me . . ." He stopped short and then turned on his heel, starting back across the school-yard.

"*Meshugah,*" Katz said, wagging his head. "He'll get in trouble yet, wait and see."

"I think he can take care of himself," Rick said.

"He shouldn't have said what he said," Katz persisted. "He knows you're married."

"Yes, that's true," Rick said, almost as if he were affirming the fact in his own mind. He'd been a little annoyed when Manners first started talking about Lois, annoyed because Manners automatically assumed something was going on between them, and then annoyed, irrationally, because Manners was stepping into the picture. For whereas Rick didn't want her, or if he wanted her he wasn't having any, thanks, there was something irritating about Manners' intrusion. A sort of unfair advantage, Rick felt, the predatory bachelor against the . . . yes, the sterile celibate. But in the short space of time between Manners' abrupt departure and Katz's profound observation on the marital state, Rick's entire outlook had changed.

Are you bored, honey? Tired with your humdrum exis-

tence? Feel hemmed in by the four walls? Long for a life of romantic adventure?

Tell you what I'm gonna do. I have here a pair of eyes that are the biggest. I have here a piner for an all-girls' paradise, a fancier of the female form, an ankle-ogler, an angle-artist, a lover from away back, Jack. I'm gonna let you have this skirt chaser, this Satan of the Satin Slip. I'm gonna let you have him, and pay close attention here, I'm gonna let you have him free of charge, absolutely free, you spend no money, not one penny, and I guarantee, I *guarantee* mind you, that this will end your boredom, that this lover boy, that this "Lover Boy" Manners will give you that life of romantic adventure. This *Deus Ex Machina*, Deus bless him, is the answer to your maidenly prayer, lady, and here he is, classic nose and all, yours for the taking, and Godspeed.

"Damn," Rick said happily, "things *are* looking up, aren't they?"

And George Katz, misunderstanding, nodded his head solemnly and said, "It's a wonderful show, Dadier."

12

The day Rick broke through was December 21st, two days before the Christmas Assembly. He would remember that day for a long time, for more reasons than his breakthrough.

His breakthrough was perhaps ironical in that it happened in his first class that day, 21–206, and it happened in a class for which he had prepared no lesson at all. He had meant to work out lesson plans for Monday, Tuesday, and Wednesday over the week end, it being a short week terminated by the commencement of the Christmas vacation on Thursday, December 24th.

But he'd got home late on Friday night after the dress rehearsal, and he'd barely had time for coffee with Anne before it was time for bed. He'd spent all day Saturday at being a husband, devoting more time to Anne than he had in the past month. On Saturday night, Ray and Dodie Crane stopped by unexpectedly, with the news that Ray had passed his state boards and could now officially and legally be called Dr. Raymond Crane. Rick had made some comment about how nice it would be having a dentist around, and Ray had promised to give the forthcoming heir free dental care for the rest of his natural days, and then they'd broken out a bottle of rye, mixed some terrible whiskey sours, and proceeded to celebrate.

On Sunday, Anne's parents dropped by in the afternoon, staying for supper, and consuming the major portion of the evening. Rick never did get to attack his lesson plans.

So on the bus Monday morning, he'd hastily scanned the text, picking out a yarn he thought was titled "The Fifty-First Dragoon." This is a war story, he thought, knowing a very little bit about dragoons. He had never read the story before, but war stories were sure-fire with these kids, and it seemed like a good bet. He'd read it to them, and then try to lead the conversation around to his own war experiences, and that would, he hoped, kill the period.

He greeted 21–206 with the announcement that he was going to read a story to them, and the kids accepted the knowledge gratefully, always willing to listen to a story being read, if it were a good story, and if the teacher didn't ask too many damned questions afterward.

Rick opened the text, a book for one of his upperterm classes, cleared his throat, and discovered right off that the story was written by Heywood Broun, a fact he had not gleaned from his hasty scanning of the table of contents on the bus. He also learned that it was not a war story titled "The Fifty-First Dragoon."

It was, instead, a story titled "The Fifty-First Dragon," and Rick felt a twinge of panic when he realized it was *not* a war story.

"The Fifty-First Dragon," he said, and the kids looked

at him with blank faces as he began reading aloud.

The story told of a young knight named Gawaine le Coeur-Hardy who was enrolled at a knight school but who did not seem to exhibit the proper spirit or zest for such knightly pursuits as jousting. In fact, Gawaine's lack of enthusiasm may very well have been termed cowardice, and the Headmaster and Assistant Professor of Pleasaunce finally decided to take the matter in hand and work out a remedy.

The Assistant Professor wanted to expel the boy, but the Headmaster had a better plan. He would teach the boy to kill dragons.

They began teaching the boy just that. Gawaine studied and learned, and studied and learned, and he progressed from paper dragons to papier-mâché dragons to wooden dragons, and each time he lopped off these dummy dragons' heads with one expert slice of his ax.

So they gave Gawaine a diploma and the Headmaster called him in for a little talk.

"It's time to get out there and meet Life," the Headmaster said, in effect, "and Life, as far as you're concerned, is dragons."

The prospect of getting out there and meeting Life did not appeal to Gawaine. So the Headmaster promised something that would help Gawaine in his slaying of dragons. Gawaine hoped this something would be an enchanted cap which would enable him to disappear at will, but the Headmaster scoffed at this, and gave him something better than an enchanted cap.

He gave Gawaine a magic word, and the magic word was Rumplesnitz.

And all Gawaine had to do was repeat the magic word once, and no dragon could possibly hurt him. Well, Gawaine went out to meet his first dragon the next day. The dragon charged at him breathing smoke and fire and Gawaine barely got the word Rumplesnitz out before he swung his ax and lopped off the dragon's head, thinking it was almost as easy to kill real dragons as it was to kill fake ones.

After that, he went out on every good day, leaving at dawn, and he rarely returned without the ears of another dead dragon. He grew more confident. He would sneeringly say Rumplesnitz and then *whoof,* swing his ax with his strong arms, and off would come another dragon's head, and home would come another pair of dragon ears.

And finally, Gawaine—who had taken to drinking at nights in the local tavern—went out after a night of revelry to meet his fiftieth dragon. The dragon shook in his boots because Gawaine's fame had spread afar. Gawaine walked up to the beast, raised his battle-ax, and then lowered it again. The dragon, knowing Gawaine was protected by an enchantment, asked the fellow what the trouble was. And Gawaine was forced to admit he'd forgotten the magic word.

Well now, this was a fine kettle of dragons.

The dragon, of course, was most helpful. He asked Gawaine if he could possibly help the knight in remembering the all-important magic word. Gawaine could only remember that it began with an "r" but that was all. And so the dragon prepared to eat him.

He charged forward, and Gawaine remembered the

magic word Rumplesnitz, but there was no time to say it, there was time only to swing his ax, and by God, off came the dragon's head, and it went flying some hundred yards, and that was the farthest Gawaine had knocked any dragon's head before.

Now this was all very confusing. Gawaine had *not* said the magic word Rumplesnitz, and yet the dragon hadn't harmed him and he'd sure as hell knocked that head for a whaling good distance. He went back to the knights' school and explained to the Headmaster what had happened.

The Headmaster admitted the truth. Rumplesnitz was not a magic word, it was Gawaine all along who was killing the dragons. The word just gave him confidence, that's all, and wasn't Gawaine glad that he finally knew the truth?

Gawaine wasn't glad. Gawaine wasn't glad at all. Why all those dragons he had killed could have devoured him if he hadn't been just a little faster than they! This was not good. This was not good at all, at all.

Gawaine did not rise at dawn the next day. At noon, he was still in bed, trembling under the bedcovers. The Headmaster and the Assistant Professor of Pleasaunce dragged him out of bed and forced him into the forest where the boy met his fifty-first dragon, having killed fifty to date.

The dragon was a small one.

Gawaine never came back to the school. They found nothing left of him except the metal part of the medals he always wore into battle. The dragon had even eaten the ribbons.

Gawaine's secret was never revealed, and he went down in the school's history as a hero. There still hangs a shield on the dining room wall, and fifty pairs of dragons' ears are on that shield. The legend "Gawaine le Coeur-Hardy," and the inscription "He killed fifty dragons," is gilt-lettered onto the shield under the dragons' ears. The record has never been equaled.

That was the story, and Rick read it well, even though he was reading it for the first time, and reading it aloud at that. He'd tried out for a good many college shows back at Hunter, and he was excellent at sight reading and interpretation.

He was delighted with the story because he had never read it before and it was a new experience to him as well as to the boys in the class. But he was sorry in a way that it was not a war story, because it was decidedly allegory, and allegory was probably far above the heads of these kids, and allegory should be taught only from a carefully prepared lesson plan.

He had no such plan, and he had already read the story, and he faced the unusually silent class and wondered just what the hell he should do next. Allegory with second termers—some of whom couldn't even write their own names.

"Well," he said, "that was a pretty good story, wasn't it?"

"Yeah," the kids said, and he could tell they meant it and had really enjoyed it.

"All about a knight who kills dragons, right?" he asked.

"Sure," the kids agreed. That's what it was about,

wasn't it? A knight who kills dragons, except he gets killed in the end, a sad ending.

"What else was it about?" Rick asked.

Finley, a kid near the back of the room, said, "He didn't really kill those dragons."

"What do you mean, Finley?" Rick asked.

"He was cheatin'," Finley said righteously. "He had a magic word."

"What was the magic word?" Rick asked, and the class chorused, "Rumplesnitz!"

"That's a funny word for a magic word, isn't it?" Rick asked.

"It wasn't no magic word," Bello shouted.

"Wasn't it?" Rick asked.

"The principal tole him it wasn't no magic word," Bello said. "That's how come he could kill the dragon without sayin' it. You remember that?"

"Yes, I remember it," Rick said slowly.

"So it wasn't no magic word."

"Yeah, there wasn't no magic word at all," Spencer said. "He was just killin' the dragons his ownself."

"Now, I don't understand that," Rick said, pleased with the response, but not for a second thinking he was going to break through. "If it wasn't a magic word, why'd the Headmaster give it to him?"

The class was silent for a few minutes, and then Shocken said, " 'Cause Gawaine was scared. He was a coward."

"But couldn't he kill dragons?" Rick asked. "He *did* kill fifty dragons, and you just told me Rumplesnitz wasn't a magic word at all."

"Sure, he killed them," Finley said. "But he was cheatin'."

"Was he cheating? Remember now, there was no magic word."

"So what?" Finley sneered. "He *thought* there was a magic word."

"Yes," Rick said, beginning to get a little excited now, surprised that they had garnered so much from the story, but still not realizing he was on the verge of his breakthrough. "That's just it. Gawaine thought it was a magic word. And did that help him kill the dragons?"

"Sure," White said.

"But how?"

" 'Cause he thought it was magic. He figured I go out there, ain't nothin' goan happen to me. Tha's how come he kill all those dragons."

"Did Gawaine need the magic word?" Rick asked.

"Sure," the kids said.

"Why?"

There was another silence, and Rick thought, *This is the end of it. The party's over. The response dies now. Now we get the blank faces.*

"He need it," Speranza said, raising his hand.

"Why?"

"He scared of the dragons. If he don't have the magic word, he run away. This way, he don't know it's not magic. He thinks it's magic, so he feels strong. He thinks he can kill any old dragon and the dragon can't touch him. That's why he needs it. Otherwise, he's a coward."

"How do you know that?" Rick asked the class.

"Well, once he finds out the word ain't magic," Daley said, "he gets et up."

"And is that why the Headmaster gave him this magic word?" Rick asked, praying the response would continue, feeling that something was happening out there, something he'd never experienced before. The kids were alive today, and he felt their life, and he responded to them the way they were responding to him, both he and the class thrashing out an allegory they had never seen before. "Is that why?" Rick asked.

"That principal, he's a smart cat," Davidson said. "He knows Gawaine need something."

"What does Gawaine need?" Rick asked. "What's the word for it?" *Please, give me the word,* he thought. *Don't let me hand it to you on a platter. Please, give.*

"What's the word?" he asked again.

"Con . . ." Daley started.

"Yes?"

"Confidence," Daley said triumphantly.

"Ah-ha, that's it," Rick said. "Confidence." He paused and made a sour face. "But that doesn't seem real," he said. "I mean, do you really think a word could give someone the confidence he needed?"

"Yeah, sure," Speranza said belligerently.

"No, I don't think so," Rick said.

"Yeah, yeah," Speranza said. "Sure, it could happen."

"How?"

"Well . . . like sometimes I'm scared before we take a test or something, an' I say three *Hail Mary's,* and I feel okay after that."

"It gives you confidence, is that right?"

"Yeah, sure," Speranza said.

"But still . . . a word like Rumplesnitz. I mean, after all, *Hail Mary* is a prayer. Rumplesnitz isn't a prayer."

"I don't think," Padres said slowly, "thees word means that. I mean, I don't think Rumplesnitz ees suppose to be nothing. You know what I mean?"

"Not exactly," Rick said. He felt hot all at once. He felt almost feverish. He was tense and tight, and he knew now that the kids were really responding, were really discussing this thing the way it should be discussed, were really giving him something, helping him. He didn't know why, and he didn't stop to ask why. He just held on and prayed almost, and he heard Padres say, "Thees Rumplesnitz, thees ees a fake, you know? I mean, the *Hail Mary*, that's real. Rumplesnitz, it don't mean nothing. Thees Gawaine, he fooling heemself."

"How is he fooling himself?" Rick asked.

" 'Cause there ain't no magic," Bello said derisively. "Hell, he coulda killed all the dragons he wanted, Rumplesnitz or no."

"Yes, then why does he need the word? Are there people like that who fool themselves? Who need magic words?"

"Sure," Price said. "My brother-in-law's like that."

"How so, Price?"

"Oh, he's a big bull artist, you know. He's always talkin' about his big deals, but he ain't really got no big deals. He's jus' a little crumb, you know? But he makes out like he's a big shot."

"And is he one?" Rick asked.

"Naw, he's a crumb. But he talks so much, I think he believes it himself."

"Like Rumplesnitz, you mean?"

Price hesitated for a moment, and then a smile flowered on his face. "Yeah," he said, surprised, "like Rumplesnitz. Just like that."

It was rolling now. It was rolling fast, and the kids out there all had their hands up in the air, and those hands were waving frantically.

"Does anyone else know anyone like that?" Rick asked. "People who fool themselves like that. People who could kill dragons if they tried, but who are too afraid to without the help of magic."

The kids were squirming because they all had something to say. They didn't call out because they wanted this lesson to proceed in an orderly fashion. They were enjoying this, and they felt something of the same thing Rick was feeling, and they wanted to express their ideas.

"This guy who pitches for our team," Finley said, "he got to chew gum or else he can't pitch. He don't need the gum. He's a good pitcher anyway."

"But that's superstition, isn't it?" Rick asked. "Is Rumplesnitz superstition? Is that what Rumplesnitz is supposed to be?"

"No," Bello said. "No, it ain't. It's what gives him the confidence. But it ain't superstition. That's different."

"How so?"

"Superstition is you're afraid of something. Like black cats or thirteens. Gawaine ain't afraid of Rumplesnitz. He loves that word. That's his courage, that word."

"That's what he leans on," Spencer said.

"A crutch?" Rick asked.

"Yeah, that's it, a crutch."

"And there are people who need crutches in life?"

"Cripples need crutches," Finley said.

"Only cripples?" Rick asked. "Was Gawaine a cripple?"

"No," Theros said, "he was strong."

"In his body," Rick said.

"Oh," Theros said, "you mean maybe like he was crippled in his head. Like maybe 'cause he was scared, he was crippled. Like that?"

"Possibly," Rick said. "Are there people like that?"

"I know a guy can't do anything without his mother says okay," Wilson said. "Like he don't trust his own . . . his own . . ."

"Judgment," Rick supplied.

"Yeah. But he's okay. I mean, when his mother ain't around, he's fine. He could do things without her. He don't need her."

"The way Gawaine doesn't need Rumplesnitz, right?"

"Right," Wilson said emphatically.

"A cripple," Rick said.

"As long as his old lady's around," Price said.

"Rumplesnitz, you mean," Ventro said.

"But I thought this story was all about a knight who kills dragons," Rick said, delighted now, pleased, almost thrilled. He knew he'd broken through, and his watch told him there were three minutes left to the period, and he wanted to round it out, wanted them to realize that the story said one thing while it meant another. "Was it?"

"Yeah, it was," Finley said.

"And only that? Just a knight who kills dragons."

"Well, you could twist it around," Price said. "Then it becomes everybody, and not just Gawaine."

"Everybody?" Rick asked.

"Everybody who needs a crutch," Speranza supplied. "Like in real life."

"You mean the story has a message?" Rick asked.

"Sure. It tells about fake words, and how you don't need them. If you're strong and quick, what you need the phony crutch for? You got it all in you anyway. You can kill dragons, not really, but you could maybe be a good mechanic, like that, you know?"

"Yes," Rick said, "exactly. And is the story a better one because it tells a second story, because it gives a message, and because it's not only about a cowardly knight?"

"It's a good story," Bello said.

"Yeah, that was a good one," Price said. "I liked that one."

"And will you remember the word for a story that tells two stories at the same time, a story that gives a message?"

"Yeah, what is it?" Speranza asked.

"An allegory," Rick said, and he wrote the word on the board, and someone behind him said, "That was a damn good story," and then the bell sounded.

He sat at his desk, and the kids crowded around him, and they asked him if there were other stories like that, where you could get something else out of them and not just the story. And one kid thanked him for showing him the second story because he'd only realized the story about the knight, and it was like finding something special, a present you didn't know was there. And another kid told him about a friend of his who was like Gawaine and had a Rumplesnitz, and another kid asked if Rick would read them another story like that.

And Rick sat there stunned, answering their questions, listening to their stories, thinking, *I've broken through, Christ, I've broken through,* and watching the kids mill around his desk while the kids in his second-period class filed in, puzzled. And at last the kids left, and he was too stunned to try a repetition of the same story in his second-period class, so he let it go, thinking all the while, *I've broken through, oh my God, I've broken through to them. I've reached them.*

And when he walked to his Hall Patrol at the end of the second period, he was stopped by kids in his seventh-term classes, kids who said they'd heard about the knight story, and would he teach them the same story. And one kid asked him what this was about Rumplesnitz, and could he learn it? And he was stopped at least a dozen times on his way down to the first floor, and each kid made the same request: teach us about the fifty-first dragon.

He would teach them now, oh God, he would really teach them now because he'd broken through and that was half the battle. He would give 55–206 the same story, and then he would give it to his seventh termers, and everything would be all right.

But he didn't give it to 55–206, and he didn't give it to his seventh termers because the messenger found him where he was sitting outside the Students' Lavatory on the first floor opposite the entrance doors, and the message told him that his mother-in-law had called, and that Anne had been taken to the hospital in labor.

The subway stop was at 77th Street, and he ran up the steps to Lexington Avenue. He turned left on the corner, realized he was heading for 78th, and then changed his course and began walking fast—almost running toward 76th Street. There was a candy store on the corner, and he crossed 77th Street and the big brown bulk of the hospital filled Lexington Avenue between 77th and 76th. Across the street, on the other side of the avenue, he saw the stores, and he watched the stores as he walked rapidly opposite them: the grocery, the luncheonette, the restaurant, another restaurant, a stationery store, and on the corner, a florist. There was a florist on his side of the street, too, on the corner of 76th Street. He turned right at the corner, looking briefly at the big church on the other side of the avenue, and then walking past another candy store, and a toy shop, and a dry cleaner's, and an electrician's shop, and then the Einhorn Auditorium of Lenox Hill Hospital.

The green canopy of the hospital reached out for the sidewalk. White letters announced LENOX HILL HOSPITAL, added MAIN ENTRANCE in a *sotto voce*. The canopy covered the center arch of three arches. Plaques with the address 111 held the walls on either side of the center arch. He mounted the steps and he glanced upward, and the arch over the inner doors was inscribed with the legend ERECTED MCMXXX.

He noticed all these things, and he thought of Anne, and he cursed because it hadn't happened while he was at home, and he worried about her at the same time, and then he was in the large entrance, and he looked first to the wall on his right, and then spotted the reception desk on his left and walked directly to it. The girl behind the desk was on the phone, and he waited impatiently, shifting his weight from one foot to the other. She put down the phone at last, and Rick said, "Mrs. Dadier."

"Maternity, sir?" the girl asked.

"Yes, my mother-in-law just call . . ."

"One moment, sir." She consulted some papers on her desk, papers he could not see, and then she said, "She is in the delivery room now, sir."

"How long . . . I mean . . . is Dr. Bradley here?"

"Yes, sir."

"Will you let me know . . . how . . . how do I find out?"

"The doctor will come down after the delivery, sir."

"Thank you."

He stood at the desk for a moment, and the girl smiled sympathetically, and then he turned and walked to the bench on the opposite wall. He sat and jiggled his feet and clenched and unclenched his hands, and when he saw Anne's mother he almost didn't recognize her. She came out of one of the arches stemming from the waiting room and walked directly to him, taking his hands.

"You made good time, Rick," she said. She was a small woman, as blond as Anne was, miraculously blond considering the fact that she was fifty-four and hadn't once used any tints on her head. She smiled now and held his hands tightly, and he asked, "Is she all right, Mom?"

"She's fine, darling," Anne's mother said.

"I came the minute I got your message. I had to clear it with the office, but . . ."

"I was in the ladies' room," Anne's mother said, as if she felt some compulsion to explain her recent absence.

"But she's all right?"

"Yes, she's fine. She called me the minute the pains started."

"She should have called me," Rick said. "I would have . . ."

"I took a cab," Anne's mother said. "I was there in fifteen minutes. I think it's going to be an easy birth, Rick."

"How do you know? I mean, how can you tell?" he asked.

"The pains were coming very fast when we got here. Dr. Bradley took her right upstairs."

"He was here when you arrived?"

"Yes. He's awfully nice, isn't he?"

"Yes," Rick said, realizing he was whispering, and wondering why he was. His mother-in-law sat on the bench beside him, and Rick turned and looked up at the face of the clock in the wall, hanging over the list of names lettered in red and black scroll. He didn't know what the names were all about, and he was too worried to read any of them. He turned from the clock without having consciously read the time, and then he looked at his mother-in-law and saw the nervousness on her face, too, and envied her for being a woman because she knew what it was all about, and he knew only the worry and the strain and the fear bred of ignorance.

His eyes roamed the room, and he knew he was consciously allowing them to roam, filling the time until Dr. Bradley appeared. He saw the sign TELE-PHONES to the left of the entrance doors, and he saw the boards flanking each side of the entrance doors, the boards holding the doctors' names, and the red IN buttons and the black OUT buttons which flashed a white arrow when the doctor was in the hospital. He was tempted to walk over to the board and see if Dr. Bradley were indeed in, but the girl at the reception desk had said he was in, and his own mother-in-law had said she'd seen him, but he still wanted to walk over there and check. He rose abruptly, and then realized how foolish he was being, but since he was standing he began to pace, and Anne's mother watched him and said nothing.

The wall opposite the entrance wall had an arch smack in its center. He could see a sign reading EMER-GENCY jutting out into the corridor beyond the arch, and he wondered if Anne were considered an emergency, and then he realized that was foolish, too. Benches flanked the arch in that wall, and two windowed doors flanked the benches symmetrically. A water fountain hugged the wall in the left corner, and a high arched window with a bench under it was on the right-angle wall that held the reception desk. On the righthand side of the arch, over the bench there, a bronze plaque and a small sign commanded his attention. He could not read the plaque, but the sign said:

SAVE A LIFE
DONATE BLOOD
For your relatives—friends
Blood Bank
11th floor

He wondered if Anne would need a transfusion, and he wondered if he should go up to the 11th floor and give some blood, and then he reminded himself he was being foolish again, and he wondered why he was being so damned foolish. Women had babies every day of the week. In China, they dropped them in the fields and then picked up their hoes again. But this wasn't China, and this wasn't a faceless woman-who-had-a-baby-every-day-of-the-week. This was Anne, this was his wife, and she was up there in the delivery room all alone and there wasn't a damned thing he could do for her. This was one battle that was all her own, exclusively, and the knowledge left him frustrated because he wanted to help her and he knew he couldn't.

All he could do was pace under the big chandelier that dominated the ceiling of the room, the ceiling with its ornate circular design. He walked to the reception desk, and then to the glass-fronted case to the left of the desk, where the carefully scripted words *Flowers For Sale* were lettered onto the wood.

He wanted to buy flowers, but the case was closed,

and the Gift Shop (magazines, candies) opposite it was locked tighter than a drum, too. He realized they were both probably open during visiting hours, but this was not visiting hours, so he toyed with the idea of running down to either of the two florists on the opposite corners of 76th Street, and then he thought he'd miss Dr. Bradley if he did that, so he kept pacing, back and forth, back and forth, and then over to the telephone booths, and then to the arch near the telephone booths, across the marbled floor, looking up at the legend on the arch:

THIS BUILDING WAS ERECTED
IN
LOVING MEMORY
OF

He did not read the rest because the "in Loving Memory of" filled him with a sudden dread. He did not know the statistics for women who died in childbirth, though he suspected the figures were very low indeed. But women *did* die in childbirth and, no, nothing like that would happen, nothing like that to Anne.

He walked back to the bench where his mother-in-law sat, and she said, smiling, "Relax, Rick. It'll be all right, you'll see."

He nodded blankly, looked up at the clock again, thought abruptly of the lesson he'd taught on "The Fifty-First Dragon," and then switched his thoughts back to Anne and the delivery room.

It couldn't have been more than ten minutes since he'd arrived at the hospital when he saw Dr. Bradley

coming through the arch where the EMERGENCY sign
hung in the corridor. Dr. Bradley was not smiling, and
he looked very tired, and Rick walked to him quickly,
seeing out of the corner of his eye Anne's mother rise
from the bench.

Dr. Bradley extended his hand, and Rick took it, and
then the doctor smiled, very weakly, like a man who has
just swum the English Channel and is too tired to pose
for pictures. Rick didn't ask anything, but his questions
were all over his face, and the doctor looked at Rick's
face, and his mouth stopped smiling. He looked very,
very tired, and the weariness showed in his eyes and
even his mustache seemed limp under the aquiline
sweep of his nose. A light sheen of sweat stood out on
his forehead, and Rick studied the doctor's eyes and then
said, "Is she all right?"

"Yes," Dr. Bradley said wearily, smiling again. "She's
fine, Mr. Dadier."

Anne's mother was standing beside them now, craning forward like someone who wants to intrude but isn't
sure her intrusion is welcome.

"She's all right?" Rick asked again.

"Yes, she's fine."

"Is it a boy or a girl?" Anne's mother asked.

Rick saw the pain stab deep into Dr. Bradley's eyes,
and the pain leaped the distance between them and
lodged in his own throat like a poisoned dart.

"The baby was stillborn," Dr. Bradley said softly. "A
boy. I'm sorry, Mr. Dadier. The umbilical cord . . . it
sometimes happens and there's no way of foretelling . . ."
He paused and wiped the sweat from his forehead, know-

ing that no matter how well he told this, no matter how honest he was, how sincere he was, there would still be doubt, that lingering doubt which silently asked, "But couldn't you do something?" The doubt which silently accused the obstetrician.

"Around the baby's throat," Dr. Bradley said softly. "Intrauterine . . ."

"The baby is dead," Rick said, stunned. "Is that it?"

"Yes," Dr. Bradley answered. Anne's mother drew in a sharp sigh, and Rick said, "Dead," dully, and Dr. Bradley said "Yes" again.

"It's . . ." Rick started, and then he forgot what he was going to say, and he thought only, *The baby is dead. A boy. And dead.*

"A perfectly healthy, normal child," Dr. Bradley said. He clasped Rick's shoulder warmly and said, "You can have others, Mr. Dadier. You're both young and . . . I . . . I know this is a shock, and believe me, I can't tell you how sorry I am."

"It's . . . it's all right," Rick said softly. "It wasn't your fault."

"An unfortunate . . ."

"It's all right," Rick said.

"Your wife is doing very well. She . . ."

"Anne is all right? You're sure . . ."

"Yes, she's fine. I'm awfully sorry, Mr. Dadier. This is always the saddest part of obstetrics, and believe me, I wouldn't . . ."

"No, that's all right," Rick said too hastily. "Please, it's all right. May I see my wife? May I talk to her?"

"She's a little weak," Dr. Bradley said, "but she asked

for you. I . . . she . . . she doesn't know about the baby yet, Mr. Dadier. I wouldn't tell her until tomorrow, if I were you. You see, she's been through a shock and it's better if we wait. Do you understand?"

"Yes, I understand. May I go to her?"

"I would also suggest that you take her home as soon as possible. It's not a healthy atmosphere, you understand, being on a maternity ward where the other women . . ."

"I understand," Rick said, wanting desperately to see Anne, wanting to see her and to touch her. "Please, may I . . ."

"Come along," Dr. Bradley said.

He followed the doctor down the corridor and they waited for the elevator, and he thought, *The baby is dead, the baby is dead*. And then the elevator took them to the fourth floor and he stepped out into a dim corridor, and his heels echoed on the floor, and the high-vaulted ceilings carried the echoes. He waited while Dr. Bradley went inside, and he heard a woman screaming with her labor pains, and then a nurse in a crisply-starched white uniform wheeled Anne out. She lay back on the table with the sheet tucked up under her chin, and the sheet was flat over her stomach, and her head was twisted to one side. Her hair was damp on her forehead, and she smiled weakly when she saw him, and the nurse said, "Not too long now. She needs sleep."

He took her hand, and she brought it to her chest and held it there, clung to it tightly. He kissed her damp forehead and there were suddenly tears in his eyes for no good reason, and he leaned over the table and held her close, and she pressed her cheek to his and he could feel the tears on her skin also.

"It was terrible, darling," she said, half-sobbing and half-laughing. "Oh, Rickie, it was really very hard."

"Do you feel all right?" he asked.

"I feel tired. I feel so exhausted. Rickie, I never knew there could be so much pain. Oh, Rickie, I'm so glad it's over, so glad." She laughed sleepily, and then she bit her lip, and the tears came again, unchecked.

"And you feel all right?"

"Just tired, darling. Darling, I want to sleep for a year."

"All right, honey, you go to sleep."

"No," she said, "no, don't go. Please don't go yet, Rickie. Wait until they chase you."

"All right," he said.

"Did you see the baby?" she asked suddenly.

"Honey, I think you ought to get some sleep. I think . . ."

"It's a boy, isn't it?"

"Yes."

"That's what you wanted, wasn't it, darling?"

"Yes. Honey, why don't you . . ."

"Are you happy, Rick?"

"Yes, darling."

"I'm glad. I knew you wanted a boy." She smiled and closed her eyes, and he thought she was asleep for a moment. He made a slight movement away from her, but she opened her eyes and held him tight. "Does he look like you, darling?" she asked.

"I . . . I don't know," Rick said.

"I'll bet he does. Oh, he was so much trouble, Rick. The little stinker." She laughed and then said, "Are you happy, Rick?"

He was ashamed of the tears that ran down his face, and he buried his face in her shoulder to hide the tears. "Yes," he said, "I'm very happy." He held her closer to him and said fiercely, "Anne, I love you so much, so terribly much."

"I know, darling," she said soothingly.

She stroked the back of his head idly, and they were silent for a few moments, and then Rick heard the click of the nurse's heels on the floor, and her voice said, "We want her to rest now," gently, because the nurse knew what had happened, too.

"I'll come tomorrow," Rick said.

"All right, darling. Take care of yourself, please. Promise. Is my mother here?"

"Yes."

"Tell her I'm all right, just sleepy. Tell her it's a boy, Rick."

"I will."

"They wouldn't let me see him. They had to clean him up. Is he big, Rick?"

"I . . . yes, Anne."

"You'll come tomorrow? You will, won't you?"

"Yes."

"All right now," the nurse said gently, "time for bed."

He leaned over and kissed Anne again, and she clung to him for a moment with a happy smile on her face, and then she leaned back and the nurse wheeled the table down the corridor. He stood under the high-vaulted ceiling, thinking nothing, feeling nothing, empty, empty, drained.

He had not known the boy, not known it as Anne had, had never felt the kicks against his stomach, had never felt the life mushrooming within him. But he felt now a great loss and a great sadness, and he stood alone in the high-vaulted room, and he wanted to say something more to his wife, wanted to share this thing with her, wanted to talk it out. He watched the table wheel out of sight, and he stood there helplessly with the sadness inside him, a weary sadness, a sadness beyond tears. He turned at last and walked toward the elevator, and on the way down to the main floor he did not look at the elevator operator, nor did he hear a word his mother-in-law said on the way home. He thought only of the son he had never known—the son he had lost.

He told Anne the next day.

They'd put her in a private room even though he'd originally arranged for a semi-private one. They felt it would be better for her, alone, without seeing another mother and her infant. When he came during visiting hours, he brought flowers, a gigantic bouquet of roses—which were her favorite—and the nurses oohed and ahhed over the bouquet and then arranged the flowers expertly in a vase beside her bed.

He sat near the bed, and she had prettied herself for the occasion. She was still pale, but her hair had been combed and it framed her face with soft gold, and she had put lipstick on her lips, and she looked very pretty even though she looked very tired.

She shifted her weight uncomfortably after he'd kissed her, and then explained, "I'm on a rubber cushion. They cut you all up, did you know, Rick? To make it easier for the baby to come out. I have stitches down there."

He smiled with a great effort and said, "They'll heal."

"My God, I hope so," she said, opening her eyes wide.

She chatted about the hospital and about one nurse she didn't like, and then she asked, "When do I see the baby, that's what I'd like to know? After all, creation is something . . ."

"Anne . . ."

". . . I don't do every other day. The least they could do is . . ."

"Anne . . ."

She stopped talking and looked at him curiously, and he knew that she knew in that moment, or at least suspected, or perhaps suspected something worse, a deformed child perhaps, something worse than death could have been.

"What is it, Rick?" she asked, her voice very low, her face resigned. Her hands were clenched against the white sheet, and he knew she was bracing herself for what was coming.

"The baby is dead," he said quickly, hoping to lessen the pain by saying it quickly. "The cord strangled him. It was nobody's fault, Anne. It just happens . . . sometimes."

She was quiet for a very long time. She did not look at him. She stared at her hands clenched on the white sheet and finally she lifted her head.

"I'm sorry," she said, "please forgive me, Rick."

He took her in his arms because she'd begun crying, and he wondered why this had to be a time of tears instead of a time of laughter, but he held her close and felt the sobs wracking her body.

"I'm sorry," she kept repeating, "oh, Rick, please, please forgive me."

"Honey, honey, don't be silly. It was something . . ."

"Rick, forgive me," she sobbed, "darling, darling, please forgive me."

"Anne," he said desperately, wanting her to stop crying, wanting to comfort her and not knowing how, "we can try again. We're young," he said, unconsciously repeating Dr. Bradley's words. "The baby was healthy and normal, honey. It was just an accident, just . . ."

"And you're not angry with me, Rick? Rick, please say you're not angry. Please."

"I'm not angry, darling. How could I be angry? Honey, I'm happy I've got you, that's all that counts. Sweetheart, I don't know what I'd do without . . ."

"Rick, I feel so ashamed of myself. The things I thought about you, and now this, I can't even give you a baby right, Rick, I'm so sorry and so ashamed, Rick."

"Come on now, Anne. Come on, honey, it's all right. Believe me, it's all right, Anne."

"You do love me, Rick? Rick, do you love me?"

"You know I do, Anne."

"Say it, Rick."

"I love you, darling."

"Even after what I thought? About those stupid notes, and Lois Hammond? Rick, I'm so ashamed I could die. Rick, please . . ."

"What notes, darling?" he asked gently.

She told him about the notes then, and he listened, and a tremendous hatred attacked him for a moment, a hatred for the unknown note-sender, but the hatred disappeared because he could not afford the luxury of hate now, and because the honest emotion inside him was something that hatred would never understand.

And when it was all over, when she'd purged herself of the doubt and the suspicion and the fear, she said, "Hold me, Rick. Hold me close, darling," and he tightened his arms around her and he murmured, "There's never been anyone but you, Anne," almost to himself, not even sure she'd heard him.

"We will try again, Rick," she said, "if you can forgive me."

"There's nothing to forgive."

"The notes . . ."

"Forget them. Some bastard . . ."

"We'll forget them," she said.

"Yes."

"And we will try again, Rick? You want to try again?"

"Yes, darling."

"I do, too."

They were silent then. They held hands, and they could hear the sound of laughter down the corridor, and they said nothing to each other. He thought again about the loss of the boy, and he didn't know what he felt exactly, except this emptiness within him. He could imagine how Anne felt, because she had been the one who'd had the baby growing inside her, feeding on her blood, a part of her, and now to lose it. He kept listening to the laughter from down the hallway, and he realized Anne was listening to the laughter, too, and because he wanted to take her mind off it, he began talking, and he told her about the school, and he told her about "The Fifty-First Dragon," but he did not tell it well because it didn't seem to matter so much now.

She listened, and she was pleased, but he could see that she was still thinking about the baby she had lost, and he knew that they would neither of them ever forget their first experience with childbirth, even if they lived to be a hundred and had two dozen kids. So he kept talking until it was time to go, and then he kissed her and left her with her own thoughts about the boy, and he wandered down to the elevator trying not to hear the proud fathers everywhere around him.

He walked out into the street, knowing he should go home, not wanting to go home, not knowing what to do with himself. He wondered if he should go back to school the next day, realizing the next day was Wednesday, the 23rd, the day of the Christmas Assembly, knowing he should be there, but not much caring whether he went there or not, except that it would keep him occupied and give him something to do. He finally went home, and when he spoke to Dr. Bradley on the phone that night, the doctor advised taking Anne out of the hospital the next day because there would be a lot of visitors for the holidays, and he did not want to risk undue depression.

So Rick stayed out of school all day Tuesday, and he stayed out of school on that Wednesday, too, missing the Christmas Assembly completely, not knowing (and not caring, anyway) that Alan Manners filled in with his small part, not knowing that Alan Manners shared the few drinks, the few toasts, the few gifts, the big present with Lois Hammond after the assembly.

And not knowing that there was another present and that this present had been purchased for Rick by the cast of the show, and that Gregory Miller had personally supervised the collection of funds and the selection of the gift which was a black-and-gold-striped necktie.

Nor did he know that the boys had prepared a little skit of their own to accompany the presentation of the gift, or that they had—on a sudden whim—given the present to George Katz because Rick was not there and they hated to see the gift go to waste. Miller had protested strongly, wanting to hold the gift until after the holidays when Rick would return to school. But the boys voted him down, saying they'd get another gift and hadn't Katz been a real nice Santa Claus, perhaps sincere in their desires to get another gift after the holidays, but never fulfilling their promise once the assembly had been forgotten.

Rick did not know anything about this, and he couldn't have cared less. He was vaguely aware of the fact that he had finally broken through in one of his classes, and he felt things would be easier when he went back to school, but he didn't think much about school now.

He took Anne home from the hospital on Wednesday the 23rd, and he didn't think about anything but her on that day.

He didn't go back to Manual Trades until January 4th, when the Christmas vacation was over, and by the time that Monday rolled around, everyone in the school had completely forgotten "The Fifty-First Dragon."

It was almost like greeting his classes again for the first time. It was almost like a beginning.

It was almost exactly like starting from scratch.

13

The door to Room 206 was locked when Richard Dadier reached it for his fifth-period English class on January 15th. He tried the knob several times, peered in through one of the glass panels, and motioned for Santini to open the door. Santini, sitting in the seat closest to the door, shrugged his shoulders innocently and grinned his moronic smile. Rick felt a sudden flow of anger, and then the anger gave way to the revulsion he always experienced lately before stepping into a classroom. He wondered briefly if Josh had felt this way, if Josh had . . .

Easy, he told himself. Easy does it.

He reached into his pocket for the large key, and then slipped it into the keyhole. Swinging the door open, he slapped it fast against the prongs that jutted out from the wall, and then walked briskly to his desk. A falsetto voice somewhere at the back of the room rapidly squeaked, "Daddy-oh!"

Rick busied himself with his Delaney book, glancing around the room, flipping cards over as he took the attendance. Half were absent as usual. He was secretly glad. He was always grateful for the cutters now, because the classes were easier to handle in small groups.

He turned over the last card and waited for them to quiet down. They never would, he knew, never.

Reaching down, he pulled a heavy book from his briefcase and rested it on the palm of his hand. Without warning, he slammed it onto the desk.

"Shut up!" he bellowed, thinking, *I'm beginning to sound just like Halloran.*

The class groaned into silence, startled by the outburst.

Now, he thought. Now I'll press it home. Surprise plus advantage plus seize your advantage. Just like waging war. All day long I wage war. Some fun.

"Assignment for tomorrow," he said flatly.

A moan escaped from 55–206, and Miller, an engaging grin on his face, said, "You work too hard, Mr. Daddy-oh."

The name twisted deep inside Rick, and he felt the tiny needles of apprehension start at the base of his spine. *So that's it for today, eh, Miller?* he thought. *Today you draw the line at Daddy-oh. Today you call me Daddy-oh and break my back that way.*

"Quiet, Mueller," Rick said, feeling pleasure at mispronouncing the boy's name. "Assignment for tomorrow. In *New Horizons* . . ."

"In what?" West asked.

I should have known better, Rick reminded himself sourly. We've only been using the book since the beginning of the term. I can't expect them to remember the title. No.

"In *New Horizons*," he repeated impatiently, "the blue book, the one we've been using all term." He paused, gaining control of himself, telling himself he lost control too easily lately. "In the blue book," he continued softly, "read the first ten pages of 'Army Ants in the Jungle.' "

"Here in class?" West asked.

"No. At home."

"Christ," West mumbled.

"It's on page two seventy-five," Rick said.

"Whut page?" Miller called out.

"Two seventy-five."

"What page?" Levy asked.

"Two seventy-five," Rick said. "My God, what's the matter with you?" He turned rapidly and wrote the figures on the board in a large hand, repeating the numerals slowly. "Two, seven-ty, five." He heard a chuckle spread maliciously behind him, and he whirled quickly. Every boy in 55–206 wore a deadpan.

"There will be a short test on the homework tomorrow," he announced grimly.

"Another one?" Miller asked lazily.

"Yes, Mailler," Rick said, "another one." He glared at the boy heatedly, thinking, *Don't start up with me today, Miller. Just don't, that's all*. Miller grinned back engagingly, safe behind the secure comfort of the arbitrary line he'd drawn. *Goddamn you and your goddamned line*, Rick cursed silently.

"And now," he said, "the test I promised you yesterday."

A hush fell over the class.

Quick, Rick thought. Press the advantage. Strike again and again. Don't wait for them. Keep one step ahead always. Move fast and they won't know what's going on. Keep them too busy to get into mischief.

He began chalking the test on the board. He turned his head and barked over his shoulder, "All books away. Antoro, hand out the paper."

This is the way to do it, he realized. I've figured it out. The way to control these bastards is to give them a test every day of the week. Write their fingers off.

"Begin immediately," Rick said in a businesslike voice. "Don't forget your heading."

"What's that, that heading?" Belazi asked.

"Name, official class, subject class, subject teacher," Rick said wearily.

Seventy-two, he thought. I've said it seventy-two times since I started teaching here. Seventy-two times.

"Who's our subject teacher?" Belazi asked. His face expressed complete bewilderment, but he could not quite hide the smile there.

"Mr. Daddy-oh," West said quite plainly. He sat in his seat next to Miller, his stringy blond hair hanging over his pimply forehead. An insolent smile perched on his mouth, and Rick looked at the smile and at the hard lus-ter of West's eyes, and then he turned his attention to Belazi.

"Mr. Dadier is the subject teacher," he said. "And inci-dentally, Whoust," he glared at West, "anyone mis-spelling my name in the heading will lose ten points."

"What!" West complained, outraged.

"You heard me," Rick snapped.

"Well, how do you spell Daddy-oh?" West asked, the smile curling onto his mouth again.

"You figure it out, West. I don't need the ten points."

"Don't worry, teach, I can spell your name all right," West said.

Rick bitterly pressed the chalk into the board. It snapped in two, and he picked up another piece from the runner. With the chalk squeaking wildly, he wrote out the rest of the test.

"No talking," he ordered. He sat down behind the desk and eyed the class suspiciously.

A puzzled frown crossed Miller's face. "I don't understand the first question, teach," he called out.

Rick leaned back in his chair and looked at the board. "It's very simple, Miltzer," he said. "There are ten words on the board. Some are spelled correctly, and some are wrong. If they're wrong, you correct them. If they're right, spell them just the way they're written."

"Mmmmmm," Miller said thoughtfully, his eyes glowing. "How do you spell the second word?"

Rick leaned back again, looked at the second word, and began, "D-I-S . . ." He caught himself and faced Miller squarely. "Just the way you want to. You're taking this test, not me."

Miller grinned widely. "Oh. I didn't know that, Chief."

"You'll know when you see your mark, Miller."

He cursed himself for having pronounced the boy's name correctly, and then he cursed Miller for simply being Miller. He remembered the day he'd come back, after the Christmas vacation. He remembered Miller stopping him in the hallway and telling him he'd heard about the baby and was sorry. He'd stared at the boy and tried to combine both halves of his character: the half that could be an angel in a Christmas show and could express concern over the death of Rick's son, and the half that raised hell in the classroom. He had given it up as a sorry task, had thanked Miller for his sympathy, and then left the boy. He knew what to expect from Miller now. Even after the show, and especially after the long talk he'd had with the boy. The easy road. That was what he would get. And the easy road was the hell-raising road, the one-of-the-boys road. *And I'm taking the same goddamned road*, Rick thought bitterly.

He sighed and made himself comfortable at the desk, and then he looked out over the class.

De la Cruz will cheat, he thought. He will cheat and I won't catch him. He's uncanny that way. God, how I wish I could catch him. How does he? On his cuff? Where? He probably has it stuffed in his ear. Should I search him? No, what's the use? He'd cheat his own mother. An inborn crook. A bastard.

Bastard, Rick mused. Even I call them that now. All bastards, all the time. I must tell Solly Klein I've succumbed. I must take Solly aside someday and say, "Solly, old boy, you were right. This *is* the garbage can of the educational system." Hell, even Miller recognized that. And then I must admit that I'm doing nothing more than sitting on the lid. And then I must look up Josh Edwards, wherever the hell he is, whatever the hell he's doing, selling shoes, washing automobiles, and I must tell him. I must say to him, "Josh, I'm a fake. You were the brave one, Josh, and I'm just a goddamned fake. It's I who's the coward, Josh."

But when did I give up, he wondered, when did I start taking the easy road, Miller's easy road? Or have I given up? Yes, I've given up. No, I haven't.

But I have, I have. And when? When the baby was born, when my son was not born. Before that? No, before that was "The Fifty-First Dragon," and oh what a lesson that had been, God what a lesson that was. Just give me a lesson like that once a week, just once a week, that's all, and I'd teach for the rest of my life. I'd take all the crap all the Millers and Wests in the world have to hand out, I'd let myself be called on the carpet every day by all the Smalls alive, if only I could reach them like that once a week, just once a week. Or if one kid, just one kid that's all, one kid got something out of it all. If I could point to one of these bastards and say, "I showed him the way," if I could only do that, but who have I shown?

I've shown no one. It's a big laugh, all right, but I've shown no one. And after all my big talk to Miller, all my big talk about hard roads and easy roads, with Miller *wanting* to be shown, and I couldn't even show him. It's Miller who's shown me. It's Miller who offered the easy road, join the crowd, fool around, play around, be a fake. Miller showed that to me, and I took it, and now we're both on the easy road, a fake student and a fake teacher. But how can I blame myself?

They're all the same, just the way they were when I first started, not changed one goddamned bit. But am I to blame?

Yes, you're to blame, all right. You're to blame

because somewhere along the line you stopped trying. And you can say it's because you don't give a damn anymore, and you can say you've got your own headaches, but you still stopped trying. When Josh Edwards stopped trying, he also stopped teaching. He gave it up, and that was the honest thing to do, but you're not honest. You're filling the chair, but you're not filling the job. You're taking the easy road, and I'm glad I don't have to live with you.

There are a lot of guys taking the easy road, Rick thought, but I never thought I'd be one of them, but I'm certainly one of them now, and that's a hell of a thing to admit. The shining example, the one who was going to show Miller all about the hard road, and Miller's skin is black, by Christ, he was born with a hard road, and yet you blamed him for taking the easy road that time you talked with him, even though you couldn't explain the hard road, even though you still can't explain it, especially not now when you've succumbed to the bastards.

Bastards again. All right, bastards.

They're all rotten, and they're all bastards, and I agree with Solly Klein now, and I should have seen it in the beginning, Solly, for you are all-wise, Solly, and you know all about baseballs crashing into blackboards alongside your head, and you know all about this machine that won't run no matter what you do to it— no, it'll run but it won't produce. You know all about this big goddamned treadmill with all its captive rats scurrying to get nowhere, scurrying to get right back where they came from. You know all about it, Solly, and you tried to tell me but I wouldn't listen because I was the Messiah come to teach. Except even a Messiah wouldn't be heard in this dump.

So why the hell bother? Why should I teach? Why should I get ulcers?

"Keep your eyes on your own paper, Belazi," he cautioned.

Everyone is a cheat, a potential thief. Solly was right. We have to keep them off the streets. They should really hire a policeman. It would be funny, he thought, if it weren't so damned serious. How long can you handle garbage without beginning to stink yourself?

"All right, Belazi," Rick said suddenly. "Bring your paper up. I'm subtracting five points from it."

"Why? What the hell did I do?" Belazi shouted.

"Bring me your paper."

Belazi reluctantly slouched to the front of the room and tossed his paper on the desk. He was a big boy with a sinewy, big-boned frame, and he stood with his thumbs looped in the tops of his dungarees as Rick marked a large –5 on the paper in bright red.

"What's that for?" Belazi asked.

"For having loose eyes."

Belazi snatched the paper from the desk and examined it with disgust. Rick stared at the boy, remembering his first meeting with 55–206, and his announcement that they'd be making a trip to the bookroom. Belazi had piped, "Is this trip necessary?" A wise guy as well as a cheat, Rick thought. Oh, the hell with them all. Belazi wrinkled his face into a grimace and slowly started back to his seat.

As he passed West, West looked to the front of the

room. His eyes met Rick's, and he sneered, "Chicken!"

"What?" Rick asked.

West looked surprised. "You talking to me, teach?"

"Yes, West. What did you just say?"

"I didn't say nothing, teach." West smiled innocently.

"Bring me your paper, West."

"What for?"

"Bring it up!"

"What for, I said."

"I heard what you said, West. And *I* said bring me your paper. Now. Right this minute."

"Aw, bring him the paper," Miller said, smiling good-naturedly.

"What the hell for?" West said to Miller. "What the hell did I do?"

"Go on, Artie," Miller said easily, "bring him the paper."

"I don't see why I should," West persisted, the smile gone from his face now.

"Because I say so, that's why," Rick said tightly.

West's answer came slowly, pointedly. "And supposing I don't feel like?" A frown was twisting his pimply forehead.

"Look, Artie," Miller said. "Why . . ."

"Keep out of this, Greg," West snapped. "Just keep the hell out of it, understand?"

Miller's eyes opened wide in surprise, but the smile clung to his mouth. The other boys in the room were suddenly interested. Heads that were bent over papers snapped upright. Rick felt every eye in the class focus on him.

They were rooting for West, of course. They wanted West to win. They wanted West to defy him, like that time he'd threatened to piss all over the floor. Rick couldn't let that happen.

He walked crisply up the aisle and stood beside West. The boy looked up provokingly.

"Get up," Rick said, trying to control the modulation of his voice.

My voice is shaking, he told himself. I can feel it shaking. He knows it, too. He's mocking me with those little, hard eyes of his. I must control my voice. This is really funny. My voice is shaking.

"Get up, West."

"I don't see, Mr. Daddy-oh, just why I should," West answered. He pronounced the name with great care.

"Hey, Artie," Miller said, "whuffo you . . ."

"Get up, West," Rick interrupted. "Get up and say my name correctly."

"Don't you know your own name, Mr. Daddy-oh?"

Rick's hand snapped out and grasped West by the collar of his shirt. He pulled him to his feet, almost tearing the collar. West stood an inch shorter than Rick, squirming to release himself.

Rick's hand crushed tighter on the collar. He heard the slight rasp of material ripping. He peered into the hateful eyes and spoke quietly. "Pronounce my name correctly, West."

The class had grown terribly quiet. There was no sound in the room now. Rick heard only the grating of his own shallow breathing. Alongside West, his eyes wide, the smile gone from his face now, Miller sat and watched.

I should let him loose, Rick thought. What can come of this? How far can I go? *Let him loose!*

"You want me to pronounce your name, sir?" West asked politely.

"You heard me."

"Fuck you, Mr. Daddy . . ."

Rick's hand lashed out, slapping West squarely across the mouth. He felt his fingers scrape against hard teeth, saw the blood leap across the upper lip in a thin crimson smear, saw the eyes widen with surprise, and then narrow immediately with deep, dark hatred.

And then the knife snapped into view, sudden and terrifying. Long and shining, it caught the pale sunlight that slanted through the long schoolroom windows. Rick backed away involuntarily, eyeing the sharp blade with respect.

Now what? he thought. Now the garbage can turns into a coffin. Now the garbage overflows. Now I lie dead and bleeding on a schoolroom floor while a moron slashes me to ribbons. Now.

"What do you intend doing with that, West?"

My voice is exceptionally calm, he mused. I think I'm frightened, but my voice is calm. Exceptionally.

"Just come a little closer and you'll see," West snarled, the blood in his mouth staining his teeth.

"Give me that knife, West," Rick said.

"Come on, Artie," Miller put in softly. "You jus' bein' . . ."

"Give me that knife, West," Rick repeated.

I'm kidding, a voice persisted in his mind. I must be kidding. This is all a big, hilarious joke. I'll die laughing in the morning. I'll die . . .

"Come and get it, Daddy-oh!" West yelled.

Rick took a step closer to West and watched his arm swing back and forth in a threatening arc. West's eyes were hard and unforgiving.

And suddenly, he caught a flash of color out of the corner of his eye. Someone was behind him! He whirled instinctively, his fist smashing into a boy's stomach. The boy brought up his head, and Rick struck again, and he suddenly realized it was Belazi, the kid who'd been caught cheating. Belazi dropped to the floor and cramped into a tight little ball that moaned and writhed on the hard wood. Rick looked at him for just an instant, satisfying himself that any danger he might have presented was past. He turned quickly to West, a satisfied smile clinging to his lips.

"Give me that knife, West, and give it to me now."

He stared into the boy's eyes. West looked big and dangerous. Perspiration clung to his acneed forehead. His breath was coming in hurried gasps.

"Give it to me now, West, or I'm going to take it from you and beat you black and blue."

He was advancing slowly on the boy.

"Give it to me, West. Hand it over," his voice rolled on hypnotically, charged with an undercurrent of threat.

The class seemed to catch its breath together. No one moved to help Belazi who lay in a heap on the floor, his arms hugging his waist. He moaned occasionally, squirmed violently, but no one moved to help him. West backed away from Rick, and Rick moved forward, passing Miller's seat. Miller sat on the edge of his chair, his hands clenching the desk top tightly. Belazi moaned again on the floor.

I've got to keep one eye on Belazi, Rick figured. He may be playing possum. I have to be careful.

"Hand it over, West. Hand it over."

West stopped retreating, realizing that he was the one who held the weapon. He stuck the spring-action knife out in front of him, probing the air with it. His back curved into a large C as he crouched over, head low, the knife always moving in front of him as he advanced. Rick held his ground and waited. West advanced cautiously at first, his eyes fastened on Rick's throat, the knife hand moving constantly, murderously, in a swinging arc. He grinned terribly, a red-stained, white smile on his narrow face.

"Come on, you stupid bastard," he said. "Come on, stupid. Come and get the knife. Come on, you dumb jerk, come and get it."

Rick wet his lips and watched the knife, and West paused suddenly and searched Rick's face. He grinned again and began speaking softly as he advanced, almost in a whisper, almost as if he were thinking aloud.

"See the knife, Mr. Daddy-oh? See the pretty knife? I'm gonna slash you up real good, Mr. Daddy-oh. I'm gonna slash you, and then I'm gonna slash you some more. I'm gonna cut you up real fine, you bastard. I shoulda done this right from the start. I shoulda realized you was too stinkin' dumb to take a hint, Daddy-oh. Come on, you sonofabitch. Come on and taste this friggin' knife."

The chair, Rick suddenly remembered. There's a chair. I'll take the chair and swing. Under the chin. No. Across the chest. Fast though. It'll have to be fast, one movement. Wait. Not yet, wait. All right, West. All right. *All right.*

"Ever get cut, Mr. Daddy-oh? Ever get sliced with a sharp knife? This one is sharp, Mr. Daddy-oh, or are you too stinkin' dumb to know that? You ever stop to figure who bitched you up with Mr. Small, Daddy-oh? You ever stop to figure that, you dumb prick? You didn't, huh, Daddy-oh? You didn't figure it, huh?" Hypnotically, advancing, closer and closer, his voice a whisper, his eyes gleaming hotly.

West, Rick realized. West. Not Miller. West. West, Westwestwest. West was the one. West told Small. West complained. Oh God, it was West.

"I shouldn'ta played games, Daddy-oh," West said. "Your kind only understands a knife in the ribs. Well, you gonna get it now, you bastard. And then you're never gonna bother us no more. No more." He smiled and advanced, and Rick backed away down the aisle. "Your wife get them notes, you bastard? Richard Dadier, 1935 East 174th Street. Straight from the phone book, you dumb bastard. Stop me from taking a piss when I have to, huh? I shoulda come there in person. I shouldn'ta played games with notes and complaints. I shoulda come to your house and give you the knife right then, right in your friggin' ribs."

Anne, Rick thought. Oh the sonofabitch. Oh, you

sonofabitch, West, you dirty maggoty bastard. So it was you. So you were the rotten little bastard who did it. You, West. He backed away down the aisle, and his thoughts were jumbled. He thought of the notes, and of West typing them up someplace, simple notes, oh the sonofabitch, and he thought, *I'll make him think I'm retreating.* I'll give him confidence. The empty seat in the third row. Next to Maglin. I'll lead him there. I hope it's empty. Empty when I checked the roll. Thank God for Delaney books. I can't look, I'll tip my hand. Keep a poker face. Come on, West, follow me. Follow me so I can crack your ugly skull in two. One of us goes, West. And it's not going to be me.

"Nossir, Mr. Daddy-oh, no more games. I'm through with games now. And I'm through with your tests, and all your goddamn noise. Just your face, Mr. Daddy-oh. Just gonna fix your face so nobody'll wanna look at you no more."

One more row, Rick calculated. Back up one more row. Reach. Swing. One. More. Row.

The class followed the two figures with fascination. West stalked Rick down the long aisle, stepping forward on the balls of his feet, pace by pace, waiting for Rick to back into the blackboard. Belazi rolled over on the floor and groaned again.

And Rick counted the steps. A few more. A . . . few . . . more.

"You shouldn'ta hit me, Mr. Daddy-oh," West mocked. "Ain't nice for teachers to hit students like that, Mr. Daddy-oh. Nossir, it ain't nice at all. Not at . . ."

The chair crashed into West's chest, knocking the

breath out of him. It came quickly and forcefully, with the impact of a striking snake. Rick had turned, as if to run, and then the chair was gripped in his hands tightly. It sliced the air in a clean, powerful arc, and West covered his face instinctively. The chair crashed into his chest, knocking him backward. He screamed in surprise and pain as Rick leaped over the chair to land heavily on his chest. The knife clattered to the floor, and Rick pinned West's shoulders with his knees and slapped him ruthlessly across the face.

"Here, West, here, here, here," he squeezed through clenched teeth. West twisted his head from side to side, trying to escape the cascade of blows that fell in rapid onslaught on his cheeks.

"Here, you dirty bastard!" and West turned his head and shouted, "Greg! The knife! Get the knife!"

The knife, Rick suddenly remembered! Where's the knife? What the hell happened to . . .

Sunlight caught the cold glint of metal, and Rick glanced up instantly, expecting to find Miller there, expecting West's friend. Belazi stood over him, the knife clenched tightly in his fist. He grinned idiotically, his lips parting over rotten teeth. He spat vehemently at Rick, and then there was a blur of color: blue steel, and the yellow of West's hair, and the blood on West's lip, and the brown wooden floor, and the gray tweed of Rick's suit. A shout came up from the class, and a hiss seemed to escape West's lips.

Rick kicked at Belazi, feeling the heavy leather of his shoes crack against the boy's shins. West was up and fumbling for Rick's arms. A sudden slice of pain started at Rick's shoulder, careened down the length of his arm. Cloth gave way with a rasping scratch, and blood flashed bright against the gray tweed.

From the floor, Rick saw the knife flash back again, poised in Belazi's hand, ready to strike. He saw West's fists, doubled and hard, saw the animal look that had come on Belazi's face, and again the knife, threatening and sharp, drenched now with blood, dripping on the brown, cold, wooden floor.

The noise grew louder and Rick grasped in his mind for a picture of the Roman arena, tried to rise, felt pain sear through his right arm as he put pressure on it.

He's cut me, he thought with panic. *Belazi has cut me.*

And the screaming reached a wild crescendo, hands moved with terrible swiftness, eyes gleamed with molten fury, bodies squirmed, and hate smothered everything in a sweaty, confused, embarrassed embrace.

This is it, Rick thought. This is really it.

"Lee him alone, you goddamn fool!" Miller was shouting.

Leave who alone, Rick wondered. Who? I wasn't . . .

"Lousy sneak," Levy shouted. "Lousy, sneaky bastard."

Who, Rick thought. What . . . ?

Miller seized West and pushed him backward against a desk. Rick watched him dazedly, his right arm burning with pain. He saw Morales through a maze of moving, struggling bodies, Morales who'd delivered the profane wire-recorder speech, saw Morales smash a book against Belazi's knife hand. The knife clattered to the floor with a curious sound. Belazi's hand reached out for it and Santini, the smiler, stepped on it with the heel of his foot. The knife disappeared in a shuffle of hands, but Belazi no longer had it. Rick stared at the bare, brown spot on the floor where the knife had been.

Whose chance is it now? he wondered. Whose turn to slice the teacher?

West tried to struggle off the desk where Miller had him pinned. Erin brought his fist down heavily on West's nose. He wrenched the larger boy's head back with one hand, and again brought his fist down fiercely.

A slow recognition trickled into Rick's confused thoughts. Through dazzled eyes, he watched.

Belazi scrambled to his feet and lunged at him. A solid wall seemed to rise before him as Carter and Antoro flung themselves against the onrushing form and threw it back. They tumbled onto Belazi, Carter's red hair flashing wildly, holding Belazi's arms, pummeling him with excited fists.

They're fighting for me! No, Rick reasoned, no. But yes, *they're fighting for me!* Against West. Against Belazi. For me. For me, oh my God, for me.

His eyes blinked nervously as he struggled to his feet. Belazi and West were subdued now, and Rick looked at them briefly and then said, "Let's . . . let's take them down to Mr. Small." His voice was very low.

Antoro moved closer to him, his eyes widening as they took in the livid slash that ran the length of Rick's arm.

"Man, that's some cut," he said.

Rick touched his arm lightly with his left hand. It

was soggy and wet, the shirt and jacket stained a dull brownish-red.

"My brother got cut like that once," Maglin offered.

The boys were still holding Belazi and West, but they no longer seemed terribly interested in the trouble-makers.

For an instant, Rick felt a twinge of panic. For that brief, terrible instant he imagined that the boys hadn't really come to his aid at all, that they had simply seen an opportunity for a good fight and had seized upon it. And then he remembered whose voice he had heard first, the voice shouting, "Lee him alone, you goddamn fool!" He looked among the crowd of faces around him, and he found Miller, and their eyes met, but he could read nothing on Miller's face.

"I . . . I think I'd better take them down to Mr. Small," he said. He stared at the boys, trying to read their faces, trying mostly to read Miller's unsmiling face, searching for something in their eyes that would tell him he had at last reached them, reached them in a different way than "The Fifty-First Dragon" had. He could tell nothing. Their faces were blank, their eyes emotionless.

He wondered if he should thank them. If only he knew. If he could only hit upon the right thing to say, the thing to cement it all.

"I'll . . . I'll take them down. Suppose . . . you . . . you all go to lunch now."

"That sure is a mean cut," Kruger said, and Miller watched and said nothing.

"Yeah," Rodriguez agreed.

"You can all go to lunch," Rick said. "I want to take Belazi and West . . ."

The boys didn't move. They stood there with serious faces, solemnly watching Rick.

". . . to . . . the . . . principal," Rick finished.

"A hell of a mean cut," Taglio said.

And then Miller came out of the circle of faces, and he stepped forward, and he chose his words very carefully, and his face was very serious. "Maybe we should jus' forget the principal, Chief, huh?" he said. "Maybe we should jus' oughta go to lunch."

Rick looked at Miller, and again their eyes met. He did not pretend to understand. He knew only that West had stepped over the line Miller had drawn, and Miller had been presented with a choice. He could either step over the line with West, or he could help in shoving West back over that line. He had chosen to help Rick. He had fought for him, and now the fight was over, and through some unfathomable code of his own, he was now turning on Rick again.

Or was he?

There was something strange in Miller's eyes, and the smile that usually dominated his face was not there now. His eyes were inquisitive and his entire body seemed to strain forward, tensed, waiting. He did not take his eyes from Rick's face, and those eyes pleaded, pleaded with a mute intensity. Rick stared at him, and he did not understand at first, and then abruptly he realized that Miller had not chosen the easy road when he'd joined the fight against West. Miller had made a choice, and for once that choice had led him down the hard road.

And now there was another choice, and Rick weighed it carefully, and his eyes held Miller's in the ring of faces around him. It would make things a hell of a lot simpler if he just sent all the kids to lunch and forgot all about Belazi and West. It would make things simpler the way things would have been vastly simpler had he not interfered in that rape so long ago. It would be easy, so easy to say, "All right, let's just forget all this," and then go back to teaching the way he'd come to teach lately. It would be easy, very easy, because the kids would all have had a good fight, and Dadier would have shown himself to be a fine guy by forgetting all about it and not getting Belazi and West in trouble. So easy.

The kids crowded around Rick and Miller, and West was smiling broadly, insolently, and everyone was very quiet, and they waited. They had heard what Miller suggested, and now they saw Rick and Miller staring at each other, and they did not know that one was deciding and the other was waiting for that decision. They themselves waited, but they did not wait the way Miller waited, and they did not know Rick was making one of the hardest decisions he'd ever had to make in his life.

When Rick finally spoke, he addressed Miller. He did not speak sternly or harshly or reprimandingly. He did not shout, and he did not whisper. He said it in a normal, conversational tone, and he looked directly at Miller when he said it, and he might have been discussing something entirely different, he might have been someone working at a bench alongside Miller's who was simply explaining a job that had to be done.

He said, "I'm taking them down, Miller," and Miller said nothing, and then Rick added, "I have to."

Miller continued to stare at him for a moment, and the circle of faces seemed to blur together, and Rick wondered if he'd made the wrong choice. And then one of the faces broke into a smile, and that face was Miller's, and Miller said, "Sure, Mr. Dadier." And then he shouted, "All right, goddamnit, le's break this up."

The circle held for just a moment, and Rick shoved Belazi and West ahead of him, not knowing whether to expect resistance or not. But the boys parted to let him through, and Rick walked past them with his head high.

He was not surprised to hear a voice behind him pipe in a high falsetto, "Oh Daddy-oh! You're a *hee*-ro."

But a second voice shouted, "Oh, shut yo' goddamn mouth!" and Rick smiled as he stepped into the corridor with Belazi and West ahead of him. He remembered what he'd thought earlier, before the fight, remembered what he'd thought about just one kid, one kid, that's all, one kid getting something out of it all, one kid he could point to and say, "I showed him the way," and that would make it all right, if he could only say that.

And so the smile mushroomed all over his face, and he walked down to Small's office, smiling all the way, smiling happily because the second voice he'd heard had belonged to Gregory Miller.

14

Solly Klein stood near the bulletin board in the teachers' lunchroom and pointed a stubby forefinger at the school page of the *World-Telegram-Sun*.

"Another list of names," he said. "All the suckers who passed the elementary school exam this time." He shook his head, tapped the tacked page with his finger, and then walked back to the table. "They never learn," he said. "They get sucked in every year."

"The way you got sucked in," Lou Savoldi said, looking up from his tea.

"I got sucked in, all right," Solly answered. "Had I known what . . ."

"Had I but known," George Katz said, smiling. "Ah, had I but known."

"Read your history book," Solly said.

Rick, entering from the stairwell behind the gym, stopped at the refrigerator in the kitchen, opened the door, and looked inside for his container of milk.

"I've got the milk, Dadier," Manners called from the table.

Rick nodded, closed the door, and then walked into the dining room.

"Look at all the happy faces," he said, smiling.

"We ought to get two containers from now on," Manners said. "I've almost finished this one."

"You're a greedy pig," Rick told him.

"I can't help it," Manners said apologetically. "I like milk."

"The trouble with you," Katz said humorously, "is that you were weaned too early."

"I was never weaned," Manners answered slyly. "There's nothing I like better than the breast."

"You owe me money on that container," Rick said. "And you haven't paid me for yesterday's yet, either."

"Wait until payday," Manners said. "I'm a little short."

"High finance at Manual Trades," Solly said sourly. "A bunch of bankers. What's the bill come to now, Dadier? Twelve cents?"

"Twelve cents is a lot of money today," Savoldi said.

Rick smiled. "As a matter of fact, it's twenty-six cents. Milk went up."

"Twenty-six cents is a lot of money today," Savoldi said sadly.

"Just endorse your paycheck over to him, Manners," Solly said. "That should just cover the debt."

"He thinks he's being funny," Savoldi said, indicating Solly with a sideward movement of his head.

"Who me?" Solly asked. "There's nothing funny about this dump, nothing. Except The Boss. He's a riot."

"He's not a bad fellow," Katz said.

"He's a prince," Solly said dryly.

"No, really. He's not bad at all."

"I said, didn't I? A prince. They should send him someplace where royalty is appreciated."

"Well, I don't think he's doing a bad job here," Katz said staunchly.

"Nobody does a bad job here," Savoldi said sadly.

"Except you, Lou," Solly said.

Savoldi shrugged. "How can you do a bad job here?" he asked. "A bad job anyplace else is a good job here."

"He's finally catching on," Solly said. "He's been teaching here for eighty years, and he's just getting wise."

"I'm one of the Original Wise Men," Savoldi said.

"It's possible to do a good job here," Rick said softly.

"Here's Dadier again," Solly said. "Dadier, you'd better be careful or you'll wind up being a principal."

"He'd like that," Savoldi said sadly. "Wouldn't you, Dadier?"

"That's what I'm bucking for," Rick said, smiling.

"You can always tell the hot-rods," Solly said, wagging his head. "I spotted you for a hot-rod from go, Dadier. That's why your arm is in a bandage now."

"It's healing," Rick said, shrugging.

"Everything heals," Savoldi said.

"Time heals all wounds," Katz put in.

"Unless they use a zip gun on you someday. Try to heal a hole in your head," Solly said.

"They won't use a zip gun on me," Rick said confidently.

"Famous last words," Solly said.

"I don't think they will, either," Katz offered. "Dadier is a good teacher."

"Oh, yeah," Rick said.

"Yes, yes, you are," Katz insisted. "You should have seen the way he handled those kids in the Christmas show."

"Are you still crapping about that show, Katz?" Solly asked. "The term'll be over in a few days, and he's still talking about Christmas." Solly shook his head.

"He believes in Santa Claus," Manners said.

"Where's your tie, Katz?" Savoldi asked. "No tie today?"

"He's slipping," Solly said.

"It was a very nice tie," Katz said, a little embarrassed.

"Who said no?" Solly asked. "It *was* a very nice tie."

"Then what was wrong about wearing it?" Katz asked.

"Nothing. But you could have stopped after you spilled catsup and coffee and mustard . . ."

"I never spilled anything on it," Katz said seriously, offended.

"How did your kids like the tie, Katz?" Manners asked.

"They thought it was very nice," Katz answered, still miffed.

"They don't know ties from garter snakes," Solly said.

"They're not that dumb," Rick contradicted.

"No, huh?"

"*I* don't think so."

"That's because you love them all, Dadier. There's

nothing like a little knifing to generate love and devotion."

"Dadier is a professional hero," Savoldi said.

"He stops rapes and knifings," Manners said, "and is also available for Christmas shows, hayrides, and strawberry festivals."

"No *bar-mitzvahs?*" Solly asked.

"Those, too," Rick said, smiling.

"What's a *bar-mitzvah?*" Savoldi asked innocently. "An Irish stew?"

"Yeah," Solly said. "With presents." He rose suddenly and walked to the window, staring out at the red brick of the housing project in the distance. "They got people living in there already," he said.

"I don't think it's proper to joke about Dadier's knifing," Katz said, really thinking it was not proper to joke about his gift tie.

"Who's joking?" Solly asked. "Dadier is a very brave man."

"A missionary," Manners said.

Solly turned, seemingly surprised. "Are you still around, Manners? I thought you'd be teaching at Julia Richmond by this time."

"I'm working on it," Manners said, smiling.

"It was," Katz said thoughtfully, "an act of bravery."

"What's that?" Solly asked.

"Dadier's knifing."

"Certainly. You have to be very brave to get all sliced up."

"You talk about it as if it were nothing at all," Katz said seriously. "As if it meant absolutely nothing."

"Knife wounds mean nothing to heroes," Manners

said. He flicked an imaginary cut on his shoulder. "Just a scratch, man."

"That's Dadier's trouble," Savoldi said sadly. "He's a professional hero."

"No," Rick said, smiling. "I'm just a teacher."

Solly turned from the window a moment and looked at Rick curiously. "Yeah," he said. "A teacher."

The men were silent for a moment, and Solly walked from the window, looped one thumb in his suspenders, and pointed the forefinger of his free hand at Rick.

"You know what a teacher is, Dadier?" he asked.

"What's a teacher?" Rick asked, straight-manning it.

"I'll tell you, Dadier. You take some slob, see? You take him when he's still in the cradle. You take this slob who doesn't know a teacher from a preacher, who doesn't even know to wipe his nose yet. You take him, and you . . ."

Rick sat and listened while Solly expounded his theory. He sat and listened, and the room felt very warm and very secure, and he was aware of the faces of the other men, all watching Solly while he talked, laughing occasionally, Solly enjoying himself as he spoke. He sat and listened, and he was very happy here with these other men in the lunchroom, hearing Solly talk.

But he was not sorry when the bell sounded, ending the lunch period, announcing the beginning of his fifth period, and he smiled when Solly said, "Well, back to the salt mines."

Biographical Notes

These are the biographical notes that appeared on the back jacket of The Blackboard Jungle *when it was first published in 1954.*

Evan Hunter was born in Manhattan, but fled to the Bronx at the age of twelve. He went through elementary and high school in the New York City school system, and the Navy claimed him in 1944. When he returned in 1946, he attended Hunter College, and it was there that he met his wife Anita, whom he married in his senior year.

His first job after graduation obviously gave him much of the background which inspired *The Blackboard Jungle.* He taught in a vocational high school. Next he answered telephones for the American Automobile Association and from there he graduated to another telephone job, this time calling restaurants and asking them if they wanted any nice fresh Maine lobsters that day.

Next, he answered a blind advertisement for an editor, and went to work for a literary agent. Up to this point his creative urge had been buckshot scattered among the arts. He had tried writing and painting—he once won a scholarship to the Art Students' League and later attended Cooper Union—and he played the piano in a jazz band. At the literary agency, he learned about plotting stories, and when his agent-boss started selling them regularly to magazines, and sold a mystery novel and a juvenile science-fiction title as well, he decided that it would be more profitable to stay home and write full time. *The Blackboard Jungle* is the first major result of this decision.

Evan and Anita Hunter now live on Long Island. They have three children—Ted and the twins, Mark and Richard.

Evan Hunter's update on what has happened since:

I now write full time *all* the time.

A year after the publication of *The Blackboard Jungle,* I invented the pseudonym Ed McBain. The first of the 87th Precinct series of mystery novels was published in May of 1956 by Pocket Books, Inc., the same publishers who had done *this* book in paperback. The series is still going strong. Simon & Schuster now publishes it. What goes around comes around.

In 1973, a girl named Amanda Finley entered my life. She is my darling stepdaughter, and she has grown to be a beautiful, intelligent, wonderful woman.

In 1997, I married Dragica Dimitrijević, the love of my life. We live happily together in a house on a river in Connecticut.